THE CAUSE

By DAN KLASING

Publisher, Copyright, and Additional Information

The Cause by Dan Klasing

Copyright © 2021 by Dan Klasing

For permissions contact: danklasing@gmail.com.

This book is a work of fiction. Names, characters, places, incidents, and dialogue are products of the author's imagination or are used fictitiously and are not to be construed as real. Any resemblance to actual events or locales or persons, living or dead, is entirely coincidental.

ISBN- 9798988149804

Editing by R. Klein
Cover design and interior design by Rafael Andres

PROLOGUE

February 29, 1928

A cold rain bounced off Edward Clark's umbrella as he walked through the dark streets of Atlanta. With the newly-installed electric street lamps on Peachtree Street barely casting enough light for him to avoid deep puddles, or worse, stepping in a pile of horse droppings, Clark chose his path carefully. In less than an hour, he was to make the most important presentation of his life before a room of multi-millionaires and appearances mattered.

Five minutes later, he finally saw the brilliant lights of the Georgian Terrace Hotel appear through the gloomy evening. Making his way across the street and past several motorcars parked under the hotel's portico, Clark closed his umbrella and wiped the tops of his boots with his handkerchief before pushing through the lobby's gleaming brass doors.

Once inside, Clark knew he had chosen the perfect venue for his meeting. Massive marble columns arranged around the circular lobby held up a muralled ceiling several stories above, giving the distinct impression of a Greek temple. All around, quiet yet efficient hotel staff dressed in black waistcoats and bow ties seemed to glide across the highly polished floor carrying silver trays of drinks or cautiously rolled brass carts piled high with luggage. To one side, an elevator operated by a red-uniformed attendant stood ready to whisk guests as high as the tenth floor.

Clark glanced at his pocket watch before presenting himself at the Concierge desk. He had a few minutes to spare.

"Ah, Mr. Clark. Welcome back," the Concierge said in a slightly nasal tone. "The preparations for your meeting are complete, and your guests have just begun to arrive. As you requested, they will be welcomed into the Robert E. Lee dining room."

"Excellent," Clark replied. "Please let me know as soon as the last arrives. I'll be in the bar."

"Very well, sir," the Concierge said, making a note with a white-gloved hand.

Clark walked across the lobby and into the hotel's bar. Unlike the gleaming white marble in the lobby, the dark mahogany interior of the bar and its leather furnishings harkened back to the days before prohibition emptied its glass shelves of liquor.

Clark sat down heavily on a barstool, thankful for a brief opportunity to rest his legs and gather his thoughts. With his nerves beginning to form a knot in his stomach, Clark longed for a shot of whiskey.

Instead, the hotel's black barman delivered a tumbler of tepid ginger ale. Clark was about to take a reluctant sip when a meaty hand appeared on his shoulder. A bit startled, Clark turned to find a tall, stocky, immaculately dressed man smiling at him through a thick black beard. Clark knew him immediately and also knew the smile wasn't meant to put him at ease.

"Clark!" the man said, almost shouting. "Stopped in here for a drink myself before having to deal with the rest of your, uh, guests upstairs."

Clark had to gather his wits quickly. Of the twelve men he had invited, Grover Jefferson Bell wielded the most money and political power. It had been a coup to get him to the meeting, and his opinion would be the key to Clark's success or failure.

"I'm honored you will attend, Mr. Bell," Clark replied as smoothly as possible.

"Barman!" Bell barked, noticing Clark's glass. "Get Mr. Clark here a glass of a real bourbon from my private stock. He'll need it."

"Thank you, sir."

"Don't thank me yet, Clark," Bell said, squeezing Clark's shoulder with a painful iron grip and leaning down to stare him in the eye. "You have talked me into coming here tonight. Your grand idea had better be worth my time. If this turns out to be some kind of scam, you won't live to regret it."

The barman placed Clark's drink on the bar and moved swiftly away.

Standing up straight again, the bearded man smiled and slapped Clark on the back.

"I'll see you upstairs."

Clark felt a drop of sweat roll slowly down his neck and form a small wet spot on his collar. Grover Bell owned half of Virginia and all its politicians. Plus, a string of newspapers in cities reaching from Richmond to Dallas gave him unparalleled ability to sway public opinion. He was more than capable of carrying out his threat.

Clark downed the bourbon in one shot, trying to shake off the surprise encounter and enjoying its momentary calming effect.

A minute later, the Concierge appeared at his side and said, "Your guests have all assembled, sir."

Clark made his way to the private dining room, paused to steel himself one last time, and then pushed confidently through the heavy double doors.

Inside, Clark found his guests seated in twelve high-backed maroon leather chairs placed around a circular table. Clark had requested the special arrangement to maintain at least a façade of equal status between men of extreme pride. Still, tension filled the room. Some of the attendees competed in the cut-throat business world, while others held grudges over perceived insults or inter-family squabbles from decades in the past. Only a truly grand common cause could have brought them together in one place.

Looking around the room, Clark knew he had pulled off a masterstroke putting this meeting together. It had taken every bit of his talent as the country's most infamous publicist and promoter. Earlier in the decade, Clark masterminded the populist message which had lifted the KKK out of back-woods obscurity and transformed it into a potent political force. Clark's brilliant political messaging had attracted millions of voters and swayed numerous elections. In the end, scandals within the organization prevented the Klan from becoming one of the dominant power brokers in American politics. When the Klan's popularity disappeared almost overnight, Clark sought another agenda to promote, one that would attract forceful men who needed or could be persuaded to need, his inherent talent at manipulating public opinion. He had selected the men at this table because he knew they wouldn't be able to resist the challenge he proposed - a plan that could change the world.

Pushing aside any lingering self-doubt, Clark began the most important pitch of his life.

"Gentlemen, my sincerest thanks for your attendance. I shall not waste your time.

"Tonight, I will lay out the structure of my plan, but I must ask now if any of you have doubts, then please excuse yourself. The government would most certainly consider what we are about to discuss an act of treason."

Clark paused for dramatic effect. As expected, no one moved or even turned to look across the room. These were not men who lived their lives in fear of the government or anyone else. Twelve deadly serious faces looked back at him.

Clark nodded somberly and continued.

"You all already know what I propose is far more than just bold and ambitious and that it cannot be accomplished in your lifetimes or those of your children or even your grandchildren. But it will come to pass."

A large man wearing a dark gray suit that contrasted with his long white beard sat forward, placed one hand on the table, and said in a deep Southern drawl: "Yes. Yes. You have explained your ideas to each of us before, and we all have always agreed, in principle, on the objective. Now, let's cut to the damn chase. What's the first step?"

Clark stepped back and spread his arms as if encompassing the entire assembly of power brokers. "Commitment. As formidable as each of you are, this, of all things, cannot be done by one man. It will take decades of concerted effort and expert leadership by you, as the directors of this great undertaking, to bring it to fruition. How often in human history has any man, standing utterly alone, accomplished greatness? Greatness such that he is revered for all time? If you stand together in this common cause, your names will be indelibly etched into history!"

Clark realized that for his plan to be successful, these men had to see each other in a different light. Not as friends, but at least as wary compatriots.

Feeling, if not seeing, an unspoken allegiance beginning to take shape, Clark went on. "This is only the first meeting of the Directors, as I recommend you be called. For now, please allow me to show you the foundation of my vision for the future."

Clark walked to an easel holding a picture draped with green felt. Slipping the cover off, he revealed an oil painting of the Egyptian pyramids standing tall in a barren landscape.

"The ancient Egyptians constructed these monoliths block by block, each level resting on the firm foundation of the one below. Yes, many years passed between laying the cornerstone and placing the pinnacle at the summit. Yet, thousands of years later, they still stand impervious to time. We shall work toward our ultimate objective in the same way - the work of one generation standing on the solid foundation laid by their forefathers. Once constructed, the result will be as unassailable as those great monuments."

Seeing his audience wanted specifics, Clark removed the painting, replacing it with a simple line drawing of a large square with an 'X' drawn through its center.

Clark continued. "This is the pyramid seen from above. Quite obviously, it has four sides. For our purposes, this represents the four parts of society that must be dominated and manipulated before our cause comes to pass. As you can see, I have marked them 'government,' 'military,' 'business,' and 'the press.'

"You, the men in this room, already possess massive holdings in each or some of these areas or have the means to control or sway others. Most, if not all of you, already have some - shall we say, influence - over a number of politicians. While we build toward our imagined pyramid, the four sides will support each other as it rises. When finished, no force on earth will be able to bring down the work of our joint enterprise, which we shall refer to as The Cause."

"And you will show us the way to build your pyramid for a price, I imagine?" one of the newly-dubbed Directors asked.

"Yes. And a hefty one at that," Clark said, without blinking an eye.

"Alright then, what's the end game?" the same man inquired. "Let's say in another eighty, ninety, or one hundred years, we and our offspring have followed your plan, and The Cause succeeds. What keeps the federal government from squashing it like a bug?"

Clark had carefully prepared an answer to this very question.

"The last piece of the puzzle, the golden capstone of the pyramid, if you will, shall be a weapon - one which you and I cannot even dream of today. A weapon that will protect The Cause from government interference or any wishing it harm. Think of it. Less than one hundred years ago, men marched into battle with a rifle that could only fire once before being reloaded and fought in wooden ships under canvas sails. But just a decade ago in The Great War, machine guns firing hundreds of rounds per minute slaughtered millions, fortresses on wheels called 'tanks' rolled over anything in their path, airplanes jousted in the skies overhead while submarines plied the ocean depths. What incredible apparatus of war will the mind of man conjure in the next hundred years?"

Clark paused and scanned the room for any reaction.

Nothing. Nobody moved. Clark feared he had failed.

Finally, Grover Bell slowly lifted his impressive frame from his seat directly across the large table from Clark. Holding Clark in a steely gaze, Bell reached down and picked up his drink. Lifting it high in the air, he looked around the room at the others and said in a loud voice: "The Cause!"

The eleven others jumped to their feet, lifted their glasses, and repeated Bell's toast in one voice.
"The Cause!"

ONE

Present Day
Groom Lake, Nevada Test Range
Area 51

The black apparition swept silently across the snowy mountain-tops of the Nevada desert, blotting out starlight as it carved a wide circle around the secret test facility. Five miles away on the edge of a secluded runway, scientists in white lab coats stood among a group of fifteen military officers, all straining to follow the new fighter-bomber's position in the night sky. A moment later, the craft stunned the observers on the ground by coming to a complete stop, hanging ominously over the nearest peak. Then, in the blink of an eye, it shot straight up and out of sight.

While the onlookers still stared into the distance, the aircraft suddenly reappeared directly over the airfield as if dropped by gods from the heavens. Without disturbing the still desert air, or making a sound, the triangular-shaped craft hovered silently for a few seconds fifty feet above the ground. Then, in a final unbelievable encore, the craft performed a slow 360-degree roll, just before three legs emerged from its belly, taking the weight of the beast as it settled onto the tarmac.

On the edge of the runway, The Chairman of the Joint Chiefs of Staff, an Air Force general, stood speechless.

"So, General, what do you think of the world's first gravity-wave aircraft?" the lead aerospace engineer on the project's development team, Dr. Dave Knox, asked with a knowing smile.

It took a few seconds for the stunned general to answer. Without taking his eyes off the strange, hyper-advanced plane, referred to internally as the Gravity Wave One - Fighter Bomber, the military man replied, "Incredible. Absolutely incredible. If I hadn't seen it with my own eyes, I would never have believed any aircraft could do what I just witnessed. There is simply no basis for comparison."

Dave had fully expected the general's reaction. The select few people that had previously borne witness to the GW1-FB had been just as confounded.

"I will be glad to answer any questions you have," Dave said, knowing the demonstration would speak for itself.

"Your briefing paper comprehensively outlined its capabilities. Although, I think you undersold what that thing can do. Where does your team stand on its fuel situation? I understand the anti-gravity propulsion system requires some new high-powered atom?"

"Correct. Element 128. It took us five weeks to produce enough 128 for tonight's three-minute demonstration, but we are hoping for substantial progress on that issue in the near future. We have our top physicists working on how to produce it in sufficient quantities to bring us up to full operational capability," Dave answered confidently.

The general took off his hat and ran one hand through his shock of white hair. Like his predecessors, who personally witnessed the first atomic explosion, he knew that once they resolved the fueling issue and aircraft in front of him became fully operational, it would change the balance of power in the world.

TWO

Two Months Later
Groom Lake, Nevada Test Range
Area 51

The breakthrough came at 2:17 in the morning.

Three shrill beeps from a computer terminal deep inside one of Area 51's underground laboratories startled Dr. Rick Donnelly, causing him to drop the chalk he had been using to scratch out a series of mathematical formulas on a tall blackboard. Except for his workspace, most of the lab he shared with two other preeminent physicists remained obscured in darkness. Completely lost in his work, Rick hadn't even noticed when his colleagues left the lab and turned out most of the lights six hours earlier. Not that he cared. Rick preferred working alone.

Without bothering to turn on the lights, Rick moved to a nearby keyboard and typed a series of commands. Immediately, a large flat-screen monitor across the room came to life, displaying what appeared to be shiny colored balls joined into a complex web by gray lines. The entire structure, a molecular model, seemed to float weightlessly, rotating slowly inside the screen.

The thirty-eight-year-old physicist scratched absently at the patchwork of two-day old stubble on his cheek as he stared intently at the monitor. Rick's stringy brown hair, wrinkled short-sleeve shirt and thin arms made him look more like an overworked store clerk than a genius with an almost immeasurable IQ. As the model rotated, Rick's mind automatically ran through calculations that would take a run of the mill physicist hours, if not days, to complete.

After two minutes of deep concentration, Rick suddenly realized the computer had, in fact, correctly identified the key molecule that would efficiently produce Element 128. The news didn't quite register fully at first. It took Rick a moment to actually accept that after five years of intense research, he had finally uncovered the answer. He imagined for a moment that this is what a treasure hunter must feel like when he finally unearths a long-lost chest of gold. His heart now pumping with excitement, Rick turned to retrieve his notebook and slide rule, only to nearly fall over the office chair he had just occupied. Clumsily pushing the offending obstacle aside, Rick used a pencil and paper to manually triple-check the computer's calculations.

The results were indisputable. With the discovery of this formula, he not only held the one and only method to efficiently manufacture Element 128, but also the key to making gravity wave technology a fully operational reality.

Rick couldn't help but bask in the moment. He had done it! Years of research, complex experiments, and innumerable failures finally culminated in this - his greatest achievement.

A grin of self-satisfaction marked the extent of Rick's celebration. He knew that if his discovery was made public, he would certainly receive a Nobel Prize – maybe two. But he didn't need recognition. The simple fact that he had profoundly advanced science afforded every accolade he required.

While Rick realized the full potential of gravity wave technology for the future, he knew its immediate application would be military. A gravity wave aircraft would dominate any battle, whether in the air or on the ground. The U.S. government would have exclusive access to a weapon much more valuable than the atomic bomb. Just a few fully operational gravity wave aircraft would once again give the United States the upper hand over the entire world. And, the very existence of the technology would trigger an arms race that would dwarf the one launched by the nuclear bomb. The implications of useful gravity wave technology were nothing less than staggering.

Rick's quiet celebration and contemplation of his discovery lasted only a minute because he knew what he had to do next. Instead of calling Drs. Thomas Grant and Phyllis Masters, the two other physicists assigned to his project, with the incredible news, Rick turned to the keyboard. With a few typed commands he permanently deleted any record the crucial molecular model ever existed. Then, opening the official logbook for his project, Rick wrote a short entry: "Molecular Modeling for Production of Element 128 #173 Partition 6 – negative results."

Without a word, Rick picked up his plastic slide rule, threw it dramatically against the nearby chalkboard, and stomped out the door. With his head down and hands stuck in the pockets of his wrinkled khaki trousers, Rick did a fine job portraying a tired and disappointed scientist who needed some rest. While he had planned this sort of ruse for when he found the critical formula, Rick struggled to contain the stress and abject fear that threatened to overwhelm him at any moment. In the past ten minutes, he had destroyed invaluable data and covered up his actions with false entries in the research logs – all acts of espionage. No place on earth had tighter security than Area 51, and Rick had no way of being absolutely certain his actions wouldn't be quickly discovered. With security cameras watching his every move, Rick managed to make his way through the underground corridor system feeling as if he was being scrutinized and dissected by unseen eyes.

Once in the relative privacy of his room, Rick's legs began to shake uncontrollably, and his breath came in quick gasps. The last time he experienced a panic attack, he had been just a boy, chased by a pack of dogs while walking home from school. He had barely made it through the door of grandmother's house without being mauled. Now, he knew he was experiencing a similar attack and forced himself to settle down. Slowly, his breathing normalized, and he was eventually able to pour himself a stiff drink. The panic subsided, but his anxiety level remained high.

Rick had few friends and only one at Area 51. Picking up the phone, he punched in the number for Dave Knox's room. Security monitored every communication at the facility, and Rick knew he would have to carefully stick to the code he and Dave set up.

"Yeah?" a groggy voice answered after a couple of rings.

"Hi, Dave. It's Rick."

"Uh, you know what time it is?" Dave asked, sounding minimally coherent.

"Yeah, sorry. But we need to talk about the last batch of tests for 128. I'm afraid they all failed, well, miserably," Rick said, unintentionally emphasizing 'miserably.'

Rick thought he could hear Dave jump out of bed.

"Miserably? Uh, that bad?" Dave asked, now wide awake.

"Yeah, I doubled check them myself. I thought you might want to know," Rick answered, fighting to keep from sounding nervous or excited.

After slight pause, Dave replied, "Okay. Well, that sucks. I have some early tests to run in the morning. Let's talk about where we stand sometime tomorrow afternoon."

"Sure. Sorry to bother you. Have a good night," Rick said, hanging up the phone.

He decided he deserved one more drink.

THREE

Exactly as planned, Rick's colleagues on the gravity wave fuel project, Drs. Thomas Grant and Phyliss Masters, left Area 51 at noon the day before the Labor Day holiday weekend, heading to Grant's secluded vacation home in the Chino Valley of Northern Arizona. Rick didn't understand the two middle-aged scientists' infatuation with each other. The fluctuations in their relationship had sometimes disrupted the group's work. He certainly wouldn't miss them in the least after he left Area 5, but he wasn't entirely comfortable with Dave Knox's request for their travel schedule. Intellectually, Rick realized the Grant and Masters knew too much about the Element 128 research and that they had the best chance of anyone in the world to replicate his results after he disappeared. Yet, the possibilities bothered him.

As soon as Grant and Masters left the laboratory, Rick sat down at the main input terminal. Layers and layers of encrypted security, firewalls, and programmed vaults protected the country's deepest secrets and blackest research. While Rick carried the entire formula for Element 128 and its production process in his exceptional brain, it would be of little use if the government could quickly rebuild his research team's process from the stored records. Sitting at the terminal, Rick knew one wrong keystroke would spark multiple security protocols. If caught now, he would disappear into whatever hellish torture chamber the military used to stash away its most dangerous traitors.

Years before, Rick had designed a clever and elegant back door through Area 51's security measures. By placing small patches of code directly into the metadata of his team's own research entries, just a few characters interspersed within the intricate mathematical models and chemical formulas, he created multiple trojan horses, just waiting for the data to be recalled. Once each file opened, the trigger code Rick now carefully entered would transform the data into useless gibberish.

For ninety grueling minutes Rick performed the complex re-programing process. When he finally hit the 'enter' key for the final time, his shirt was nearly soaked with sweat, but he knew he had succeeded. The government would have no chance to replicate his discovery by building on his past research.

With his mission at Area 51 complete, all he had to do now was get out.

Rick had booked his travel plans almost two weeks before and his corporate employer, as well as the security office, knew he would be flying out of Las Vegas to Atlanta. Rick didn't travel often, but he had planned similar trips over the years to visit his aging grandmother in a small town in South Carolina, a few hours' drive from Atlanta. His travel schedule would raise no red flags, at least until he failed to return to work at the end of the long weekend. He had three days before that happened and he would take good advantage of the time.

Rick kept to himself as he waited to board a large unmarked orange and white airliner for the short flight from Area 51 to Las Vegas. Everyone at the facility more than earned their off time. They worked long hours, often under extreme stress. Once on board, some of his anxiety receded. Against all odds, he had managed to steal one of the country's most valuable secrets from under the noses of the government and military. For the moment, Rick felt like a million bucks. A million exhausted bucks.

The feeling wouldn't last.

FOUR

J.P. Hoffman slid the barrel of his M24 sniper rifle over the crest of a rock-strewn hill, letting its heavy noise suppressor come to rest on a small canvas bag filled with sand. He lay prone on the rough ground, his muscular, tattoo-covered arms protruding from a sleeveless tee shirt. An old ball cap, turned backward, covered blond hair so short it almost didn't exist. J.P. sighted his weapon through a military-grade night vision scope, giving him perfect visibility of the lonely two-lane road below. Several hours earlier, he had received the call. His quarry had left Area 51 and begun their journey to Arizona.

Temperatures in the desert drop quickly after sunset. A cool breeze chilled the sweat on J.P.'s neck, while a pair of curious rodents scurried across his jeans. He didn't notice, hyper-focused on the shot he would need to make perfectly. He rehearsed it in his mind over and over again. *Identify the car. Place crosshairs on left rear tire. Breath. Hold. Squeeze the trigger.*

Not a single vehicle had passed his position since darkness fell, so when he first detected headlights in the distance, J.P. felt sure it was his targets. They were right on time. Finding the vehicle in his scope, the gunman identified the white Volvo SUV as Dr. Thomas Grant's car. A wry grin crossed his face as he centered the crosshairs on the car's tire.

As the Volvo approached, the target grew larger in his sights. When it reached the perfect position, he stilled his breathing and squeezed the trigger.

As he expected, the tire came apart, causing the big SUV to swerve violently. The destroyed tire slapped drunkenly on the asphalt as the vehicle quickly slowed to a stop just below his sniper's nest.

J.P. expertly chambered another round and waited. Just a few seconds later, he watched the car door open and a thin man wearing glasses emerge scratching his balding head. J.P. recognized Grant immediately from a picture provided by his employers. As the scientist knelt down to examine the destroyed tire, J.P. placed his crosshairs on Grant's temple and fired. The gun recoiled under his arm, emitting only a low cough as the round left the barrel.

Grant's head jerked to one side, blood and brain matter splattering over the car's white paint.

"Tom? Tom? What happened?" a woman's voice called as the passenger door opened.

J.P. could see his next victim stepping around the front of the car, light from one headlight and then the other clearly illuminating Dr. Phyliss Masters.

"Tom!"

Masters died instantly. J.P.'s third shot of the night snuffing out another brilliant mind in less than minute.

J.P. moved quickly now. He temporarily stashed the two bodies in a shallow ditch while he drove the SUV slowly toward a murky water reservoir a hundred yards away. As he approached the edge, he lowered the windows and simply stepped out of the still-rolling vehicle as it limped into the black water. He didn't wait to make sure it sank. He knew it would.

Anyway, he still had two bodies to hide, and one of those would be a pain in the ass to move.

J.P. dragged Phyliss Master's body backward, bearing the weight of her upper body by the underarms. Her chin rested on her chest, allowing the night breeze to blow long strands of gray hair into the killer's eyes and mouth. Wickedly hooked cactus needles grabbed at the woman's white lab coat and skin, further slowing his progress. With each pull, the heels of her ugly black shoes etched shallow furrows into the rough desert sand, the last mark the genius physicist would ever make on the face of the earth.

His thighs burned and sweat poured down his face until he finally arrived at the crude oblong hole in the desert floor he had dug earlier in the day. He unceremoniously dropped the dead woman nearby, her head making an audible thud as it impacted the ground.

Exhausted, J.P. sat down on a nearby rock and reached around to find the gallon of water he had stashed there. After downing almost half of the overly-warm liquid, he stepped over to the hole looking down to where Grant's body already rested on its back. With its arms askew and legs bent unnaturally, the dead man looked like a life-sized marionette, all dressed up like a doctor.

"Hey, Doc. I found your woman," J.P. said, chuckling at himself.

With that serving as the two scientists' only eulogy, J.P. rolled the woman into the pit. She landed face down, her massive body completely covering Grant's, except for two open eyes staring lifelessly over the dead woman's shoulder.

FIVE

Rick settled himself into the window seat for the commercial flight to Atlanta and immediately fell asleep. The stress of the past three months, not to mention the last twenty-four hours, had finally caught up with him. He didn't stir when another passenger maneuvered into the seat next to him, or even when the big airliner took off from McCarran Airport in Las Vegas.

He finally awoke when a flight attendant leaned across and asked if he wanted something to drink. Foggy from the brief nap, Rick asked for a cup of coffee, and looked around trying to get his bearings.

"Glad to see you're okay," his seatmate said, amiably.

Rick looked at the man in the seat next to him. A cold chill ran down his back despite the stranger's smile and friendly manner. *Who is this guy?*

"Uh, yeah, sorry," Rick said, pulling himself together. "Heavy few days, I guess."

"Casinos?"

Rick paused before replying. He felt trapped in the cramped seat pinned against the window. If the tall man in a rumpled dark suit was on the plane to stop him, there was nowhere for him to run. He was trapped. He had no choice. He had to play it cool.

Rick almost agreed he was a tourist, weary from several long nights of gambling. But if this guy worked for the feds, he would know that was a poor lie. Then he remembered the government knew he was on this flight, so he didn't need to try and make up some awkward story.

"I wish. Just a rush government contract. I've been putting in too many hours trying to make a bunch of generals happy with their new airplane," Rick replied, as casually as possible.

"Yeah? Generals and government contracts sound like serious stuff. By the way, I'm Drew. Drew Campbell," Drew said, reaching into his jacket pocket.

Rick's eyes grew wide and he felt an icy knot in the pit of his stomach.

"Uh, you know, I guess so," Rick managed to say more calmly than he felt.

Rick watched Drew closely, fearing he was about to produce an FBI badge, or worse. He suppressed a strong impulse to jump out of his seat despite the fact he was confined in an airplane thirty-thousand feet in the air.

"What kind of plane, if you don't mind me asking?" Drew asked, finally pulling a cell phone out of his inside jacket pocket.

Rick sat up, relieved. But the question kept him on edge.

"Uh, new fighter. Cool stuff really."

"Anything you can tell me about it? I'm sort of an aircraft buff. New military planes especially." Drew said, momentarily distracted by his cell phone before looking up at Rick. "Hey, no chance you worked out at Groom Lake is there?"

"Well, uh, yeah. We do a lot of testing out there," Rick answered, now obviously shaken.

"Oh, man. Look, I'm sorry. I think I've been too nosy," Drew said, quickly.

Rick could tell Drew felt honestly embarrassed. His nerves calmed a bit realizing his own imagination had run away with him.

"I'm Rick. It's no problem. Really. They don't let me out of my lab much, I guess. I wish I could tell you more. But, you know, it's all classified. I work on engines for one of the major suppliers. All pretty dry technical stuff," Rick replied, now much less jumpy.

"No problem. I completely understand. But I never thought I'd meet anyone that actually works at Area 51!" Drew exclaimed.

"Yep. I can't tell you much about that either, but it's awesome," Rick said, glad to see Drew's genuine reaction.

Rick's paranoia slowly subsided. No federal agent was this friendly.

"If you don't mine me prying further, are you an engineer?" Drew asked, trying not to sound too in awe of Rick.

"Aeronautical," Rick answered. "I also get a chance to use a lot of physics. I guess you'd say I'm a high-functioning airplane mechanic. How about you?"

That made Drew laugh. "Well, I imagine it's a fascinating job. I'm a lawyer."

"You don't sound too thrilled with it," Rick observed.

"Not today. A long week in Los Angeles with a bunch of hothead lawyers, grumpy judges, and epic traffic have soured me on the whole lawyer thing for the moment. I usually stay close to home in Banebridge. I guess I'm ready to get back there."

"I don't have any real idea about what lawyers do outside of what I see on T.V.," Rick said. "But give me your card and I'll send some promotional pictures of military aircraft my company puts together. They're pretty cool."

Drew quickly agreed, handing Rick a card from a small leather case.

"I have to visit some suppliers before going back. You can give the pictures to your kids or whatever," Rick said smiling, finally deciding Drew was actually the small-town lawyer he claimed to be.

"I'll look forward to it. Thanks," Drew replied. "But we both know I won't be giving them to my kids."

The two men chatted amiably for another thirty minutes discussing various aircraft. Seeing Drew's evident interest in anything aeronautical, Rick even offered a few facts about the engines on the airliner they sat in at that moment.

When Drew could see Rick getting tired, he said: "That was just fascinating. But maybe you should catch some shuteye for a while. You look beat."

"I think I'll do just that," Rick said, folding his arms and leaning back in his seat.

As he was just closing his eyes, Rick asked: "You a Star Trek fan by any chance?"

"How did you know? I'm a Next Generation nerd," Drew answered.

"Well," Rick said, quietly. "We got most of that stuff already."

Before Drew had a chance to ask any more questions, Rick turned his head toward the window and fell fast asleep, leaving the astonished lawyer to ponder the meaning of his last remark.

Three hours later, the airliner's tires slammed into the runway in Atlanta, jolting Rick awake.

Naptime was over and he had less than seventy-two hours before his absence would trigger alarm bells at Area 51. He needed to be safely tucked away at the new laboratory in Texas Dave Knox had told him about long before that time expired. But first, he had to keep a promise.

Once off the plane, it took only minutes for Rick to rent a car for the drive to South Carolina. But before he left, he stood in the parking lot absently folding his last credit card in half until it split down the middle. After flipping the two halves into a trash can, he tossed his bag into a nondescript white sedan. Once the feds began searching for him, his electronic trail would end at this very spot, a dirty curb at the Atlanta airport.

Three hours later, Rick rolled through the town of Aiken, South Carolina, his hometown and home to the only person in the world he cared about.

SIX

315 Miles West of Austin, Texas

Dr. Dave Knox stood next to Governor Margie Franks of Texas inside a gleaming stainless-steel elevator anticipating what he would find when they finally stopped plunging deep into the earth.

After receiving the coded message from Rick while at Area 51, Dave simply returned to his apartment in Las Vegas, packed a bag, and drove his car out of town. They planned to meet in Austin, but Rick hadn't appeared yet.

Rick's sabotage of the project at the beginning of a holiday weekend bought them three full days before security at the base discovered their disappearance. Now, time was running out, and Dave began to worry. While he could build the gravity wave craft, only Rick could recreate the precious formula for producing its fuel.

After an exhausting drive from Las Vegas to the outskirts of Austin, Dave met helicopter that whisked him across the desert to a tiny abandoned airfield where Margie's private jet sat alone at the edge of the tarmac. When his helicopter landed, he was surprised to be led into the single ramshackle hangar alongside the runway, instead of being invited into the governor's brand-new

Gulfstream G500. Inside, he found the Margie Franks waiting next to an open elevator door concealed in the hangar's back wall.

Foregoing any greeting, Margie ushered him inside for the quick descent to what turned out to be an underground laboratory. Rick had expected a top-notch facility to build a prototype gravity wave aircraft and fuel system, but he could never have imagined the vast area that opened up around him. The scale hit him first. The brightly lit space expanded in all directions, the view in front of his eyes only infrequently blocked by support pillars. To one side, a laboratory and computer center filled with every conceivable diagnostic, testing, and analytical device he had ever used or was even aware of, sat unmanned but ready. In the other direction, a gantry supported the beginning stages of an airframe under construction. Beyond that, he could see a complete materials warehouse and fabrication shop.

Speechless, Dave walked forward, taking a first look at the rudimentary airframe that would become the Directors' secret weapon.

To the untrained eye, the skeleton-like frame looked like one of those unfathomable pieces of modern art stuck in front of a glass office buildings. But to Dave, the roughly triangular assembly of carbon nanofiber tubing was a glorious scientific sculpture. Moving underneath, he took several minutes to closely examine one of the structural elements. With his nose six inches from the surface, the material looked just as he expected, but no less awesome. The tubing appeared to have no surface whatsoever. Instead, it seemed to be made up of separate particles each shimmering within its own space. In fact, Dave knew that's exactly what it was: a collection of specially designed molecules that clumped into particles of three distinct types. Each attracted two of the others without actually touching one another. One of Dave's latest creations, he never tired of grasping the material in his hand, knowing that as solid as it felt to the touch, radar waves, and even light in some of its forms, passed right through.

"Margie," Dave said, turning to his host for the morning's tour, "I think I'm in love with you! In my wildest dreams, I didn't expect a place like this. And you've already made progress on the prototype airframe."

"Don't be an ass, Knox," Margie scoffed. "But yeah, it's damn impressive if I do say so myself. The structural components are manufactured here on-site to the specifications you provided. Deliveries of materials, tooling, testing equipment, and everything else are made by vendors, sold to several dummy companies, and then delivered here."

"Where's the test range?" Dave asked.

Margie tapped a command into a small tablet computer and pointed at the far wall. Seventy-five yards in the distance, two enormous doors began opening smoothly and quickly away from each other, revealing a black gaping void almost two hundred feet wide and three stories tall. A second later, the darkness disappeared into the distance as the tunnel illuminated one section at a time.

"Good god! How far does that go?" Dave asked.

"Seven miles, give or take," Margie said, smiling.

"Is the testing range at the other end?"

"Yep. Weapons depot and a three hundred-square-mile test range. Nobody will know we have a new super plane until it's ready to go into action," Margie said proudly.

"Where'd you get that much land?" Dave asked.

Margie shrugged. "I'm the governor. We have near unlimited resources. And it's a big state. Once the prototype is finished, we'll go into production at the French airliner manufacturing plant near Mobile. We have another fully-equipped lab over there set up for final shakedown flights with full armament."

Dave turned back to his boss. "I appreciate the tour. But how did I get lucky enough to have one of the Directors as a tour guide? I imagine the governor of Texas has better things to do," Dave inquired.

"Nothin' as important as this," Margie said.

Dave looked down at a woman somewhat shorter than average, but with an ego as big as the state she ran. Piercing blue eyes burned into his and he could smell a slight lilac scent from her short straight gray hair. Despite her having to physically look up at him, in more ways than one, he felt she was actually looking down her nose.

"Let's talk straight," she began. "You and Donnelly have done us a great service. So great, in fact, that we are on the cusp of achieving our goal. *But we ain't there yet.* Secret plans and that crap get us nothing. We need the real deal and time's short. The feds will mobilize every law enforcement agency to look for you and Donnelly and they will be highly motivated."

"I get it, Margie," Dave replied, too lightly for the governor's liking.

Margie put one finger on Dave's chest. "No, I don't think you do. We're playing high stakes poker here. We're all-in on this airplane and what it can do. And you and Rick Donnelly are at the table. We've got two, maybe three months tops to get your toy put together and in the air. It's do or die time. We win, and you'll be rich and powerful beyond your dreams. Lose? Well, I hear the government just loves to execute traitors like you."

"We'll get it done," Dave said, doing his best to sound more confident than he felt.

Margie backed off a step. "Good. That's what the Directors want to hear. Now, where's your partner?"

"Uh, I'm not sure. I think he'll be here tomorrow or the next day. I left early. We couldn't risk anyone connecting us, could we?" Dave answered.

Margie immediately recognized that Dave's over-confident sarcasm had suddenly gone missing. "Call him," she ordered, a tinge of ice in her voice.

Dave looked back at Margie. While never warm or easy-going, he could feel her mood had gone from business-like to cold and threatening.

"Yeah, I would, but there's no way he kept his cell phone on. It can be tracked too easily. And I don't have any other way..."

Margie cut him off. "Are you telling me we don't know where the only man on earth that can produce Element 128 is right now?"

"Margie, he'll be here," Dave said, trying to sound calm and reassuring. "I know he planned to fly into Atlanta. He probably just wanted to see his grandmother. She raised him and I think she may be in bad shape."

Margie held Dave in the most malevolent stare he had ever seen. "You get him here in twenty-four hours or I'll take it out on your ass. Understand? In the meantime, get to work."

After Margie took the elevator, Dave looked around the cold empty space that suddenly felt a lot like a giant mausoleum. He had no idea how to reach Rick and his head quickly filled with worst-case scenarios. Could he have been caught already? Had he sold the process to someone else? Had he turned them in?

Yet, his logical mind wouldn't let him accept any of these fear-driven explanations. He knew Rick was loyal. He knew it. But...

Where are you, Rick??

Margie Franks didn't like loose ends. She didn't press Dave further about Rick's whereabouts, but she needed to know.

After one of the organization's long-term assets had approached her three years earlier about the possibility of acquiring a gravity wave weapon, she had pitched the prospect to the other Directors. It hadn't been easy, but they eventually green-lighted the plan and provided staggering amounts of funding for the underground laboratory and other facilities in the Big Bend desert of southwest Texas. She 'owned' the entire gravity wave aircraft project and failure wasn't an option.

The success of the entire endeavor rested on one man – Rick Donnelly. And nobody knew where he was.

Once in the air heading back to the capitol in Austin, Margie called the Chief of the Texas Ranger Division, commonly known as the Texas Rangers. Chief Randall Snow was not only one of the governor's staunchest political supporters, but a loyal member of The Cause and Margie's right-hand man. He answered on the first ring.

"Good afternoon, gov..."

Margie detested small talk. "Stow it, Snow. I got a special project for you."

"Yes, ma'am. What can I do?" Snow responded, used to Margie's abrupt style.

"I need you to find Dr. Rick or Richard Donnelly. He's an egg-head scientist working on jet engines or something. He's supposed to be working with the Directors on a special project and he hasn't shown up yet. Track him down, hog-tie his ass if you need to, and get him out to the lab."

"Yes, ma'am."

"Keep this private, Snow. Very, very private. Use only loyal internal resources, but get it done asap. This is for the Directors. You understand?" Margie asked.

"Indeed, I do, Madam Director."

"He may be headed towards wherever his grandmother is in South Carolina. Find him."

SEVEN

Members of the First Baptist Church still remembered the strange boy raised by his paternal grandmother – the venerated Irma Donnelly. 'Mrs. Donnelly,' as everyone in town called her, had been a pillar of the community for longer than anyone could remember. Her well-connected late husband had owned multiple metal-fabricating companies and left his wife the richest widow in Aiken County. And when her own deadbeat son dropped a baby on her doorstep, Mrs. Donnelly raised the boy as her own. As he grew up, the close-knit town began to notice the child's extreme intelligence and marveled at how Mrs. Donnelly worked tirelessly to nurture and care for a child who devoured college-level physics, chemistry and engineering textbooks and blew through high school assignments as if he had been asked to finger paint a duck in kindergarten.

Rick passed through the center of town just as dusk faded into night, slowing as he passed the old Aiken County Courthouse. He wanted to see the monument his grandmother had not only funded but fought to place prominently on the grassy square. The names of every Confederate soldier from Aiken appeared on the twenty-five-foot granite obelisk, including Rick's own ancestor, Lieutenant Richard J. Donnelly. In the springtime, the Daughters of the Confederacy carefully tended to rows of flowers planted at its base. A smile crossed Rick's face as he drove by, and he couldn't help but feel pride well up inside his chest.

Rick had come to see his grandmother, perhaps for the last time. She had remained loyal to the same cause he now served. He wanted to tell her they would succeed. He wanted her to know he too had remained loyal. But most of all, he wanted her to be proud of him.

A few minutes later, Rick pulled into the rehabilitation center's nearly deserted parking lot. He chose a spot near the far end, well away from the few dim overhead street lights. He had been here before and knew the limited number of security cameras on the property focused on the front entrance. The parking area and side entrance were simply ignored.

Rick moved quickly to a door that led directly into the first-floor residence hall. Tapping a code into the electronic lock, he stepped inside, ready to meet any staff with a smile and an explanation about a surprise visit. But it wasn't necessary. The hall was empty and quiet except for the muted sound of a baseball game seeping out from someone's room.

Just two doors down on the right, Rick opened his grand-mother's door and slipped inside. It had been almost a year since his last visit and he didn't know what to expect.

Mrs. Donnelly, the strongest person he had ever known, looked like death itself. She lay curled into a tight ball, several blankets covering her emaciated body despite the room being almost eighty degrees. Thin strands of grey hair fell from her nearly bald head and wrapped around her slack jaw. Rick could barely hear her shallow breathing, but each one sounded like it could be her last.

Pulling up a chair, Rick tenderly brushed several strands of hair off her face.

"Mama? Mama, it's me, Ricky," he said, leaning in close and using the name he had always called his grandmother.

When she didn't stir, Rick put a hand on her shoulder and tried again. This time, the old woman's eyes fluttered and then opened. A scowl crossed her ancient face.

"Mama? It's me, Ricky."

"I know who you are, boy," Mrs. Donnelly said, her voice harsh and cracked. "Why ain't you in school?"

"Mama, you know I graduated a long time ago. I gotta tell you something," Rick answered in a voice that sounded more like a child than a man.

"Where's Bonnie?" the old woman asked.

Rick had no idea who Bonnie was.

"Mama listen," Rick said, ignoring the question. "I've done it. I've got the formula. The federals will never have the weapon. We will be free again. You understand? Just like we always talked about."

For an instant, fire burned in Mrs. Donnelly's glassy eyes and a look of defiance crossed her face. "You're a good boy," she said, just before she closed her eyes.

It wasn't much, but it was enough. Rick could see it in her eyes.

He had kept his promise.

Confident his visit had gone unnoticed by the staff; Rick made his way back outside. He was just about to cross the lawn and walk to his rental car when he froze. Something wasn't right. Just across the street from the retirement home, two men sat in a black pickup. He could clearly see that the driver held a pair of binoculars to his eyes focused on the building's front door. He also couldn't miss that the same man wore a cowboy hat. The country road from the middle of town out to his grandmother's home saw little traffic during the day, much less at that time of night. He had to assume the men in the truck were looking for him.

Rick's blood ran cold as he backed slowly into the shadows of the building.

Calm down. Think.

He had left Area 51 just over thirty hours ago. The Element 128 project should be dormant, shut down, until almost two days from now when he and Masters and Grant were supposed to return from their vacation. There was no way, *no way,* the feds could have been on his trail this fast. *Was there?* Rick had been looking over his shoulder ever since he stole the formula and he now realized that if the feds had discovered what he did, they would absolutely stake out his grandmother's home.

Then, an even more disturbing thought crossed his mind. One that caused a wave of nausea to wash over his whole body. What if his bosses, the Directors, decided he wasn't invaluable after all? What if they planned to force him to give up the formula and then dispose of him, like he assumed they did to Grant and Masters? Did they somehow believe he would sell the formula to someone else? Why wouldn't they? Rick knew one thing for sure – someone wanted him found.

Rick peeked around the corner again, the truck hadn't moved. Suddenly, the cowboy hat made sense. They had to be Margie Franks' men!

In less than a minute, Rick had gone from proud of himself for living up to his grandmother's expectations, to paralyzed by imagined threats from all directions. Even the genius part of his mind couldn't deal with the sheer terror that made his knees shake and his hands sweat uncontrollably. And to make matters worse, he was trapped. He had no way of getting to the car without being seen.

With no place to go, Rick stayed by the back door, his back pressed against the side of the building. If someone suddenly decided to come outside, they would be startled to find him lurking by the door and would almost certainly give him away. He could go back in, but he didn't know if there was an agent or someone already inside just waiting for him to appear.

Over the next five minutes, the tension became nearly unbearable.

Finally, Rick heard an engine start in the distance and the crunch of tires on gravel. Daring a brief glance around the corner, Rick saw the pickup making a U-turn and drive off back in the direction of town.

Without waiting, Rick walked quickly back to his car and drove away in the opposite direction.

EIGHT

Rick spent the entire night holed up in a seedy hotel that didn't mind taking cash. The next day, after mustering enough courage to take some sort of action, Rick abandoned the rental car in the motel's back lot and called one of Aiken's only taxis. The run-down old sedan dropped him at a used car dealership on the southern edge of town. Now, he stood in the hot sun while an excited salesman boasted about the quality of his inventory and his five-star customer satisfaction rating.

"That's great," Rick said, trying not to sound in a hurry. "I'm looking for something for my son. He's about to go off to college, and he needs something cheap but reliable. His mother worries about him enough already, and I don't want him broken down on the road somewhere between here and Clemson."

"No problem!" the salesman replied. "I bet he wants a truck."

Rick could almost hear the guy licking his chops at the prospect of an easy sale.

"Well, he sure does! How'd you know?" Rick asked, attempting to sound impressed.

"Most boys around here do. Anyway, I think I've got a few that might work."

They walked to one side of the lot where several pickups sat in a row facing the road. Prices had been scrawled in white shoe polish on their windshields.

Rick immediately picked out a red 1992 Ford Ranger priced at $2500.00.

"Tell me about this one. It's in my price range," Rick said, peering inside.

"Good eye!" the salesman commented. "I got this one in on trade just last week. Sixty thousand miles. Air conditioner is broken, but she drives out real smooth."

Rick examined the tires and took a few minutes inspecting the four-cylinder engine for leaks. He needed to fit into the countryside, and the little truck's slightly shabby appearance would do so nicely.

After a short test drive, Rick agreed to pay the asking price.

The dealer couldn't believe his luck. Rick hadn't even tried to negotiate the price lower! And he paid cash!

A few minutes later, Rick found himself inside the dealer's office, a battered metal shed with a window unit that made more noise than cool air. "Yes sir, you're all set. She's ready to go," the used car salesman said, beaming and handing Rick the keys.

Rick got up and headed for the door.

"Mr. Crandle, don't forget your bill of sale!" The salesman called, holding up a single sheet of paper. "You'll need it to get a permanent tag. That temporary one on the back window is only good for thirty days. I hope your son enjoys it!"

"I'm sure he will. Thanks again," Rick said, taking the paper and smiling. "Have a good day."

"Already did, sir. Already did," The salesman answered with delight.

Rick drove out of Aiken about eleven o'clock in the morning in the old truck. His original plan was to simply drive the rental car to Texas after visiting his grandmother. He had plenty of time before the discovery of his theft. But the appearance of the stakeout at the retirement home had forced him to rethink everything.

Rick knew that he couldn't do anything except run if the FBI or other federal agencies were already this close. But, if the Directors were looking for him, his only hope was to have an insurance policy – a threat to reveal everything if some harm came to him. Terrified and confused, he wasn't thinking as clearly as he should. He had been loyal. He had the information that would give his employers the weapon they desperately needed. But he just couldn't shake the feeling he was being hunted.

Am I crazy? Did I make too much of the two guys in the truck last night?

Thoughts raced through his head, one moment convinced everything was fine and he had just been paranoid the night before. Then, in the next second, he became obsessed with the idea of building his "safety net." Rick had no friends, nobody to turn to for help. He and Dave Knox had been friendly but not close. And he had no idea whether he could trust him anymore. But then he remembered the exceptionally friendly lawyer from the university town of Banebridge. He seemed trustworthy and would probably be glad to maintain some important information for a nice fee. He finally decided on a course of action and turned west. It would take him six hours or more to reach Banebridge on back roads - if the ancient pickup held together.

A couple of hours later, as he passed south of Atlanta, Rick had calmed down somewhat and decided to make a call to Dave Knox. He rationalized the call by telling himself he would keep it short and untraceable. He figured that if Dave had betrayed him, he would know by the sound of Dave's voice. Digging in his bag, Rick retrieved one of the cheap burner phones he had purchased at the Atlanta airport. A few minutes later, and after taking a few deep breaths, he dialed Dave's number.

"Oh man, I was worried. You were supposed to be here yesterday. Are you okay?" Dave sounded genuinely concerned.

"Yeah, no problem. I'm on the road. I'm on my way there now," Rick replied, doing his best to sound natural.

"Driving?" Dave asked. "Where are you coming from? Will you be in town soon?"

"I'm actually near Nashville," Rick replied. "I should be there sometime tomorrow. No worries."

"How about letting us pick you up in, say, Memphis? We could fly you down here right away on the G-500," Dave suggested. "We need you as soon as possible."

"No thanks, I'll drive. Chill out. I'll see you tomorrow. It's been a long time since I've been out of the lab, let me have a little free time and we'll knock the thing out when I get there."

Dave had put Rick somewhat at ease by sounding perfectly normal and anxious for his help.

"Well, alright, buddy, I'll cover for you until then, but we have to get moving. Our employers need the product, and we're behind. Tomorrow for sure?" Dave asked.

"Absolutely. I'm going to find a good barbeque place and pig out. Ha! Pig out! Get it? I'll be there no later than tomorrow evening. See you then."

Rick hung up feeling slightly better and congratulating himself on his performance.

After more thought, he finally concluded that even if the Directors had no intention of killing him and did indeed want his expertise, and he was far from convinced that was the case, he still needed a safety net. He would be in Banebridge now in less than three hours, about the time a lawyer should be wrapping up his day.

In Austin, Chief Snow scowled at his computer screen. Tapped into NSA surveillance systems, Snow's office could filter cell phone calls, texts, and emails through sophisticated algorithms, looking for names or combinations of words that met particular search parameters. Once they flagged a call, they could peel back the metadata embedded in the signal, find the specific telephone number, and track the telephone through cell tower intercepts.

One such call had just been identified and even included a transcript of Rick's recent conversation with Dave Knox. According to the data embedded in the call, Rick Donnelly had been just southeast of Atlanta a little less than two hours ago. However, the cellphone had gone dead immediately after the call ended and, the NSA's system had picked up no further information.

One thing was clear though, he had lied about being near Nashville.

But Snow also knew that if Donnelly used the phone again, he would be able to pinpoint the wayward physicist's location immediately.

NINE

Rick drove through southern Georgia on back roads and state highways, making sure to stick to the speed limits. The area had a reputation for setting speed traps meant to collect funds from tourists avoiding the crowded freeways on their way to Florida. The last thing he needed was some Barney Fife deputy lucking into the biggest arrest of his life.

Evening approached as Rick's old truck rolled across the border into Alabama. After joining an interstate highway for twenty minutes, he found the exit to Banebridge and Southern University. Tired and sweaty from the summer heat and lack of functioning air conditioning, Rick picked up a burger and extra-large soda at a fast-food place before parking in the shaded lot of the Hillmont Hotel, just across the street.

After taking a break long enough to get revived by the cold drink and food, Rick fished around in his bag for the burner phone. Hoping Drew Campbell would still be in, Rick dialed the law firm's main number. Knowing that he couldn't loiter in Banebridge overnight, he needed this to work.

"Drew Campbell's office," an overly-cheery woman's voice said when the phone picked up.

Rick asked for Drew in what he hoped was a businesslike voice.

"I'm sorry, Drew just left for the day. Can I give him a message?" the woman replied.

Dammit!

Rick had to think fast.

"Oh, no! I'm an old friend of Drew's from college. I'm just in town for the night and sure hoped he might be in so I could buy him a beer," Rick said, sounding disappointed.

"Oh my, that's too bad. But he just left a few minutes ago headed to the gym. It's on second avenue downtown. He won't let me give out his cell number, but you could probably catch him over there."

"I'll do that. You are very nice, and I'm going to tell him so," Rick replied.

After hanging up, Rick turned off the burner phone and tossed it into the now-empty fast-food bag. He stepped from the cab of the truck, stretched his muscles, and then threw the remnants of his meal, along with the phone, into the hotel's dumpster.

Chief Snow nearly jumped out of his office chair when his computer flashed an alert that the same cell number Rick Donnelly had used earlier in the day was once again in use, this time in Banebridge, Alabama. Snow had no way to hear the actual conversation, but he could pinpoint where it originated. Typing a few commands into the tracking program brought up a map of the area showing the precise location - a hotel.

"Now I got you," Snow said, just before dialing Governor Margie Franks' private phone line.

"Madam Governor, I found him. He's at the Hillmont Hotel in Banebridge, Alabama," Snow reported when Franks answered.

"Excellent. Who do we have in the area that can pick him up?" Franks asked.

Snow checked the location of his men. The news wouldn't please Franks.

"I'm afraid none at the moment. I can have some of my Rangers there by morning," Snow responded, bracing for the verbal assault he knew was coming.

To Snow's surprise, though, Franks remained silent - which was worse.

"I'll take care of it," Franks said after a few moments. "We have other assets in the area. Get your men on the move. I'll have Donnelly delivered to them."

The gym turned out to be a new, modern YMCA. After explaining that he was just looking for a friend, the bored front desk clerk informed him Drew Campbell had checked in almost an hour earlier and that Rick could wait for him at a small seating area just off the lobby.

After keeping a lookout for only five minutes, Drew emerged from the men's locker room headed for the front door, looking down at his cell phone.

"Drew?" Rick said, as the lawyer walked by.

Drew looked up from his phone and turned in Rick's direction.

He didn't recognize Rick at first. Rick's beard and slightly disheveled clothes didn't help.

"Yes," Drew said politely. "Can I help you?"

Rick threw on a smile and stood.

"Hi, I'm Rick. Rick Donnelly. Uh, we met on an airplane out of Las Vegas a few days ago."

Recognition dawned on Drew's face.

"Of course! The glorified airplane mechanic. Now I remember. How are you?" Drew said, offering his hand.

"Oh, fine. Sorry to catch you off guard," Rick said. "I've been on the road visiting suppliers and stopped in Banebridge for the night. I called your office, and your friendly secretary said you had left for the day, but kindly told me you might be here. I was hoping to catch you while I was in town."

A little confused, Drew asked: "What about?"

A chance conversation on a random flight rarely led to continued contact with the other person. Drew was wary, but not worried.

"I know, I know, this is a little weird," Rick said, seeing the concern on Drew's face. "I'm just in need of some simple legal services. I found your card, and since I was in town…"

Disarmed by Rick's friendly manner, Drew looked at his watch.

"Sure. Why not? Why don't we just sit down right here? I'm meeting my wife, but I have a few minutes," Drew said.

The sun still shone brightly outside as Rick explained how he was thinking about leaving his company and starting a consulting firm of his own. He had concocted the story on his long drive to give Drew a plausible reason for seeking him out. Rick went on to explain how he needed help setting up a company and a lawyer he could trust to handle some sensitive documents.

"What kind of 'sensitive documents'?" Drew asked.

Rick had anticipated the question.

"I've developed a few ideas for vastly increasing the efficiency of jet engines. It's groundbreaking work I've done on my own time," Rick explained. "The truth is, every major manufacturer would like to get their hands on my designs. And I know it sounds egotistical, but they know I'm the guy that could make such a discovery."

"And you want a lawyer to hang on to this for you? Why? Why not just stick it in a safe deposit box or something?" Drew asked.

"Well, I've done that," Rick said. "But I need a lawyer to hold another complete set of the plans and specs in case I need them and I can't get to the bank. I spend a lot of time with European aircraft manufacturers, so I'm on the road or in the air most of the time. Once I leave my current job, I'll be in a position to get a patent and all that legal stuff. I'm not quite ready to do that yet."

"Why me?" Drew asked. "I'm not a patent lawyer."

Rick gave Drew his most earnest look.

"Simply put, because I think I can trust you. That may sound naive, but that's the truth," Rick said. "Like I said on the plane, I don't know any lawyers. None in fact."

"I have to ask," Drew responded seriously. "Are you involved in anything illegal? Because I'm out if there's anything, and I mean anything, shady going on."

Rick gave a quick laugh.

"No. Not at all, I swear," he said without hesitation. "This is about me protecting my ideas and hopefully making a great big pile of money. That's it."

Other than the odd circumstances of the meeting, Drew couldn't come up with a reason to distrust Rick. He had decided during their time on the plane Rick was brilliant and nerdish, but a good guy.

"Alright, then. You got yourself a lawyer," Drew said.

"Awesome! I have a couple of things for you," Rick said, reaching into the black backpack he had carried into the gym. "First things first, here's a five-hundred-dollar retainer. Other than holding the documents, there won't be much to do on your end for a few weeks at least. You can bill against that for now."

"That's plenty," Drew said, sticking the cash in his wallet.

"Now for the important part," Rick said, pulling a fat shipping envelope from the bag. "Keep these someplace safe."

Drew took the envelope and turned it over in his hands. He could tell it contained a thick stack of documents.

"This contains the plans or whatever?" he asked.

"Yes. Hard copies and a thumb drive. Formulas, technical specs, calculations, some drawings," Rick explained. "Feel free to look through them if you want, but it's pretty dry technical stuff."

"I'll put it in the firm's safe as is. I wouldn't understand it any-way," Drew replied, placing the package in his gym bag.

"Thanks. I'll be in touch in a week or two when I sort out my situation," Rick said, standing.

After parting, Drew drove back to his office to tuck Rick's package into his safe, completely unaware that plans for the world's newest superweapon lay nestled next to his sweaty workout clothes.

TEN

In the end, Rick's decision to meet Dave Knox in Austin came down to a simple risk analysis. If the feds caught him, he would spend the rest of his life in a windowless cell deep inside a super-max prison - or worse. On the other hand, his fear that the Directors didn't need him might be been nothing more than his imagination. Plus, now he had his 'insurance policy'.

Unfolding his paper map, Rick traced out a route that took him on backroads into Mississippi, through Louisiana, and across eastern Texas. Using the interstate system would have saved almost six hours but would also be heavily patrolled. Mustering his courage, Rick aimed his truck west. If he drove through the night, he would arrive in Austin around six o'clock the following evening.

Downing cup after cup of coffee, Rick passed countless small towns, modest farms, ramshackle mobile homes, and ancient barns slowly disintegrating back into the earth. Seemingly unending hours passed on roads that all looked pretty much the same. Having spent his life either in college or cocooned in gleaming laboratories, Rick hadn't been exposed to the rural south since leaving South Carolina many years before. Sometimes lushly beautiful, but often dismally poor, the view from his pickup re-introduced the brilliant scientist to his true home. A home he loved.

Stopping only to fill up the truck with gas and grab the next cup of bad coffee, miles rolled by under the old truck. Despite his high caffeine intake, Rick's energy slowly ebbed close to empty. He almost stopped to catch a couple of hours of sleep several times, but he needed to keep his promise to meet Dave in Austin that evening. Even though he was still anxious about his decision, he knew he couldn't afford to give the Directors any reason to doubt his loyalty.

Finally, Rick stopped the truck at a crowded shopping mall outside Austin and used his last burner phone to call Dave Knox.

"Oh, man! Am I glad to hear from you!" Dave said, sounding genuinely excited. "Where are you? Please tell me you're in town."

"Yeah, I'm at, uh, North Austin Mall. It's been a long drive. Where do I need to go now?" Rick asked, his voice betraying his exhaustion.

"No place. Just sit tight and we'll pick you up. You don't need to be seen," Dave replied.

"What do I do with my ride?" Rick asked, having become somewhat attached to the faithful old Ford that managed to get him halfway across the country without trouble.

"Leave it. Our guys will take care of it. Anyway, you won't be needing a car for a while. Man, I can't wait for you to get out here and see our new, uh, workshop! You won't want to leave," Dave said confidently.

"Dave, I'm sorry I'm late," Rick said, trying to keep doubt out of his voice. "Am I cool with, you know, the Directors?"

Dave didn't hesitate. "Absolutely. Nothing has changed. But, man, a lot is going to change when we get this thing done! Are you ready to change the country forever?"

"I'm ready."

He might have been less enthusiastic if he had known about what transpired in Banebridge just hours after he drove away.

ELEVEN

Southern University
Banebridge, Alabama

Michael King threw one arm up on the door, sat back in the bucket seat, and felt the sun on his face. Driving his old Mustang convertible slowly under the live oaks on University Avenue, Michael couldn't deny the sense of freedom that came with leaving his suburban family or the anticipation of everything his sophomore year might hold in store. All his emotions rolled up on that beautiful afternoon equaled one thing – happiness.

With a grin on his face, Michael flicked the wheel right and turned into his favorite place on earth, the Eta Mu fraternity house. His tires crunched across the packed gravel parking lot while he searched for a spot as close as possible to the front door. Getting lucky, Michael spun the wheel with one hand, hit the brakes, and skidded to a stop, the nose of his car just peeking over the concrete curb. He was home.

Sitting still, Michael took a moment just to look around, thinking about how the house hadn't changed at all since he left in May. The five gleaming white columns still stood two stories over the wide front porch, dormers on the third floor still kept watch over much of the campus, and the enormous live oak trees standing in the expansive front lawn still cast their broad cooling shadows. As always, it looked the part of an old Southern plantation. Michael realized he was being a little silly thinking about how glad he was everything was just as he left it, but he was anyway.

Ready to get inside, Michael opened the car's long door, noticing just in time Hunter Ewell's black BMW parked right next to him. Denting the pristine paint of the new fraternity president's car would have made for a poor start to the year. Had he been less in a hurry, he would have chosen somewhere else to park. One of the few brothers Michael didn't get along with, Hunter had taken a little too much pleasure hazing the pledges, particularly Michael, often making pointless demands that he wash his precious vehicle over and over.

Determined not to let Hunter's past antics ruin his mood but making sure to avoid Hunter's car, Michael grabbed one of the two big canvas duffle bags from his back seat. Inside, the house was busy, filled with brothers moving in, fathers hefting their sons' belongings into rooms, and mothers fretting over details their sons cared little about.

Michael tossed hurried greetings to friends as he passed through the frat house parlor. Strictly reserved for entertaining alumni on football weekends and formal parties, Michael made sure to skirt around the room's expensive furniture, which sat carefully placed across from an ornate faux fireplace mantle. He didn't understand all the fuss made over the room and how it looked. Sometimes he just had to chuckle at the absurdity of it and especially the wallpaper that depicted an English fox hunt, complete with red-coated hunters, bugles, and a snarling fox trapped by dogs against a tree.

Even though he had to move in by himself, Michael hadn't taken his parents up on their offer to come along. They both worked full-time. And, the long trip from their home near Birmingham to Southern University's campus in Banebridge would have meant them taking a vacation day, which Michael wanted them to use for just that - a vacation. Anyway, they didn't understand why Michael wanted to spend money joining a fraternity, and he, in turn, didn't relish the idea of fielding their well-meaning questions about the frat, how it spent his money, and the like. While his family helped Michael pay for college when they could, he had contributed the lion's share of his college expenses; so, joining Eta had been his decision. Sure, he had to work all the jobs he could get and take out loans, but he knew it took a lot of pressure off his family.

Moving into the stairwell, Michael thought about how his parents might be surprised by the frat house's spartan, even institutional, nature beyond the ground floor parlor. The brothers lived on the top two floors, each side lined with basic dorm rooms with metal beds and desks jammed inside. Most brothers cleverly arranged their rooms to take advantage of the limited space. Only the officers' suites on the top floor provided some amount of privacy. The mansion-like exterior, vast front lawn, and parlor were just a shiny veneer. The luxury ran only skin deep.

Finally reaching his room, Michael pushed down the door handle with his foot and kicked the door open.

"Hey, dude! What the hell!"

Startled, Michael saw a blanket being yanked up over the lower of two bunk beds.

"Really?" Michael said to the covered lump as he dropped his duffle and backed quickly out.

"Sorry!" said a different voice, this one clearly female.

As he shut the door, Michael shouted: "No problem! But I'm coming back in fifteen minutes with the rest of my stuff!"

He didn't wait for a reply.

Michael could only shake his head at the exploits of his roommate. A good guy, but altogether too focused on chasing girls, and not at all on college. Michael was actually kind of surprised his parents had sprung for a second year. Unless his roommate's grades improved this year, his chances of seeing a third year seemed slim.

Now having a few minutes to kill, and hungry from his drive, Michael trotted back downstairs and into the restaurant-sized kitchen.

"Hey, Carl!" Michael said, smiling after seeing the fraternity's long-time head staffer looking over a new food delivery.

"Mr. King!" Carl said, turning away from several boxes of dry goods. "I see you made it back for a second year. That's just fine! How was your summer? Good?"

"Yeah, fine," Michael replied, perching on a stool next to one of the long stainless-steel prep tables. "Worked. Went to the beach for a week. Stuff like that. Got any sandwiches around? I'm starving!"

"You know we do," Carl replied. "I put some chicken salad in the refrigerator over there just a few minutes ago. I'll get you some lemonade too. It's from that powder, but it's cold as can be."

"Thanks, man. You're the best."

Michael attacked the sandwich, downing two large glasses of lemonade along the way.

Finished, Michael thanked Carl again, left through the kitchen door and walked around the building back to the parking lot. The sun had grown even hotter as the afternoon went on and Michael could barely touch the surface of his car after it sat baking outside for less than an hour.

After tossing the second duffle on the sidewalk, Michael opened the trunk and reached inside. Some of the college stuff he had haphazardly loaded into two laundry baskets had managed to escape in transit. Leaning over and trying to corral a bunch of notebooks and pens, he didn't see Hunter Ewell come up from behind.

"Hey, King! Welcome back!" Hunter laughed, slapping Michael on the back. "I can't believe that old POS is actually still on the road."

Michael generally tried to avoid Hunter. He had a hard time dealing with Hunter's exaggerated sense of self-worth that sprouted from the Ewell family's wealth and political clout. And, when he became fraternity president last spring in an uncontested race, Michael knew he would become insufferable.

"Funny as always, Hunter," Michael replied, not amused by the joke. He and his father had worked together on its restoration, and they had done excellent work.

"Wow! I must have hit a nerve. Sor-ry," Hunter said, his voice dripping with sarcasm.

"No problem," Michael said, turning back to finish unloading his car and hoping Hunter would move on.

As Michael wrestled a laundry basket up out of the trunk, Hunter slapped him on the back again and said, "King, I hope you have a *great* year, dude!"

Michael didn't have time to reply before Hunter ducked into his car. He decided just to forget the whole incident. It wasn't worth his time to deal with someone as self-important as Hunter Ewell.

TWELVE

Later that afternoon, Hunter sat sprawled on his leather couch enjoying the evening's first sips of whiskey. Moving into the president's suite on the top floor of the frat house had been a breeze. The big room came fully furnished, and as president, the house staff moved in all his personal belongings. For the moment, he just relaxed, congratulating himself on rising to the top of the university's most prestigious fraternity.

Nobody believed for an instant that Hunter did anything to earn the position. In fact, everyone knew his family's reputation made his ascent to fraternity president a foregone conclusion. Hunter knew it too and couldn't have cared less – he was entitled to it all. Simple as that.

As the shadows on the lawn outside grew longer and the air cooled, he grabbed a folding chair and stepped through one of the dormer windows onto the roof of the expansive front porch. Flicking the chair open with one hand, Hunter sat down to admire his new domain. It was good to be the president!

Thirty minutes before dinner would be served in the dining room, Hunter decided maybe one more drink would be in order. But as he got up, his plan got interrupted by the ring of his cell phone deep in the pocket of his khaki shorts. Pulling out the phone, he looked for the name of the caller. No name appeared on the screen, only a number and 'Austin, Texas.'

He didn't need a name. His father had made him memorize the number - it belonged to the Directors. Hunter's stomach churned, and his hand shook as he came to grips with what this call might mean.

Just before Hunter started college three years earlier, his father, Richard S. Ewell, IV, sat him down in his plush office perched atop the tallest building in Mobile. With an expansive view of Mobile Bay at his back and a portrait of Confederate General Richard S. Ewell scowling down from one wall, his father had revealed information provided to only a select group of young men and women. That conversation came flooding back to Hunter.

"Son, this is important. In fact, what I'm about to tell you will affect the rest of your life. So, listen carefully," Richard began, standing proudly in front of his desk.

"Yes, sir," Hunter replied, recognizing the tone his father used for the most solemn occasions.

"You are part of a grand and historic family that stretches back to the Civil War. Since that time, our fathers and grandfathers have built this family's fortune to a truly remarkable level. You should be proud of that."

"Yes, sir. I am," Hunter said, already wondering where this conversation was going.

"Now, you must begin preparing to carry our family forward, and I'm going to tell you the first steps. This information is for you alone. Revealing it to anyone would be dangerous to you, me, and the entire family. Do you understand?" Richard asked, sitting down behind his desk.

"Yes, sir. I understand," Hunter said, his curiosity piqued.

"The Ewells are part of a special group of people. Many years ago, your great-great-grandfather formed an alliance with several other families. They worked together where possible, aided each other's endeavors – all with the goal of advancing every families' wealth and

influence. That alliance has carried forward even to today. Do you understand so far?"

"I think so," Hunter said, without confidence he actually did.

"You'll learn more later. For now, I can tell you that twelve men and women serve as the Directors of our group. You would know some, but not others."

"Are you a Director?" Hunter asked.

"If I was, I couldn't reveal that to you. Not yet," Richard replied. "But that's not important now. What you must do now is prove you can one day step up, become a leader, and represent your family within this alliance. You are about to enter college. Your first step, once there, will be to join my old fraternity and become part of The Tyros."

"Isn't The Tyros that sort of secret organization that controls campus politics?" Hunter asked.

"Yes. That will be your training ground, for lack of a better term. You will not only join the fraternity; you will control it. You will not only be a part of The Tyros; you will be become president of the Student Government Association. How you accomplish this is up to you. The Directors will be watching, as will I."

Hunter already controlled the fraternity. And, in the next few months, he would use The Tyros political machine to be elected president of the Student Government Association. As a sign he was on track and noticed by the Directors his father had given him the telephone number that now appeared on the front of his phone. He also had to memorize a code to be used if the Directors ever called. Richard Ewell's only instructions had been to obey whatever orders he received without question. Most importantly, though, he was not to fail at whatever task the Directors assigned.

"Hunter Ewell, 6158," Hunter said tentatively into the phone.

"Richard Ewell's boy. I've heard good things," a raspy female voice said without further identifying herself. "Are you ready for your first task?"

Gathering himself as best he could, Hunter said, "Yes, ma'am. I'm ready."

"Excellent. The Directors are looking for a scientist named Rick Donnelly. He's at the Hillmont Hotel there in Banebridge. I'm going to give you a number for a man named J.P. Call him, meet him in person, and have him find and hold Donnelly until I call you again. J.P. will do the heavy lifting, but it's your responsibility to make sure it gets done. Do you understand these instructions?"

"Uh, yes. I mean, yes, ma'am. I understand," Hunter said.

"You don't exactly fill me with confidence, Mr. Ewell," the voice said.

"It will be no problem. I'm to have this J.P. find and hold Rick Donnelly until you call again. I can handle it," Hunter replied, sounding somewhat surer of himself.

The voice read out J.P.'s number and provided a brief description of Rick Donnelly.

"Mr. Ewell, this is your chance to prove yourself. Don't fail us."

The call ended abruptly, and Hunter sat back down. *Did she mean to have him participate in kidnapping someone?* Of all the things he had imagined the Directors might ask him to do, he hadn't imagined anything like kidnapping!

Two more hefty shots of whiskey made him feel a little better. After a third, he had enough courage to call J.P.'s number and arrange a meeting.

THIRTEEN

To celebrate their first day back on campus, Michael met his long-time friend, Zach Self, for a beer at Smokey Joe's Bar. Conveniently located across University Avenue from the frat's front yard, the old bar had catered to students for over five decades. Michael couldn't help but love the dark, shabby interior and its pervasive odor of spilled beer, with undertones of urine and cigarettes. Its single, scarred oval booth near the door seemed out of place among thirty or so rickety wood tables and chairs, not one of which sat squarely on the floor.

Nearly empty on a weekday afternoon, Michael and Zach had grabbed one of the three pool tables arranged side by side in the bar's backroom. Stained but straight and level, generations of Southern students had lined up shots across these same tables. Now Zach sighted down his own cue, hoping to bank the eight ball into a side pocket. The ball missed, scratching into the corner.

"Crap!"

As Michael grabbed his cue to break, Zach's phone rang. Michael waited for the short conversation to end.

"What's up?" Michael asked, seeing the confused look on Zach's face.

"Hunter wants to see me right now," Zach said, his eyebrows raised.

"That sucks. But I guess you better see what our fearless leader wants. I'll see you for dinner," Michael said. "By the way, you forfeit."

Zach trotted across the street and into the frat house, stopping in the bathroom before continuing up to Hunter's room. He didn't want the beers his just drank interfering with whatever Hunter wanted.

After climbing to the top floor, Zach knocked on Hunter's door. "Yeah! Get in here, Self."

Zach opened the door and found Hunter restlessly pacing up and down in front of a heavy oak desk.

"Hi," Zach said, noticing the drink in Hunter's hand and a half-empty bottle of Jack still sitting on the coffee table.

"Sit down, have a drink," the Eta president said, handing Zach a glass and waving vaguely at the bottle of liquor. "I just might have something for you having to do with the elections."

Zach poured a shot of the whiskey into the glass. "Okay," he replied a little warily.

"Me and The Tyros watched you last year. Even as a freshman, you campaigned harder for our candidates than anyone."

"Just trying to do my part I guess," Zach replied.

"Ha! That's funny! You can't bullshit a bullshitter! You're ambitious and in a hurry to prove what you can do. Right?"

Confused, Zach just said: "I suppose."

"Aww, don't be shy. What do you *really* want? What's your goal here? We're just friends talking," Hunter said magnanimously.

"Alright. Fine. I want to be the President of the Student Government Association, go to law school, and one day become a United States Senator from Alabama," Zach replied, every word the truth.

"And how you going to get all that done?" Hunter asked, trying to draw more out of Zach.

Still not understanding where all this was going, but knowing that his answer would be important, Zach took a second before answering.

"Loyalty," he said. "To the school, the frat, and the state."

Hunter grinned. "Close. What about The Tyros?"

Dammit! I'm an idiot! Zach thought, chastising himself for missing the obvious answer. His father had always told him that the men from the fraternity, and everyone in The Tyros, had stayed loyal to him his whole life and that they had been instrumental in his success.

"Of course, The Tyros," Zach answered. "My grandfather and father were both Tyros men, I'm loyal to The Tyros and in twenty-five or thirty years or so my sons or daughters will be too."

"Okay then. Better. I'll get right down to it," Hunter said, half-sitting on the edge of the desk. "Look, I got a problem. One of The Tyros candidates for senate this year dropped out. I think I can get a second Eta into the senate. If I can, you interested?"

Zach couldn't believe his ears. The Tyros never ran sophomores for any office, and it was unheard of to have two senators elected from the same fraternity!

"Well?" Hunter asked when Zach hesitated.

"Uh, yeah, sure! I'm your guy. Just tell me what you need me to do," Zach said, his eyes betraying the immense ambition that could be very useful to Hunter.

"Now, that is *exactly* what I wanted to hear. I got a little job for you tonight."

FOURTEEN

"Who did you say you are meeting?" Zach asked from the driver's seat of Hunter's car.

"I didn't say," Hunter replied, his voice slightly slurred. "I got to meet some guys for a minute. Your job is to just drive me there."

"Okay," Zach said. He didn't mind driving Hunter around a little, especially after being offered the senate candidacy. Hunter clearly shouldn't be behind the wheel, but Zach didn't like the way Hunter was acting secretive or the fact he looked nervous and more than a bit scared.

Hunter directed Zach away from campus and out to the Moon Glow truck stop near the interstate highway.

It had grown dark, and the giant neon crescent moon hanging over the parking lot cast a yellow glow visible for a half-mile in either direction. Rolling past the diesel pumps used by truckers, Hunter had Zach stop near the back of an expansive but dimly lit parking area usually reserved for tractor-trailer rigs.

"You're meeting someone *here*?" Zach asked. "Hey look, I appreciate your offer, but I don't want to get mixed up in anything ...."

Even through a whiskey-induced haze, Hunter played it cool. "Naw, it's nothing like that. I just have some business with this guy. It won't take long. When he gets here, just stay in the car. Okay?"

"Yeah. Yeah, sure," Zach replied, unconvinced, but without any real options.

Hunter checked his watch. "They should be here by now."

As if on cue, headlights swept across the parking lot, followed by a car and an old pickup truck. The bright green muscle car looked like a classic of some kind but was obviously new. Its engine emitted a deep, ominous rumble as it slowed to a stop about fifteen feet away. The old pickup hung back, pulling to the far side of the lot.

Zach didn't like the look on Hunter's face. The usually over-confident fraternity president didn't want to be here, which did nothing at all for Zach's growing anxiety level.

After taking one more swig of liquor straight from the bottle to bolster his courage, Hunter turned to Zach and said, "Seriously, stay here. I'll be right back."

As Hunter climbed out of the car, Zach watched the driver's door of the green car open and a tough-looking white guy in jeans and sleeveless t-shirt step into the light. With tattoo-covered arms and very short blonde hair Zach instantly thought he must be a skinhead.

As Zach sat back a little further into the shadows, he noticed his window was still a third or so open. He would have rolled it up right then, but everything about the situation told him not to draw the attention of the skinhead staring malevolently at Hunter.

Hunter walked as steadily as he could over to J.P. Hoffman.

"Oh, holy crap!" J.P. said, as Hunter approached. "You're wasted!"

Unfortunately for Hunter, the alcohol had loosened his inhibitions. "I'm Hunter Ewell, dumbass and I got orders...."

Before he could finish, J.P. smashed a fist into Hunter's gut, then snatched and twisted one arm behind his back while the other locked Hunter's face down against the hood of his car.

"Now what were you saying, frat boy?" J.P. asked. "You were about to greet me nicely and just misspoke. Am I right?"

J.P. grabbed Hunter by the hair and smashed his face even harder against the hood.

"Yeah, you're right, man! Sorry!" Hunter cried, helplessly pinned.

J.P. yanked Hunter up and let go.

"Now that we have the pissing order all lined up correctly, what do you want?" J.P. asked as if nothing had happened.

Hunter smoothed his clothes and hair as best he could. "*I don't want anything. Like I said on the phone, it's the Directors. They give the orders. I don't know why they didn't just call you themselves.*"

"They don't call me because they can't have someone like me connected to them. So, they use expendable dumbasses like you. Well? Spit it out. What do they need?" J.P. growled.

"They want you to find a guy named Rick Donnelly. Doctor Rick Donnelly. They want him grabbed and held until they can get someone here to pick him up. He's supposed to be at the Hillmont Hotel. I think it's up at the next exit. White, mid-forties, looks like a nerd scientist. They need it done now."

"Is that all? Just grab one guy and sit on him?" J.P. said, acting surprised at the simplicity of the job. "Okay by me, but they could have sent a flabby college boy like you to do something as simple as that."

Hunter wisely chose not to respond to the insult.

Zach couldn't hear everything J.P. and Hunter said, but what he did hear made him wish he had rolled up the window all the way so he couldn't hear any of it. *Did Hunter just tell that skinhead to kidnap someone?*

J.P. laughed out loud. "Get out of here, frat boy. And next time...."

The pickup parked at the edge of the lot suddenly honked twice, stopping J.P. in mid-sentence.

A second later, a police car drove slowly around the building, its headlights landing squarely on J.P. and Hunter. Although neither had committed any crime, they knew meeting in a dark parking lot would look suspicious. Sure enough, the policeman flipped on flashing blue lights and accelerated up to where J.P. and Hunter stood.

"Be cool," J.P. hissed. "I'll handle this."

A short, hefty police officer stepped out of the car and aimed a flashlight at Hunter and J.P.

Back in Hunter's car, Zach ducked down below the dash just before the cop swung his flashlight across the windshield.

"Good evening, gentlemen. Nice night for a drug buy?" the cop said in a mocking tone.

"Uh, no officer, that's not it at all...." Hunter said.

"Have you been drinking, sir?" the officer asked. "You seem impaired to me."

"Officer, my friend here just needed a ride. I was about to take him home when you pulled up," J.P. offered.

The officer looked J.P. up and down. He obviously didn't buy J.P.'s story.

"Yeah, right. Let's see some I.D. gentlemen," the officer ordered. "Then I'll have a look in your vehicles. College boys and skinheads don't mix unless the college boys run out of weed or coke."

J.P. stole a look over his shoulder at the pickup that had accompanied him. He gave a quick nod of his head to the side. The message was clear– *get out of here.*

"Look officer. Nothing is happening here. I got nothing...." J.P. pleaded.

J.P. had to try something. If the cop got a look in his car, he would find some weed. But he would also find several highly illegal firearms– unregistered fully automatic assault rifles and one high-power sniper rifle with scope and silencer.

Already wary about J.P. because of his rough appearance, the officer decided not to take any chances.

"Get your hands on the car. Now!" the officer ordered, cutting off J.P. and placing his right hand on his pistol.

Out of options, J.P. struck like a snake. In one smooth and unbelievably quick motion, he snatched the shorter man's head between his hands, and with one vicious twist, broke his neck.

Hunter only realized what J.P. had done when the officer's body slumped onto its knees facing J.P.'s car. He almost screamed when he saw the policeman's dead face plastered against the fender with a pair of dead eyes staring out into the distance.

"Get out of here. Now!" J.P. ordered as he shoved Hunter back towards his own car.

"But…" Hunter said, backing away.

"You breathe a word of this, and you're dead too," J.P. threatened. "I'll hide this guy, and then I'll take care of Donnelly."

"Okay. Yeah. Okay," Hunter said, turning and running back to his car.

Zach hadn't seen a thing. He had remained as low in the car as he could get until Hunter opened the passenger door. Even then, he didn't sit back up all the way.

"Let's go!" Hunter said. "Go! Go!"

Zach finally pulled himself upright, just in time to see the police car driving away. Hunter was obviously freaked out.

"What happened?" Zach asked, starting the car and driving out of the parking lot. "You okay? What happened with the cop?"

Hunter didn't respond. His eyes looked as big as saucers, and sweat ran down his neck, soaking his shirt. With shaking hands, he found the bottle of Jack Daniels and lifted it to his mouth.

All the way back to the fraternity house, Hunter alternated between taking swigs out of the bottle and mumbling obscenities. Zach knew something insane had happened, but except for the strange partial conversation he overheard about finding and holding on to some guy, he had seen and heard nothing. Now, he was worried about Hunter, who looked like he was going into shock.

When they finally pulled into the parking lot back at the house, he asked, "Hey, Hunter. You okay? Is there anything I can do?"

"Yeah," Hunter snarled. "Keep your mouth shut. Breathe a word of this to anyone, and I'll kill you. Understand?"

"Yeah," Hunter snarled. "Keep your mouth shut. Breathe a word of this to anyone, and I'll kill you. Understand?"

FIFTEEN

Inside, Hunter disappeared into his room, leaving Zach alone and as confused and troubled as he had ever been. He started walking back to his room, but he decided that sitting by himself trying to make sense of what happened wouldn't help. So, he turned to the one person he could always count on.

Still shaken from the odd experience, Zach stuck his head into Michael's room. His best friend lay in bed propped up on some pillows, deeply engrossed in one of his car magazines.

"Hey! What's up?" Michael said amiably.

Zach slipped into the room and shut the door.

"You alone?" he asked.

"Yep. What's going on? You look like you've seen a ghost or something," Michael said, sitting up straighter.

"Something weird. Real weird," Zach said, his voice betraying the adrenaline still flowing through his system.

"You better sit down and tell me about it. You want a beer? There's some in the fridge right behind you," Michael offered, now fully aware of Zach's agitation.

"I'm not sure I believe it myself," Zach began, ignoring the beer.

For the next few minutes, Zach told Michael about how Hunter offered him the chance to run as a Tyros candidate for senate and about how Hunter had gotten drunk and insisted he drive him out to the truck stop for a meeting. Hesitating briefly, he then described Hunter's encounter with the skinhead in the green car, how he had ordered the skinhead to abduct someone, and the sudden appearance of the police.

"Are you telling me Hunter ordered this guy you think is some kind of skinhead to commit a kidnapping?" Michael asked, incredulously.

"Yeah. I know. It's hard to believe. I don't understand it either. And I didn't see what happened with the police. I ducked down like a wuss," Zach said, looking to Michael for some help piecing together what he had just witnessed. "Oh, and Hunter literally said he would kill me if I told anyone about what happened. And I seriously don't think he was kidding. What do I do? Call the police or something?"

"I don't know," Michael replied, trying to make sense of Zach's story. "And tell them what? You're pretty sure the president of our fraternity ordered a skinhead to kidnap somebody? Did you get the guy's name? Anyway, the police were already there weren't they?"

"Yeah, I think the cop thought Hunter and the other guy were doing a drug deal or something. And yeah, I didn't hear the skinhead's name. But the guy they wanted was like 'Duncan' or 'Donny' or something like that. He's supposed to be at a hotel here in town. I couldn't hear which one. And the cop just drove away. I saw that much."

"I'm not sure the police wouldn't just blow you off. You said the skinhead was driving a bright green car. Do you know what kind?" Michael asked, doing his best to help Zach think through the situation.

"You're the car guy," Zach answered. "It was definitely a new car but looked like an old classic like you and your dad go for. But man, it was a really bad light green."

Michael thought a minute then went to his desk and rifled through a stack of magazines. Pulling one out, he flipped through the pages until he found the picture he was looking for. Showing it to Zach, he asked, "Is this it by any chance?"

Zach took the magazine. "Yeah! That's it exactly!"

"Dodge Challenger. Nice. Not many of those around, particularly in bright green," Michael said, taking back the magazine.

"I'm glad you like the skinhead's car, but do you have any idea what we should, you know, *do*?" Zach asked, still freaked out.

Michael thought for a minute. What had Zach actually witnessed? He thought he heard Hunter giving some rough-looking guy instructions to kidnap someone just before a policeman pulled up. After that, he saw the police leave and Hunter badly upset and frightened.

"I don't know. I wish I did. Something must have happened after the cop got there, but we don't know what. Not much, I'm guessing, because the cop left. Sorry, I'm not much help," Michael said, wishing he could find a way to help.

"Uhhh! This sucks!" Zach exclaimed, placing his hands over his eyes.

Michael couldn't stand seeing his best friend tormented. He needed to think of something.

"Hey, I have an idea! Let's go see if we can find this skinhead's car. You said they're going to a hotel in town. There's not that many. Maybe the police would listen to you if we could give them some more information. More than you kinda overhearing a vague conversation anyway," Michael suggested, sounding a little excited.

"Really? You and me go out hunting for a skinhead? That sounds pretty dumb to me. There was another truck there too. Some old beater with one of those camper shells on the back," Zach said. "And just what will we do if we find them?"

"Look, we won't get close and we won't take any chances. If the skinhead is at a hotel, we can take pictures or something. At least we'll have something to back up what you overheard if we do call the police. Or, you could just go ahead and call them now, I bet Hunter would tell them the whole story, being the upstanding guy that he is," Michael replied, trying not to sound too sarcastic.

Zach didn't like the plan but he needed to do *something*. It just wasn't in his nature to walk away if he thought someone was in trouble. And, he didn't exactly have a better suggestion.

"Well, crap. It's still a bad idea," Zach complained.

"Tell you what, we'll bring Bubba along. He's always up for most anything. Plus, we'll take my car. We'll just drive around looking. You can sit in the back in case we actually run across these guys. It's not like I want us to be like superheroes. Let's just go see if what you heard plays out at all," Michael said convincingly.

"I guess riding around wouldn't hurt anything. But if Hunter sees me leaving with you and Bubba, he might get suspicious," Zach said.

"No problem. I'll call Bubba. You walk out through the kitchen. Nobody would think twice about you looking for something to eat. We'll meet you a block behind the house."

At six-foot four inches tall, Lawrence "Bubba" Adcock had to fold himself into the front seat of Michael's convertible. His beer belly, which he proudly told everyone was 'bought and paid for,' strained the seat belt.

"So little buddy, you really think Hunter is into something?" Bubba asked Zach, who sat in the car's small back seat. "That boy's a real piece of work, but getting mixed up with skinheads? Seems like a stretch, even for him."

"Yeah, but I was there and that guy Hunter met was a badass. Tats, almost shaved head, arms like a pro linebacker. He had Hunter's face smashed into the hood of his car just like that," Zach said, snapping his fingers.

"Pretty impressive," Michael agreed. "I've seen Hunter muscle two guys out of the frat house by himself. And he was full-bore wasted at the time."

"I gotta say, of all the stuff I thought about doing tonight, I didn't expect to be looking for skinheads in a green muscle car. Where are we going first?" Bubba asked.

"I heard Hunter say this Duncan or whatever was at a hotel. I couldn't make out which one. There aren't that many, and most are up by the highway. Let's head up to the first exit," Zach suggested.

Michael took the on-ramp and gunned the engine.

"All right!" Bubba cried, grabbing the door frame. "You and your daddy must have worked on this thing over the summer."

Michael downshifted, causing the rear tires to chirp loudly.

"Yeah, a little," he said, smiling.

SIXTEEN

J.P. slammed his hand against the steering wheel of the police cruiser. A dead cop was a problem he didn't need.

After breaking the policeman's neck, J.P. threw the body into the police cruiser's back seat, jumped behind the wheel, and drove casually out of the parking lot. It took only minutes to reach a web of backroads that twisted through dense uninhabited woods.

J.P. knew the secluded area well. After navigating a maze of dirt roads that twisted, turned, and undulated through the trees, J.P. eventually stopped near a steep slope above a creek hidden by dense undergrowth. J.P. quickly arranged the body in the driver's seat, wadded up a few sheets of paper, stuffed them in the glove compartment, and lit them on fire. An old trick used by arsonists, J.P. knew the fire would spread to the interior, and in just minutes, engulf the entire car.

J.P. waited only long enough to ensure the fire spread adequately before pushing the car into the ravine. The big sedan bounced down the hill, flames erupting from the windows. In twenty minutes or less, the car would be a smoldering burned-out shell.

Retracing his route through the woods on foot, J.P. swiped open his phone.

"We picked up your car, and Skeeter is bringing it your way," Mitch Singleton, J.P.'s second in command, said as soon as he answered.

"Good. We got a job," J.P. responded. "The Directors want a guy named Dr. Rick Donnelly picked up down at the Hillmont Hotel. We're supposed to sit on him until they can get some people up here."

"So that's what the frat boy wanted," Mitch, commented. "What do you need us to do?"

While Mitch didn't sport the same bad-boy look J.P. preferred, he was just as tough and nearly as ruthless. Unlike J.P., Mitch could move around in public, even posing as a college student, without attracting unnecessary attention - something he used to his advantage.

"For now, you and Gina get down to the Hillmont. It's one of those new hotels one exit up the interstate from the truck stop. There's a service road that goes around the back of the hotels and restaurants over there. Find a quiet place to park where you can keep an eye on the place. If a single white guy leaves, you call me immediately. It's late, so most guests should be in for the night."

"You got it, J.P.!" J.P. heard Mitch's girlfriend, Gina, squeal.

"Shut her up. She gets too hot and bothered when it comes to this stuff," J.P. said, not hiding his irritation.

"Don't worry. We got it covered," Mitch answered.

As the conversation ended, J.P.'s Challenger emerged out of the darkness and skidded to a stop. J.P. climbed in the driver's seat. "Okay, Skeeter, we got some planning to do."

Skeeter, who got his moniker from the initials of his full name, Frederick Leonard Yeager, possessed the mind of a genius, but the personality of a mad scientist. Skeeter resembled the tiny insect he was named after. Skinny to the point of emaciation, his clothes hung limply off every part of his body. He wore round wire-rimmed eyeglasses that made his eyes look half again larger than normal and his hair was an uncontrollable brown greasy mess.

Without saying a word, Skeeter just nodded, slinking around to the passenger side of J.P.'s car.

"You're the genius. How do we get one guy out of a hotel in the middle of the night? Put a gun in the desk clerk's face and politely as for the guy's room number?" J.P. asked.

Skeeter looked at him for a moment, his eyes blinking rhythmically, like a poorly programmed robot. J.P. had become used to Skeeter's odd behavior and had learned to let the man's brain work at its own pace. He had come to rely on Skeeter's innate ability to define problems, plan operations, and foresee the outcomes.

Skeeter slowly turned his eyes forward. "That would be unwise. First, it is improbable, given the circumstances, that Donnelly checked in under his own name. Second, security cameras would certainly capture such rash action. You would have to wear a mask, thus compounding the probability of someone seeing you, rightly concluding a crime was underway, and calling the police. Finally, it would take a considerable amount of time to find Dr. Donnelly's room, extricate him quietly, and transport him to our vehicles. No, that plan is fraught with unnecessary risk."

J.P. just shook his head at the odd little man and how he spoke. "Do you have to sound like an uptight prick every time you open your mouth?

Skeeter just looked quizzically back at his boss. "I convey information efficiently, leaving no doubt about my meaning."

"Alright, alright," J.P. replied, knowing it didn't do any good to get irritated at his resident genius. "Then how do we find his room and get him out of the place?"

Skeeter turned back to J.P., looking perplexed that J.P. had not seen the solution.

"We don't, of course," Skeeter replied.

"What? All right, all right, why don't you just explain just how we get this done," J.P. said, trying not to get irritated. If Skeeter became frightened, his brain tended to lock up for an hour or so.

"He'll walk right out the front door any time we want him to. There will be crowds around and they'll be upset. Covertly taking him away from such a scene at gunpoint will be simple," Skeeter said.

"I don't get it," J.P. said.

"It's actually quite an elegant plan if I do say so," Skeeter said, one side of his mouth rising in a slight grin.

"Just explain it, please, you bug-eyed insect. I'm losing it," J.P. said, gripping the steering wheel so hard his knuckles started turning white.

"Have Mitch set it on fire," Skeeter said at last.

"You're serious," J.P. said.

"Absolutely. A small fire in a bathroom should do the trick."

"Then what? So, the people all spill out into the parking lot. How do we pick out Donnelly? We didn't exactly get a picture of him," J.P. asked.

"Again, simple. We quietly approach any unattached white male and ask if he's Donnelly. I'm sure his reaction will give him away immediately. Then, as I said, we just walk him away from the chaos caused by the fire," Skeeter explained patiently.

"Why Mitch?" J.P. asked.

"Because he looks substantially less like a mass murderer than you," Skeeter responded, not a hint of sarcasm in his voice.

"Don't try to kiss my ass with compliments or anything," J.P. said, smiling.

SEVENTEEN

Mitch looked up from his cell phone. J.P.'s orders surprised even him.

"They want you to burn it? Oh, Baby, can I come with you?" Gina asked, breathlessly.

"Not this time. I need you to stay right here with the truck. If the cops show up or something weird happens, call me," Mitch said. "This should only take a minute. When I'm done, I'll walk around the back and meet you right here."

Gina pouted. "I want to go."

"Next time, Baby," Mitch said, climbing from the cab.

Pulling an old ball cap over his eyes, Mitch made his way across a vacant lot behind the hotel and walked inside. A single clerk sat behind the check-in desk at the far end of the lobby. J.P. and Skeeter had suggested setting a small fire, perhaps in a bathroom. The smoke would set off the fire alarms, waking the guests and forcing an evacuation. But as soon as he entered the building, Mitch realized he would have to walk right past the front desk to find a restroom.

To the right, Mitch saw a seating area, nicely furnished with low couches, a few club-style chairs and a grouping of fifteen or so tables where the hotel served a free breakfast.

Avoiding the bored clerk, Mitch made his way across the dining area. At the far end, he found a door marked "Employees Only."

Mitch bent to get a close look at the lock. *No sweat.* He pulled a short knife from its belt-mounted scabbard. After some quiet and expert fiddling, the door opened, and he stepped inside.

He now stood in a small kitchen that serviced the dining room. Mitch smiled, knowing that the kitchen would be covered by several smoke detectors and that he could easily set a fire that would be effective and look like an accident at the same time.

Moving quickly, Mitch set a large pan on the stove and poured an inch of cooking oil in the bottom. Turning the burner on high, he was about to turn and leave when he heard footsteps approaching down a long service hallway that connected the kitchen to some other part of the hotel. *Crap.* He couldn't get caught in the employee area and he had no way to bluff his way out. Even if he could sneak out now, the hot oil would be discovered, ruining the plan. Most importantly, Mitch knew J.P. did not tolerate failure. He had to see this through.

The footsteps continued slowly toward the kitchen, so Mitch moved again, silently concealing himself against a side wall at the end of the hall. Then someone called, "Rosa?"

A short dark figure emerged from the hall, walking right past Mitch into the kitchen. He appeared to be looking for someone.

The oil-filled pan was just beginning to smoke on the stove, the unmistakable odor filling the kitchen. "Que es esto? What is this?"

Realizing he had only a second before the man turned around, Mitch acted. Taking two quick steps forward, he wrapped his left arm around the man's neck, sliding his right arm behind the head and grabbing his left upper arm - putting his target in a classic chokehold. The other man should have passed out almost immediately, but Mitch didn't have a good angle. Mitch stood over six feet two inches tall, while his opponent was a good seven or eight inches shorter and built like a tank. Mitch never fought anyone so compact and muscular. The short Latino grabbed at the arm locked around his neck and pulled down with all his might. Mitch strained to pull the man backward, increase the pressure on the carotid artery, and stop blood flow to the brain. But he couldn't get enough leverage. The two men were deadlocked, neither able to gain an advantage. Suddenly, Mitch's training in hand-to-hand combat kicked in. Since he couldn't pull the man backward, Mitch suddenly stopped trying.

The tough Latino's immense effort now worked against him. He tried to take one step forward but lost his balance, falling face first with Mitch's arms still locked around his neck. Now trapped under the larger man, the chokehold took quick effect. The Latino passed out, his body relaxing and his eyes rolling back in his head.

The fight didn't last fifteen seconds, but the oil was already smoking furiously. Mitch suddenly had a problem, he couldn't very well carry this guy outside; and, there was at least a small chance he could identify Mitch later. He didn't have a choice. He had to eliminate the evidence.

Finding several bottles of lamp fuel the hotel used in warming tables, he doused the entire kitchen, taking a few seconds to thoroughly soak the still unconscious stranger.

Shaken and sweating from the mortal struggle, Mitch smoothed his clothing and his hair, took two deep breaths, and noiselessly left the kitchen, his hands still shaking from the massive adrenaline release.

Back in the safety of his truck, Mitch considered whether to tell J.P. about his encounter with the Latino, but decided against it. J.P.'s reactions could be unpredictable.

Gina wrinkled her nose as soon as he climbed back in the cab. "You smell weird."

"Yeah, well I think they've been cooking a little Mexican in there," Mitch replied with a straight face.

EIGHTEEN

Michael, Bubba, and Zach drove slowly past several hotels, looking for any sign of the skinhead's bright green car.

"Hey, brother, I'm getting hungry over here," Bubba complained after nearly an hour without success.

"Dude, you ate three helpings of spaghetti for dinner. How can you possibly be hungry?" Zach asked from the back seat.

"It ain't the size of the dinner, it's the size of the man," Bubba replied. "A skinny little fella like you don't need much sustenance. Anyway, Michael promised me a pizza if I rode along on your little private eye adventure."

"You did?" Zach asked Michael.

"Nope," Michael said with a chuckle. "But there's some late-night burger places up ahead. Let's take a break and think this thing through while Bubba gets something to eat before he starves."

After making a circuit around the drive-through lane of a fast-food restaurant, Michael parked facing the road and just across the street from two multi-story chain hotels.

"I don't know Zach," Michael said, thoughtfully. "Maybe I just got us chasing our own tails. I don't doubt what you saw and heard, but for all we know, they might be headed toward a hotel someplace else. Maybe we should...."

"What's that light?" Zach interrupted, pointing between the seats and out the front window.

Michael and Bubba immediately saw what had caught Zach's attention. A red light on the side of the Hillmont Hotel had suddenly come to life, blinking brightly.

"That's weird. I wonder if that means something," Michael said.

Bubba knew immediately. "That's a fire alarm. It's supposed to help the fire department find the exact building quickly. Kinda useless these days."

A few moments later, people began streaming from the hotel's main entrance. Dressed in pajamas, robes, or hastily thrown on clothes, the hotel guests gathered outside. Hotel staff stood at the door, urging people outside. Families and couples stayed close to each other while single travelers milled about on their own.

As they watched, plumes of dark smoke began rising menacingly from the rear of the building, partially blocking the hotel's pinkish outdoor lighting.

"Wow! Do you think we should go over there? Help out somehow?" Michael asked.

He was about to get out of the car when Bubba grabbed his arm.

"Hold on a second, is that the car y'all are looking for?" Bubba said, as a bright green muscle car rolled past them and pulled to the curb just past the hotel entrance.

Zach had seen the car as well and had no trouble identifying the driver. "That's it! And that's the guy Hunter met," he exclaimed.

J.P. and Skeeter came to a halt, their eyes scanning the crowd gathered outside the burning hotel building.

"May I suggest having Gina and Mitch approach the gathering from their position behind the building?" Skeeter suggested. "You and I can start from here. I think we should move rather quickly in case Donnelly decides to move on."

J.P. just nodded and called Mitch. "You and Gina, move into the crowd. Casually, ask any white guys standing around alone if their name is Donnelly. He won't tell you if he is, but if he looks freaked out by the question, back off, watch, and call me."

Everyone in the parking lot stared as the first tongues of bright yellow fire danced over the top of the building. Nobody noticed four extra on-lookers mixing into the crowd.

J.P. and Skeeter moved through the guests and staff but had no luck finding Donnelly. Skeeter approached two single men but dismissed them as possibilities. One looked like a biker, sporting a beard, tattoos and wearing only a pair of leather pants - definitely not a scientist. The other, short and balding, held a small trembling dog in his arms. Nobody on the run would be coddling a lap dog.

Just minutes later, J.P. and Skeeter ran into Gina and Mitch, who quickly reported they had found no one fitting Donnelly's description.

"I hear sirens," J.P. said. "We're out of time."

"Indeed, we are," Skeeter agreed. "I strongly urge us to make our exit now."

"You two get back to the workshop," J.P. ordered. "Skeeter and I will meet you there later."

"Why are they going into the crowd?" Zach asked, seeing J.P. and Skeeter leave the car and saunter through the hotel's parking lot.

"Looking for the guy they are supposed to kidnap?" Michael suggested. "And who's the little dude with glasses? Did you see him before?"

"He might have been in the truck, but the blonde skinhead didn't have anyone with him when he met Hunter," Zach said.

"There's one way to find out what they're up to. Me and Michael will go see," Bubba suggested. "We can't be positive they didn't see Zach at the truck stop, so he should stay here."

"Ya think?" Zach said, not without sarcasm. "But I don't know, that sounds dangerous."

"Aww come on. They don't know us. We're just two curious gawkers," Michael said. "Come on Bubba."

Michael and Bubba crossed the street, looking at the fire, which by this time could be seen burning furiously through the lower floor windows.

"I hope everyone got out of there," Michael said.

"I see the skinhead and little guy right up there. They're not too interested in the fire. They seem to be looking for someone," Bubba observed. "Stay close."

Without raising any attention, Michael and Bubba got within twenty feet of the pair they were following. A moment later, they stopped and watched with one eye as the big skinhead talked with a tall man in a baseball cap and a girl that looked overly excited by something. When sirens approached, the skinhead got visibly concerned.

"Wait, they're leaving," Bubba said, putting his arm around Michael's shoulder and turning him toward the fire.

As J.P. and Skeeter walked right behind them headed back toward the road, Bubba stole a glance.

"Let's stay right here until they pull out," Bubba said.

"Okay, but what's the matter?" Michael asked, sensing Bubba tense up slightly.

"They're armed. They both had handguns stuffed in their pants," Bubba answered quietly. "And, they lit out of here as soon as they heard the sirens."

Michael resisted an urge to turn and watch the skinheads walk away.

"Do you think they noticed us?' Michael asked.

"I hope not."

NINETEEN

"What in the hell just happened?" Zach asked as Bubba and Michael got back into the car. "You guys look a little shaken up."

Michael started the car and pulled out into the road before speaking.

"I think you were right. Those guys were definitely looking for someone, and they weren't alone. They met up with another guy and a girl, but I don't think they found whoever they were looking for," Michael said.

"Those boys were serious, that's for sure," Bubba added.

Michael managed to catch Bubba's eye and give an almost imperceptible shake of the head before Bubba could say they were armed. Zach didn't need the extra stress.

"So, what do we do? Call the police *now*?" Zach asked.

"Well, if anyone cares what I think, I don't think we should call anyone," Bubba responded. "We have got what? A conversation overheard at a distance and some shady characters walking around - maybe looking for someone?"

"I don't know either. Maybe we should go ask Hunter what's going on after all," Michael suggested.

"No way! He's a loose cannon on a good day. We go in there and accuse him of like attempted kidnapping or something? He'd kick my ass and then get me kicked out of the frat. Then good old Roger Self would kick me out of the family. No way!" Zach responded, talking way too fast.

"Yeah. It's cool, man. Don't freak out. I know Hunter and your dad both have short fuses," Michael said, worried about his friend.

They drove on for a few minutes in silence, each thinking about what they had just seen and what they could do about it.

Finally, Zach leaned into the front seat. "My dad's a blowhard and a jerk. But yours isn't," he said, talking to Michael. "Your parents are the best. I bet if you called your dad, he could help us out. Maybe he'd have an idea about what we should do."

"Ugh, I don't know. I don't really want to tell him we were out chasing skinheads," Michael objected.

"Zach's got himself a good idea," Bubba said. "We can't go to the cops or even campus police. But we can't just let this go either."

Michael thought for a minute, then looked at his watch and picked up his phone.

Michael's father listened to his son explain what Zach saw and heard. Michael even ended up telling him they found the skinhead's car and how they watched the skinheads looking for someone at the hotel fire. Michael left off the part about how he and Bubba had followed the skinheads into the hotel parking lot.

After hanging up, Michael relayed his father's suggestion.

"Well, you probably heard most of that. I'm going to have some serious explaining to do next time I see him. But for now, he thinks we should go talk to a friend of his in town. A lawyer. Dad knows him through work and says he's smart and would be willing to listen to us."

"A lawyer?" Zach asked, incredulously.

"Sounds right to me," Bubba declared. "What's his name?"

"Drew Campbell. Dad will give him a call in the morning."

"Alright! Now that that's all settled, you boys owe me a pizza. Four or six beers wouldn't go down too bad either," Bubba exclaimed.

"Don't you ever worry about gaining weight?" Michael asked with a chuckle.

"How much more could I gain anyway? I'm just trying to maintain what I got, brother!"

The trio drove back to the frat house, convinced they at least had a plan.

As they got close to the house, Zach suddenly pointed out the window. "Oh man! What's Hunter doing out by the road?"

"Duck!" Michael said quickly. "He doesn't need to see you with us right now. No reason to make him suspicious."

Zach made himself disappear into the back seat as Michael drove right by Hunter. Michael gave him a perfunctory wave, but Hunter didn't respond. Instead, he just glared for a moment and then turned to look down the street once more.

"When I park, get out and act drunk," Michael said to Bubba. "Zach, you chill out. We'll call as soon as the coast is clear."

Michael parked the car and Bubba popped out the side door, closing it quickly behind him. "Hey, Hunter! Come on up! Me and Michael's gonna have a par-teee!"

Hunter looked back but just shook his head.

"Come on, big guy, let's get you a sandwich or something," Michael said, pulling Bubba by the arm.

"Naw! Just get me another beer!" Bubba said loudly, playing a convincing drunk.

As expected, Hunter ignored Bubba's antics. Once inside, Michael sprinted up to Bubba's room and found a place he could see Hunter through the window. It was dark, but he could make out Hunter pacing nervously and talking on his cell phone.

A moment later, Bubba came in and asked, somewhat out of breath: "What's he doing?"

"Not much, just talking on the phone," Michael answered. "Wait! You aren't going to believe this!"

Bubba looked over Michael's shoulder just as the skinhead's bright green muscle car pulled up right next to Hunter.

As J.P.'s car came to a stop, Skeeter rolled down the window.

"Get in," J.P. said, leaning across so Hunter could see his face.

Hunter, knowing better than to argue, did as he was told.

"What the hell happened, frat boy?" J.P. said as he pulled away from the frat house entrance. "Donnelly wasn't there. You wasting my time?"

"Hey, man," Hunter said from the back seat. "I was just passing along orders. That's it."

"That's not going to cut it. The Directors expect results, and you made me look bad. Someone must have tipped him off. You had someone with you at the truck stop tonight. Who?" J.P. demanded.

"I got a kid to drive me. Zach Self. He doesn't know anything," Hunter explained nervously.

"Goddammit, Hunter! Are you sure? I don't have to tell you some heavy crap went down tonight. How do you *know* he didn't see anything?" J.P. demanded.

"He didn't see you kill that cop. I know he didn't. He ducked down when the cop pulled up, and he asked me about what the cop wanted. If he had seen it, I would have known it," Hunter said, with more confidence than he felt.

The night had gone poorly, but Hunter had no desire to put Zach in real danger. If J.P. believed Zach witnessed the murder, Hunter realized J.P. wouldn't hesitate to kill again to protect himself.

"What did you tell him was going on, then?" J.P. asked. "He saw me kick your ass. He had to ask about that."

"Uh, yeah. I told him I owed you on a bet," Hunter replied.

"Anyone see you waiting for us just now?"

Hunter almost said 'no,' but he wasn't sure if Bubba and Michael made it into the house before J.P. and Skeeter arrived.

"Just a couple of frat brothers. They'd been out partying," Hunter replied. "They didn't see me talking to you ...."

"Names, please," Skeeter demanded.

"Michael King and Bubba Adcock," Hunter answered. "King's a nobody, and Adcock is a drunk. Nothing to worry about, and like I said, all they saw was me walking through the parking lot."

"You have no way of confirming what they saw and what they did not," Skeeter replied without emotion.

"Skeeter's right. They better not have seen us, or I'll figure maybe you've lied to me. And I don't like liars," J.P. said menacingly.

"Are Michael King, Bubba Adcock, and Zach Self friends?" Skeeter asked.

"Hell, I don't know," Hunter said, obviously getting nervous.

"I think you do," Skeeter replied. "The question caused you concern."

"Okay, I guess I've seen them hanging out sometimes. I never really thought about it," Hunter answered. "Look, J.P., we shouldn't be riding around like this. We shouldn't take the chance on being seen together, should we?"

"For once, you're right," J.P. said slamming, on the brakes. "Get out. I'll find this guy Donnelly myself if he's still around, and then I'll actually kick your ass. Or, you find him, let me know where he is, and maybe I'll let you off the hook."

Hunter climbed out of the car without saying another word. It was over two miles back to the house, but he didn't dare complain about it.

Back in the car, J.P. asked: "Was he lying?"

"Most certainly," Skeeter said.

"What went wrong at the hotel?" J.P. asked.

"The plan was solid. If Donnelly had been in the hotel, we would have him now. Therefore, he was not in the hotel. Either Hunter Ewell's information was faulty or Donnelly simply wasn't there."

"What's your recommendation?" J.P. asked.

"Vigilance. I recommend keeping an eye on this Zachary Self. He is the only possible witness to your, uh, treatment of the police officer. As you heard, we also established a connection between Zach Self, Bubba Adcock, and Michael King. I don't believe in coincidence. Their presence outside the fraternity house at the exact moment Hunter came out to meet us is of concern." Skeeter said, repeatedly pushing his glasses up on his nose. "Authorize surveillance of all four of our fraternity members. Hunter, Zach, Michael, and Bubba."

"That's a lot of manpower. You think we really have to go that far?" J.P. asked.

"Yes. We cannot chance anyone connecting us with The Tyros organization. The security of the Directors depends upon it. If Hunter and therefore The Tyros is suspected of any criminal wrongdoing, investigations by the authorities might ensue. We cannot be certain Hunter won't reveal that the Directors gave the order to make a deal to save his own ass," Skeeter replied.

"You are one goddamned nerd, boy," J.P. said, shaking his head.

"Thank you, Mr. Hoffman," Skeeter replied earnestly.

TWENTY

The next day, Michael, Zach, and Bubba found themselves sitting in attorney Drew Campbell's conference room while Drew's secretary fretted over them, offering coffee, Cokes, and snacks.

"Michael, I just love your father. He's such a nice man," the secretary gushed. "Are you sure I can't get you anything? I have some homemade cookies in the back."

Just as Bubba was about to accept the offer, Drew entered the office holding a legal pad.

"Thanks, Tracy," Drew said. "Would you mind closing the door, please?"

Disappointed at not getting to hear what three young college boys needed to see her boss about, Tracy reluctantly returned to her desk.

"Michael, it's good to see you again. You don't remember, but your father brought you here when you were a little boy," Drew said, trying to put the three friends at ease.

After introducing Zach and Bubba, Michael said, "Thanks for seeing us. Dad said you might be able to help or at least give us some idea about what to do with a, well, situation we got into. We won't take much of your time."

"Don't worry about that, your father is a good friend. Now, what's going on?" Drew asked.

Michael retold the same series of events he had told his father the night before, but this time included the fact that Hunter had once again met with the same skinheads Zach saw at the truck stop outside the fraternity house.

Drew listened carefully, jotting notes on his legal pad. After a moment he asked, "I heard about the fire on the news. What made you think to go out looking for these, uh, skinheads after Zach took Hunter to meet with them at the truck stop?"

Zach answered for the group. "After I told Michael about how Hunter had kinda ordered the skinheads to kidnap someone, I wondered whether we ought to call the police. But then we thought, they probably wouldn't believe us."

"So, you just got in Michael's car and drove around hotels looking for this green muscle car?" Drew asked, a bit incredulously.

"Yeah, I guess that's my fault," Michael said. "It was my idea."

"Don't get me wrong, guys. I'm not judging. But it does seem like a wild idea," Drew explained.

Bubba spoke up for the first time. "Maybe so. But Hunter is the president of our fraternity and he might have gotten Zach involved in something illegal or worse. We just wanted to know for sure."

Drew sat back in his chair and considered the young men. He already knew Michael's family and considered them good and honest people. Zach and Bubba impressed him with their candid answers. He concluded he liked all three and took their story at face value.

"Zach, you said you heard Hunter name the guy to be abducted. Who was it?" Drew asked.

"I couldn't hear perfectly, but it sounded like Duncan or Donny. It definitely began with a 'D' anyway," Zach said.

"Okay, Michael and Bubba, when you were at the fire, did you see the skinheads do anything illegal, or overhear them say anything that might indicate they were doing going to commit a crime?" Drew asked.

Michael and Bubba looked at each other for a moment, but neither could come up with anything, other than the fact they seemed to be looking for someone.

Drew thought for a moment. "Well, I think y'all stumbled into something strange. The president of a fraternity meeting with skinheads and ordering them to commit kidnapping is certainly concerning. And later those skinheads showing up at a hotel fire looking for someone seems like more than just a coincidence. Zach, do you think anyone else witnessed Hunter meeting with the skinheads at the truck stop?"

"Another vehicle followed the muscle car into the parking lot, and I'm sure they were together. Other than that, we met way back in the corner of the truck stop. I doubt anyone noticed," Zach replied.

"It's totally up to you, of course, but if you go to the police and accuse Hunter of ordering a kidnapping, it will be your word against his. Is this Hunter a good guy? Would he tell the truth?" Drew asked.

Bubba's loud laugh answered the question for all three young men.

"I guess that's a big 'no'?" Drew asked.

"Hunter's family is one of the most politically connected in the state. He lies at the drop of a hat and gets away with it. Nobody wants to mess with him because of his family's money and power," Zach responded, sounding disheartened.

"Yeah, and he would totally destroy all of us with the fraternity and probably the university," Michael added.

"And my father would pull my butt out of college," Zach said, softly.

Drew could see the dilemma Zach and his friends faced. If they went to the police with the slim information at hand, they jeopardized their college lives. If they didn't, they risked Hunter and the skinheads possibly committing a serious crime.

"I'm not going to tell you what to do here," Drew said. "But I'll offer this. Whatever you decide, I'll support and represent you if necessary, pro bono. In fact, I'm going to consider myself your counsel unless you tell me different. And, I'm going to give each of you my cell number. If you need me, or just want to talk things over, call me."

"Damn! That's nice of you, Drew!" Bubba said.

"No problem. But in return, I ask only one thing - stay safe. Don't go playing secret agent and following skinheads around anymore," Drew said in his most serious adult voice.

Michael answered for all three. "Yes, sir."

TWENTY-ONE

FBI Special Agent Frank Deal's boots kicked up small clouds of dust as he strode across the dry dirt of southern Spain. Sweat ran down the gray stubble on his square chin and soaked into the front of his khaki-colored shirt. While the quaint Andalusia region offered travelers countless vacation opportunities, Deal and his hand-picked team were not there for fun. They had spent the last three weeks searching for a lost nuclear bomb that had been accidentally dropped by the Air Force back in 1955. That morning, Deal had ordered yet another full visual sweep, on foot, of a sun-bleached open area covered in rolling hills.

Deal felt good, totally immersed in his work, directing a talented team and pursuing a clear objective. He didn't need nor want vacations, a characteristic his team didn't necessarily share but tolerated since working for the preeminent WMD hunter in the world meant making sacrifices.

Deal currently led the FBI's Fast Response team, the FBI's secret weapon for locating weapons of mass destruction of all kinds. Deployed anywhere in or outside the country within hours, Deal's team took immediate control of any case involving the use or planned use of WMDs. It wasn't unusual for allies of the United States to request Deal's help - the very reason his team had been in Spain for almost a month.

His current assignment arose after military intelligence agencies uncovered new clues about the Air Force bomber's exact flight path. Unfortunately, they also learned the same information may have fallen into the hands of several terrorist organizations. After intense research of the area, hundreds of interviews, and analysis of the latest satellite surveillance and imaging, Deal knew he was close. Damn close.

Engrossed in directing his team, Deal didn't hear his phone ringing at first. When the trilling became loud and insistent, he reluctantly pulled the irritating device from his pocket.

"Deal," he barked after swiping the phone open.

If he had taken the time to look at the face of the phone, he would have seen it was the Director of the FBI, William Glover, himself.

"Frank, we need you back in the country. We have a situation." Glover said without having to identify himself. Deal would know his voice immediately. He also knew Deal wouldn't like being pulled off his current case, especially after making significant progress.

"I'm going to find this thing, sir. I can smell it," Deal said, wiping the sweat from his scowling forehead.

"Yes, I know. This is more important."

"I have a hard time believing..."

Glover cut him off. "Stow it, Frank. There's transport for the rest of your team waiting at Jerez now. One of our private jets will be landing at the airstrip outside of Arcos de la Frontera in forty-two minutes to pick you up. You will be there waiting on it, and I will brief you personally over secure lines in flight. Just get your butt on that plane. That's an order."

Deal's phone went silent.

Glover didn't enjoy yanking Deal's leash, but everyone knows it's hard to get a pit bull to let go once it locks its jaws down on its prey. But he didn't have a choice. He needed Deal and his team to recover a weapon far more dangerous than a lost nuclear bomb. And he didn't have time to argue the point.

Deal had to move fast after Glover's call, barely having time to get his team organized for its surprise relocation and arrange for Spanish security to guard his search area until they could return and finish the job. After a rushed drive across mostly dirt roads to the small airfield, Deal quickly found himself forty-thousand feet over the Atlantic Ocean, ensconced in a buttery soft leather chair. He didn't appreciate his opulent surroundings or the exclusivity of being whisked across the ocean in a private executive jet. Such things were merely part of the job. And, the fact that he was still wearing sweaty, dusty clothes didn't bother him at all.

Upon boarding, he was offered a bottle of water by a sharply uniformed young Navy lieutenant and ushered to his seat, where an open laptop already sat open. The lieutenant disappeared into the cockpit, not to reappear.

Deal sat down and ran a hand over his silver crew cut, still angry about being pulled out of Spain but more concerned about why. Not many things took priority over a lost nuke. Thankfully, he didn't have to wait long for an explanation.

The screen came to life with a live picture of the FBI Director's private conference room. Glover sat at the head of a long, slightly oval table. A tired-looking middle-aged man in a rumpled suit sat at his right, nervously polishing a pair of wire-rimmed glasses. Nobody else appeared to be present.

Glover looked up from his ever-present tablet. The deep worry lines on his dark brown face now deepened into black crevasses.

"Christ, Frank, you look like a desert rat," Glover said, skipping further niceties. "Let's get to it. This is Dr. Smith. You don't need to know his real name. He's here to brief you on the subject of your assignment. First, I'll explain why you were ordered back to the U.S. You can read the detailed briefing documents after we talk."

Deal just nodded.

"At zero eight hundred yesterday, some seventy-two hours ago, four top scientists failed to report for work at the Groom Lake research facility in Nevada. Three of the four scientists, Doctors Phyllis Masters, Thomas Grant, and Richard Donnelly, were working on the same project - a new type of fuel for a ground-breaking aircraft propulsion system. The fourth, David Knox, was assigned to the engineering team for the same propulsion system. Multiple efforts to contact the scientists failed. At zero nine hundred, security protocols automatically triggered a review of their work. That audit revealed the records of Donnelly's research had been irretrievably sabotaged.

"Internal security at Groom Lake and state law enforcement immediately undertook an investigation into the whereabouts of the missing scientists. Arizona State Troopers did an excellent job tracking Grant and Masters. Unfortunately, they were both murdered and their bodies concealed about twenty miles south of the Nevada border. Preliminary coroner reports indicate the time of death to be some time the previous Friday evening. Doctors Knox and Donnelly are still missing. At this time, we consider them suspects in the murders of Grant and Masters as well as suspects in the theft of highly classified research. Obviously, they have several days' lead on us now. The FBI was immediately informed of the security breach and the missing persons; however, we have just learned about the critical nature of their research. I'll give you more on that later.

"The Las Vegas field office has confirmed Knox's car is missing from his home. We have a BOLO alert out to all state and federal law enforcement. We also know Donnelly boarded a flight to Atlanta on the same Friday evening Doctors Grant and Masters were murdered.

"You and your team are to locate and apprehend Knox and Donnelly and recover the research. The remainder of this briefing is classified black. Per protocol, you must verbally acknowledge your understanding of what that means."

The 'black' designation meant Deal could never reveal any part of the information he was about to receive to anyone. Further, he would report exclusively to Glover.

"I understand the black designation, sir," Deal said, trying not to sound irritated. He hated useless procedures.

Glover turned to 'Dr. Smith,' motioning him to proceed with his part of the briefing.

Smith quickly put his glasses back on and fumbled for a moment with his computer. The picture on Deal's screen changed to a strange black triangular aircraft flying over snow-covered mountains.

"This is the GW1-FB. Its official designation is Gravity Wave One - Fighter Bomber configuration," Smith said, his voice tinged with both nerves and pride.

Deal heard the words, but their meaning didn't sink in immediately.

Smith continued. "As the name suggests, this is a gravity wave propulsion aircraft. As you can see, there are no engines, wings, or control surfaces as on all other aircraft. Manipulation of gravity waves both propels and controls the aircraft...."

Deal interrupted. "Hold on a second! Gravity waves? I don't understand."

Smith looked up from his computer so Deal could see his face.

"Technical explanations will have to wait, but in short, we have learned to create and manipulate gravity waves. The waves are produced by a gravity wave generator and then directed around the aircraft through the two large round openings, or projectors, you can see in the area of the triangular fuselage that you may think of as 'wings.'

"The gravity wave generator uses a unique high atomic weight element as fuel. This element, number 128, must be created in a laboratory. Currently, it takes over six weeks to manufacture enough Element 128 to fuel the GW1 for a few minutes of flight. Needless to say, that is insufficient. However, the team of three scientists identified by Director Glover were working on a process to mass-produce this element."

Deal summed it up. "So, you have a new super-plane, but you don't have the gas to fly it?"

"Yes, Agent Deal, that is essentially the problem. Their last report indicated they were close to making a breakthrough. Now, however, their research is gone. To start the research over again would take at least five years. Five years that we don't have," Smith explained.

"Why not?" Deal asked.

Glover answered the question. "Because detailed plans for the GW1, the gravity wave reactor and projectors were stolen as well. With the right expertise, whoever has the technical data can produce a fully-functional gravity wave aircraft. You'll understand why the theft of this technology is a greater threat than the loss of a nuclear weapon after you read the briefing materials."

"Absolutely," Smith agreed.

"I'll set up shop in Atlanta. That's the last known location for Rick Donnelly," Deal stated. "I'll leave the investigation of the Grant and Masters murders to the Las Vegas office."

Glover had anticipated Deal's first move. "I've already ordered your team's plane directed into Atlanta. They should be landing shortly. Anything you need?"

"Yeah, a change of clothes. I think these might stink now."

After the somewhat cryptic conversation with his boss and the rattled 'Dr. Smith', Deal still didn't fully appreciate the urgency of this assignment. He settled back in his leather seat, placed reading glasses on his nose, and opened the encrypted file materials. While not formally trained in physics, chemistry or engineering, Deal had acquired vast experience in many disciplines while chasing down WMDs and their makers.

Agent Deal had served four tours in Afghanistan and Iraq as a Judge Advocate General investigator with the United States Army. Despite being a JAG officer, one of the Army's lawyers, Deal's job in the middle-east was neither clean nor safe. The Army had assigned him to a highly-trained unit of WMD hunters, which had brought him into contact with enemy insurgents and terrorists on many occasions. Gunshot injuries to his right leg and shoulder, courtesy of a couple of perturbed insurgents, earned him the

Purple Heart. After an outstanding military career that included several successful missions to find and stop terrorists from making and using WMDs, the FBI had recruited Deal into its specialized WMD investigation division.

Deal soaked up information on the gravity wave aircraft. It read like science fiction.

Gravity waves were first proposed as a means of propulsion in the 1940s by none other than Nicola Tesla. After Tesla died alone and penniless in a New York hotel, the FBI broke into his room and took the vast majority of the genius's research, including his gravity wave theories, calculations, and experiments. Using Tesla's work, the government conducted decades of ultra-classified research into the viability of gravity wave energy.

Then, in the 1960s, physicists from the University of Chicago discovered the key that would open the door to the practical production and use of gravity waves - Element 128. With continued experimentation, scientists learned how to project gravity and manipulate the waves to propel an aircraft - the GW1.

While Deal found the background interesting, he needed to know what made gravity wave technology so incredibly dangerous. Two hours later, as the jet began its initial descent, he finally understood the Director's alarm.

This technology could not be allowed loose in the world.

TWENTY-TWO

The basement of Atlanta's federal courthouse buzzed with activity as Deal's team rushed to get set up before their boss arrived. Despite fighting cruel jet lag and exhaustion from being pulled out of Spain at a moment's notice and then flying over ten hours through the night into Atlanta, the team worked with the efficiency that only came with constant training. Deal's technical experts unpacked mobile computer equipment, mounted high-definition monitors, ran cables, and set up workstations. Once up and running, Deal would have the same access any analyst at the Washington headquarters enjoyed. In fact, Deals 'techs' always made sure they had far better. At the same time, Deal's two groups of tactical operators, Red Team and Blue Team, located space inside an abandoned warehouse just outside of downtown for their weapons, vehicles, and equipment. Deal expected his team to assemble the mobile command center and be fully functional in less than one hour. Fifty-five of those sixty minutes had already passed when the door crashed open.

"What have we got so far?" Deal barked as he sat down at the cheap but functional conference table placed just minutes before in the center of the room.

Deal's agents instantly took seats. Agent Stella Sims, Deal's second in command, remained standing while a map of the United States flashed onto one of the monitors mounted on the far wall.

"Knox left Groom Lake Research Facility the same day as Donnelly. He filed an itinerary that simply took him back to his home in Las Vegas," Sims began as lines appeared from the middle of Nevada to its biggest city.

"Donnelly boarded a flight from Las Vegas to Atlanta on the Friday before Labor Day weekend. The flight manifest shows him on the aircraft," she continued. "The bodies of Masters and Grant were found four days later, yesterday, in the Arizona desert." More lines appeared on the map connecting Las Vegas to the other points the agent just mentioned.

"Not what I was looking for, Sims. Let me be clear, what *else* do we have other than the obvious?" Deal growled.

"Just getting there, boss," Sims replied, calmly. "We have nothing else on Knox. In the three days between the time he left Groom Lake and when he was first reported absent, he could have driven anywhere in the country. He has not used credit cards or his cell phone. To put it bluntly, he's in the wind."

"What about Donnelly?" Deal asked, now scowling deeply.

"Nothing firm after arriving in Atlanta and renting a car. He has traveled here on three other occasions in the past four years. The itineraries he filed indicate past visits to his elderly grandmother, Irma Donnelly. Ms. Donnelly is currently alive and residing in a rehab facility just over the border in Aiken, South Carolina," Sims reported, pointing to a small town highlighted on the map.

"Has he been there?" Deal asked.

"We think so," Sims said, knowing Deal wouldn't like the answer. "I contacted the nursing home and spoke with the charge nurse on Irma Donnelly's floor. She reviewed their visitor logs but didn't find where Dr. Donnelly signed in. But, and here's why we think so, she reported that Irma Donnelly, who suffers from dementia, kept insisting her grandson had visited her," Sims explained.

"Okay. Sims, you get over there and talk to Ms. Donnelly. Use that South Carolina charm you grew up with. Sweet-talk her. Determine whether he was there or not."

"Okay, boss," Sims said in the Southern accent she had worked to drop for years.

"Where are they from anyway? Where are their families?"

Another agent took over from Sims., "David Knox, Ph.D. in aeronautical engineering from Georgia Tech. Grew up right here in Georgia. His parents live in a small town south of here, Claxton."

"Donnelly?" Deal asked.

"Richard Donnelly, Ph.Ds. in physics and aeronautical engineering – both from the University of North Carolina. Raised by his fraternal grandmother, Irma Donnelly, as Agent Sims noted, in Aiken."

"Get people to both places. I want their life stories in excruciating detail. You know the drill, if either had a goddamned pet turtle, I want to know its name. Get help from the Atlanta field office if necessary. If we know these guys, we can find them," Deal said.

"I'll take Donnelly. I'm going over there anyway," Sims volunteered.

"You want help?" Deal asked.

"No, boss. I know the people in small Southern towns. They don't like feds. If we go in there, flashing badges and demanding answers, they'll clam up. I don't recommend the heavy-handed approach - in either town," Sims said.

"I agree. Now, what do we have on motive? Why did they steal government secrets? Why did they commit murder? If the motive is money, then who are their customers? Where they are now will depend on where they intend to go and why," Deal said, as he paced back and forth at the end of the conference table.

Sims spoke up again. "The first run-through by NSA didn't find any suspicious communications between Knox and Donnelly or the two suspects and unknown parties. Just two nerdish, hyper-intelligent scientists focused on their projects."

"Political leanings? Could this be some kind of a move toward domestic terror?" Deal asked.

"No evidence of that yet, boss," Sims answered.

"So, to f-ing recap, we have two missing scientists, two dead scientists, and a stolen secret weapon. On top of that, we have no idea where they are or why any of this happened. Let's keep the NSA and CIA digging. People, we were basically out of time on this one before we even got started. Let's get moving!"

TWENTY-THREE

Agent Stella Sims drove into Aiken early the next morning. She found the town familiar, even comfortable, having been raised in a similarly sized town on the other side of the state. After a brief Google search, she found her first stop - a family-owned diner called Brenda's, where she knew locals would gather for morning coffee and a hearty breakfast. Every small town in the south had a place like Brenda's.

Sims grabbed a seat at the counter and ordered eggs, sausage, and a biscuit covered in white gravy. When the food came, she chatted up the waitress who had probably worked there for decades. Sims' South Carolinian accent raised no suspicions when she asked about the Five Palms Rehabilitation facility.

"Got family out there, honey?" the waitress asked.

"Sure do. My mother's great aunt, Irma Donnelly. You know her?" Sims said, hoping that the name drop would bring a response.

"Mrs. Donnelly? Honey, everybody in town knows her. She's a treasure!" the waitress said. "You know what? You just have to meet Pastor Ken. He goes to see her all the time."

"Well, I'd love to!" Sims exclaimed. "Mama is getting older and just wants to know everything about her family."

The waitress craned her head around the crowded restaurant.

"You're in luck hon, he's right over there. Pastor! Pastor Ken," the waitress said, waving at a balding fifty-ish man wearing a short-sleeve shirt and flowered tie.

Introductions made; Sims sat down with the minister.

"I'm afraid my mother never knew her great aunt very well. When I told her I'd be passing through Aiken, she just begged me to look her up and find out more about her family and all. I know she is out at the nursing home and has some dementia, so this might be a waste of time," Sims explained.

The pastor seemed to want to talk.

"I didn't know the Donnelly family had people outside Aiken County. But I guess that makes sense. What's your mother's name?" he asked.

Sims had to think fast.

"Simons," she said quickly, using her own name as a template. "Anne Simons. She's into all this genealogy and I'm trying to help her where I can."

"Well, I'm sure Nancy told you," Pastor Ken said, referring to the waitress. "Mrs. Donnelly is a hero around here. She did more for Aiken after her late husband passed away than anyone could have possibly expected. She kept the people employed at the plants, practically built the new addition to the church all on her own, and even erected the confederate soldiers' memorial outside the courthouse. And that's not nearly all."

"Does she have children or grandchildren? Mother would just love to know them."

"Not in town. Sadly, Mrs. Donnelly's only son left town long ago. He met a woman of poor character, and they had a son. Soon after, that woman abandoned Mrs. Donnelly's son, and he left his baby, Ricky, with Mrs. Donnelly. He hasn't been seen since that day, and some people say he just went out into the woods and drank himself to death," the pastor explained.

"And the baby?" Sims asked.

"Little Ricky turned out to be a prodigy. God gifted that child with incredible intellect but little faith, I'm afraid. He's a scientist of some kind and doesn't come home much. But he loves his grandmother and makes sure she's well cared for."

Having obtained as much information as she could from Pastor Ken, Sims headed out to visit the famous Mrs. Donnelly.

As soon as Sims drove away, Pastor Ken made a call on his cell phone and left a short message.

"This is Pastor Ken, identification four-two-seven-two, in Aiken. A federal agent posing as a long-lost relative of Irma Donnelly showed up in town this morning digging for information. She'll be visiting the old woman but won't get anything. Mrs. Donnelly is in the advanced stages of dementia."

Pastor Ken hadn't always been a man of God, but he had always been loyal to The Cause.

TWENTY-FOUR

Sims had no trouble locating the Five Palms Rehabilitation Center on the outskirts of town. The sparsely populated parking lot seemed a sad testament to how often the elderly are forgotten in such places.

Entering the building, Sims found the atmosphere unexpectedly inviting. Skylights provided natural bright light to a central living space furnished with comfortable chairs, soft sofas, and game tables. Several residents sat in wheelchairs watching a large flat-screen television. Along one side of the room, several nurses sat at a reception desk.

As Sims approached, a friendly woman wearing pink scrubs looked up from her computer.

"Welcome to Five Palms," she said cheerily. "May I help you?"

Keeping her FBI identification tucked in her jacket pocket, Sims responded in her Southern accent: "I sure hope so, Ma'am. I'm looking for my mother's cousin. Irma Donnelly?"

"Oh, yes. Pastor Ken called a few minutes ago and said to expect you. I don't know if Mrs. Donnelly is awake this morning, but you're welcome to visit. I guess Pastor Ken told you she hasn't been, well, able to talk that well lately," the nurse said, handing Sims a paper name tag on which she had scrawled 'Visitor' and the day's date.

"Yes, he did. What a kind man. You're lucky to have him in town," Sims replied, looking around to get her bearings.

"We sure are. Mrs. Donnelly is in room A121 down the A-wing, near the end of the hall. I can show you if you want," the nurse said politely.

"Oh, no. I can find it. That way?" Sims said, pointing down one of the four corridors that intersected the main meeting area.

The curtains in the room were closed, making the room seem gloomy, despite the bright afternoon sun outside. The infamous Mrs. Donnelly laid in her bed clutching several blankets with bony blue-veined hands.

Sims pulled a chair close and sat down. Mrs. Donnelly appeared to be asleep. Wisps of white hair hung over a near skeletal face. Sims leaned in close and turned back the clock in her mind, trying to picture Mrs. Donnelly as a younger woman. The fact that this had once been a formidable woman became readily apparent.

"Mrs. Donnelly?" Sims asked gently. "Mrs. Donnelly, are you awake?"

The old woman didn't stir.

After a couple more attempts, Sims tried another tack. "Mrs. Donnelly, Ricky needs your help."

Irma Donnelly slowly opened her eyes and tried to focus on her visitor. After another moment she managed to say, "Ricky? My Ricky? He's here?"

"No, Mrs. Donnelly, but he needs your help real bad like," Sims said, still using her natural Southern accent.

Mrs. Donnelly struggled to comprehend what she was being told. She said nothing but looked into Sims' eyes. She wanted to know about Ricky.

Sims took the clue. "Ricky needs you to show him how to come to Jesus, Mrs. Donnelly. He wants to but don't know how."

Ruth's eyes opened a bit wider but then dimmed again. She managed a small shake of her head and closed her eyes. No response. *A lost cause?*

Sims thought for a moment and decided to try something else.

"Mrs. Donnelly?" This time Sims talked a bit louder and lowered her face close and gave her shoulder a tender shake. "Mrs. Donnelly. They want to take down the Confederate Memorial in the square. Ricky needs your help. He needs to know how to stop them. It's important!"

Ruth's eyes slowly opened again, and her eyebrows furled together. For the first time, she looked directly at Sims' face. The FBI agent couldn't help but feel she was being judged. Then, without releasing Sims from her gaze and in the voice of the ancient, Ruth spoke again, clearly, but softly. "My Ricky's a good man. He'll know what to do. My Ricky's a Southern patriot." Sims could barely make out Ruth's words, but there was a recognizable pride in her voice. Her eyes closed, and she pulled the blankets further under her chin.

Thinking Ruth's dementia clouded her thoughts, Sims knew she was just about out of time. Ruth's coherence would be fleeting.

"Mrs. Donnelly, how do you know Ricky's a Southern patriot?"

Without opening her eyes, a brief smile crossed Ruth's face.

"He told me so."

TWENTY-FIVE

"Let's think a minute, people. What do we know as fact?" Deal said loudly as he entered his current headquarters in downtown Atlanta. Twenty-four hours had passed since Deal and his team initiated their search for Donnelly and Knox, and they needed a break. Deal knew that each passing minute increased the chances the two suspected traitors would escape along with the gravity wave technology.

Sims had just returned from Aiken and had been looking over the team's progress.

"I think we have a lead, Boss," she said, looking up from her notes. "We know Donnelly flew into Atlanta from Vegas. So, we've been investigating the movements of everyone on that flight. Every passenger and crew member had a cell phone, so we can track their post-flight movements. One older lady had no phone, but she's an eighty-year-old widow with a bad gambling problem. Donnelly had a cell phone at one time but must have dumped it in Las Vegas - that's the last hit we got on its location. Anyway, nothing suspicious turned up, so we began interviewing the passengers and crew and got lucky. One of the flight attendants remembered Donnelly because he fell asleep on the plane before it even took off. Later, she recalls Donnelly chatting with his seatmate, a tall white, middle-aged guy in a business suit."

"That's not much, Sims," Deal commented, taking his seat. "White guys in suits on airplanes aren't exactly rare."

"Ah, true. But remember. This was a flight out of Las Vegas, the party capital. People dressed casually, lots of pictures, and not so many business types. So, we vetted Caucasian males on the plane by age. Then, we checked social media for pictures, posts and such and I think we found who Donnelly sat next to on the flight - a lawyer from Banebridge, Alabama. His name is Drew Campbell."

"Have you interviewed him?" Deal asked.

"We just ran this down a few minutes ago. Anyway, I figured you would want to talk to him in person," Sims replied.

"Isn't there a college in Banebridge?" Deal asked.

"Yep, Southern University. We haven't had a chance to dig deeper on Campbell but we know he's married, two children, a member of the local bar association, runs a small law firm, pays his taxes, and is as squeaky clean as they come."

"Yeah, I'm going down there and meet this guy. He sounds like an upstanding citizen, but I don't trust people who are *too* squeaky clean."

"You want company?" Sims asked.

"No. You stay here. If a guy like Donnelly got friendly with some Mr. Clean lawyer, I have a feeling he had a reason. Get Red and Blue Teams on standby. I may need them."

"You onto something?" Sims asked.

Her boss had an uncanny ability to sift through scattered bits of evidence and find the one that meant something.

"I'm sniffing around Sims. I might smell an opportunity, yeah," Deal replied.

Drew Campbell had just unwrapped a turkey sandwich to eat at his desk when his secretary appeared in his office door out of breath. An overly excitable woman, she now seemed nearly hysterical.

"Uh, what's going on?" Drew asked, unconcerned.

"Drew," his secretary said through gasps of air. "There's a, there's a..."

"There's a what?" Drew replied, allowing a bit of irritation to creep into his voice.

"There's an FBI agent in the waiting room. He wants to see you," she said, her eyes the size of dinner plates.

Drew got up from his desk, more irritated that his brief lunch had been interrupted than worried about his secretary's news.

Walking to the front of the office with his secretary trailing close behind, Drew found a large man standing rigidly in front of the reception desk. With a gray crew-cut, dark suit, and square jaw, the visitor certainly looked the part of a federal agent.

"I'm Drew Campbell. How can I help you?" Drew asked, entering the reception area.

Deal pulled his identification from his jacket pocket and displayed his badge. "I'm Special Agent Frank Deal. Is there somewhere we can speak in private?" Deal asked, looking over Drew's shoulder at the secretary.

"Certainly. Let's step into the conference room," Drew said, leading Deal through a pair of frosted glass French doors.

Once inside, Drew gestured at one of the chairs arranged around the conference table.

When they were both seated, Drew asked again, "Now, how can I help you, Agent Deal?"

Deal took a picture out of a leather briefcase and slid it across the desk.

"Do you know this man?" Deal asked.

Drew picked up the picture. A middle-aged white male wearing a lab coat and round black glasses looked back at him from the photo. At first, Drew didn't recognize the face. When it dawned on him a moment later, his stomach turned to ice. Not only did he meet with the man in the photograph less than a week before, but his mind snapped together another connection. Michael, Zach and Bubba's fantastic story of the president of their fraternity ordering the abduction of someone with a name very similar to Donnelly.

The lawyer suddenly found himself at the center of a hurricane.

"I do. That's Rick Donnelly," Drew answered, trying and failing to keep the nerves he felt from invading his voice.

"Correct. How do you know Donnelly?" Deal asked, pulling a pad of paper from his briefcase and jotting notes.

"May I ask what this is about?" Drew asked.

"Mr. Donnelly is a suspect in a serious federal crime. That's all you need to know," Deal said, gruffly. "Now, please answer the question."

"I met Mr. Donnelly on a flight from Las Vegas to Atlanta last week," Drew answered, truthfully.

"And have you seen Mr. Donnelly since then?" Deal wanted to know, looking up from his notes as if he already knew the answer to his question.

"Yes, as a matter of fact. A couple of days ago, Rick, uh, Mr. Donnelly showed up at my gym. I never thought I would see him again, but he said he was in town, remembered me from the plane, and looked me up. Apparently, my secretary told him where I would be."

"When exactly was this?"

"Last Friday," Drew said, thinking back.

"What did he want?" Deal asked.

"Ultimately, he wanted a lawyer to represent him. I agreed," Drew answered.

"Representation for what?"

Drew hesitated, but he didn't have any choice about his answer. "That, I can't tell you. Attorney/client confidentiality. I'm sure you understand."

Deal looked up from his notes. *Damned lawyers!*

"Mr. Campbell, this is a matter of national security. I must insist."

"I don't mean to be rude, but you may insist all you like. Unless you have an order from a court compelling me to answer your questions, I can't help you," Drew replied.

After staring into each other's eyes for a few seconds, Deal backed off. This guy wasn't going to cave. He needed a different tactic.

"Alright, counselor. Let's try again," Deal said, sitting back down.

"Agent, our meeting is over," Drew declared, moving toward the door.

Deal didn't budge. "No. It's not. You need to hear what I have to say."

Drew looked into the Deal's steel-blue eyes. The man was serious.

"Fine," Drew replied, retaking his seat.

Figuring he would have to give this lawyer a reason to cooperate, Deal decided to tell Drew as much as possible. Even if he had the time for the red tape involved in getting a court order, he couldn't reveal the gravity wave technology, even to a federal judge. He needed Drew to open up as quickly as possible.

"Mr. Campbell, Dr. Rick Donnelly is a preeminent physicist. He disappeared just over a week ago along with the technology he and two other scientists developed at the Groom Lake laboratories in Nevada. The technology he stole is irreplaceable, expensive, but most of all dangerous. On top of that, the other two scientists working on the project were brutally murdered and their bodies left to rot in the desert. So, when I tell you what you know about Donnelly is vital to national security, I'm not being dramatic. Your country needs your help."

Drew sat back in his seat, considering Deal's story. After a moment, he said, "I'll tell you everything I can."

Drew recounted the flight from Las Vegas in as much detail as he could remember. Rick's explanation of his background in physics and aeronautics, his work on jet engines, and the fact that he worked at Area 51. He even told Deal about how he had given Rick his business card and Rick promising to send photos. Deal listened carefully and took notes.

"Alright, but why did he show up here? What did he want?" Deal asked, thinking Drew had agreed to volunteer the information.

"As I said before, he wanted a lawyer. I can't and won't tell you specifics, but I can tell you what he needed from me is not illegal in any sense."

Deal nearly exploded. "Goddammit! You are letting some jack-ass lawyer rule stand in the way of protecting this country! Did he give you anything? Any information? Any documents?"

At the mention of Rick giving him documents, a look of concern swept across Drew's face, and Deal saw it.

"I can't answer that either," Drew said quickly.

He didn't have to, Deal already knew the answer, and would get his hands on whatever it was another way. His way.

"You're skating on thin ice here, Mr. Campbell. You are being evasive. And, since you're a lawyer, I'm sure you know that lying to the FBI is a federal crime. There's something else. Something you haven't told me. What is it?" Deal demanded.

Just as he agreed to represent Rick, he had also told Michael and his friends he considered himself their lawyer. His hands were tied. He couldn't just tell the FBI what the young men had brought to his attention. But they could.

"There is something else you need to hear. Give me a couple of hours to discuss it with some other clients. I'm sure they'll want to tell you their story, but it will have to be their decision," Drew said.

Deal could see that going another three rounds with this lawyer wouldn't get him any more information, but he was intrigued.

"Make your calls, counselor. I'll wait right here."

Drew went back to his office, leaving Deal planted in his conference room. He wanted to break something, release the overwhelming stress. Instead, he slammed his fist down on his desk. *Goddammit! How the hell did I get myself into this?*

"Are you okay?" Tracy asked from his doorway. "Can I do something?"

Drew looked up, and for once was grateful for his assistant's motherly nature.

"Yeah, I'm fine. I just don't have an FBI agent interrogating me every day," Drew answered with a wane smile. "Do me a favor, call Michael, Zach, and Bubba and ask them to get down to my office as quickly as possible. It's important."

"Can I tell them what it's about?" Tracy asked.

"Just tell them it's important enough for them to miss class if they need to."

TWENTY-SIX

An hour later, Tracy ushered Michael, Zach, and Bubba into the conference room. Drew stood and introduced Deal.

"Have a seat guys," Drew began. "And thanks for hurrying down here. Let me explain what's going on. Agent Deal here is part of a nationwide manhunt. He wants to ask you some questions. Because I'm your lawyer, I haven't told him anything about what we discussed the other day, so it will be your decision whether to answer his questions. As I understand it, he's looking for information. You understand all that?"

"Yeah, I guess so," Michael said.

Zach just nodded, obviously anxious.

"Yep," Bubba agreed.

"Good. Alright, Agent, go ahead," Drew said.

Deal passed around photographs of Rick Donnelly. "Do any of you know this man?"

All three boys looked at the photo.

"I don't know him," Michael said.

"Me either," Zach added.

"Who is he?" Bubba asked.

"He's a wanted felon. His name is Rick Donnelly, and it's critical we find him as soon as possible. Mr. Campbell here said I should talk to you three, and I want to know why.

The three friends looked at the photo again and then back at the FBI agent. Finally, they pieced together why Drew thought they should meet Deal.

"Donnelly? That's this guy's name, right?" Zach said, excitedly. "That's the name I heard, Drew. That's the name of the man Hunter sent those skinheads to kidnap!"

"You sure about that?" Michael asked.

"Yeah. All I had to do was hear the right name - and that's it! Donnelly," Zach replied without a hint of doubt in his voice.

"What?" Deal asked, surprised by Zach's announcement. "What the hell does that mean?"

"Is it alright if I explain?" Drew asked the boys. "If I get something wrong, you guys can let me know."

"Sure," Zach said, after making sure Michael and Bubba agreed.

Drew turned back to Deal. "That's what Michael, Zach, and Bubba came to see me about. Several days ago, Zach drove the president of his fraternity to what appears to have been a clandestine meeting with some men Zach described as 'skinheads.' At that meeting, Hunter Ewell, their fraternity president, ordered the skinheads to abduct a man named Rick Donnelly. Later that night, these guys all witnessed the same skinheads apparently looking for someone outside of a hotel - from which all the guests had been evacuated because of a fire. They later witnessed Hunter meeting with the skinheads outside the fraternity house. They came to me for advice about what to do, although at that time Zach didn't recall Donnelly being the name mentioned by Hunter."

"And when they came to you, you didn't connect what they told you with the Rick Donnelly you agreed to represent?" Deal asked, obviously suspicious of Drew's explanation.

"No. I didn't make the connection until just a little while ago when you told me Rick Donnelly was wanted by the FBI. Zach didn't recall Donnelly's name until he heard it from you," Drew explained.

"I'll take your word, for now. Tell me about this Hunter, uh, Ewell," Deal said, looking down at his notes. "Why would he be giving skinheads orders?"

Michael answered first, "Hunter James Ewell is his real name. He comes from a very well-connected and very wealthy family that has basically run the politics in this state for generations. Hunter's an ass, but I never thought he was a criminal. None of us know why he would even be meeting with skinheads or gang members or whatever they were. Excuse my language."

I'd say a major-league ass*hole*," Bubba added.

"Bubba!" Zach exclaimed.

"Well, he is," Bubba said, shrugging.

Deal frowned but didn't react to Bubba's comment. "Okay, I need to talk to this guy. Where is he?"

"Probably at the house. He doesn't make it to too many classes," Zach answered.

"But Agent Deal?" Michael interjected. "I don't know if talking to him will do much good."

"And why not?" Deal replied, surprised at the young man's comment. "The FBI can be pretty persuasive."

"I think I know what Michael is getting at," Drew added. "The Ewell family is indeed powerful. Along with the state government, it's common knowledge they have bought off the courts through big campaign contributions. Anyone running for office either accepts their money or the Ewells just give it to the competition. Either way, the judges all owe them. So, let's say you bring Hunter in for questioning. He likely won't tell you anything, and his family will surround him with heavy-hitting lawyers in less than an hour. Unless you have some strong evidence that Hunter committed a crime, you won't be able to hold him, and you'll lose any chance he'll tell you about the skinheads or Donnelly."

"And once that happens, any connection to the skinheads will disappear? Is that what you're saying?" Deal asked.

"No doubt about it," Bubba added. "Look, if I know skinheads, and I do because we got plenty of them where I'm from, they'll just disappear back into the woods."

Deal stood and walked around the room, considering his options. Unfortunately, Drew and the college boys were probably right. To be sure, he'd have his team check on the Ewells, but Hunter and the skinheads were the one thin thread they still had to Donnelly, and he needed to protect that thread. While Donnelly had told Drew he was returning to his job with the engine manufacturer, that hadn't happened. But it appeared someone else wanted Donnelly. Deal wanted to know who and why.

"I see your point," Deal said, sitting back down. "Does Hunter suspect Zach knows what actually went on at the meeting with the skinheads?"

"I don't think so," Zach answered. "He hasn't acted any different around me since then."

"Alright, what do you all think about keeping an eye on Hunter for me? Not spy on him, but just let me know if he does anything else suspicious and ..."

"Hold on there just a second!" Drew said, interrupting. "These are college kids. You can't ask them to get involved."

"No, counselor, you're wrong there. The FBI has always relied on civilian help. These men are all of legal age. Besides, I'm not asking they do anything out of the norm. Just watch and report to me. That's it. We may bring Hunter in for questioning, but in the meantime, I need to keep an eye on him and I can't very well send an undercover agent into a fraternity house who isn't a member."

"We'll do it," Zach said. "No problem."

"Don't worry, Drew. It's no big thing. If Hunter does anything else shady, we'll just call or text Agent Deal and report," Michael added.

"I can't stop you, but I still don't like it," Drew said, finally. "I don't like it at all."

TWENTY-SEVEN

That night, Deal implemented his plan to find and recover any documents Rick might have given Drew. By twelve-thirty, two members of Agent Deal's tactical Blue team had set up overwatch. Blue One provided surveillance from a car located one block west of Drew Campbell's office building while Blue Two took up position in a plain white panel van one block to the north. Red team's three members would enter the building, breach the security system and locate any suspect documents. Voice-activated radios kept the teams in continuous communication with each other. White One, Deal, monitored the operation from team headquarters.

About the size of a residential house, Drew's single-story office building faced one of the streets leading from campus into downtown Banebridge. A sidewalk ran from the building's front door to a tiny parking lot. Six-foot tall windows lined the sides and front entrance. Once obviously residential, that particular part of Banebridge had changed use over the years to professional offices.

Thick clouds hid the moon, and light rain kept people inside. Only one house, across the street and two doors down, showed lights in its windows. Two other small office buildings on either side of the law firm remained utterly dark. At the back of the property, an old privacy fence behind separated it from the back of a closed dental office. A solitary streetlight down the block cast only a faint orange glow.

Red team stepped casually from Blue Two's van and walked across the street. Passing behind an accounting firm next door, they paused.

"Red One, you are clear," Red Team's leader heard in this ear. The operators moved swiftly across the damp parking lot. Even if someone had passed by on the street at that exact moment, they would have missed the three indistinct black silhouettes hidden in deep shadows. The plan entailed picking the back-door lock and shutting down any alarm system. When Red One reached the back door, he removed a lock pick set from a covered pocket on his combat-style pants. Just as he was about to insert the first pick, he heard, "Red One, hold. You aren't going to believe this." Red One looked back. Red Three was lifting one of the windows.

"Alright, plan deviation, move in through the window," Red One said quietly.

Led by Red Three, they each ducked through the window. "White One, we're in," Red One reported.

"Acknowledged. Proceed."

"Red Team, switch to night vision," Red One ordered. "No lights. This place is like a fishbowl with all these windows. Red Two, alarm check."

Red Two pulled a device from her pocket and turned it on. "I read two commercial quality motion sensors. Probably pointed down each hall. Wireless signal to a pad hardwired to the phone. Child's play."

Red Two disappeared through the office door. A loud chirping began almost immediately but fell silent less than five seconds later.

"Disarmed. No signal out. We're clear," Red Two reported.

"Alright, let's get it done," said Red One.

Deal didn't entirely trust that Drew Campbell wasn't working with Donnelly and decided to install some surveillance devices along with recovering Donnelly's documents. Each team member moved swiftly and efficiently. Red Two strategically placed six digital microphones so that all conversations anywhere in the office could be monitored and recorded. In Drew Campbell's office, she hid the device inside a wall outlet behind his desk. Finally, she opened both motion detectors and installed wireless video cameras with a view down the two main hallways.

Red Three quickly located the firm's sole computer server. Inserting a thumb drive, Red Three copied the servers' entire contents in less than two minutes. A second thumb drive installed a program that allowed a remote computer at their headquarters to mirror every computer in the office, constantly uploading new emails, documents, court filings, and male enhancement advertisements. In less than fifteen minutes, the FBI possessed every byte of information that touched the firm's computers and could monitor each in real-time. A search of the office located no old computers that might contain more information.

In the meantime, Red One searched for the paper documents Deal wanted. Finding every desk unlocked and paper files arranged in open filing cabinets, his search proceeded quickly. *These must be the most trusting lawyers in the whole world*, he mused. Thinking they must have some kind of on-site secured storage, he swept the entire office again, finally locating a small fireproof safe deep inside a utility closet. Examining it closely, Red One determined that anyone could purchase that make and model at a big box office supply store for less than fifteen hundred bucks. It would pose no challenge.

"Red One to White One," he said, contacting the operation's command center.

"White One," he heard.

"White One, I need the combination for a Nicholas Safe. I'll read you the number." Red One found the identification plate on the side of the door and read out the numbers.

"Stand by."

Red One sat down in front of the safe. After about thirty seconds, Deal read the combination to him over the radio. The FBI did not have the authority to hack into the computers of safe manufacturing companies and appropriate combinations at will; but, since they were already breaking dozens of state and federal laws tonight, cracking one safe wouldn't matter much anyway.

Using the combination to unlock the heavy door, the highly trained agent checked that his headlamp could not be seen from outside, turned it on, and looked inside. Half the safe was stacked with legal-size brown envelopes, but Red One immediately noticed that one envelope's color differed from those below. He removed it, turned it over, and identified the logo of a prominent jet engine manufacturer. After carefully opening the envelope and removing the two-inch-thick stack of papers stuffed inside, Red One saw that he held the target of the night's infiltration in his hands - multiple miniature blueprints for an advanced military aircraft.

"White One, all mission objectives successful. Red Two and Three, time to go," Red One ordered.

TWENTY-EIGHT

It didn't take Deal long to look through the documents. While he didn't understand the technicalities, he could easily discern that what he held was, indeed, at least the basic plans and specifications for the gravity wave aircraft. Once he had made the initial identification, his team uploaded the documents to FBI headquarters where they could be further evaluated.

Forensic analysis of the envelope revealed fingerprints from both Rick and Drew Campbell. However, the seal had remained intact and Drew's fingerprints could not be found on any of the materials it contained. Drew had not opened the envelope and probably had no idea he had possession of one of the nation's most closely guarded secrets resting in his office safe. Deal concluded that Rick had used Drew to hold a set of the plans, probably as insurance against a double-cross by a co-conspirator - most likely Dave Knox.

Just an hour after uploading the file, Deal was summoned to a secure office for a video conference with FBI Director Glover and the anonymous Dr. Smith.

"Frank, Dr. Smith has reviewed the documents you recovered. I'm not going to ask exactly how you got them. I'll think I'll just let him explain his findings," Glover said.

The skittish scientist looked just as worried as he had when Deal first video-conferenced with him on the way back from Spain.

"Yes, well, the documents you found are relevant to the GW-1 project. They consist of airframe, instrumentation, and radar plans and designs. I also found some prospective armament proposals. However, they are far from complete. Most notably, the formula for Element 128 is missing as are the designs for the gravity wave reactor and dispersal units."

This confirmed Deal's theory. "So, would you say that with the file we recovered Donnelly could prove his bona fides, but wouldn't reveal any crucial information?"

"Yes, that's exactly it," Dr. Smith said, readjusting his thick black glasses.

"Alright, Frank, good work. But until we find Donnelly and Knox, the gravity wave technology is still out in the open. We need to put it back in its box."

"Yes, sir," Deal replied. "Donnelly's still ahead of us, but we're on his trail now. Any hint the technology has been put on the market?"

Glover shook his head. "No. NSA hasn't gotten even a whiff that a new superweapon is for sale. Has your team run down a motive yet?"

"No. But we're working on it. We're deep-diving on Donnelly and Knox's backgrounds. As you know, they were vetted heavily before ever being allowed to work at Area 51, so anything we find will have to be very, very deep," Deal explained.

"You don't think they did it for a big paycheck?" the Director prompted.

Deal frowned thoughtfully. "No, I don't think so. Hyper-intellectual scientists like Donnelly and Knox aren't generally motivated by money. They find reward in the success of their work and the process of achieving that success. Their willingness to commit treason arises from one of two types of motivation. Either they believe they can advance the science further on their own or they have a duty to something more important than loyalty to their country."

Dr. Smith agreed. "Yes, perhaps they felt a duty to pure science. I can at least see that point of view as being relevant."

"Or maybe they aren't the honorable citizens they appeared to be and have some devotion to some other agenda altogether," Deal suggested.

"What's your next move?" Glover asked.

"I'm taking the entire team down to Banebridge."

"That's your call. Keep after it, Frank. We can't let that technology get into the hands of an enemy of this country," Glover said.

"Yes," Smith added, somberly. "Testing wasn't complete, but the GW-FB1's maneuverability and speed are well beyond the capabilities of even the most advanced anti-aircraft missiles. And, its third-generation stealth technology make it completely invisible to all forms of radar. Not to put too fine of a point on it, but there is no current defense against a fully-functional gravity wave aircraft. None."

TWENTY-NINE

The Georgian Terrace Hotel
Atlanta, Georgia
One week later

Governor Margie Franks stood before the other eleven Directors holding a remote control that would allow her to scroll through the most important video presentation of her life. Her tailored Tom Ford suit, Saint Laurent pumps, and lack of jewelry had been carefully chosen to portray a formidable presence amid eleven alpha-male egos.

Franks had fought for this opportunity her entire life. She had been loyal to The Cause from her first breaths as a newborn. Her father had been a Director. Although disappointed at not fathering a son, he made sure Margie became as tough and hard-nosed as any man. After inheriting the controlling stock in her father's oil empire and becoming its first female CEO, she had entered the cutthroat world of Texas politics. Backed by The Cause and its Directors, Franks became the state's first female senator, gaining the reputation of a political brawler, willing to personally attack and destroy her competition or their families, if necessary. She didn't hesitate to use every dirty trick available, including feeding completely untrue stories of criminal or sexual misconduct to media outlets hungry for sleaze.

The men around the table she now faced had been instrumental in her success, but with tonight's announcement, she knew she would become their leader.

"Gentlemen, thank you all for being here," Franks began. "We are all busy, but I can assure you, this *will* be worth your time."

"I goddamn hope so, Governor," growled a bald man seated to Margie's left. "I'm supposed to be in Washington right now, preparing for a meeting with the Joint Chiefs of Staff, and you didn't give us any idea why you insisted we be here tonight."

"General, we all appreciate your time," Margie said, unphased. "You'll be particularly interested in this briefing. So, I'll get right to it. From the days of our grandfathers, we always knew that for The Cause to succeed we would have to accomplish innumerable nearly impossible tasks. But I'm here to talk about the one indispensable thing we still needed - the weapon. The weapon that Edward Young Clarke could not describe to our forefathers but knew would exist one day."

General Sean Brady stood. "Are you talking about the gravity wave technology we've spent so much on? Are you saying you have it?"

"Yes, General, that's exactly what I'm saying," Margie replied. "Now if you'll sit down, I'll get on with it."

Brady smiled at Margie and took his seat. "Please do, Madam Governor. Please do."

"Eighteen months ago, the Directors authorized a full-scale effort to gain access to a very special weapons system. We now have the technology for that weapon in our hands. And more importantly, we have been able to ensure the United States government will be deprived of that same technology for at least the next five years," Margie explained, not trying to keep her pride in the accomplishment hidden.

The intense interest of the Directors was evident in their body language. They sat forward in their seats, eyebrows raised and eyes opened wide.

"How did you accomplish depriving the U.S. of their own secret? That seems incredible," one of the Directors, a small balding man with glasses, asked.

Franks didn't want the other Directors to know about Rick and Dave yet. The men in the room with her, while loyal to The Cause, wouldn't hesitate to make a power grab for themselves. No, for the moment, they didn't need the particulars.

"That will have to wait. But you'll meet the genius scientists who pulled off that coup and are now in charge of the gravity wave project in due time. Now, let me show you the weapon and explain its capabilities," Margie said, turning to the giant projector screen slowly lowering from the ceiling. "This, gentlemen, is the key to our success."

Margie pushed a button on her remote, turning on an overhead projector. She said nothing as a video began playing, opening on a wide shot of a desert, obviously taken from high on a mountainside looking down into a valley. Indecipherable technical readouts appeared along the bottom of the video, but everyone in the room saw the time and date stamp showing the video was recorded three months earlier. A small U.S. Air Force insignia had been placed in the upper right corner.

Thirty seconds elapsed with no change to the scene. Then, what appeared to be a black triangle suddenly appeared at the far end of the valley. It seemed to have come from nowhere, and just sat there, barely visible hovering in the distance. Then, within less than three seconds, the triangle shot forward, directly at the camera lens. Incredibly, it then simply stopped, hanging in the air just ten yards in front of the camera. Two pilots could be seen sitting side by side in the cockpit.

The Directors reacted just as Margie had when she first saw the astonishing video. The vehicle moved at a speed they simply couldn't comprehend, leaving them speechless. A voice from the video, probably the photographer, vocalized what they all felt.

"Holy shit!"

Margie paused the video.

"The U.S. Air Force designated this aircraft as the GW-FB1 or Gravity Wave Fighter Bomber number 1. As you can see, it is roughly triangular, and a bit larger in overall length and width from a current F-22. But this aircraft makes the F-22 as obsolete as Orville and Wilbur Wright's flying machine."

Margie advanced the video in slow motion. As the aircraft turned away, the perspective changed, revealing large holes in each of what they would have called wings.

"As you can see, this aircraft has no engines, at least in the traditional sense, and no tail, flaps, or control surfaces of any kind. These openings emit and control gravity waves produced by an internal gravity wave generator," Margie explained, using a laser pointer to highlight important parts of the plane.

"Good lord!" the balding Director exclaimed. "How the hell does that work?"

"Think of it this way," Margie replied. "We think of gravity as something that holds us down to the earth, like a magnet. In fact, gravity is a force that actually pushes us and everything else down. That same force could just as easily lift us up or propel us forward. Simply put, we have learned how to create and control gravitational force."

"What's its top speed?" another of the Directors asked.

"Well, as you can see from the readouts at the bottom of the video, that short burst across the desert was Mach 3.3 or 2,531.99 miles per hour. But I'm told top speed is unknown because air friction is not a factor with gravity wave engines. Airspeed is always limited because conventional aircraft must plow through the atmosphere. However, gravity waves completely displace the air ahead of the plane. This plane can fly backward, up, down, or sideways as fast as it can fly forward. Its lift does not depend on air moving across wings."

Margie could see several directors didn't believe her last statement, so she restarted the video saying: "Keep watching."

The GW-FB1 turned slowly away, pirouetting on one wing until it faced away from the camera. Then, in a series of maneuvers impossible for any other craft, it transitioned from a hover in mid-air to standing on its tail. A second later, it launched, missile-like, into the sky and quickly receded from sight. In the next moment, the plane reappeared in front of the camera as if conjured by magic.

Franks turned off the video.

"What you just saw was a fully functioning gravity wave military aircraft. Impressive? Yes. But *that* plane is nearly worthless," Margie said.

"And why is that?" General Brady asked.

"Because they don't have enough fuel to fly it," Margie answered, expecting the same looks of confusion that appeared on her audiences' faces. "You see, the production of gravity waves requires an energy source far more powerful than the fusion or even fission of natural elements. Scientists quickly realized it would be necessary to invent a new and extremely heavy atomic element to generate the necessary power. It took decades of research, but such an element now exists. It's called Element 128, and it's a real bastard to manufacture. It took five months of exacting laboratory work to produce enough of it to power the plane in the video for the three-minute test flight you just saw."

"Then what the hell good does it do us to have the same plane?" General Brady asked, irritation building in his voice.

Margie gave the general a sneer of victory. "Good question. And the answer is simple. Because we have the ability to not only build the same aircraft, but also manufacture all the Element 128 we want, and the government can't."

The general, for once, was stunned. "Tell me that thing can be armed."

"If you have it, my plane will be able to carry it, shoot it, or drop it, anywhere, any time."

"When?"

"Soon."

THIRTY

It took days for Hunter to work up the courage to call his father and he agonized over whether to do it at all. The Directors gave him a simple task, relay their orders to J.P. But he screwed it up. He had gotten drunk and brought along someone who shouldn't have been there at all – Zach Self. His father had been clear. The Directors rewarded success but harshly punished failure.

Hunter thought about throwing the blame on J.P. The skinhead didn't have to murder the policeman, and he didn't locate Rick Donnelly at the hotel. But that explanation sounded hollow even to him. He knew what his father would say. *Only a failed leader blames others for a botched job.*

Hunter had to force himself not to take several shots of bourbon before dialing his father's number. And he almost hung up before his father answered but didn't.

Much to his relief, the conversation went better than he expected. His father could be harsh, but above all, the man was a pragmatic problem-solver. The incident with the police at the truck stop had been a turn of bad luck, and he didn't blame Hunter for J.P.'s actions. Yet, Richard Ewell would report the incident, and Hunter would have to live with whatever action the Directors decided to take. For the next two hours, Hunter felt better. Then his phone rang – the Directors.

"Our asset you met the other night already reported the incident," a voice stated before Hunter said a word. "Does the person with you in the car that night suspect anything?"

Hunter knew better than to use Zach's name. "No. Nothing. And he has shown no signs otherwise."

"We are watching the situation there carefully. You will report any changes in your, uh, companion's behavior. You have other responsibilities. Do not fail in those."

Hunter knew the Directors meant the elections. "Understood. I won't."

In Austin, Margie Franks stood next to Chief Snow, who had just ended the call with Hunter Ewell.

"Goddammit, Snow, what the hell is going on?" Franks demanded.

"It's been forty-eight hours since J.P. Hoffman reported he had to take out the Banebridge police officer. As I expected, there is a wide-ranging search for the missing officer being conducted by law enforcement from several jurisdictions. J.P. must have done an excellent job covering his tracks," Snow responded.

"I can't have the FBI connecting J.P. Hoffman to the murder and this Hunter Ewell kid," Franks observed. "That one connection could lead the FBI deeper into our organization. Potentially even right to our front door. I know Hunter Ewell's father. He's a good man and loyal to The Cause. But his son seems like a weak link. The other Directors know about the gravity wave plane, but I sure didn't share the cluster fuck in Banebridge with them. Will this be a problem?"

"I don't know yet, Madam Governor. It depends on Hunter Ewell. If he's right and this, let's see, Zachary Self, doesn't suspect anything and Hunter stays strong, we'll be fine. Otherwise..."

"Otherwise, I'll make other arrangements," Franks said.

THIRTY-ONE

After meeting Agent Deal at Drew Campbell's office, Michael, Zach, and Bubba did their best to resume their normal college lives while keeping a watchful eye on the president of their fraternity. Somewhat to their frustration, Hunter Ewell had done nothing they felt would remotely interest the FBI. Surprisingly, Hunter had been on his best behavior, even attending classes and staying mostly sober.

"So, what do you think?" Zach asked quietly one evening after supper while the three friends relaxed on the front porch.

"About what?" Bubba asked, cracking open a can of cola. "You mean our little spy mission?"

"No, he's curious about your love life," Michael said, smiling.

"Don't worry about that, little brother," Bubba responded. "I got more offers to tutor engineering co-eds than I can handle."

"I thought aerospace engineering students were all nerds with thick glasses," Zach kidded.

"Maybe so. But being two years ahead of where I should be and the *numero uno* engineering brain in the whole school has its advantages. Plus, this amazing bod makes me..."

"Okay, okay, that's not what I was asking. I mean Hunter. You guys think I got any of this wrong after all?" Zach asked.

"No," Michael answered. "Definitely not. He's being un-Hunter-like now, and that, in and of itself, is suspicious. But I have a feeling he'll slip up eventually."

Just as the small group settled back into a comfortable silence, Michael nudged Zach with his elbow. Zach looked across the lawn in the direction Michael had nodded.

As they watched, Hunter walked into the parking lot to their right from behind the house. This wouldn't have raised any particular suspicion except for the fact that Hunter was vigorously arguing with someone on his cell phone. Hunter's appearance also caught Bubba's attention, and all three tried to remain as inconspicuous as possible. But Hunter had his back to the group and was becoming angrier by the second. They couldn't catch much of what he was saying, but they could make out several expletives before he climbed into his car and slammed the door.

"Looks like our esteemed president is a little pissed off," Bubba observed as Hunter's BMW launched across the parking lot.

"Yeah, that was a little weird, even for him," Zach added.

"Well, what are we waiting for?" Bubba said, standing. "Let's go."

"Let's go where?" Zach asked.

Bubba gave Zach a withering look. "Really?"

Michael caught Bubba's suggestion, stood, and said: "He's right. Let's go. Bubba, we need your car. Mine's too recognizable."

They all stood, but Zach hung back. "Hey! Are we really going to follow him? Deal said to just, you know, observe."

Hunter didn't scare Zach, but the thought of what his father would do if he got in any kind of trouble made him hesitate. Michael and Bubba understood.

"Hey, buddy," Michael said, walking back to Zach. "Let me and Bubba do this. It's probably nothing anyway. You stay here in case Hunter comes back."

"Yeah, no problem," Bubba agreed. "But we need to move our butts."

THIRTY-TWO

Hunter had no idea Bubba and Michael were following him. Earlier in the evening, he had gotten word that a poll conducted by the campus newspaper had shown him tied with the independent candidate for the Student Government Association presidency. To make matters worse, Hunter could feel the eyes of the Directors and his father bearing down on him and judging if he would be able to meet their heavy expectations. Winning the election should have been a cakewalk. Losing would label him unworthy of any help from the Directors and, worse, irreparably damage his family's standing in the very organization that had made them incredibly rich and powerful. The words *'failure is not an option'* rang loudly in his head.

With the news of his dropping poll numbers, Hunter began calling the chosen presidents of the other fraternities and sororities, demanding an immediate meeting of The Tyros' controlling committee. Such a meeting was unusual at best, but he didn't care. He wasn't going let a goddammed independent take away his presidency and spoil his life.

The Tyros and its block voting strategy was the worst kept secret on Southern's campus. But only a select few knew that special representatives from the top Greek organizations hand-picked the candidates and then controlled their votes and other decisions after they got elected. Hunter realized an impromptu meeting of the controlling committee could be dangerous. If it got out the committee even existed, The Tyros would be exposed for what it truly was – a corrupt political machine.

Hunter drove angrily through campus and its quiet surrounding neighborhoods, fuming at his bad luck in getting mixed up with J.P. Hoffman and blaming his precarious status in the election on the other Tyros committee members' lack of loyalty and hard work. He vowed to fix that problem tonight.

A few miles out of town, Hunter arrived at the Sunshine Motel. Old but well maintained, the two-story motor lodge hadn't changed much since the 1950s. While not luxurious, staying at the Sunshine for football games at the university had become a tradition. For a hefty monthly fee, its owner maintained a special conference room just for The Tyros' leadership meetings.

Hunter whipped his car around the back and parked.

The conference room had been constructed from two hotel rooms. Several committee members mingled around a bar that stretched across one wall while others had already taken seats at a long conference table.

The Directors controlled The Tyros through this committee, and Hunter controlled the committee. Only Hunter, as a member of one of The Cause's most loyal families, even knew The Directors existed. The remainder of the committee came, for the most part, from affluent, influential Southern families. While their motivations differed, they all believed at least one thing: the university could not be subject to the needs of the poor independents, the complaints of minorities, or the whims of the liberal arts students.

The room grew quiet as the members moved quickly to their seats. Hunter remained standing and leaned forward, placing his hands flat on the table.

"Listen up. We have to do something, and we have to do it now. You know the problem. The Tyros' opponent for president, this Mary O'Dell, is popular. Too popular. And she has a better than even shot at beating us for the first time in decades. This looks bad for everyone. We are not going to fail! Not on my watch. We need a solution, and nobody is leaving until we have one."

For the next fifteen minutes, the members made various suggestions but rejected each in turn. Hunter listened to the discussion but quickly became irritated by his committee's lack of imagination. The members were proposing only safe and conventional remedies to a problem that required altogether new thinking. Plus, many independents loathed The Tyros, and an independent winning the presidency would spell disaster.

Conventional means won't work this time; the opposition is too close to victory. We need something more. We need something nuclear!

"No!" Hunter barked. "We can't out-campaign O'Dell, even with what some might call 'dirty' politics. We don't have time to convince five or ten thousand idiots not to vote for her, and they'd just see right through anything we try. So, if we can't beat her, we have to remove her, uh, convince her to get out of the race."

Hunter's solution was simple but elegant, and it took the committee members a few seconds to catch up.

"How are we supposed to do that? O'Dell isn't going to quit just because we ask her real nice," one of the committee members asked, causing a brief chuckle in the room

"Then we don't ask *real* nice," Hunter responded. "Yeah, I think we should have a serious face-to-face talk with her in private. We need to ... uh ... un-gently persuade her to give up. Leave her no choice."

The room went silent as Hunter's purposefully vague suggestion sunk in. As it did, some faces in the room turned stony and determined, while others looked more than a little concerned.

"You're not seriously considering hurting anyone, are you?" a sorority president asked.

"Of course not. But she needs a reason to pull out of the race, and we can certainly give her one," Hunter replied, his tone intentionally less threatening than it had been a moment before.

"Who do you think is going to make this, uh, suggestion to her?" the same sorority president asked. "If anyone gets even a hint The Tyros is involved..."

"Don't worry about it," Hunter replied. "This committee's only job is to be sure all our other candidates have the support they need to win when the time comes. I'll take care of my own competition."

Bubba and Michael parked at a strip mall across the street as soon as they saw Hunter's car pull into the Sunshine. They wanted to get closer but couldn't take the chance of being seen.

"Now, just what do you think he's doing out here?" Bubba asked. "I saw him with some girl at the house earlier, so I doubt he's here to get laid or something."

"I have no idea," Michael replied. "Let's hang out for a while and see if anything happens. I've got nothing better to do."

"Sure, but I thought you were meeting Sarah tonight," Bubba said, referring to Michael's long-time girlfriend.

"She had to cancel. Some kind of meeting about the student government elections. You know how she is with all that stuff."

"Yeah, she's like the dynamo powering her sorority's candidate. That little girl has more energy than any three other people I know," Bubba agreed.

Michael smiled because it was true. When Sarah committed to something, she held nothing back. "Tell me about it. But sometimes, I don't get it. The Tyros always wins the elections. All the frats and sororities know who to vote for already. But don't tell her I said that."

"Well, she loves it, and that's cool. Me? I don't give a rat's ass about politics, and the whole Tyros 'secret society' thing seems kinda juvenile," Bubba said.

"I guess it's all pretty harmless," Michael observed, crossing his arms and settling down in his seat to keep watch.

Almost an hour later, Michael and Bubba couldn't decide what to do, finding themselves profoundly bored but still intensely curious. If Hunter stayed at the motel all night, they would feel stupid for sitting in a parking lot for hours. But they couldn't find a logical reason for Hunter's abrupt exit from the frat house and rushed drive to the edge of town.

Bubba was about to complain about being hungry again when Michael sat up in his seat and pointed out the front window. A pair of headlights swung around the hotel and into its front parking lot. Hunter's black BMW sedan paused briefly before turning back toward campus.

"Should we keep following him?" Michael asked.

"I don't think so. I bet whatever he needed to do just happened. Let's wait here just another second or two before going home," Bubba suggested.

As they watched, almost a dozen more expensive vehicles emerged from the back of the motel and turned toward the university. Michael and Bubba found themselves even more puzzled at the night's events when they recognized several of the drivers to be fraternity presidents.

"Uh, what the hell was that about?" Michael asked. "There must have been eight or ten frat guys over there."

"And a few sorority bigshots," Bubba added. "What were all those Greek officers doing at a secret meeting in the back of an old motel?"

"No idea," Michael answered, clearly bewildered. "But I just bet it wasn't anything good."

Across the same parking lot from where Michael and Bubba sat speculating about the gathering of Greek presidents, J.P. Hoffman's overly-clever advisor, Skeeter, sat comfortably ensconced in Mitch's pickup truck with Mitch's cousin, Dog. Unlike the amateurs they had followed from the fraternity house, Skeeter and Dog had been trained in covert surveillance. Michael and Bubba had no idea they were being watched.

"What are they doing now?" Dog asked in his simplistic way.

"They are getting caught doing something they shouldn't," Skeeter replied.

"You want me to go snatch those two? I bet J.P. would like a chance to ask them personally why they're following that dumbass Hunter around," Dog suggested.

"No. That would be rash," Skeeter said. "But J.P. needs to know."

THIRTY-THREE

The following Thursday night, Hunter met J.P. in the Camellia Gardens Apartments parking lot, one of the many small off-campus complexes rented exclusively to students. Like many in the area, this building had two stories, with all of the units facing the street. It was eleven-thirty, and the lot was dark and quiet. Nobody would look twice at two guys casually leaning on a truck.

"It took a big set of balls to get me involved in this thing," J.P. said, lighting a cigarette. "We have a common problem because of that cop in the parking lot. Otherwise, I'd have told you to go to hell."

J.P. kept the fact his men had been keeping a close eye on him, Michael, Bubba, and Zach since the night of the fire to himself.

"Yeah, I get it. But this is important, and I needed the best," Hunter replied, knowing he was taking a chance by asking J.P. for help.

"Bullshit!" J.P. hissed. "You're too chickenshit to do it yourself, and you think you have some leverage. Let me give you a piece of advice. Don't play that card again. You're the only other witness, and I don't like witnesses. Get it?

"I got it," Hunter said, fully understanding J.P.'s meaning.

J.P. snuffed out the cigarette under his boot and laid out the plan.

"She lives alone and hasn't been out since she got back from some kind of meeting at about nine o'clock. Her place is on the bottom floor of the building one street over," J.P. reported. "I got two of my guys and one of their girls with me. We can use the girl to get our subject to open the door. Once we get in, it's easy."

Hunter was on edge. This had to both go well and be effective. He'd taken a big risk involving J.P.

"Okay, do it fast. But be sure she gets the message."

J.P. smiled. "Oh yeah, dude. We'll deliver the message. I'll call you when it's done, and we're out of town."

J.P. turned and walked south, quickly disappearing around the side of the building. Hunter waited a moment and absently checked his phone, mostly for show, before moving away in the opposite direction. But he didn't leave the area. He had too much riding on this operation and needed to see what happened next, so he turned left at the next block. At the corner, he found a spot where he could get a view of the entire front side of O'Dell's complex without being seen.

Exhausted from a long day of classes and campaign meetings, Mary O'Dell had trouble concentrating on her Spanish 410 assignment. *Maybe it's time for a break.*

Mary lived in a one-bedroom apartment furnished with items her family would have otherwise donated to charity. Faded yellow paint covered the cinder block walls, and the only door opened directly into the main room. Right next to the door, a clattery air conditioner pierced the outside wall under the room's single window. Though spartan, the college senior had decided against a roommate for her last year in college and found she enjoyed the privacy of living alone.

At that moment, Mary was in her favorite spot, curled up on the end of a massive faux leather tan couch. Her parents claimed the couch came directly out of her grandfather's office when he was president of a small bank in Mary's hometown. It was definitely from the sixties, maybe even the fifties; its thick fake leather would probably never wear out.

Mary was stretching her arms over her head and yawning luxuriously when a soft knock at the door startled her. She looked at the clock - 11:35. Puzzled but not concerned because college students often kept late hours, she got up, walked over, and looked through the door's peephole. A short blond girl in a t-shirt and jeans stood there looking a bit anxious.

"Hi! I'm Gina," the girl said, smiling when the door opened. "I live upstairs, and I'm real sorry to bother you, but, uh, I knew a girl lived here, and I, well, was wondering if you might have a pad or something I could borrow?"

Mary had a soft heart, and she understood Gina's predicament.

"Hey! Nice to meet you. I'm Mary. And, yeah, sure. Come on in and I'll grab some."

Mary found a pad and a few tampons in her bathroom and went back to the door. The girl wasn't there!

Surprised at Gina's disappearance, Mary looked outside. Without warning, Mitch and Dog pushed her back into the apartment. J.P. followed behind, quietly closing and re-locking the door. All three men wore identical black sweatshirts, jeans, and full-face black ski masks.

Dog grabbed and held Mary from behind while Mitch covered her mouth and bound her hands and ankles with black duct tape. Neither spoke a word. The three intruders moved so quickly Mary had no time to react. When she finally grasped what was happening, it was too late to scream.

Without J.P. having to give an order, Mitch and Dog lifted Mary roughly off her feet, and half dragged, half carried her into the bedroom and threw her face-up onto the bed.

Mary's wide and unblinking eyes stared up at her attackers. Her chest heaved, and panic robbed her of rational thought.

J.P. stepped over to the bed. "Mary," he said calmly, grabbing her face between his hands and placing his face close to hers. "Mary, look at me. We are not going to hurt you. I need you to listen."

Uncontrollably terrified, Mary tried to shake her head from side to side and began kicking her legs. Dog jumped onto the bed, straddled her legs, and held her down by her hips. Mary thrashed as if fighting for her life.

J.P. slapped her.

"Mary. Look at me," he said again. "Stop."

He raised his hand for a second strike.

Mary finally looked J.P. in the eye.

"We're not going to hurt you," J.P. said. "But listen. Are you listening?"

Mary blinked a few times, then nodded slowly.

"You have to get out of the election. Do you understand me? Withdraw from the election for president. Get it? Get it?"

Mary's brow furled. *What was he trying to say?*

"Get out of the election, or we'll be back. And next time I won't be this nice. Do you understand? You will get hurt, and your family will get hurt. Your dad Warren, mom Judy, and little sister, what's her name? Oh yeah, Kim. Understand now?" J.P.'s tone had turned deadly serious.

At the mention of her family, Mary's mind engaged fully. She understood.

"Do it tomorrow and come up with a good excuse. If you tell anyone what happened here, well, I don't want to come back here or take a trip to that little town of yours to ask your family why you were so stubborn. Got it?"

Mary nodded again. Suddenly, she began struggling again, and a stifled scream escaped through her taped mouth.

J.P. looked back and saw Dog yanking at Mary's shorts. Incensed, he backhanded Dog across the face.

"What the hell?" Dog cried.

"Get out of here," J.P. ordered.

"Yeah, okay," Dog muttered, disappointed. But he obeyed J.P.'s order and climbed off Mary's legs. "I'll be right outside in case you change your mind."

J.P. looked back at Mary, still holding her face in one hand. "We're leaving. Do what you're told, and this will be the last time you see us. Take my advice. You don't want to see me again, ever. Do you agree? Nod."

Mary did.

With that, J.P. stood and left the bedroom, finding Mitch watching out the front window.

"We're good to go," Mitch reported.

After they removed their masks and sweatshirts and stashed them in a backpack, J.P. turned and smashed his fist into Dog's face.

"I said no extras tonight."

Mary withdrew from the race the next day.

THIRTY-FOUR

"What's the difference?" Michael asked Zach on the Monday afternoon after Mary O'Dell dropped out of the SGA election. The two buddies sat out on the front porch of the frat house, enjoying the warm afternoon sun, having completed their last classes for the day.

"Are you serious? We're unopposed for president! That's the difference. The Tyros is a lock now for the top spot."

Zach was incredulous. He couldn't believe his best friend could be uninterested, even apathetic, about the elections.

"That's great. But The Tyros was going to win anyway. It always wins, doesn't it? So, yeah, what's the big deal?" Michael repeated.

"The Tyros doesn't always win, dumbass. Most of the time, sure. But in the past few years, more and more non-Tyros people have been working their way in, and O'Dell had a real shot at becoming president. If she had gone on to win, well, I can't even guess what would happen. You like our seats at the games, don't you? And being left alone by the university P.D.? That's the difference," Zach pronounced.

"Plus, Zach gets a seat at the table with the big boys, right buddy?" Michael slapped Zach playfully on the back. "Hey man, I play by the rules. Straight Tyros voting for me, that's for sure.

And, I suppose I'll even vote for you since I have to and all," Michael kidded.

"Gee, thanks a lot! I've only known you since the sixth grade," Zach laughed.

"Well, how about buying my vote with a beer?" Michael suggested. "I'm still sittin' on the fence."

"Buy your own. Stephanie's coming over, and you know how that girl likes a cold beer," Zach answered.

Zach certainly had a way with the opposite sex. He exuded confidence, never doubting that he deserved the best-looking girls. But that was just Zach, certain everyone he met liked him.

Michael lacked that level of confidence and had always been just a little jealous of Zach's prowess, luck, charisma, or whatever it was. Michael had been dating the same girl now for three years.

"Don't give me that crap!" Zach said. "Sarah's a great girl, and you know it. Better than you deserve, that's perfectly obvious."

"So, what are you and Stephanie going to do?" Michael asked.

"My master plan is to hang out here, share a few cold beers, see what happens around the house, and then let nature take its course."

"No campaigning tonight? I thought you were going to talk to some club or something. You blowing that off?"

"Nope. Canceled. When O'Dell dropped out of the race, I guess several other independents lost their will to fight, including the guy running for my place. Michael, as I said before, life is good. I don't even need your vote. You're looking at the next Place Six senator."

Michael suddenly realized that Zach's unexpected luck, along with that of Hunter and other Tyros candidates, had materialized only days after the strange meeting he and Bubba had observed. Mary O'Dell reportedly said she had to withdraw from the race to care for some aging relatives. Yet, rumors flew around campus that The Tyros forced her out. Michael had laughed off even the suggestion that The Tyros could be involved - until now. What if the fraternity and sorority presidents at that meeting decided to pressure the independent candidate out of the race? He now found the idea implausible but not impossible. Some people took The Tyros and student elections way too seriously. He had never considered The Tyros to be anything other than a simple agreement by Greeks to vote for other Greeks, but he now began to question that belief.

Michael didn't respond to Zach, stunned by the realization that The Tyros might be more than a harmless college political organization. He simply couldn't dismiss O'Dell's withdrawal so soon after the clandestine meeting as just a coincidence.

When his thoughts turned to Hunter meeting with skinheads and ordering a kidnapping, Hunter Ewell suddenly seemed a lot more dangerous.

"Man, The Tyros rules!" Zach said as he got up to get ready for his date, not noticing the scowl that had crossed his best friend's face.

Just a week later, Zach's prediction came true. The Tyros swept the elections in a landslide. While it had engineered big wins in the past, the scope of this election victory was unprecedented. Every Tyros candidate won. A few independents were elected, but only because The Tyros decided not to run a candidate for a few relatively unimportant positions.

While independent students outnumbered the Greek population three to one, only a fraction bothered to vote in SGA elections. The Tyros' electoral power came from the allegiance and dutifulness of its members - who were required to vote.

A united and obedient minority easily overcomes a fractured and apathetic majority.

THIRTY-FIVE

Michael kept his theory about a link between The Tyros, Mary O'Dell's sudden departure, and Hunter's meeting with the skinheads to himself until after the elections and things on campus returned to normal. He didn't want his thoughts about The Tyros to spoil Zach's big win. But suspicions haunted him day and night, and he needed to do something. Finally, Michael reached out to the one person he trusted more than any other.

A week after the election, Michael invited Sarah to their favorite coffee house. After placing their usual orders, they settled into an oversized red couch near the back of the store.

"Ah, this is just what I needed. Thanks for calling!" Sarah said after taking a long sip of the hot drink. "What happened to the warm weather?"

After the unusually bright warmth of the day before, the unpredictable Southern fall played its usual trick, turning the weather suddenly cool and damp.

"I don't know. But I sure liked it better than this crap," Michael said, vaguely waving his cup at the outdoors.

"Me too. But at least I have you to keep me warm," Sarah said, smiling as she pulled her feet up under her and snuggling up under Michael's arm.

"Any time!" Michael said, enjoying Sarah's closeness. He would gladly have just stayed sitting there forever, but he needed to talk to her about his growing skepticism about Hunter and The Tyros.

"Hey, as comfortable as I am, can I ask you about something?" he asked reluctantly.

"Does that mean I have to move?" Sarah said with a pout.

"I'm afraid so. But you can come back in a few minutes."

"Okay, but I'm not done with you yet. So, make it quick," Sarah said as she turned around so she could see him. "What's up?"

"Well, here's the thing. I'm trying to find out some stuff about The Tyros, and I thought maybe you might know more than me," Michael said, sounding uncomfortable.

Sarah had two sides. One was fun, flirty, and adventurous, but the other was all business. Her serious side appeared as soon as Michael asked about The Tyros.

"Sure, I guess. Are you having a problem with the frat or something?" Sarah asked.

"No. Nothing like that. I've been thinking, and I guess I'm curious about what it really is. Uh, it's hard to explain. Like, is The Tyros a real organization of some kind or just a thing we use to pull together votes? I always thought it was just a cool name someone came up with and a deal between the Greeks to vote together. Now I think it may be a real secret society that actually meets and decides everything ahead of time."

"Like a cult or something? You've been watching too much television," Sarah replied.

"No, I'm serious. I know the question is weird, but humor me a second," Michael said.

Sarah could tell when her boyfriend worried about something. "Okay, well, that's a good question, but why do you care? It's not like you want to run for office or anything. And I don't buy that you're just curious. You're all tense for some reason. What's really going on?" Sarah wanted to know.

"I'm just looking out for Zach. He's really into all this election stuff, and I'm afraid he's getting a little brainwashed by the whole thing," Michael tried to explain.

"Brainwashed!" Sarah laughed. "Really? Zach's more likely to do the brainwashing than the other way around. He's living his dream of being elected to the SGA senate as a sophomore. So, I'm calling bullcrap on that, Michael King! Try again, and this time find a better story!"

Michael's already unbelievably poor ability to mislead people became non-existent with Sarah. After thinking for a few seconds, he realized he had to fill Sarah in on what he had been doing, at least partially anyway. He also figured the FBI would be more than a little pissed if they knew he was telling Sarah anything at all.

"Okay, listen. What I'm going to tell you will sound stupid and unbelievable. And, I'm not supposed to talk about it. But I could really use your help," Michael said, earnestly.

Sarah's eyes opened a little wider as genuine concern crossed her face. "Maybe you better tell me about whatever it is that will be stupid and unbelievable. You know you can trust me. Always," Sarah said, touching Michael's face.

Michael took her hand in his and began quietly explaining how Hunter had taken Zach to the meeting with the skinheads and the other strange events of the evening culminating with their witnessing a hotel fire. He left out the fact that he was essentially an FBI undercover agent and about the search for Rick Donnelly. When he finished, he waited for Sarah's inevitable response.

"Just what the hell did you think you were doing going out chasing skinheads in the middle of the night? Have you lost your mind?" Sarah said, angrily hitting Michael's shoulder with her fist.

"Ow! Yeah, I know. But can we set my stupidity aside for just a second?"

Still fuming, Sarah said, "I guess so, but I'm still mad at you about it."

After pondering over Michael's story, she asked, "So what does all that have to do with The Tyros? Do you think it's involved with the skinhead guy somehow?"

"Dang girl, you sure connected the dots fast. But, yeah, I think there could be some connection between The Tyros and the skinheads. I don't know. I told you it would sound unbelievable. But that's the thing. If it's true, then Zach is in way over his head," Michael explained.

"Yeah, I see what you mean. But just because Hunter knows this skinhead and he's a member of The Tyros doesn't necessarily connect Tyros to the skinhead," Sarah correctly observed.

"Maybe. But I don't want to take that chance," Michael said, leaving out for the moment what he and Bubba had seen outside the Sunshine Motel after following Hunter a few days earlier.

Sarah looked around the coffee shop carefully to see if anyone could hear what she was about to say. Only two other customers sat at tables – both near the front windows and both engrossed with laptops.

Satisfied they were alone, Sarah said quietly, "This probably means nothing, but one of our candidates got drunk after winning the election and ended up in my room. I arranged all her meetings, campaign events, signs, tee shirts, and stuff. I guess I was her campaign manager. Anyway, she started thanking me over and over. Then, at one point, she said, 'Aren't you glad Hunter got rid of that crazy Catholic girl?'. She was pretty plowed. And, until you asked whether The Tyros had some formal organization, I forgot all about it. Hunter is the president of your frat, but I have a hard time believing he would 'get rid' of a candidate or how he could even do such a thing. Crap, you've got me thinking in circles!"

"Wow. That fits," Michael said, thinking out loud.

"Fits what?" Sarah asked.

"I'm probably going to get hit in the shoulder again, but Bubba and I followed Hunter out to that old motel, The Sunshine or whatever, yesterday and... ow! Hey! Nothing happened!" Michael exclaimed, rubbing his shoulder where Sarah's punch landed for the second time.

"I don't care," Sarah said indignantly. "You deserved it."

"Geez, okay, okay, I get it! Anyway, Hunter and a bunch of other fraternity and sorority presidents met out there for some reason. A couple of days later, O'Dell suddenly pulled out of the election and left school. I wish we had a way to figure out what's really going on."

"I'm a little freaked out right now," Sarah said slowly. "But I might know a way we can learn more if we want to. But I'm not sure I actually want to."

Michael heard the conflict in his girlfriend's voice. "Well, let's just say you did for a second. What's your idea?"

"Paige Wilson. She's president of my sorority and Hunter's girlfriend. She's full of herself and has a big mouth. She constantly brags about how Hunter is the big man on campus and makes all the decisions. If anyone knows something about all that, it's her. I'm not sure how to get anything out of her, but I'll think of something."

"So, you think you can find out from Paige Wilson the real story? I'm not asking you to get involved...." Michael began.

Sarah cut him off. "Look, this all still sounds like a series of coincidences to me. It's my bet The Tyros isn't some major conspiracy or secret society and had nothing to do with Mary O'Dell dropping out of the race. I think it's just a way to get our candidates elected. No big deal. But I want to be sure for me and you and Zach. Let me think about it some more."

"I don't want you getting in trouble or anything," Michael told Sarah as he reached out to pull her back close to him. It wasn't lost on him that Agent Deal gave him those exact instructions.

"Don't worry. I won't." Sarah snuggled back into Michael's side and enjoyed the warmth and safety of his presence.

"I mean it."

"I know."

A few days later, Sarah had an idea.

THIRTY-SIX

Bubba sat hunched over his personal workbench in the basement laboratory of the engineering building. Other students had come and gone during the evening, but now Bubba sat alone under a bright work light in an otherwise dark room. With a set of magnifying goggles perched on his nose, and exotic electronics piled at his elbows, anyone would be forgiven for mistaking him for a mad scientist. The fact that from time to time he chuckled at his own genius, or cursed a tiny error, only added to the effect. Bubba was happily soldering together the last bits of minute electronic circuitry when the overhead lights for the entire lab unexpectedly flickered to life.

"Dammit!" Bubba cried, bumping his head into the light-emitting diode lamp hanging over his head.

"Sorry, dude," Michael said, stifling a laugh. "Didn't mean to scare you."

"Yeah, you did," Sarah said, walking into the lab behind her boyfriend.

"I always knew I liked her better than you," Bubba replied, rubbing his unkempt mass of reddish-brown hair. "But you got lucky, I finished just the second y'all walked in."

"You did it? You actually made the thing?" Michael asked excitedly.

"Yes, and you're welcome. Child's play really," Bubba said, holding up a black plastic tube eight inches long and two inches in diameter.

"How does it work?" Sarah asked. "You said it could hear people talking through windows or something?"

Bubba proudly lifted the finished device. "Yep. When you told us about the officer's meeting at your sorority in Paige Wilson's president's suite, I had an idea. You said that Paige always held officers' meetings in private, right?"

"Yes. They decide a lot of things, but this month's meeting is one of the most important ones of the year. After this Tuesday's meeting, she'll reveal the slate of new candidates for next year's sorority officers," Sarah agreed. "After talking to Michael, I realized that the whole election at our sorority is rigged. She won't announce candidates, she'll basically just tell us who is going to be 'elected'. It makes me mad."

"It's like that at the frat too," Michael responded.

"Yeah, and I bet corruption like that infects the entire Greek community," Bubba agreed.

"I think we should find out for sure. I don't want you guys following Hunter Ewell around anymore, so I asked Bubba if there was some way we could hear whatever goes on in Paige's meeting without anyone knowing," Sarah explained.

"And you came to the right guy, if I do say so myself," Bubba said with false modesty. "You just shoot this here laser at a window. The vibrations on the window pane from people's voices deflects the returning laser, which is read by this little device, a photodiode. From there it sends a signal to a standard digital recorder. Presto! You have a recording from the room without ever stepping inside!"

"That's just too awesome!" Michael exclaimed. "Can we try it out? I mean, is it ready to go?"

"Sure, we'll have to do it outside and find a target. But that shouldn't be a problem. It needs to be calibrated anyway," Bubba agreed, gathering the device and a few small tools. "Sarah, I have to say you're pretty brave for agreeing to let us listen in on your sorority sisters."

"Honestly, I still bet this is a waste of time, but I need to know one way or another," Sarah said. "And let's call it what it is. I'm spying on them."

"After considering Michael's theory about The Tyros, I think we're justified in simply seeking out more information. A well-considered hypothesis deserves to be explored through experimentation," Bubba pronounced, putting a hand on Sarah's shoulder.

"Oh, man," Michael responded, used to Bubba's ability to naturally transform from country-boy to scientist and back. "Don't try and impress my girl with your science genius."

"It's working, ain't it?" Bubba joked. "Anyway, where's Zach? He'd get a kick out of this too."

"Well, I haven't exactly told him about what I think about The Tyros yet. Maybe I should have already, but he's been so happy doing the senator thing I didn't want to spoil his party," Michael explained.

"He's actually been working with Hunter on SGA stuff a lot too. We were afraid if he knew about Michael's hunch, he might, I don't know, act weird around him?" Sarah added.

Bubba scratched his chin. "Hmmm. That's good thinking, but we have to tell him pretty soon."

"Yeah, we will. For now, let's see if your toy actually works," Michael said, heading for the door.

"It's not a toy," Bubba protested, following Michael and Sarah outside. "Wal-Mart don't carry none of these, you know."

Standing on a courtyard surrounded by three buildings, the trio searched for a window to test the laser-microphone. But it was late, and they could locate only one widow that showed a light inside.

"Let's be careful," Michael warned. "I'm not sure the campus cops would understand what we are doing out here."

"I'll keep an eye out," Sarah volunteered, as Bubba quickly attached a digital recorder to the laser microphone's output jack.

After inserting batteries, Bubba said, "Okay, I'll shoot the window and see if anyone's awake inside." Taking aim, Bubba pushed a button on the side of the plastic tube. Nothing seemed to happen.

"I don't see a laser beam," Sarah said, peering into the darkness.

"Yeah, I know, but it wouldn't be much of a spy thing if it shot a bright red line across the sky," Bubba responded. "I can see where the laser is hitting. If someone is talking inside, we should hear it."

All three listened intently for any sound coming through the recorder's small output speaker but heard nothing at all.

"Either it's not working, or nobody is home," Sarah said.

Bubba fiddled with the laser for a moment before trying again.

"Wait!" Michael said in a whisper a moment later. "I think I hear something."

Sure enough, they all could hear faint Latin music. While distorted, the sounds were being picked up from a window at least fifty yards away. Then, someone began singing in Spanish.

Astonished, Michael and Sarah looked up at the third-floor window to see someone emptying a trash can and dancing to the same music they heard coming from Bubba's device.

"Es muy bueno, si'?" Bubba said, his hips swaying back and forth to the music.

"Si'" Michael responded, profoundly impressed with his extroverted genius friend.

Sarah hugged Bubba's neck and pecked him on the cheek, making the big guy blush.

Thrilled with their new spy equipment, none of them noticed a white pickup truck parked across the street. Inside, Mitch and Gina peered through binoculars at the three college students.

"What are they doing, babe?" Gina asked. "They keep pointing that thing around and listening to a voice recorder or something. I don't get it."

"I'll be damned. I think that's some kind of listening device, maybe even a laser-mic. J.P.'s gonna want to know about this!" Mitch said, excitedly dialing J.P.'s number.

After listening to Mitch's description of the listening device, J.P. made a rare call to the number provided by the Directors. When the line picked up, J.P. said: "Hoffman 4883 in Banebridge. Subjects King and Adcock have a laser microphone and intend to use it. We will continue surveillance. Requesting instructions from the Directors in case they proceed with some sort of covert action."

"Hold one," the voice on the other end of the line said.

A minute later, J.P. had his answer. If Michael and Bubba tried to use the microphone, J.P. was to interrogate the subjects, determine their motivation and extract what they knew.

If necessary, elimination was authorized.

THIRTY-SEVEN

Weeks had passed since his team learned Rick Donnelly had been in Banebridge and left the highly classified documents with lawyer Drew Campbell. Now, except for that connection and somewhat sketchy information that a group of skinheads had been ordered to kidnap the missing scientist, Deal's team had nothing. The NSA detected no online chatter about a new weapon on the market, and CIA assets reported no new inquiries from foreigners about stolen U.S. technology. Deal desperately needed another lead. If they just knew why two highly respected and brilliant scientists committed treason, they could deduce their next move and be ready when they made it.

Early in his investigation, Deal had charged Agent Stella Sims with compiling deep background profiles on Rick Donnelly and Dave Knox. Sims approached this daunting task methodically. The life of any human being is a complex web of associations, decisions, and consequences. From those webs, as spun by Donnelly and Knox, Sims hoped to find a common thread – the particular intersection of common interest that compelled both men toward the same goal and reveal their elusive motive.

Using the full resources of the FBI, Sims sent agents into the field to track down and interview anyone with a connection to either scientist. Other agents gathered and analyzed documents ranging from high school grades to published scientific papers. She considered the scope of her inquiry unlimited. No matter how small, any fact could turn out to be the one clue she needed.

On the surface, the two scientists didn't appear to have known of each other's existence, except through reading each other's academic papers, until they both took jobs at Area 51. Even then, sources from the facility related that while the two men knew each other, they never worked closely and appeared to be little more than acquaintances. But this didn't surprise the FBI agent. If they had been working together clandestinely to steal the gravity wave technology, they would have maintained a certain distance from each other - rather basic spy tradecraft.

Sims strongly believed the Rick and Dave shared some other connection, not to each other, but to some third person, country, or cause. *But what? Who?*

Sims dug in again, considering and reconsidering possibilities. Rick came from a broken family in rural South Carolina and was raised by his paternal grandmother. Dave was born in a small town outside Savannah, Georgia to two devoted parents - both school teachers. Neither man grew up wealthy. Each scientist displayed remarkable intelligence at an early age, graduated from high school well before they should have, and won scholarships to prestigious universities.

Rick attended the University of North Carolina and majored in physics and aerospace engineering. Dave received a double major in physics and chemical engineering from Georgia Tech. After receiving doctorate degrees, both men entered the private sector and vaulted to the top of their respective fields.

After joining different but highly respected aerospace companies, their lives seemed to be an open book. Basic searches of public documents garnered multiple academic papers and patents. Over the years, their work advanced the state of the art in aircraft design, jet engine efficiency, and spacecraft performance. While Rick and Dave weren't famous in the popular sense of the word, they were widely known and respected in the aerospace industry, not only in the U.S. but around the world.

Sims decided to focus on their time in college and explore their lives before becoming top-flight scientists. What shaped the young men? What influence could have re-directed the course of their lives so drastically?

Sims deployed agents into the field to interview as many of Rick and Dave's college friends, associates, and professors as possible. Reports from the investigators painted similar but distinct pictures.

Rick reluctantly joined one of UNC's fraternities during his sophomore year only after being heavily recruited. His fraternity brothers remembered him as a bookworm, not overly sociable, but nonetheless popular because he brought the fraternity's overall grade point average up considerably. Around the frat house, the brothers referred to him as 'the Professor.' Rick's instructors remembered him as driven, quiet, but most of all - brilliant.

Dave immediately joined a fraternity at Georgia Tech as a freshman. His outgoing personality, loyalty, and willingness to help get his fraternity brothers elected to student government organizations led to his eventual election as president of the fraternity. Dave never lacked female companionship but never formed an attachment to any one girl, preferring to play the field. As a student, he mastered the sciences of physics and engineering with little effort. His professors and advisors all relayed that Dave seemed to intuitively comprehend advanced mathematics and chemical formulas rather than learning them through hard work and determined study habits.

While none of this information surprised Sims, she had at least found a common thread between the men. Each had been a member of a prestigious fraternity. This alone wouldn't have meant much to her, except for the odd reports generated from the interviews conducted by her field agents.

On several occasions, fraternity brothers of each man had seemed reluctant to talk about the fraternities and their members.

One ex-president of Rick's fraternity became overtly hostile, even after the agent explained the interview was nothing more than a routine background investigation. Sims never understood college fraternities to be anything more than social clubs of sorts. Sure, they all had 'secret' handshakes and such, but she had never believed any of it was taken too seriously. She now realized she would have to reconsider that belief.

But some of the interviews proved unusual in another way.

A few ex-fraternity members remembered both Rick and Dave receiving special treatment and expressed some resentment toward them. Several interviewees reported that after being in the fraternity for only a short time, neither were required to pay dues. On top of that, two distinctly recalled Dave suddenly driving a new expensive convertible - a far cry from the decrepit old Nissan he brought to campus as a freshman. Another report indicated that Rick always seemed to have large amounts of excess cash. The agents conducting these interviews noted that each person giving such a statement denied any knowledge about how or why Rick and Dave gained such advantages.

Sims poured through the interview transcripts and field agents' notes again and again. Both men, at different universities, in separate states, received very special treatment from an on-campus fraternities. She didn't have an answer, but she could sense progress.

THIRTY-EIGHT

With Rick's arrival, the monstrous underground lab beneath the Texas desert came to life. While technicians in white lab coats quietly calibrated a vast array of aerospace, navigation, communication, and armament hardware, highly skilled machinists, mechanics, and welders filled the space with the sounds of sputtering torches, hissing lathes, and the pops of rivet guns.

After seeing the progress Dave made on the gravity wave aircraft and propulsion system and the staggering facilities, Rick all but forgot his fear that the Directors might have targeted him for elimination. Now engrossed in his work, Rick had to admit he was as happy as he had ever been.

In the weeks since his arrival, he and Dave had perfected the process for manufacturing Element 128 that Rick had discovered and then stolen from Area 51. It had been a time-consuming challenge. But by working in collaboration, the two scientists had finally presented Governor Margie Franks with a real-world, portable prototype device capable of creating enough Element 128 to sustain a squadron of gravity wave aircraft.

After Margie reported their success to the other Directors, Rick and Dave found their funding unlimited, allowing them to make further improvements to the incredible weapon.

Two months after teaming up, Rick and Dave laid on their backs under the nearly- completed airframe of the gravity wave aircraft. Perched on a scaffold six feet off the ground, the two brilliant scientists struggled to install one of the plane's gravity wave generators.

While the unusual shape of the triangular craft had taken form, it was still unfinished. An entire cockpit needed to be installed in the gaping orifice on the top of the fuselage. Underneath, empty weapons bays hung wide open with numerous colorful wiring harnesses spilling out like odd jungle vines. But even in its unfinished state, the craft was both elegant and fearsome to behold.

"Damnit!" Dave shouted suddenly.

"What's the matter?" Rick said, not able to look around due to his cramped position. "You hurt yourself again?"

"Yeah, some clown didn't grind the edge off of this titanium alloy bracket, and it cut my hand!" Dave hissed through clenched teeth.

"I keep telling you to wear gloves and to be more careful. This entire aircraft is one hundred percent handmade, and that means there may, in fact, be a few rough edges. Just as you have encountered."

"I'm an engineer and not a damn grease-monkey mechanic," Dave responded. "Since you're so interested, it's not a bad cut, thank you very much. Geez, let's see if we can get this thing mounted once and for all."

Dave had a point. Neither he nor Rick usually turned the wrenches. But by taking the installation of the reactor into their own hands, they could develop a detailed procedure that would speed the manufacturing of future aircraft.

"Okay, Cinderella let's see if this glass slipper will fit now," Rick said, chuckling.

Three critical components comprised the gravity wave propulsion system. The gravity wave reactor created the immense power necessary to fuel the gravity wave generators. The twin generators created densely-packed gravity waves and fed them into the round reflectors on each wing. Each component took decades of research to perfect and only one other example of each existed anywhere in the world - Area 51.

Rick and Dave had completed the final installation of the reactor a week prior with little trouble. But the generators, although built to exacting specifications, needed several modifications before mounting in the airframe. Once they were successfully installed, they could begin work fitting the reflectors.

The afternoon spent on their backs didn't go to waste. The pair managed to properly install the generators with few further setbacks, carefully documenting the installation procedure for future use. After noting problems and writing the final guidelines, they decided to call it a day. But unlike the other craftsmen and mechanics assembling the aircraft, Rick and Dave couldn't chance being seen in public. The FBI and almost every other intelligence and law enforcement agency in the country had mounted an exhaustive search for the missing scientists. So, for the time being, they had to be satisfied with remaining in their snug but comfortable quarters tucked inside the laboratory.

Dave ambled toward his living area, quite pleased with their progress. He stretched his arms over his head, trying to work out the kinks in his back from lying on a rigid platform for almost eight hours. He looked forward to a shower and a couple of cold beers, but he also wanted to talk to Rick about the projected timeline for installing the reflectors. Like many scientists absorbed in their work, Rick and Dave thought about little else and were perfectly content sequestered away with their project.

Dave's phone rang just as he reached his small suite of rooms. Pulling the device from his pocket, he didn't need to check who was calling. He knew already.

"Hello, Margie!" Dave said without hesitation. "How's my favorite Governor this fine evening?"

"How'd you know it was me? These phones are supposed to be secure!" the Governor of Texas demanded.

"It doesn't take a genius to establish a pattern in the timing of your calls, Margie, although I certainly qualify for that esteemed status. Plus, it's not like a lot of people have this number. I just bet you are going to ask for a progress report on the Revolution 1," Dave said, using the plane's new name.

"You're damned right I am, you egg-headed prick!"

Everyone knew Margie Franks could cuss the skin off of a rattle-snake, but she and Dave had long ago developed a mutual respect. The coarse exchange was just a part of their usual banter.

"Oh my, such language!" Dave responded. "You need to broaden your repertoire of insults. I believe you've used that one before."

"Just tell me how long it's going to be before I can show off your invention to General Brady. The old hard-ass won't make any final decisions about the military phase of The Cause until he sees the technology in action with his own two eyes."

"The good general is most assuredly a hard-ass," Dave agreed. "But I think he's just your kind of hard-ass, if I'm not mistaken."

"I admit I prefer a real man," Margie shot back. "Unlike you!"

"Ouch! You wounded me with that one!" Dave laughed. "Alright, here's the latest. We will complete the airframe in less than a month. But the propulsion and weapons systems will take another 90 to 120 days. We could get into the air faster, but that would seriously jeopardize our ability to produce the next several examples with any efficiency. If we take a little longer now, it will pay us back many times over with the ability to quickly make duplicates."

The only response to Dave's report was silence, followed a few seconds later by a dull crash and a grunted "shit."

"Margie, are you alright?" Dave asked tentatively.

"Yeah," Franks answered finally. "That's longer than I told Brady it would take. I don't suppose shouting at you would speed things up. You'd just shoot back some scientific bullshit I couldn't argue with. Anyway, I'd rather have half a dozen aircraft in a year than one right now."

"What was that crash I heard?"

"I threw a glass paperweight the president of Mexico gave me. It knocked the arm off that ugly statue of Sam Houston over in the corner. Just be glad *you* weren't standing in my office a few seconds ago."

"Can't argue with that," Dave agreed, fully aware of Franks' volatile temper.

THIRTY-NINE

The beautiful Four Seasons Hotel stands at the southern end of San Jacinto street in Austin, Texas. Its Governor's Suite offers stunning views of Lady Bird Lake through its floor to ceiling windows and from the hotel's only balcony. At night, the brilliant lights of the hotel reflect clearly off the calm waters. Tonight, one more small red flicker could be seen in the reflections - if someone were to look carefully enough.

General Sean Brady stood on one of the suite's balconies, seven floors above the water, the end of his cigar glowing brightly. A cool night breeze blew the smoke away in long, velvety fingers with each exhale.

Dressed in one of the hotel's plush and unbelievably expensive bathrobes, Brady leaned against the rail on his meaty forearms, scowling across the water at nothing. Consumed by his thoughts, he didn't hear the French doors open behind him.

Governor Margie Franks stepped lightly onto the balcony wearing an identical robe and carrying two crystal tumblers of fine bourbon whiskey. Franks set the glasses gently on a small wrought iron table, took another step, and slid her hand under Brady's arm.

"What's on your mind, General?" Franks softly inquired into his ear. "Feeling guilty about cheating on your wife with a governor?"

Brady looked down at Franks. With the cigar still clenched between his teeth, he simply smiled back. *This one's as tough as nails, but a dang little wildcat in bed!* Brady thought to himself. He didn't answer Franks' question.

"Playing tough guy, huh?" Franks asked, looking out over the lake. "Tough enough to go another round?"

This made Brady laugh out loud. "Lady, the answer to that is no! Is that my drink?" he asked, looking over his shoulder. "Or do you need two after dealing with a general for the last two hours?"

"Okay, you big 'ol cowboy. Why don't we go inside and talk? Since you're done exercising for the night, we have a few things to discuss."

"Is it secure here?" Brady asked, suspiciously.

"Darlin', this here's the Governor's Suite! Plus, the Rangers swept it minutes before we got here and two of my best men are standing guard outside."

The couple made their way inside to the sumptuously decorated main seating area. Brady put out his cigar and tossed down his entire drink before taking a seat in a soft leather club chair. Franks sat at the end of the sofa and placed her drink on the table between them. The decorator of the room put comfort front and center when picking out the decor. Soft neutral upholstery combined with carved mesquite tables and ironwork lamps making the space perfect for high-level meetings and tough negotiations. Franks often chose to utilize this suite when her imposingly grand office didn't provide the correct atmosphere.

Tonight, however, Governor Franks had two reasons for choosing the suite. She needed to talk over her plan to become the first president of their new country with the Director in charge of military matters for The Cause. And, she wanted to get Brady into her bed. She had already accomplished one of those.

"You have the floor, Madam Governor. How may I be of service?" Brady said, with a flourish of his now-empty tumbler.

"Well, Sean," Margie replied, leaning forward and placing a hand on the general's knee. "Without trying to be too abrupt, I want to solicit your support."

Brady had been expecting Frank's overture for some time. He had pre-planned his response.

"I'm honored that you think you need me standing behind you. But your brilliant acquisition of the gravity wave aircraft has, I believe, given you all the clout you need to outright claim the presidency after the secession takes place," Brady said.

"Maybe. But with the leader of our military by my side, I'd be much more, uh, comfortable," Margie responded, smiling.

"I'm all yours, Margie," Brady replied, without meaning a word of what he just said.

Margie cocked her head slightly. "Just like that? It's not like you to be so, well, agreeable."

"Oh, Margie, don't take my quick response the wrong way. I have my own ambitions. I'd be lying if I said otherwise. But I have more than enough on my plate as it is. Once we break away from the United States, we'll have to work together. You know politics, I know the military. From where I sit, I think we make a good team. Let's keep it that way," Brady said.

Margie hadn't gotten to the pinnacle of Texas politics by taking anyone at their word, and she didn't fully believe Brady would be content with his position in the new country for very long. No, this man had much higher aspirations for himself.

"Well, Sean, that was a very nice speech. Now, what do you want?" Margie asked, looking Brady in the eye.

Brady gave Franks a shocked look. "I'm wounded, Margie. I think you doubt my sincerity."

Brady gave her a big grin which made Franks laugh out loud.

"Now that we have all the bullshit over with, what's your price?" Margie asked, getting up to pour them both another drink.

"Easy enough," Brady replied. "I want control of the gravity wave plane. I'll need it when the time comes and I can't be asking a committee whether I can play with their toy or not."

Margie hadn't expected Brady's response, although she chastised herself for not considering it beforehand.

"She has been named 'Revolution I'" Margie said, handing Brady back his refilled glass.

"Nice name. Appropriate, I suppose," Brady said.

"You want me to hand over exclusive control of the most lethal weapon since the atomic bomb. Have you lost your mind?"

Brady didn't take the bait. "Not at all. It's a military weapon, it should be under military control. The situation after our announcement will be fluid, to say the least. It's idiotic not to handle it my way."

"And if I just give you operational control of the craft, you will stand behind me when the Directors choose the first president?" Margie asked.

"Absolutely," Brady answered.

"Sean, let me say this as sweetly as I can. There isn't a chance in hell I'd give you the Revolution I. I found a way to get my hands on it for The Cause. I took all the risks talking the Directors into funding its development. And I own the scientists that built the damn thing. It's mine."

Brady didn't even flinch at Margie's flat denial. He knew she wouldn't consider his request and he didn't care. He had plans of his own.

FORTY

After returning to his office at Fort Benning, Brady called together his staff. Comprised of hand-picked officers, Brady had personally guided their careers since each graduated from the United States Military Academy at West Point. Brady had used his position to carefully evaluate cadets from the south. He chose one or two a year to mentor and groom for promotions and coveted commands after graduation, making sure each developed a personal loyalty to him. The best of these men and women became his staff officers.

The six men and one woman that now filed into his office had been working with the general for months, quietly creating a military operation that was meant to vault General Sean Brady to the presidency of their new country.

Brady stood with his staff in the General's lavish office studying a map of southeast Georgia.

"I have news," Brady began. "Per your recommendations, I offered Governor Franks my support in exchange for control over the gravity wave aircraft. As we knew she would, Franks refused."

"Excellent, sir," a Calvary major said. "Do you plan on making the request formal with Directors?"

Brady smiled. "That's an affirmative, Major. As soon as Franks refused, I contacted the Directors and demanded operational control of the aircraft for when the time comes. Franks threw one of her tantrums and accused me of trying to usurp civilian command and control of the military."

"When are they going to learn that bureaucrats are not equipped to effectively make military decisions?" one of Brady's staff scoffed.

"Never," Brady replied. "That is precisely why we must not hesitate to take things into our own hands. The bureaucrats and other civilian toadies should serve the needs of the military and not the other way around. But let's not get ahead of ourselves. Once The Cause has an operational gravity wave fighter, we will announce the formation of our new country. When Franks obtained the plane and its fuel source, she cemented her claim the interim presidency. I want to be in a position to take the permanent presidency when the first elections are held. What we need to do today is to review our little, uh, side operation."

"Yes, sir!" the major said, enthusiastically. "If you'll turn your attention to the map on the screen, General, we have finalized Operation Longbow. Captain Jennings, who will lead the operation on the ground, will brief you and explain any changes made since our last planning exercise."

Captain Paul Jennings, a strikingly handsome blond man of thirty-eight strode to the front of the room. Wearing his camouflage uniform and tanker-style black boots, Jennings carried the no-nonsense air of a combat veteran.

"Carry on, Captain. Everyone, take a chair," Brady said, seating himself behind his desk for the briefing.

"Thank you, sir. I will begin the timeline of my briefing at the jump-off point on the north end of the base. I will be in command of one headquarters battalion, fourteen M-1 Abrams tanks. On your orders, General, the battalion will proceed north at top speed, moving in platoon column formation until we split into two elements at the intersection of these two county roads located 6.7 miles outside the town of Ellerslie. One platoon will then take up positions on this hill overlooking the Georgia National Guard base. Their objective will be to draw out the Guard units."

Jennings circled the Guard base with his laser pointer. "The other platoon will loiter three miles to the rear."

"Excellent. And your orders of engagement?" Brady asked, already knowing the answer.

"After we draw the Guard units out with several well-placed rounds, the lead platoon will retreat back toward Benning and take up defensive positions alongside the rest of the battalion. From there on, we will only respond as necessary, sir," Jennings answered.

"What are the chances, the Guard will deploy armor?" Brady asked his staff.

"Near one-hundred percent, sir," one of two Lieutenants answered, looking at her computer pad. "The Guard is scheduled for live-fire exercises that day on a range just east of the base."

"I need this to look authentic. Once you draw them out, make it look like they attacked you on their way to Benning. I need the people to see us as the heroes who stopped a federal incursion into Southern territory," Brady said, standing.

"Yes, sir."

FORTY-ONE

The same night that governor Franks was locked in a battle of wills over who would wield control of the Revolution I, Drs. Dave Knox and Rick Donnelly stood beneath the craft in its new testing hangar near Mobile, Alabama. They had moved its location east so that the French contractors could use the original plane as a template.

Dave looked straight up at the underbelly of the craft hovering twenty feet above his head while Rick watched the expression on his face. With the smell of cordite hanging in the air, Dave slowly lowered the forty-five-caliber automatic he had just fired at the priceless hand-built aircraft.

"Now, put your gloves on and hold out your hand," Rick prompted.

Still looking up, Dave holstered the pistol and slipped on a pair of work gloves.

"Okay. One. Two. Three. Catch!" Rick called out, pushing a button on a small remote control.

Dave reached out his gloved hand and caught the bullet he had fired moments ago. He looked down at the pristine piece of lead and looked up at Rick.

"That was awesome! I mean, too cool! I shot, and the next thing I see is this bullet hanging in the air. What? Ten centimeters below the second electronics housing access door? Oh, my friend, you have outdone yourself this time!" Dave could barely contain his enthusiasm. "How did you manage that?"

The pair walked out from under the hovering aircraft as it began slowly descending back to the hangar floor, eventually coming to rest on its tricycle landing gear.

"It wasn't difficult," Rick answered without any trace of sarcasm. "I just realigned the gravity wave reflectors so that twelve point four percent of the exterior wave pattern produced fluctuating wave apogees. I was playing around with the amplitudes and found that the gravity waves could hold an object on one side within a narrow bandwidth while still smoothly propelling the craft from the other. Pretty neat, huh?"

"Pretty neat? Do you know what you've done? You just made this thing invulnerable to small arms fire! You're a genius, boy!" Dave exclaimed like a man who just found the proverbial pot of gold.

"First, the fact that we are both geniuses is a bit of an understatement, as you well know. Second, the wave modulation won't just stop little bullets like that one. A RIM 174 Standard ERAM wouldn't get any closer than your forty-five-caliber round," Rick said with the same amount of emotion he would have used telling Dave what he had for lunch.

"Wow! Holy-crap! Wow!" Dave pronounced, shaking his head at the extent of Rick's accomplishment. "Even a three-thousand-pound missile would just stop and hang there like that bullet?"

"No. In a real-world application, the system will automatically change the amplitude of the waves upon contact with an object and then just release it. It would look like the missile bounced off the craft. But in reality, it would be caught in the gravity wave for only a millisecond," Rick explained.

"The Directors are going to love this! Love it! I can't wait to tell Margie! She's going to flip a shrimp!"

"Flip a shrimp? I don't get it," Rick responded, looking at Dave quizzically.

"You'll see what I mean, man! You'll see what I mean."

"I would think she would be more impressed with how efficiently we can produce Element 128. Comparatively, finding a way to simply manipulate the gravity waves was child's play," Rick replied.

"I agree. But finding a way to bombard three elements with light atoms instead of just two was inspired. It increased the chance they would fuse into 128 and remain stable when most artificial elements decay in milliseconds. It's just not as sexy as our baby streaking across the sky," Dave agreed.

"As long as we're patting each other on the back, I think you should get more credit for taking all the bulky lab equipment I used and miniaturizing it into one self-contained and portable unit," Rick said. "By the way, where is your invention? I haven't seen it in the lab for a day or two."

"Thanks. The Directors are certainly happy with our work. Anyway, Margie has it locked away somewhere. Don't worry. We have enough 128 on hand to keep three Revolution aircraft in the air for a year nonstop," Dave explained.

Rick just shrugged. "Speaking of flying, what's on the test schedule for tonight?"

Dave pulled his phone out of his shirt pocket and consulted the work schedule. "Looks like a high-speed run over Cuba, Jamaica and over to Africa. It's a max velocity test. Shouldn't take but a couple of hours or so. I'll enter the flight data later and get a precise timeline."

"If that long," Rick observed after doing some mental calculations. "Is your plan to top the Mach 4 we achieved a couple of days ago?"

"Hell, yeah! Mach 5 should be easy. After tonight though, the speed and altitude testing will be done. Shoot, at Mach 4, we can just outrun any missile, even if it didn't just bounce off," said Dave.

"I told you that it doesn't actually bounce off; it gets caught and then released," Rick objected.

"You're a double genius, my friend. But you're a geek," Dave chided.

"I know you are, but what am I?" Rick deadpanned.

Dave just laughed. It had been a very good afternoon indeed. "Hey, how would you like to go along on the flight tonight? You can ride in the observer's seat! You've never taken a ride. What do you say?"

"I'd find that quite fascinating!"

"Alright then. Test flight at zero two hundred hours. Daniel Zafran will be in the left seat," Dave said as he headed toward his room.

"That Israeli pilot?"

"Yeah. Good guy."

FORTY-TWO

Major Daniel Zafran had found himself in Texas one month earlier. A decorated F-15 Strike Eagle pilot of the Israeli Air Force, Zafran's other occupation made him perfect for this assignment. The Mossad, Israel's intelligence agency, recruited Zafran at an early age. Gladly accepting the chance to be of service to Israel as both a pilot and a spy, Zafran's training with the air forces of other countries provided the Mossad with an invaluable stream of intelligence.

Just before his flight to the secret facility built by the Directors, Zafran met with the Deputy Director of the Mossad, Ariel Behrmann. A small man with an unkempt suit and a ring of white hair around his head, the seventy-seven-year-old sat straight in his overly large leather desk chair, a small pair of reading glasses propped on the end of his nose. Zafran stood rigidly on the other side of the desk. In stark contrast to the second most powerful man in the Mossad, Zafran sported a full head of jet-black hair and wore an impeccably pressed uniform that looked tailored to his still powerful forty-five-year-old body.

Behrmann let his visitor stand in silence while he poured over the latest intelligence on Zafran's assignment. When he finally looked up, the lines of his forehead and a downturned mouth made him appear even older than his already advanced years and betrayed the gravity of the meeting.

"I've asked you here to give you new orders and explain the background of what you are about to embark on and why," Behrmann began. "What I'm about to tell you is incendiary at best and not to be repeated. Clear?"

"Yes, sir," Zafran responded. "Clear."

"Good. Now, you have been chosen because you are one of Israel's finest pilots and have proved yourself to be an exemplary agent."

"Thank you, sir."

"Save your thanks, Major," Behrmann said, waving his hand dismissively. "The information you bring back will decide major issues related to Israel's foreign relations and security. Now you will just listen."

Behrmann sat back in his chair and folded his hands under his chin.

"In 1949, the United States of America was the first nation to recognize the State of Israel. This you know. But what is not part of history is why. You see, President Harry Truman had no real interest in our statehood. Yes, he had several Jewish friends, even did business with Jews when it wasn't popular. But Truman would rather have seen us give up half our territory to the Arabs and Palestinians. In truth, that would have been the better political move for him. But luckily for us, Truman's decision was influenced by others. Who do you think did such a thing?"

Zafran had no idea.

"Of course, you don't know. Why should you? So, I'll tell you the answer. Several congressmen and senators approached the president at just the right moment with an intriguing offer. One he couldn't pass up. In exchange for immediate recognition of Israel as a sovereign country, they promised he would win the presidential election of 1948, an election he was certainly going to lose to the Republican Thomas Dewey. At the same time, this same group of legislators came to our people and made a bargain.

They promised Israel recognition as a nation, but we, Israel, had to make a promise in return. You see, these particularly important and powerful Americans were all from the states of the American South. The states that once rebelled in their country's civil war. What did they want in return? Simple. All they asked was that when the time came, Israel would immediately recognize the new country when their states once again separated themselves from the United States of America."

Zafran had to let this sink in a moment. *A new country? The breakup of the American states? How? And what would we have to do with this?*

Behrmann watched the questions roll through Zafran's mind and was impressed by the younger man's ability to absorb such a bombshell with little more outward expression than raising his eyebrows. Then he continued.

"I see you have many questions. Good. But let me go on. These men made compelling arguments. They told us how they would convince Truman to change his mind. I was told by people at that very meeting there was never a question about whether to accept the southerners' proposal. Our people simply didn't believe that any attempt to carve a new country out of the United States would ever occur. So, we agreed. In return for nothing but a promise, Israel would become a nation! Truman did as they wanted. We became a nation, and Truman retained the presidency of his country. An amazing story, yes? But true! What do you think?"

"I'm not sure what to think," Zafran said, honestly. "Certainly, it's of historical significance, but I don't see the relevance today. Although, I'm sure you are telling me these things for a reason."

Behrmann plucked a pair of wire reading glasses off his nose and leaned forward in his chair. "The relevance today, Major, is that we might have to make good on our deal with those Southern statesmen. And, your intuition is correct. I do have a reason for telling you this. You are going to go and meet with the successors of those men who helped us create the State of Israel," Behrmann explained. "We were contacted a year ago by the descendants of the men who made the original bargain, 'Directors' of their cause I believed they called themselves. We were told they would require our recognition within the next several years. The Mossad has been looking into it, privately, as you might expect. But we have, so far, uncovered nothing but vague rumors of powerful families from the Southern states influencing foreign investments and becoming quite friendly with several foreign governments. We must assume that this group, or conspiracy of persons, is making overtures so that other countries will be ready to recognize their new country as well."

Zafran listened to all of this with patience but mounting curiosity and then asked, "So, Mr. Deputy Director, how may I be of service?"

"Yes, yes! You deserve answers! When we were contacted again a year ago, we naturally had many questions for the representatives of the new would-be state. One of those questions was about the viability of their government after they announce their secession. How would they counter a military response to their rebellion? They assured us they have a new weapon that will 'level the playing field', as the Americans say. Now, they want us to see it, prove they are serious and that our recognition will not be a futile gesture. This is your job. Go there. See this new wonder weapon. Fly it. Do as they ask. This is where your military knowledge will be critical.

"But also, we need to know more. Who is behind this movement? Are they indeed serious? Will this succeed? That is your task."

"Sir, may I ask a question?" Zafran asked.

"Of course."

"Why would Israel even consider such a thing and jeopardize its relationship with the strongest and richest country on the planet? Why not tell the Americans about this planned rebellion and be done with it?" Zafran asked, without sounding like he questioned his orders.

Once again, Zafran had impressed Behrmann with this grasp of geopolitical maneuvering.

"For two reasons. First, when our representatives made the bargain back in 1949, they signed a document that would hold them to their promise and described in detail the agreement concerning Truman. But even beyond the obligation it imposes, if that document is released, our enemies will have a legitimate argument that the recognition of Israel by the United States was illegal, not based on our right to exist - but on nothing more than a political deal. This must not happen. Second, if the aircraft is half of what they claim it to be, we want it."

FORTY-THREE

Inside the Revolution I, Rick's knees pressed uncomfortably against the opposite side of the crew access corridor. The small metal jump seat installed just behind the usual two-person crew cockpit allowed him only a limited view out through the front windows, and he had to twist his head to the left just to see outside. But Rick's almost child-like excitement and fascination with the performance of the new technology completely overcame his discomfort. Zafran sat in the pilot's position while Dave Knox monitored the aircraft's flight instruments and test data from the co-pilot's seat. Neither the pilots nor Rick wore a G-suit or helmet like those required in conventional modern military jets.

After leaving the Mobile test facility, Rick knew their course would take them soaring southeast over the Gulf of Mexico toward the island of Cuba. But even from his cramped position, it didn't feel like flying at all. Except for occasional radio communications, the inside of the craft was silent. He found it somewhat disturbing that the usual noise from jet engines did not assault his ears. The Revolution I rode so smoothly that Rick didn't even experience that 'pit of the stomach' response most people have during high acceleration. Upon takeoff, they had simply shot straight upward into the air, a maneuver that would have caused immediate loss of consciousness had they not been encased in an invisible gravity wave field. The sensation for the Revolution I's pilots was more like playing a video game than actually flying.

"Approaching Cuban airspace," Zafran reported in the emotionless monotone pilots use.

"Descend to Angels 10 and reduce speed to twenty percent below Mach One," Dave ordered.

"Angels 10, speed 530 knots, heading 275," Zafran responded.

Dave looked over his shoulder at Rick, who was grinning from ear to ear. "Hey, buddy, what do you think so far? We just flew over the Gulf of Mexico in about ten minutes!"

"I know. I've been watching the Mach Indicator. Not too bad, but she can go a lot faster!" Rick almost shouted. "Why are we slowing down over Cuba? Isn't that risky? We're not invisible."

"Whoa there! No need to yell. We can hear you just fine. And, I know. We break speed records every time we fly. But tonight, we have orders to make a lap around the Presidential Palace. Sort of a demonstration, I guess. The Directors sent over the authorization just before we left. I'll tell you what, we'll give her the spurs on the way over to Israel," Dave explained.

"I thought we were just going to the African coast and back. More new orders?" Rick asked, sounding concerned.

"Yep, same deal. Zafran requested we do a flyby for his guys just north of Tel Aviv. The Directors agreed. It's no problem. We got plenty of gas!" Dave answered jokingly. They both knew the Revolution I could stay comfortably in the air for a week utilizing just the unique Element 128 fuel they had on board.

Rick shrugged. "Okay, then. I've never been to Cuba or Israel."

Dave turned around and began entering waypoints into the navigational computer for what was turning out to be a goodwill tour. The U.S. Navy often visited foreign ports to show off its latest ships and make valuable local connections. It also didn't hurt to let the world know how easily the U.S. could project its power. The Directors just borrowed this time-honored strategy.

Despite his excitement, Rick had to admit to himself he was uncomfortable with tonight's mission. The aircraft had passed every test so far, but it wasn't, at least technically, fully operational. It seemed a bit reckless to reveal even the existence of their gravity wave craft. If someone in Cuba or Israel leaked that it existed or published photos or videos, it might be impossible to contain the news of a silent, hyper-fast aircraft from spreading like wildfire. In the end, Rick simply had to find contentment by hoping the Directors knew what they were doing. They had managed the project perfectly up to this point, so Rick gave them the benefit of the doubt. Still, *Cuba?*

"Approaching waypoint and slowing to fifty knots. We are descending to treetop level per flight plan," Zafran reported.

"Look, Rick! The Presidential Palace is coming up. It's lit like they're having a big party or something!" Dave said, excitedly pointing out the front window.

Rick leaned a bit further forward. Outside, he could see a magnificent house perched on a high rocky peninsula overlooking the Straits of Florida, the fifty miles of water separating Florida from Cuba. As they got closer, Rick could see three men standing on a wide veranda, staring into the sky in their direction. Another sat hunched in a wheelchair.

Zafran stopped the aircraft only two hundred feet from the observers. After hovering for a moment, he twisted the joystick controller slowly to the left. The scene in front of Zafran, Dave and, Rick flipped upside down as the craft slowly rotated onto its back. But inside the aircraft, they felt nothing at all. By all rights, their bodies should have been straining against their safety harnesses with blood rushing to their heads. When Zafran first began training in the Revolution I, this maneuver and others like it proved challenging to understand. Now, however, his mind and body fully accepted the unnatural experience.

"Now that's fun!" Rick cried from the jump seat.

On the ground, four men dressed in uniforms weighed down by rows of gaudy medals stood holding cigars and staring wide-eyed at the incredible aircraft hovering silently in the night sky.

One of the men, a tall general sporting a Fidel-like long beard, took a step forward, stuck his cigar firmly between his teeth, and began slowly clapping his hands. The other three men joined in, the excitement of the moment nearly overwhelming.

"Madre de Dios!" the bearded general cried. "Cuba must have that!"

"Okay, show's over. Looks like they enjoyed it. Let's go, heading 090. And let's give them a thrill on the way out, Zafran," Dave said.

"Yes, sir. Heading 090. Speed - Mach four."

"Initiate," Dave said gesturing forward with his hand.

The Revolution I flipped back upright and, at least to the eyes of the astonished Cubans, disappeared, slipping silently over the horizon to the east.

FORTY-FOUR

After leaving Cuban airspace, the morning sun didn't rise in the cockpit windows; it popped into view all at once. Dave, Rick, and Zafran flew east over the Atlantic at Mach 4, three thousand sixty-nine miles per hour. Except for the white clouds flashing past the cockpit window, the occupants of the Revolution I didn't notice the tremendous speed.

Their flight across the ocean, northern Africa, and part of the Mediterranean Sea would last only a couple of hours. Rick made himself as comfortable as possible in his small jump seat. Even though physically cramped and uncomfortable, he beamed with pride over the capabilities of this technology. He mentally calculated that the regular flight time by commercial aircraft between Cuba and Israel would be fourteen hours.

"Ten minutes to waypoint two. We have confirmation the observers are present and waiting," Zafran reported.

Looking forward to showing off his pride and joy for a second time, Dave said, "Good! Let's not disappoint them. Do they have something to shoot at us with? That would be so cool!"

Zafran looked over at Dave and raised his eyebrows. "Are you sure you want to do a live test of the system while the craft is occupied?"

Dave said, "Absolutely! Okay, Rick?"

Rick was surprised, but only at Dave's question. "Of course. The defense system is fully operational, and the system is nominal."

Zafran didn't respond other than to type a quick message into the communications system. After a moment, he turned back to Dave. "They can deploy a fifty-caliber mounted on a Humvee."

"Ask them to give us a few hundred rounds as soon as we show up!" Dave said, barely containing his excitement.

"Confirmed," Zafran said shortly afterward. "Two minutes to our next waypoint. Descending to treetop level and slowing to fifty knots.

The Revolution I skimmed over the top of the Mediterranean Sea before passing into Israeli airspace. A lone fisherman throwing his line into the water near the beach caught a glimpse of a strange craft coming out of the sky. His jaw dropped to his chin, and his fishing pole fell from his hands as he turned to watch the object glide silently over the dunes behind him and disappear into the desert.

Ariel Behrmann stood next to several IDF vehicles about twenty-five miles deep into the Israeli desert. After sending Zafran to America, the pilot had kept him informed about the day-to-day testing of the incredible new aircraft. Behrmann wasn't easily impressed, but if the information he received about the weapon about to appear was accurate, today would be different. Much different.

The head of the IDF, General Eli Kahn, stood next to Behrmann dressed in simple but immaculately pressed fatigues and highly polished black combat boots. He stood at least a head taller than the elderly Behrmann and peered through a pair of high-power binoculars to the northwest. His Chief of Staff, a Major, stood just behind the General, ready to relay orders should any come.

Atop the General's Humvee, Master Sergeant Ben Zeit handled the mounted machine gun. His weapon's fifty-caliber rounds could penetrate light armor at distances of up to a mile. A few moments ago, the General unexpectedly ordered him to prepare to fire. Despite being confused about the need for such firepower this far inside Israeli borders, he dutifully checked, loaded, and charged the gun. Now ready to fire, he shifted the gun from left to right, looking for a target that didn't exist.

Behrmann looked serenely at the desert in front of him. But inside, he had to admit he was both excited and tense. He needed to suitably dazzle the head of the IDF and gain the support of the military before the Israeli government would agree to recognize a new country sliced out of the southern United States.

"I thought you said they were only minutes away," the General growled, still holding the binoculars to his eyes. "There's nothing out there but sand and ..."

The General stopped talking when the view in his binoculars suddenly went dark. As he pulled them away from his face, a demonic black craft filled his vision. Without a sound, the monster had seemingly fallen from the sky and now hovered motionless in front of the small group of men.

Behrmann rarely smiled. But he couldn't suppress the grin that cracked his face.

After entering Israel at treetop level, Zafran put the Revolution I into a rocket-like vertical climb to thirty-five thousand feet. When he reached the target coordinates, he dropped the craft at supersonic speed to make it appear as if the Revolution I had blinked into existence in front of his boss.

Not waiting for orders, Zafran pitched the plane onto one side and flew a perfect circle around the group, all of whom turned in place to follow, unable to wrench their eyes away from what should be impossible. Zafran stopped again in front of the group and then pitched the plane's nose up, presenting its underside as a target!

Behrmann reacted first. "General, please ask your gunner to fire."

The General simply nodded at his aide, who looked up at the gunner motioning him to open fire.

Although a seasoned combat veteran, Zeit wasn't paying attention. His gaze and mind were locked on the Revolution I.

The General looked at the Major and raised his eyebrows. He wasn't used to a delay in his orders being carried out. The Major, recognizing the General's expression, turned back to the Sergeant and screamed. "Sergeant Major! Fire that weapon!"

The Sergeant responded instinctively, unleashing a ten-second burst directly at the Revolution I. He didn't need to aim, at point-blank range, he couldn't miss.

The terrible ripping sound caused Behrmann to cover his ears with his hands. Hot brass casings flew from the weapon, spilling off the Humvee and into the sand while bright red tracer rounds flashed across the short distance.

Inside, Dave looked around at Rick. "Have they fired?"

"Yes, no damage at all, of course. Shall I release the bullets now?"

"Yeah. I just wish I could see their faces."

General Kahn couldn't believe his eyes. Without looking away from the bottom of the craft, he shouted, "Are my eyes deceiving me, or are those rounds, uh, stuck fast to that thing?"

Just as he spoke, all two hundred rounds fell off the craft and landed in the sand. A distinct tinkling sound reached their ears as the steel-jacketed bullets landed atop one another.

The demonstration over, Zafran pointed the nose of the craft at the sky and unleashed the power of the gravity wave propulsion system. The Revolution I disappeared before the men on the ground could fully re-gather their wits.

When they were alone again, General Kahn walked out into the desert just far enough to find the spent rounds. He picked one up and turned it over and over, looking for any imperfection. It was pristine.

"Sababa! Sababa! Behrmann, my friend, Israel must have this machine!" Kahn called back to the short, balding man who was grinning from ear to ear.

Behrmann waved back. "We shall see, my good General. We shall see."

FORTY-FIVE

The twin Baxter dorms stood at the edge of Southern's campus, providing a total of thirty-six floors of housing for the university's incoming freshmen. New to campus, the dorms quickly became the first choice for underclassmen. The addition of a recreation center, workout facility and wide outdoor study terrace covering the entire top floor of both twin towers enhanced their appeal. Overlooking the back of sorority row, and particularly the windows of the president's suite of Sarah's sorority house, it was those same terraces that attracted Bubba, Michael, and Sarah to the top of Baxter II. But Michael and his friends weren't there to study or relax. They came to spy.

After Sarah figured out the date and time Paige Wilson set for the closed-door officers' meeting, she, Michael, and Bubba determined that the rooftop terrace atop the second Baxter dorm would provide the perfect line-of-sight vantage point to use Bubba's laser-microphone.

"Will this rain affect the laser?" Michael asked, as Bubba set up the equipment along the wall surrounding the terrace.

"No, not at all," Bubba said, without looking up. "If it was pouring, I might be a little concerned, but this little drizzle just gives us some privacy."

"I've got Sarah inside with a story that the area is closed, just in case," Michael replied. "The physics department experimenting with lasers."

"Perfect cover story," Bubba said, absently. "This is almost set and it looks like we have about thirty minutes to hang out before the meeting is supposed to start. You still good with doing this?"

Michael hadn't seemed too enthusiastic about their unauthorized surveillance mission that evening.

"Yeah, I'm good. I guess I'm feeling a little guilty or something about not bringing Zach into the loop," Michael explained.

"I know. I miss the little guy, too. But I think you were right. He's been all-consumed with the SGA, and if we get caught, I wouldn't want his daddy comin' down hard on his butt," Bubba agreed.

"Hey, y'all worried about Zach?" Sarah asked, walking up behind Michael and slipping her arm through his. "I think we did the right thing. He might end up feeling a little hurt and he'll definitely wish he had been here, but he'll understand."

"I sure hope so," Michael replied, not sounding convinced. "I haven't even mentioned our theory about The Tyros to him."

"Well, we got a job to do. I've set everything up and we'll be able to hear if anything strange happens inside," Bubba said, turning back toward his equipment.

"It's almost time. Would you keep watching the door?" Michael asked Sarah.

Sarah took up her position just inside the door to the terrace while Michael joined Bubba against the short wall that overlooked the sorority house. Bubba had the laser aimed at the window and the device plugged into the voice recorder. They sat waiting for someone to enter the room below, all but invisible in the gloomy weather.

Moments later, they could hear the door to the room open and a female voice apparently chatting on the telephone. Michael gave Bubba a thumbs-up. While the voice emerging from the small speaker was somewhat distorted, they could make out the girl complaining about a lack of clothes for an upcoming event. A knock at the door ended the telephone call and what sounded like a group of girls entered, all talking over one another.

Michael looked over the wall, but the blinds on the windows were closed, keeping him from seeing anything taking place inside. But amazingly, they could hear everything being said.

Concentrating on the voices coming from the device, neither Michael nor Bubba heard Sarah approaching. Finally, seeing her out of the corner of his eye, Michael turned around to find Sarah standing ten feet away with a gun pointed at her side.

"What the hell..." Michael exclaimed, jumping to his feet just as the gun shifted its aim in his direction.

Behind Sarah, a man wearing a black ski mask said, "Stay right there, boy."

Michael raised his hands and looked at his girlfriend. The expression on her face showed more anger than terror. "You okay?"

Sarah nodded.

Now Bubba was on his feet as well and took a step toward the armed man, but stopped dead when a second gunman appeared from behind the first holding a small but dangerous-looking pistol.

"What do you want?" Bubba demanded.

"Shut up. You're coming with us," the second man said.

Bubba put his head down and took a few steps forward as if in surrender. Suddenly, he rushed the second gunman, who deftly sidestepped Bubba's clumsy attack and smashed the butt of his pistol into the back of Bubba's head. Bubba ended up on his hands and knees, not unconscious, but badly dazed.

"And here they said you were some kind of genius," the second assailant scoffed. "Try that shit again and I'll splash your smart-ass brain all over the floor."

Sarah tried to go to her friend, who had recovered enough to stand, but she was held back by the first gunman.

"You okay, buddy?" Michael asked.

Bubba just nodded, one hand planted on the back of his head, a thin trickle of blood emerging between his fingers.

"Now, we are going to walk out of this building. I don't want to hurt any of these sweet little college kids in the halls, so don't make me have to. Understand? And bring your little spy camera or whatever it is."

The two kidnappers removed their masks but kept their three captives in front of them as they quietly took the elevator down to the lobby and out the door. A bored student checking the student identification cards of anyone entering the building late at night sat at a metal desk. He didn't care who left.

J.P. pushed the three students into the back seat of an enormous black SUV, while Mitch climbed into the driver's seat. J.P. looked back at his new guests and handed each a black cloth hood. "Put these over your heads. Stay calm and nothing will happen to you. There're some people that want to talk to you. Once that's done, you can go back to your cute little dorm rooms."

Sarah had had enough. "You can't..."

Michael put a hand on her knee. The meaning was clear - don't provoke these guys. He had recognized J.P. from the night of the hotel fire and knew they were in deep trouble.

"Good choice," Gina said from behind Sarah. "I wouldn't want to hurt such a pretty young thing. Now put on the hood."

Leaning forward, Gina used the barrel of her gun to gently caress the side of Sarah's face. Recoiling, Sarah quickly slipped the bag over her own head and moved closer to Michael.

She was scared. They all were.

FORTY-SIX

Zach was sitting in Hunter's room when Hunter's phone buzzed. He could see Hunter's mood turn black as soon as he looked at the number.

Snatching up the phone at once, Hunter answered: "Hello?"

Zach watched as Hunter visibly stiffened and glanced in his direction.

"He's here, uh, in the house...yeah, I'm sure."

The hairs on the back of Zach's neck stood on end as he realized the conversation was about him. The call continued for another minute, while Hunter rubbed his forehead with his free hand.

"Spying on who?"... "Took them?"... "Okay, alright. I'll take care of it..." Hunter said, before unmistakably turning his attention to Zach.

Zach got up and moved toward the door. "Look, we can talk about how to vote on that funding thing later. You look busy," Zach said, trying to sound unfazed by Hunter's now malevolent stare, but failing.

"Get your ass back over here," Hunter demanded, his eyes fixed on Zach.

"Hey, man. I don't know what all that was about, but whatever it was, its none of my business," Zach said, backing toward the door.

"You little bastard! What are you and your stupid buddies up to? Why were they spying on a Tyros meeting at the Pi house?" Hunter shouted, coming around the desk.

Zach didn't wait around to see what Hunter meant. He'd seen Hunter angry before, but the murderous look in his eyes terrified him to the core. In a flash, he squirted through the door, ran down the hall and bounded down the stairwell. At the bottom, he paused. He could hear Hunter's heavy footsteps not far behind.

Zach sprinted through the house and into the kitchen, startling Carl who had been unpacking a new set of glasses.

"I wasn't here!" Zach said, his voice stressed and pleading.

Carl didn't have time to respond before Zach ducked out the back door. Then, just seconds later, Hunter burst through the swinging double doors into the kitchen.

"You seen Zach Self?" Hunter blurted.

Carl never liked Hunter Ewell and his demanding tone did nothing to change that assessment.

"No, Mr. Ewell, hadn't laid eyes on him since breakfast," Carl responded, returning to his unpacking.

"Dammit!" Hunter shouted, before turning back into the dining room.

Carl's little subterfuge gave Zach time to find his car parked behind the house and drive quickly out the back entrance. Checking his mirrors, Zach thought he caught a glace of Hunter dashing into the parking lot.

Zach drove aimlessly, unsure what to do next, and completely in the dark about what had triggered Hunter's sudden attack. He just needed to get away and find somewhere to think.

What had Hunter meant about spying? And why did he ask what we were up to? This doesn't make sense!

All he could come up with was that Hunter, or someone, discovered he and Michael and Bubba had been watching Hunter for Agent Deal and the FBI.

Needing to warn Michael and Bubba, Zach snatched his phone off the passenger seat and texted Michael - *Call me asap.* After a few seconds with no response, he sent the same message to Sarah. Still nothing. Then it hit him. He remembered Hunter also saying something on the phone about 'taking them.'

Zach's mind often considered the worst-case scenario first - and that's where it led him now. More than a little rattled, Zach called Bubba's number. *Please pick up!*

In the black SUV, Bubba's tiny wireless-enabled earpiece vibrated. At the first tickle behind his ear, Bubba knew they had gotten lucky. While J.P. had grabbed his, Michael's, and Sarah's cell phones before they ever left the Baxter dorm's terrace, they hadn't thought to turn them off. Plus, the skinhead's cursory search hadn't found the miniature earpiece Bubba had built for himself. An ingenious design, the inch-and-half long device looked like a thin flesh-colored wire that tucked neatly into the crease between his ear and skull that picked up both incoming sounds and relayed his voice through the mastoid process bone. More ingenious yet, all Bubba had to do was touch his right ear, slightly compressing the wire, to answer a call.

Not able to risk making a move that might give away his secret, Bubba leaned to his right and gently bumped his ear against the top of Sarah's head. He could tell Sarah was startled and probably confused, but she didn't say anything.

Once he heard Zach's voice, Bubba cleared his throat as loudly as possible. This had the desired effect - shutting Zach up for a second.

"Hey, man, I can't breathe in this hood," Bubba said quickly. "How about giving us some air while you kidnap us?"

The reaction from the front seat was swift, violent and came without warning. J.P. simply turned in his seat and smashed his fist into Bubba's jaw, knocking him into the blackness of unconsciousness.

But not before Zach heard everything.

FORTY-SEVEN

"What? Bubba? Bubba?" Zach nearly shouted into his phone over and over. Nothing. No response.

Zach stopped his car and kept listening. He thought the line was still open, but except for some faint sounds of wind noise from a car, he heard nothing. He didn't want to hang up, but he had to do something, call someone. His friends were in serious trouble and it fell on him to act. Now.

Reluctantly, Zach ended the call.

Okay, Okay, calm down. Think.

Stressed nearly to the point of paralysis, Zach forced himself to make a decision. With shaking fingers, he called Drew Campbell.

"Hello?" a female voice said when Drew's line picked up.

"Uh, hello?" Zach stammered. "I'm trying to reach Drew Campbell. Is, is this his phone?"

"Yes, may I tell him who's calling?"

"This is Zach Self. Please, ma'am, it's real important..."

"Okay, Zach, this is Lex Campbell, I'm Drew's wife. Just a second."

Zach sat with his head resting on one hand as he waited. Prone to worry anyway, his mind now mercilessly tortured him with thoughts of his friends getting hurt...or worse. Each second drove

Zach closer to complete panic and it took every bit of his resolve to remain calm enough to clearly communicate what he knew.

Finally, he heard Drew's voice say, "Zach? What's going on? Are you alright?"

Like a dam bursting from too much pressure, Zach spewed out what he knew - how he had been in Hunter's room when the call came in, Hunter's violent reaction, how he had been accused of spying and being a traitor, his escape, and finally, the terrifying sound of Bubba's voice letting him know his friends had been kidnapped.

"Alright, slow down. I hear what you're saying, Zach. Where are you? Have you called the police?" Drew asked in a calm, measured voice.

"I'm in my car near the south end of the stadium. I haven't called anyone but you. I...I didn't know if I should. Maybe I should have called Agent Deal. What do you think? This has got to be something to do with Hunter and those skinheads! Hunter asked what me and my buddies had done. He said they were spying on a meeting of The Tyros at a sorority house or something," Zach replied.

"What do you think he was talking about? Isn't The Tyros that supposedly secret campus club or whatever? What would that have to do with the skinheads?" Drew asked.

"I have no idea. I have no idea about any of that. Nothing. I swear. Nothing!" Zach said.

"You said you called Bubba. Do you have one of those apps or whatever that tells you where his phone is? Lex uses one to see where our kids are all the time," Drew said.

Zach thought for a minute. *Of course! Bubba even installed it on all our phones. Why didn't I think of that?*

"Yeah! I'll check, hold on a minute," Zach answered.

"You do that and call me back in two minutes. I'm calling Agent Deal. And Zach, listen to me. Stay where you are. No use you disappearing too," Drew counseled.

Zach found the right app and immediately tried to track Bubba's telephone. *Yes!* A tiny blue circle appeared on a map of the area showing Bubba about twenty miles south of Banebridge. Then, just as he took a screen shot, the blue dot simply disappeared. Bubba's phone had been turned off or, perhaps, destroyed.

He lost them.

"Drew, what's going on?" Lex asked her husband. Drew's face had become a hard-set scowl. She knew that face well. It meant her husband's stress level had maxed out.

Drew didn't answer.

Lex stepped out of the room. He didn't need her hovering over him while he dealt with whatever crisis Zach Self had just reported. But she stayed close enough to overhear her husband's side of the conversation.

"Agent Deal, its Drew Campbell. I think we have a problem. Zach Self just called and he believes Michael, Bubba, and Michael's girlfriend, Sarah Marshall, have been kidnapped ... Yes, Hunter Ewell accused him of spying on The Tyros. ... Alright, yes, I'll tell Zach you're on the way to meet him."

Drew called Zach back and told him Deal and his team would be at his location quickly and reminded him to stay put.

As he hung up, Lex came back in the room, understandably concerned.

"Hey, you okay?" Lex asked, placing a hand on Drew's chest.

"Yeah, I think so," he said.

"You want to tell me what's going on now? Who is Zach Self and this Agent Deal? I don't want to pry, but I don't like how you got so stressed out."

Drew tried to produce a smile but barely managed to raise the corners of his mouth. "Maybe you can help," he said a moment later. "You were in a sorority here at Southern, weren't you? Zach said that the president of his fraternity accused him and his friends of trying to spy on a Tyros meeting at a sorority and called him a traitor. I know The Tyros is some kind of secret club at the university. Apparently, from what I could get out of him, a group of skinheads stopped them and, geez it sounds crazy, kidnapped them. Does that make any sense to you at all?"

Lex thought a moment before saying: "When I was here a hundred years ago, The Tyros was just a deal of sorts between the fraternities and sororities to get Greek candidates elected to the student government association. People back then tried to make it into some kind of secret society or something, but it wasn't. I don't know about it today, but I know it's still in the school paper editorials and even makes the local news sometimes. But I have no idea why anyone would even think about trying to spy on a sorority meeting or why anyone else would care enough to stop them - much less kidnap them."

"That's exactly what I thought," Drew said, his mind churning. "Would the president of Zach's fraternity be a member of this Tyros group?"

"Sure, but every member of a frat or sorority is a 'member,'" Lex said, making little quotation marks in the air with her fingers.

"Well, there has to be some connection between the skinheads that Zach says kidnapped Bubba, Michael and Sarah and Hunter Ewell, the president of Zach's fraternity. And if Zach's a traitor for spying on The Tyros - then maybe they are involved too."

"I don't know," Lex said. "That theory sounds pretty farfetched to me, at least The Tyros part."

"Maybe so..." Drew said, obviously lost in thought.

"Hey, I'm going to run up to the store and get a bottle of wine for us. What do you think?" Lex asked.

"Yeah, sure. Thanks, Hon," Drew replied, barely noticing Lex grabbing her purse and keys.

Lex climbed into her luxurious new SUV and headed for the store. Once parked outside the local supermarket, Lex dug her cell phone out of her purse and dialed a special number given to her by her father. She had committed the number to memory long ago.

When the other end answered, Lex didn't wait for a greeting. "This is Alexandria C., identification 1966 in Banebridge. This is a priority one message. A federal agent named Deal is in pursuit of a kidnapping that involves the local Tyros. Known names of those involved include Hunter Ewell, Zach Self, Sarah Marshall and two others. Local militia probably involved. Immediate action necessary."

"Message received. We will pass it on to our local assets."

FORTY-EIGHT

Deal's black SUV sped through downtown Banbridge, its tires launching intermittent explosions of water from puddles formed from the early evening rain. As the huge vehicle swung around the university's football stadium, Deal pointed at a small gray sedan sitting by itself in the shadows of a wide VIP parking lot. After skidding to a stop, Deal opened the door and stepped out.

Zach sat in the driver's seat, his eyes wide with fear and confusion as he stared at Deal approaching through the rain-spattered windshield.

Deal walked directly to Zach's door and opened it. The kid looked almost in shock.

"Zach, we need to go," Deal said, trying to sound compassionate, but mostly failing.

When Zach didn't move, Deal reached in, unhooked his seat belt and pulled Zach out of the car. As soon as he had Zach standing, he could tell the young man truly believed his friends were in deep trouble. He could tell when someone was too scared to lie.

"Okay, okay," Zach said, wrenching his arm out of Deal's grasp.

"Zach, I need the coordinates where you last tracked Bubba's phone. We don't have time to screw around here, son," Deal demanded.

Immediately after Drew's call, Deal's team had tried to track the telephones of all three of Zach's friends. But none had returned a ping off any cell tower in the past twenty minutes.

Zach pulled out his phone and showed Deal a screenshot of the last place his phone had tracked Bubba's. Comparing his team's information about the last cell towers connecting to Bubba's phone with Zach's information, Deal could tell whoever had Bubba, Michael, and Sarah had turned west, just before all signals were lost. They needed to get to that location in a hurry and Deal had already arranged transportation that would do just that.

"Zach, quickly, what can you tell me about what Michael and Bubba were doing tonight?" Deal asked, while scanning the sky.

"I don't know. I had a meeting with Hunter. Michael talked about getting together later for a beer, but that's it. Really. If I knew anything else, I'd say," Zach answered.

"Do you think Hunter Ewell found out you guys were keeping an eye on him? Could that be it?" Deal asked.

"It must be, I guess. But he's been acting perfectly normal, at least right up until he got that call during our meeting. Then he just went nuts. He accused me of spying on The Tyros. But that doesn't make any sense. The Tyros is a campus political group. It doesn't have anything to do with Hunter and the skinheads."

Deal looked puzzled. "The Tyros?"

Zach gave Deal a short rundown about The Tyros, how they worked to win campus elections and how some people thought they were part of some kind of secret society like Skull and Bones at Yale.

As he finished his description, Zach turned to see a black helicopter landing forty yards away on the damp tarmac. The long, sleek machine settled gently onto its landing gear, its rotors emitting only a muted whump-whump sound that probably couldn't be heard from a block away. Zach had never seen a helicopter like it. The cockpit's pyramid-shaped canopy stood high on the pointed nose of the craft. The entire body was diamond-shaped with no tail rotor assembly visible at all.

Deal grabbed Zach and headed for the helicopter's side door along with two members of his Blue Team. As they ran under the rotors and climbed inside, Deal gave orders through a headset he took from his pocket. "I need everything you have on a college organization called The Tyros. You know what I want, articles, news stories, rumors - everything. Get back to me."

Zach could hear most of what the FBI agent wanted. When they had climbed inside the aircraft and buckled themselves in, Zach said, "Agent Deal, The Tyros isn't that big of a thing. It's just college students playing at politics. It's not, like, a *real* secret society. At least I don't think so. Everything about The Tyros is out there for everyone to see."

"Maybe so. But I've found that when people act in secret, they usually have something to hide."

Stella Sims had been listening carefully.

"Boss, as soon as we finish here, we need to talk about Rick Donnelly and Dave Knox. I may have something that could tie them into this Tyros thing," Sims said, before turning back to her computer.

Deal heard Sims, but he had to resolve the immediate crisis first.

Two minutes after lifting off, the ultra-quiet stealth chopper shot over the landscape at harrowing speed. Invisible to radar and nearly silent, the deadly-looking aircraft could appear directly above a target before anyone even thought to look up.

"I have five minutes of tasking authority for a Nimbus 15 satellite coming up in two minutes," Agent Sims reported from her seat right next to Deal.

"Five minutes?" Deal exclaimed. "We need more than that, dammit."

"I know, boss. But apparently, the military is more interested in Russia, China, and North Korea. We were lucky to get this much. Nobody put much thought into satellite surveillance coverage over rural Alabama," Sims replied.

"Alright, at least the traffic out here is practically non-existent. If they're still on the move, we have at least a shot at running them down," Deal observed. "Zach, I know you called Bubba's phone. How did he answer it? The kidnappers must have taken their phones away."

"Like we said before, Bubba looks and acts like a country boy redneck, but he's a genuine genius. He made himself a little set of earphones that he can hide way back behind his ear. You can't see them because they're so tiny. They send sound right through the bones in his head - or something like that. When he got the call, all he had to do was touch his ear to answer. Cool, huh?" Zach explained.

"Just how smart is he?" Deal asked, impressed.

"I hear the aerospace engineering professors don't want him in their classes because he ends up knowing so much more than they do. How smart is Bubba? Einstein smart. And that's no joke," Zach said, seriously.

"Sounds like he could have put together something to spy on a sorority meeting then," Deal concluded.

"Child's play," Zach responded, snapping his fingers.

"Let's hope he can use some of those smarts tonight," Deal said before turning his attention back to Sims, who was about to begin controlling the surveillance satellite.

FORTY-NINE

J.P.'s SUV came to a stop. Bubba heard one of the kidnappers get out followed by the long squeal of a gate swinging open on rusty hinges. Bubba knew the sound well - they were about to enter a field that held cows - or did at one time.

As he expected, the ride became bumpy as the SUV's suspension bounced over a rough track. Bubba could hear gravel crunching under the vehicle's tires and soft splashes as they encountered puddles in the path's ruts. If he was right, they would stop again while a door was opened to a barn or other building.

Sure enough, they stopped again for a moment before pulling into some kind of structure.

"Get them inside and secure them in the back room."

Bubba, Michael, and Sarah were ordered out of the car and led through what smelled, to Michael, like a mechanic's shop with the slightly sweet odor of machine oil mixed with acrid gasoline. In the background, he heard the fast-chugging whirl of a commercial-sized air compressor.

The kidnappers lifted the three friends' hoods long enough to slap duct tape across their mouths before binding their wrists behind their backs and winding more of the sticky silver tape around their knees and ankles. The kidnappers couldn't see it through his hood, but their use of duct tape made Bubba smile.

The kidnappers left, locking the door behind them, leaving Michael, Bubba and Sarah standing awkwardly unbalanced.

As soon as the tape went over his mouth, Bubba began forcing his breath through his lips. After a couple of minutes, the water vapor loosened the tape's adhesive backing, making it possible for him to speak.

"Stand still a second," he managed to say.

Michael and Sarah tried to reply, but only managed some muffled grunts.

Bubba began forcing his wrists apart by bringing his arms as far forward as possible, essentially wedging his body between his forearms. The repeated pressure stretched the tape binding his wrist. In less than a minute, he was able to free his hands, remove his hood and break the bindings on his knees and ankles.

Moving quickly now, Bubba snatched the hoods off Michael and Sarah. The two looked bewildered, but neither showed any signs of panic.

"Where are we?" Michael asked quietly. "I think we walked through some kind of auto shop getting in here."

"Yep, and we drove through a pasture after turning off the road. But I don't know where we are on a map, that's for sure," Bubba added. "You have any guess how many bad guys are out there?"

"Three guys and one girl brought us here. I thought I heard a couple more walking through the shop, but I can't be sure," Michael added. "I guess you noticed the lead skinhead is the same one we saw at the hotel fire."

"Yep, but it doesn't really matter. They have guns and we don't. And I'm bettin' we ain't got much time before they come back," Bubba said.

"So, let's leave," Sarah said in an excited whisper from the back of the room.

Bubba and Michael looked around to find Sarah kneeling at the back wall of the storage room that served as their temporary jail cell. While they had been talking, Sarah had made a quick inspection of the space, finding a loose portion of the corrugated metal wall. Near the floor, one corner of the gray galvanized sheet metal had pulled loose from the bare wood framing.

"Looks like raccoons forced that open going in and out. But I'm never going to wedge my big butt through there," Bubba observed.

"Maybe we can push it out some more," Michael said, pushing on the metal sheeting, testing its strength.

"Probably, but we don't want to, you know, disturb our hosts," Bubba quipped.

The excitement they felt at Sarah's discovery faded quickly. The opening just wasn't big enough.

Suddenly, Michael perked up. "Bubba and I can't fit. But you can," he said, looking at his girlfriend.

"I'm not leaving you here," Sarah replied. "No way. Where would I go anyway?"

"Find the front of the building and follow the track through the field back to the road. From there, find a phone," Michael said. "We don't have time to debate this."

"He's right," Bubba added. "We'll be fine."

"Crap," Sarah said, spitting the word out of her mouth.

Michael got on the floor and pushed on the metal, using the strength in his legs to give Sarah as much room as possible.

Without another word of protest, Sarah leaned over and gave Michael a quick kiss on the lips and snaked her way headfirst into the small opening. As small as she was, and even with the few inches of extra clearance Michael could generate, she barely fit through. Using her elbows to pull herself along the mud on the other side of the wall, she finally managed to get her legs clear and stand up.

Bending quickly to look back through her escape hole, she said, "I'll be right back. I love you guys."

With that, Sarah found her bearings. The storage room was at the back of a windowless, barn-sized building set in the middle of a wide-open field.

Approaching one side of the structure, Sarah glanced around the corner. With the moon making only occasional appearances from behind the clouds, Sarah couldn't make out much detail, but she was reasonably sure that their kidnappers hadn't posted any guards outside. Across the field, Sarah could see a line of trees.

She steeled her nerves for a second and then sprinted across open ground, making for the concealment of the tree line. Sarah wasn't an athlete, but the adrenaline in her system gave her a burst of speed that surprised even her. In less than fifteen seconds, she crashed through some scattered underbrush and found herself in deep blackness.

With Michael and Bubba's lives hanging in the balance, Sarah's only thought became making it out to a road and finding help. Ignoring the thorns that scratched at her face and arms, and roots that reached out of the ground to trip her feet, Sarah fought her way through the darkness.

Keeping the open field on her right, Sarah managed to find the fence that surrounded the pasture. She knew it would eventually lead to the gate Bubba said they came through earlier. Stumbling along, covered in mud and bleeding from several deep cuts, Sarah began to doubt herself.

Had she gone the wrong way? Was she moving farther from the road or closer?

When she finally emerged from the trees, she could make out the gate twenty yards ahead. Better yet, the road was right there!

It seemed like an hour since she climbed through the raccoon hole in the wall. In fact, it had been less than five minutes.

In the fast-moving helicopter, Sims widened the view on her laptop. The satellite's optics cut through the darkness, allowing her a clear, near-daylight view of the southeast Alabama countryside. As she suspected, only sparse traffic along the state highways and county roads appeared on her screen. She had only a short time to find a large SUV or van that could transport three captives and several kidnappers. Despite knowing they were looking for a needle in a haystack, the young FBI agent operated with cool efficiency. Slewing her cursor between vehicle contact signatures, Sims ruled out open pickup trucks, small cars, and motorcycles.

The spy satellite's capabilities also allowed Sims to identify license plate numbers, which were automatically transmitted back to Deal's technical experts. Moments later, names, addresses, and pictures of each target vehicle's owner flashed up in a sidebar. Yet, even with the stunning technology at her fingertips, Sims' efforts weren't producing results.

With less than a minute left of satellite coverage time left, Sims changed her strategy. Instead of looking for cars and trucks on the move, she began identifying properties showing late-night activity that appeared unusual. Sims desperately scanned houses, barns, and outbuildings using the satellite's infrared mode. The number of living people and animals could be determined inside each structure from bright red signatures the specialized camera picked up from body heat. Still nothing.

Then she saw it - a mere speck of heat on a lonely road at the edge of her screen. Sims swung the camera south and brought the heat signature into the center of her screen. Zooming in, Sims could see it was a single female running down the side of a road.

Sims zoomed in as close as possible. Yes! Just as their time with coverage ended, Sims saw the woman or girl look over her shoulder.

"Boss, I may have something," Sims said, rewinding the video of the overhead surveillance.

Deal leaned over and watched. "Maybe," he said.

From the seat opposite Sims, Zach stretched forward. "Can I see?"

Deal motioned for Sims to turn the laptop around so Zach could take a look.

Zach stiffened visibly. "That's Sarah! I know it is!"

FIFTY

Michael couldn't believe the pain. A detached and objective part of his brain somehow registered that he had never experienced anything like the explosions of agony inflicted by the tattooed skinhead standing in front of him.

"Where's the girl?" J.P. demanded.

Michael looked up through a haze of blood. "What girl?" he croaked, hoping the smile he tried to produce had actually appeared on his face.

A savage blow to his gut bent Michael over at the waist and left him gasping for air. No longer able to stand, his knees buckled, but he didn't fall. Two immense men holding him from behind kept him on his feet and pulled him back up to face another question.

"What were you assholes doing on that roof?"

Michael could barely breathe. In the past five minutes, his entire world had become one of pain and defiance. But, as long as the skinheads were focused on him, maybe they wouldn't be as concerned with Sarah - or Bubba.

"Like I said, dude. A goddamned science project. That's it! What the hell!" Michael managed to say through gritted teeth.

The unexpected left hook landed against Michael's jaw. His vision went fuzzy and he began to lose consciousness.

J.P. stepped forward, his murderous eyes inches from Michael's face. Even through his agony, Michael recoiled from the monster's stinking cigarette breath.

J.P. tapped Bubba's laser microphone on Michael's nose. "This, smart ass, is a laser mic. And now you're going to tell me what you were using it for. I'm losing my patience here, college boy."

"Too bad," Michael said, spitting blood from his mouth onto the floor.

J.P. stepped back and considered his captive. Whether stupid or brave, he wasn't getting quick results out of him.

"Well, you should have cooperated, mister he-ro," J.P. said. "I ain't got time for more games, as much as I'd enjoy massively fucking you up."

Before Michael's mind could register what was happening, J.P. drew his 9mm, aimed at Michael's head, and pulled the trigger.

The bullet scorched across Michael's ear, slicing a bloody furrow through skin and cartilage. When Michael's eyes opened again, he was looking straight down the blackness of the pistol's barrel.

Sarah couldn't run any farther. Exhausted, she walked along the deserted road desperately looking for help. A mile or so back, she had found a house with a couple of junk cars on cement blocks in the driveway. She briefly considered knocking on the door, but a vicious-looking dog chained to the front porch railing frightened her away. Just after that, headlights appeared in the distance. She thought about trying to stop the car, but she couldn't take the chance the kidnappers were out looking for her. When the vehicle approached, she took cover in some tall grass growing in a ditch at the side of the road.

Now near panic, Sarah worked to remain calm. Michael and Bubba's lives were in her hands. She couldn't let them down but she didn't know what to do. Sarah choked back a strong urge to cry and walked on in the darkness.

Suddenly, she became aware of a strange sound coming from over a line of trees across a field to her left. The rhythmic whooshing sound seemed to come and go but was definitely becoming more distinct. Not knowing what to make of it, Sarah took refuge in a small stand of pine trees, her back plastered against a trunk just big enough to hide her from whatever was coming.

Without warning, a huge gust of wind shot through the trees throwing clouds of dirt and pine straw into the air.

Sarah shut her eyes against the blast but didn't dare move.

"Sarah! Sarah! It's Zach! Where are you?"

Not believing her own ears, Sarah didn't move a muscle, her exhausted mind warning her this could be a trick.

"Sarah! Where are you?"

Sneaking a peek around her tree, Sarah caught a glimpse of - Zach! He was moving across the field in her direction holding his hand up over his eyes against the debris thrown up by the blades of a black helicopter.

"Zach! I'm over here!" she shouted, finally emerging from hiding and running into the field.

Zach saw his friend and wrapped her in a warm hug. "You okay?"

"Uh, yeah. I think so anyway."

"Come on, Agent Deal is in the helicopter. We've been looking for you," Zach said.

"I know where Michael and Bubba are. We have to go get them," Sarah said, looking up at Zach, her eyes filled with tears of relief.

J.P. gazed steadily at Michael, the sights of his gun lined up perfectly with the space between Michael's eyes. Less than a pound of pressure on the trigger would send a 9mm round through bone, brain, and life itself. This was the moment J.P. relished – the second before he pulled the trigger. The second when he was a god.

Then his phone rang, ruining the moment.

Without lowering his weapon, J.P. withdrew the offending device from his pocket and answered.

"Yes, sir," he said.

The voice on the other end said, "Abort all operations, imminent FBI threat. I repeat, imminent threat."

The phone slid back into J.P.'s pocket.

"Listen up!" he announced. "Imminent threat. Plan B. Execute!"

Responding like trained special forces, J.P. and the rest of the skinheads jumped into their cars and trucks and roared out of the old mechanic's shop. At the squeaking old gate, they separated. In less than ninety seconds, they had all disappeared into the dark countryside.

It took a minute for Michael to understand what happened. He knew the skinhead was going to kill him. He could see it in his eyes. And then, he just drove away!

Michael wiped blood out of his eyes with his shirtsleeve. While still in pain, he knew he wasn't seriously injured. He had taken a beating, but he had come through without any broken bones. He also knew he had been lucky as hell.

Bubba!

Michael walked slowly to the storeroom door and opened it. He found Bubba lying on his side, hogtied and blindfolded.

"Damn, they got you tied up right this time, didn't they?" Michael asked as he pulled the black hood off Bubba's head.

Bubba couldn't respond. After finding their captives had escaped from the duct tape binds and gags, the skinheads had used nylon rope and wound tape around Bubba's head five times to keep his mouth shut.

Five minutes later, a black-clad FBI agent appeared in the doorway holding a fierce-looking assault rifle.

"White One, Blue Two," the agent said. "I have the two male victims at the rear of the building in a storage closet. No suspects present."

FIFTY-ONE

Sarah climbed out of the helicopter as soon as Michael and Bubba emerged from the front of the shop. She gasped when she got close enough to see Michael's face. The swelling around Michael's left eye had nearly shut down his vision on that side, crusted blood covered his cheek and under his nose and an angry red bruise spread over the other side of his jaw. Another line of drying blood painted an ugly line from his ear, down his neck and disappeared under his shirt. But when he saw Sarah, his injuries didn't stop him from smiling with delight.

Sarah ran to her boyfriend, throwing her arms around his chest. Michael flinched but said nothing.

"Are you okay?" he asked, putting a hand on Sarah's head.

"Me? I'm fine. We need to get you to a doctor," Sarah said pulling away and looking up into Michael's eyes.

"I'm fine. Nothing a little ice and Tylenol won't fix. How about you? No offense, but you look like you've been lost in the woods for a week," Michael responded.

Sarah looked down at herself. Michael was right.

"I guess I do. At least we match - sort of."

Moments later, Bubba appeared at Michael's shoulder.

"Hey, sorry to break up the reunion, but Agent Deal wants to see us inside the shop. He's set up a command post. Agent Sims and the guys with the guns are about to take off. I'm going with Sims. We're going after the bad guys."

"Michael needs a doctor," Sarah objected.

"There's a medic inside. Anyway, Michael don't look all that much worse than usual. Maybe even an improvement," Bubba joked. "Zach's there too."

"Is Zach pissed at us?" Michael asked, worried about how they kept their attempted spy mission secret from his best friend.

"Naw," Bubba said in his Southern drawl. "I got him all straightened out on that. He's just happy we lived to tell him about it. I gotta go."

After Bubba jogged off to join Sims in the helicopter, Michael and Sarah went back inside to find Deal at a makeshift desk made from a three-foot-square piece of plywood and two paint-covered saw horses. Deal stood on one side, talking into a hand-held radio. When he saw Michael and Sarah walk in, he motioned them over.

Zach, who had been sitting on an old folding chair, greeted his friends warmly, but quietly, not wanting to disturb Deal as he gave orders.

"What's your current position?" they heard Deal ask. "We need to run down at least one of the suspect vehicles."

While Deal consulted a map, Michael walked over next to him and said: "Tell them they're looking for a new Dodge Challenger Hellcat. It's bright green and will be showing only three headlights."

Deal looked up, momentarily irritated by the interruption.

Michael didn't care. "The skinhead that did this - that's his car. It was here, in the shop. The other cars were less noticeable. An old white pickup and a black SUV. I didn't get a look at any others. The Challenger will stand out and be moving fast."

Deal relayed the information to Sims in the helicopter. Maybe it would help.

FIFTY-TWO

J.P. loved his ride. The big muscle car's engine could produce seven hundred horsepower and J.P. unleashed every one of them as he sped away from the machine shop building on long, straight country roads.

The warning call from the Directors advising of an 'imminent threat' had put into motion a pre-planned escape and evasion protocol. Taking separate routes, J.P. and his men would meet again in a small town outside Pensacola to await further orders.

J.P. would have loved to waste the irritating frat-boy, but he didn't like to leave bodies lying around. Bodies tended to make people angry. Anyway, he didn't have orders to take him out - just extract information. And J.P. prided himself on being a professional.

Sitting next to him in the car, Skeeter calmly consulted a map program on his laptop, providing J.P. with turn-by-turn directions. As J.P. floored the throttle down a long straight section of road, Skeeter noticed the fact they were traveling at over 130 m.ph.

"It is generally considered unwise to exceed the posted speed limit in an escape and evade situation. Conventional doctrine would suggest a less noticeable speed, particularly while fleeing from law enforcement," Skeeter said, looking up at J.P. and pushing his wire-rim glasses higher on his nose.

"That right?" J.P. said. "Well, it sure ain't as fun."

"Nonetheless," Skeeter said simply, looking back at his screen.

Sims, Bubba and two of Deal's Blue Team operators flew over seemingly never-ending pine forests as they searched for the escaping skinheads. They had chased down several vehicles, but none turned out to be one of the vehicles Michael described.

"We don't have any satellite access," Sims complained. "Without it, we're just flying circles in the dark."

Bubba sat forward. "Agent Sims, I think I can help."

"I thought you might come in handy," Sims replied. "What have you got?"

"I'd bet my last beer that they're using GPS devices for directions. All those systems work off the GNSS or Global Navigation Satellite System. The devices detect microwave signals from satellites. I might know a way to hack into those signals. It's not strictly legal..."

"Do it," Sims said, handing her laptop to the engineering genius.

Working furiously, Bubba used a code-breaking program, available from certain hacker-sites, to break into the Air Force's GPSS system. Then, writing new code on the fly, Bubba locked onto signals from the four satellites currently providing signals to the southern United States. Backtracking those signals to receivers was the hard part, requiring a complex algorithm to sift through the thousands of receivers in use and narrowing the search to a comparatively small area of south Alabama.

"Alright. It looks like I've got three possibilities. One is stationary. Another appears to be in a field. Probably a farmer up early using GPS to control a harvesting machine of some kind. But this one here is moving at over a hundred miles per hour," Bubba said proudly.

"And you'd bet your last beer that's our bad guy in a, what was it? Hellcat?" Sims asked.

"Oh yeah. It looks like it's on Highway 54 about twenty miles north of the Florida line," Bubba said.

Sims relayed the suspected coordinates to the pilot, who threw the helicopter into a tight bank to the southwest.

"Hell, yeah!" Bubba crowed.

FIFTY-THREE

"I must once again recommend slowing considerably before reaching the border," Skeeter said. "There is a high probability of State Troopers lurking in the area."

"Dammit, Skeeter, I hate it when you're right," J.P. replied, about to follow Skeeter's recommendation.

"*When* I'm right?"

"Shut up, you ain't..."

J.P.'s comment got cut off in mid-sentence as five incredibly bright lights suddenly flooded the interior of the car.

J.P. instinctively turned the wheel hard right and stomped the brake pedal. It was the wrong move. At over one hundred miles per hour, the tires' friction with the pavement caused the bright green car to flip over into a deadly roll.

J.P. retained consciousness for only the first of six times the car rolled over its roof. The remains of the once-stunning muscle car finally came to rest against the trunk of an ancient oak tree, its thick trunk absorbing the vehicle's last bit of momentum.

J.P. came to slowly at first, but with a quickening realization of his situation, started extricating himself from the wreck. He climbed up and pulled himself through the driver's side window. Once outside, he peered back down into the blood-splashed interior. The dim light revealed Skeeter's face staring back at him. J.P.

grimaced at the odd little genius's crushed skull and leaking brain matter.

"That's as dead as you can get, bro," J.P. said to the corpse. Without further requiem for his comrade, the skinhead jumped down from the car and rolled behind the oak tree.

As he watched from hiding, the lights that forced him off the road descended to the ground, revealing the outline of a helicopter. J.P. correctly assumed the FBI had somehow located him. He didn't know how, but he wasn't about to wait around to find out. He didn't waste any more time. His only tactical option was to withdraw and regroup.

J.P. pulled his sidearm from his shoulder holster, checked to be sure it was loaded and moved out, confident in his ability to escape and evade capture.

After running across a small field, a quarter mile from his wrecked car, he stopped to rest, listen, and choose his next path. As he knelt behind a clump of scrub brush, J.P. became aware of a pain in his right side and the fact that he was panting, out of breath. He didn't understand. He had always been able to move through any terrain smoothly, like a ghost, leaving no trail to follow. Slowly raising his white sleeveless shirt, J.P. could just make out a dark bruise on his side. He touched the spot and found it tender and hot.

Ignoring the pain, J.P. moved deeper into the trees, eventually finding a small stream. Pausing again to listen for any pursuit, he pulled his shirt over his head, dipped it in the water and touched it to his side.

Agony ripped through his abdomen, causing him to gasp and breathe through clenched teeth, trying not to scream.

"You have internal bleeding my friend," a voice said from somewhere in the darkness.

J.P. pulled his revolver out of its holster and tried to raise it in the direction of the voice. "Awwww!" The pain from his side doubled and he dropped the pistol from his shaking hand into the running water.

A cold gun barrel touched the back of his neck. "Stay still," a voice over his head ordered.

J.P couldn't move anyway. The slightest twitch of a muscle caused unfathomable torture. He was fighting just to breath and stay conscious.

A second voice said, "Weapon secure."

J.P. never heard the second member of Blue Team. Losing his battle with reality, he fell over, a broken, tattooed, shirtless corpse.

"White Actual, Blue Two. Suspect two is dead. I repeat, suspect two is dead."

At the workshop, Deal slammed his fist into the plywood tabletop. His best lead in months had just died face down in the mud.

FIFTY-FOUR

Back in Deal's Banebridge headquarters, Michael, Sarah, and Zach sat in Deal's conference room exhausted but relieved. Sarah fretted over Michael's deepening bruises, checking and rechecking the bandages covering the three stitches expertly applied by Deal's medic on his wounded ear.

"I'm fine," Michael protested for the tenth time.

"You've been shot. Hold still," Sarah commanded.

Michael gave Zach a look.

"I'd do what the lady asks," Zach said, smiling at Michael's predicament. "Anyway, you look like crap."

"I'm going to find some more ice," Sarah said, getting out of her chair and walking out the door.

Michael took the opportunity to look at Zach and ask: "You think Hunter's part of this? If so, I think I need to pay him a visit."

"No doubt about it. He got really mad when he got that call. Somebody told him what you guys were up to. He's part of it at least somehow. I know it," Zach said, quickly.

"Hunter is part of what? The kidnapping? The Tyros? Or both?" Deal asked, entering the room with Sims and Bubba following close behind. Neither Michael or Zach had seen them come in.

Michael and Zach didn't respond immediately. Deal had caught them off guard.

Michael recovered first. "Hunter is definitely Tyros. But I don't know if he's involved with our kidnapping. I know this, though, that skinhead knew what we were doing with Bubba's laser microphone and he got serious on my face trying to get more information out of me."

"Michael's right. I don't think Hunter knew about the kidnapping in advance. He seemed, like, surprised when he got that call," Zach added. "But whoever called him asked where I was. I guess they thought I knew about what Michael, Bubba and Sarah were up to."

Deal nodded. Michael and Zach's analysis about Hunter made sense.

"The suspects in the car Sims and Bubba chased down were a J.P. Hoffman and a Frederick L. Yeager," Sims said, glancing at her notes. "Do you know those names?"

"Never heard of them," Zach responded.

Michael agreed.

Deal pulled up a picture of J.P.'s face on his phone and showed it to Michael and Zach.

"That's the guy Hunter met with!" Zach blurted. "Is he dead?"

"Yeah," Deal replied. "His car hit a tree during the pursuit."

"That's definitely him. I wish I could say I was sorry," Michael added, absently rubbing his jaw where the now dead J.P. had landed a vicious blow.

A moment later, Sarah came back in with a bag of ice, moved Michael's hand and laid it gently on the spreading bruise. Deal filled her in on the night's events.

"A lot happened tonight, so let me get this straight," Deal said. "You guys took it on yourselves to try and listen in on a private meeting at Sarah's sorority house. And you did this - why?"

Sarah responded for the group. "You wanted to know why we would be listening in on my sorority's officers' meeting? It's because we think The Tyros may be something more than some silly campus political party. We thought it might have something to do with that scientist y'all are looking for. And for the record, Zach knew nothing about our plan."

Sims sat quietly, extremely interested in Sarah's description of The Tyros' possible involvement with the search for Rick Donnelly.

Michael turned to Zach. "We're sorry about that. We didn't want you to get in trouble, especially with your father, you know, if things went wrong."

"Alright. We'll get into all that later," Deal said. "Michael, what happened just before we arrived at the workshop? What made the kidnappers scatter so quickly?"

"I'm not sure, other than that J.P. guy suddenly got a call..." Michael began, but became silent for a moment as he remembered the pistol pointed at his face. He hadn't told Sarah how close he came to getting a bullet in the head and decided to keep that to himself, for now, anyway.

After a few seconds Michael went on. "Sorry. Uh, yeah. He got a call, gave an order and they all just dropped everything and disappeared. I wasn't sorry to see them go."

"Sounds like they were warned we were coming," Deal observed. "Zach, you talked to Drew Campbell before calling me."

"Yeah, but Drew knew everything from the start. If he wanted to warn someone about us and the FBI, or whatever, he could have done it a long time ago."

Deal knew he was right. "Did you tell anyone else? Call anyone else?"

"No. Wait. Well, Drew's wife answered the phone. I suppose she could have overheard what I told Drew or something," Zach said. "But I don't know for sure."

"Okay. You all go home. And for God's sake, stay out of trouble. We'll be in touch if we need anything else," Deal said, sternly.

Even though perturbed by the way they took matters into their own hands, the young college students impressed Deal with how they had all handled themselves in a true crisis. And, he had to admit they had become an important part of the investigation. Their suspicions about The Tyros remained his one lead.

FIFTY-FIVE

After being dropped outside Sarah's sorority house, Michael and Zach decided to walk the short distance back to their rooms. They needed to talk and Michael didn't want Sarah to fret about what he had in mind.

Heavy, boiling, low-hanging clouds blocked any light from the moon and stars, blotting out any chance of a beautiful sunrise and promising more rain. Michael's mood matched the weather. Usually easy-going, Michael rarely became angry. But as he walked across campus, his face reflected the fury building inside his head.

"Hey, you look like you might murder someone. You okay?" Zach asked.

Without looking at Zach, Michael said, "No. I don't think I'm okay. I'm not okay with someone kidnapping Sarah, Bubba and me. I'm not okay with getting the shit kicked out of me and nearly having my ear shot off. And I'm not okay with Hunter, my own fraternity 'brother', being somehow connected with the people that did it."

"I hear you, buddy," Zach said. "I don't want to jack you up any more than you already are, but like you said, I think we owe Hunter a visit."

"We sure as hell do," Michael agreed. "And right now."

"Hold on. Hold on," Zach answered, stopping Michael with a hand on his shoulder. "I have an idea."

"What are you talking about?" Michael asked, seemingly ready to take on Hunter right then and there.

"Chill a second," Zach said, looking Michael in the eye. "I think I've got a way to screw Hunter. But you'll have to wait to go all Rambo up on his ass."

Zach's language made Michael break a grin. "Rambo on his ass? Really? We'll see. Tell me what you got in mind."

Zach explained his idea. When they reached the fraternity house, Michael went straight to his room. Zach checked the charge on his cell phone, turned on the recording app and knocked loudly on Hunter's door.

After Hunter's violent reaction to the telephone call earlier in the day, Zach didn't know what to expect. But he had to try.

It took several attempts to stir Hunter out of bed. When the door opened, he appeared wearing an old t-shirt, boxer shorts, and a bad attitude.

"You've got to be kidding me, Self. After what you and your friends did? Spying on The Tyros? Now you have the balls to come back here?" Hunter growled.

Without warning, Hunter reached out and pulled Zach into his room and slammed the door. Zach realized he had only moments to convince Hunter not to beat him to a pulp.

"Hey! Hold on a second. You need to hear what I have to say," Zach said, stepping back and putting up his hands in surrender.

"I know enough to take out your sniveling traitor ass," Hunter said, beginning to advance on the much smaller man.

"Look, Hunter. Why would I come back here just to get my ass kicked? This is important," Zach replied, standing his ground.

Hunter could understand simple logic like that and hesitated.

"If it's important, why'd you bolt out of here yesterday? Answer me that?"

"Are you kidding?" Zach responded. "You weren't exactly in the mood to listen and only a dumbass would take you on, man."

Flattery was Hunter's Achilles heel and Zach knew it.

"Uh-huh," Hunter scoffed. "You just bought yourself two minutes. What's so important?"

Zach had to sell his next answer. If he could get Hunter to buy into the story he put together just a few minutes ago with Michael, he would own Hunter and get the information he needed to help Agent Deal.

Zach looked Hunter straight in the eye. "Alright, I'm not a traitor to The Tyros. If you had given me two seconds yesterday, I would have told you it was me that made the call about what Michael and Bubba were doing."

"Bullshit. You're telling me *you* called the Directors' number?" Hunter said, folding his arms across his chest.

Hunter's answer couldn't have been any better! He now knew The Tyros was a functioning organization and that some people called the Directors had a hand in it. But he needed more.

"Of course not. I called my father. He must have called the Directors, whoever they are. Like I told you before, my family has been loyal for decades."

Hunter hesitated, obviously considering Zach's statement. Before offering Zach the candidacy for SGA Senator, he had carefully confirmed that the Self family had attended Southern, joined fraternities and sororities and been steadfast supporters of The Tyros for generations.

"But they're your friends," Hunter objected.

"Yeah. So? If I caught my own sister spying like that, I'd have no choice but to turn her in too. You know the rules," Zach said, convincingly.

Hunter visibly relaxed and Zach knew right then his and Michael's plan had worked to perfection.

"Yeah, I do," Hunter said, smiling for the first time.

Having earned Hunter's trust, Zach baited Hunter one more time. "By the way, my father said you did a fine job getting that Catholic girl out of the race for president. She had no business running in the first place."

Hunter fairly beamed thinking someone high enough in The Cause to call the Directors had heard about what he considered his own master-stroke of genius. "It didn't take much convincing. I ordered some of our experts to break into her place and scare the crap out of her. The next day, poof! She's gone."

"Nice. Real nice," Zach said, smiling to cover his disgust. "I didn't know we had access to guys that would take care of business like that."

"Oh, yeah. I can handle whatever needs to be done. You make sure and tell your daddy Hunter Ewell's got this covered. By the way, you heard from Michael or Bubba?" Hunter asked, clearly not knowing what happened to Zach's friends.

"As a matter of fact," Zach said, slowly pulling his phone from his pocket. "Michael has been listening and recording our entire conversation."

"What are you talking about?" Hunter said, not understanding the implications of Zach's answer.

"I'm talking about you admitting to a crime that could land you in prison," Zach said, replaying Hunter's own words.

"... *I ordered some of our experts to break into her place and scare the crap out of her...*"

FIFTY-SIX

Dr. Dave Knox reached out of an access port on the side of the Revolution I aircraft to answer his ringing telephone. He had climbed through the small door to install an update to the aircraft's radar hardware, and he had left his phone on a rolling workbench just outside.

"Margie! My favorite lady governor of all time! What can I do for you on this beautiful day?" Dave said, not revealing he was quite awkwardly lying on his side with his head and arm hanging out of the plane's side.

"Cut the crap, Knox. Do you always have to be so cheerful and condescending when I call?" Margie Franks was as caustic as usual.

"Well, governor, I think our history together says the answer to your inquiry is 'yes', don't you? I can't help it - I get so excited when I see it's you calling!"

"I need an update on the project," Franks demanded.

"Certainly. As I said during our last pleasant exchange no more than three days ago, the Revolution I is fully operational. Our French partners on the other side of the airfield report the second aircraft has passed its initial flight evaluations and is within days of beginning advanced protocols. Work has begun on airframes three and four. I must say, the French are surprisingly efficient.

Not German efficient mind you, but quite good nonetheless. Why the need for an update today?"

Dave knew something must have changed if Franks needed another status report so soon.

"None of your business. I just need to know that she's ready to go into operation today if necessary. And Knox, try to just answer the question this time," Franks said, flatly.

"Yes. I was just installing a radar hardware update, but if you needed her, she could be armed and rolled out of here in fifteen minutes. No question. But I hope that's not necessary," Dave added.

"No. Not today," Franks answered. "But maybe soon. I want the Revolution I kept at standby from this moment forward. Understood? And stick one of the nukes on her."

Dave started to respond, "Yes...". But Franks had hung up. "Ma'am." Dave kept looking at his phone, trying to process Margie's order. *Had he really just been ordered to arm the Revolution I with a nuclear missile?*

"What's up? You look confused, and that's not a good look for someone as intelligent as you are," Rick Donnelly said as he walked up to where Dave's head still stuck out of the side of the plane.

"Dr. Donnelly," Dave said formally, covering the fact he had just been shaken to the core. "I believe something's afoot. I just got a call from Margie. She ordered that our baby here be kept on ready standby from now on."

Dave had no intention of telling his sometimes-skittish partner about the nuke.

"What? That can't be correct. We're only about three quarters through flight testing! And we've only run four armed strike exercises! I'm uncomfortable in the extreme with ending our test protocol now and taking this craft to operational status!" Rick protested.

"I know, I know. But it's not our call. Hold on a minute," Dave replied as he reoriented his body and dropped out of the access panel feet first. He tossed the old radar circuit board on the workbench along with several small tools he had been using for the installation.

"We both know our baby here is ready. Yes, we haven't completed the testing protocol. But in every test so far, every single one, she has exceeded our criteria. Not met, mind you, exceeded. I'm not in total agreement with our orders, but I'm confident in what we've built here. Aren't you?" Dave asked earnestly.

"Yes. I am confident. It just goes against every fiber of my being to disestablish a protocol once it's in place. We developed our test parameters correctly and I want to see them through," Rick explained.

"Me too, buddy. Me too. But we have orders for now. Let's hope we can start testing again soon. For now, we'll have the pilots run more armed scenarios on the simulator. Hell, they're so good now, I don't know that it's really necessary but you can use your overactive mind to try and find something the pilots and this craft can't handle. How about that?" Dave suggested, trying to placate Rick's disappointment.

"Okay, but I don't withdraw my objection," Rick said, obviously unconvinced.

"I'll tell you what. Later tonight we'll run through a couple of ideas I have for improvements. What do you say?"

Dave knew that Rick would obsess over the lack of testing unless given a new challenge. And his ploy worked. Rick brightened up immediately.

"Yes! Certainly! What are you thinking about?" Rick asked with genuine enthusiasm.

"Not what, but where," Dave responded. "Start thinking about the deep blue sea and the blackness of space."

Rick's eyes lit up. "I've had a few ideas on those particular operational areas! Must we wait until later tonight?"

"You get started putting your thoughts on paper. I have to speak to the ground crew for a few minutes, then I'll join you," Dave replied.

After Rick left to start working on his theoretical designs, Dave met with the ground crew and ordered that the Revolution I be kept ready for operations. No ordnance would be loaded until further orders were received, but a full range of armaments was to be organized and placed at the ready.

An hour later, the ground crew had finished clearing the hangar of unnecessary tools and equipment. The tow vehicle was attached to the front landing gear and rows of various missiles and smart weaponry were arranged behind the craft.

After the crew finished, Dave stood alone in the now darkened hangar. The black skin absorbed light, but the polished concrete floor reflected just enough to give the aircraft an eerie, almost supernatural aura. An unexpected chill ran up his spine as he suddenly felt the true power of his newborn weapon, and he reveled in the consequences of releasing its potential into the world.

It took a moment before Dave could turn his thoughts back to the job at hand. Margie Franks wanted the Revolution I armed with a nuclear weapon, and Dave needed a way to obey that order without raising objections from Rick or anyone else.

And he knew just how to do it.

FIFTY-SEVEN

The kidnapping of the three college students went terribly wrong. Margie Franks fumed at the stupidity and lack of foresight that led to one of her field operators landing in FBI custody when they were so close to success. Somehow, they had dodged a bullet after J.P. Hoffman killed the police officer. Now, his capture could lead to revealing the Directors and directly threaten the success of The Cause. She knew one fumble could cost the game, and she had no intention of missing her opportunity to become president of the new country.

Chief Snow's deeply embedded sources within the FBI had reported the capture of J.P. Hoffman during the FBI's rescue operation. However, they didn't know where he was being held, if he talked, or any other information. Deal had intentionally released the false information and strictly limited knowledge of J.P.'s death to his team members.

Margie realized they had no choice. The Cause must make its move now.

Margie's emergency meeting convened just eight hours after the kidnapping. Once assembled in the same room where their predecessors initiated The Cause, she explained the reason for the meeting.

"My fellow Directors. Thank you for getting here so quickly. I apologize for the short notice, but the matter is of utmost urgency. A situation has developed that will require us to move our timetable forward.

"The FBI is currently looking for suspects in the unfortunate abduction of several college students; and, our last report indicates they have taken at least one of our field assets into custody. You have been kept apprised of the situation, and we now believe it's under control. However, we cannot be certain. There is a chance, a small chance, but a chance nonetheless, that The Cause may face exposure for the first time in its long history."

A couple of discrete gasps underscored Franks' revelation.

Franks continued. "Yes, I agree. Such a thing would be devastating. Therefore, I propose that we take this evening to discuss whether we are even now fully prepared to move forward. Whether we have taken the necessary steps to fulfill the journey our forefathers began almost a hundred years ago.

"I now move that before any of us leave this room again, we decide whether to proclaim our independence from The United States of America. Please stand if you agree with this course of action."

Without hesitation, ten of the other eleven Directors of The Cause stood as one. Immediately, all eyes in the room turned to the one man who remained planted in his chair.

"General? You have an objection?" Margie asked, trying to control her anger at General Sean Brady's surprise move.

"I do," Brady replied calmly.

"Then I guess you better explain what that might be because you seem to be outvoted here," Franks said, sweeping her hand across the room and the Directors all standing in place.

"Outvoted?" Brady chided. "Do you somehow believe this is a democracy or that I am here to do the bidding of a majority of the Directors? I think not. This body has always acted unanimously or not at all."

Brady's argument cornered Franks. He was right. The Directors could only act effectively if they all agreed on a course of action. If any Director refused to support the efforts of The Cause, the entire enterprise would be weakened to the point of ineffectiveness. And Brady, controlling the military strategy, was indispensable.

Brady understood this perfectly. The Cause, revolution, secession, or whatever they chose to call their joint enterprise would never succeed without military support. Brady had played his trump card, and Franks, and the rest of the Directors, would have to listen.

"Then I guess the floor is yours, General," Franks said with some reluctance as she and the other Directors took their seats.

"Thank you, Governor," Brady said, rising to his feet.

Brady stood in the full-dress uniform of the United States Army. He wore every medal and ribbon he earned during his long and successful career. Standing with his arms locked in the parade rest position, the general slowly scanned the faces at the table before beginning.

"A hundred years ago, the Directors initiated The Cause with one objective – to create a new sovereign nation, a new Confederacy. A bold and noble undertaking to be sure. But times have changed. We are no longer here to raise the Confederacy from the grave, proclaim Southern independence and thumb our noses at the rest of the states. No, we are here and ready to form a new country for one reason. It benefits us, the Directors.

"Let me speak in terms you all understand. What's the return on your investment here? We all know the answer – it's immeasurable. Once we take Texas, Louisiana, Mississippi and Alabama out of the union, the Directors will have more than just money. The Directors will wield total power and everything that brings. You will control international trade, do business without regulation, manipulate the media, or, Governor, become the mother of a new nation."

"Ambition is no sin, General," Franks said.

"Of course not. You all will make billions and stand on the world stage alongside presidents, prime ministers, and dictators. But, and here is the crux of the matter, what do you think I stand to gain?"

"My God, General. You'll be in charge of every aspect of the new nation's military. Next to the president, you will be the most powerful person in the country!" Franks exclaimed.

Brady paused a moment and then laughed out loud. "Ha! I essentially have that now! I'm a member of the Joint Chiefs of Staff of the most powerful military the world has ever known. If you believe I will blindly follow along and obey orders, you are very sadly mistaken. I suggest that you give that some thought before this group begins the final phase."

Franks had expected Brady to use his position to leverage some advantage for himself. He made that clear when he requested control of the Revolution I. But she hadn't thought the general would essentially threaten to bring down The Cause. Franks could see the other Directors looking to her to get Brady under control. She coveted becoming the mother of a new country, but at the moment, she felt her deepest desire slipping through her fingers.

"Alright, *Sean*, you've stated your case," Franks responded, using Brady's first name on purpose. "Put your cards on the table. Everyone else here is all in. The rest of us have bet our families, our fortunes, and our very lives on The Cause. Now, why don't you just spit it out? What do you want?"

Franks had thrown Brady's power play back in his face. With eleven extremely powerful Directors staring at him, Brady knew he hadn't won. But he hadn't lost either. Of the several demands he considered before the meeting even began, he decided on a middle road.

"Madam Governor, if you're implying that I am less loyal or have less to lose than you, you are wrong. But, since you demand an answer, I do think some assurances from this body are appropriate. First, I want control of the Revolution I, beginning today. Second, I nominate myself for interim vice-president with you as interim president until we set the first elections. In those elections, I will run for president unopposed, except for yourself, of course."

Having no idea what Brady would demand, the tension in the room seemed to ease. Brady's demands seemed reasonable. While the other Directors relaxed a bit, Franks knew Brady didn't make threats to achieve *reasonable* results.

"No, to the first. Yes, to the second. I will not relinquish control of the Revolution I until after The Cause has succeeded, if then. I found and acquired that plane and technology. But I would welcome you as interim vice-president and head of our military. Is that acceptable?" Franks asked, putting the question to the Directors.

"I shall accept your kind offer," Brady said, smiling and looking Franks in the eye. "As long as approval is unanimous, of course, Madam *President*."

Franks smiled back, but she knew Brady wasn't finished.

FIFTY-EIGHT

With Brady's objections satisfied, the Directors got down to work.

Over the next six hours, their nerves frayed and the tension in the room built until it became palatable. The discussions required precise language, attention to detail, and unanimous agreement. The outcome of the meeting would decide whether they would light the fuse of open rebellion. And once lit, the work and planning of generations would result in an event so explosive the entire world would feel its effect.

The Directors reviewed the four sides of the brilliant strategy first developed by Edward Young Clark in the 1920s and 1930s. The pyramid plan required slowly constructing, brick by brick, support for the secession of the South in four key areas. Economic strength through business and manufacturing, the backing of the Southern people, control of state governments, including their diplomatic relations with foreign countries, and military protection.

The Cause's method of building economic power had been brilliant. At the beginning of the last century, labor unions had gained immense power. By monopolizing the labor market, unions raised the price of manpower to ever-higher levels. Major manufacturing corporations, located mainly in the northeast and upper mid-west, felt they had to close plants and move America's manufacturing overseas. The Cause supported the unions with both money and political power for decades. Then, in the mid-1980s, The Cause turned the tables through its control of Southern politics. Using its political muscle, the Directors engineered passage of legislation which effectively killed the power of labor unions in the South.

The Southern states could then entice foreign manufacturers by offering them a comparatively well-educated and trained workforce at bargain prices. Combined with significant gifts of land and immunity from taxes, foreign corporations enthusiastically moved assembly and manufacturing plants to the South.

The Cause's business/commercial side of the pyramid plan not only brought economic independence but created well-paying jobs, close relationships with foreign governments, and the ability to manufacture military arms.

The population's support had been a bit trickier, but The Cause's success in this area couldn't be questioned. Southerners had always considered themselves different in many respects from the rest of the country, and The Cause worked to maintain and amplify those feelings decade after decade. Newspapers owned by the Directors propagandized the South's unique character, then later adapted the same message to television and, more recently, to all forms of social media. The politicians bought off by the Directors made it their goal to further separate the South from the rest of the country. And it worked. With jobless rates at historic lows and companies opening manufacturing plants where cotton crops once grew, the Directors felt confident that the South's population was ready to accept the new reality and pride of living in a country of their own.

Later in the evening, Governor Margie Franks explained the status of their foreign diplomacy efforts aimed at seeking pledges of recognition from other countries.

"As you know, we have been working toward the birth of our new nation for many, many years. With the promise of gravity wave technology and the Revolution weapon system in our hands, we currently hold pledges of recognition from thirty-seven countries, including three of the five permanent members of the United Nations Security Council - France, China, and the Russian Federation. Japan, Uruguay, and Ukraine are currently sitting on the council and have also pledged their support and recognition."

"What promises have been made to these countries?" one of the Directors asked from across the table.

"Very few. Our economic development program has resulted in a trading boon for Japan, France, and China. For instance, the French are thrilled with their new aircraft plant down in Mobile, and the Chinese have taken full advantage of the decreased importation duties we have kept in place for decades by keeping them on the Most Favored Nations list. The Russians still owe us because certain Directors insisted the U.S. send vast amounts of arms to them during World War II. Without our work to bail them out, the Germans would have quickly rolled over Moscow. But to be honest, they would be thrilled to see the United States divided in two with no incentives whatsoever."

"And the Revolution I?" General Sean Brady asked, entering the conversation. "We're not going to give that to the Russians and Chinese, are we?"

"No, General, of course not. They know we have it. But that's all. We can expect them to be quite generous and supportive in hopes of obtaining the technology for themselves. However, we have promised to supply the Israelis with one of our creations. In return for the security it will provide them against the Arabs, they will recognize us immediately. Plus, they know we can prove Truman only recognized Israel back in 1949 because of our promise to get him re-elected. The Israelis are hard-nosed horse traders, but they keep a bargain. We also made a deal to provide one example to Cuba. We'll decide whether we'll keep that particular deal later. With that, I'll hand over the table to General Brady to explain how he will forestall any U.S. military response."

Brady stood again and brought up a map of the southeastern United States on a large monitor mounted on the wall. A series of red dots of varying sizes were scattered across the map.

"Fellow Directors, these dots represent the United States military and major National Guard bases in and around the future borders of our new country. The bigger the dot, the bigger the base, airfield, or port. As you can see, there are almost too many to count," Brady began, sweeping a laser pointer across the map. "To be clear, every dot on this map represents a potential threat to The Cause."

"I had no idea there were so many!" one Director exclaimed.

"Most people don't. But I think this map demonstrates the scope of the problem we have been working on for many years. How can we possibly sustain a takeover when the U.S. government has such vast resources already within our borders?"

Brady posed the question because the answer was obvious. Such a task would be impossible.

"So, how do we neutralize this threat?" Brady asked, pressing another button on the remote.

Suddenly, a spider web of lines appeared, running from dot to dot and off the screen in all directions.

"These are hardened specialized communication lines, telephone lines, and fiber optics. And here," Brady explained, changing the map's orientation, "are the satellites tasked to each base, airfield, dockyard, and such.

"We have studied all the ways the base commanders communicate with their superiors at the Pentagon. It took a great effort, but we have found a weakness we can exploit. A hacker from the outside could not get anywhere close to this system. But my people are already inside and have found several critical junctions. The details are complex, but it boils down to this. If we disable this network at nine points, we can disrupt communications between commands for up to seventy-two hours."

The Directors all knew that their success didn't depend on defeating a military response by the United States. Instead, it was crucial they avoided armed conflict. The lynchpin to the entire operation was time. If they could stall the president from taking any overt action against the rebellion for several days, other nations would recognize their country as legitimate. Once that took place, the United States would be forced to back down or face overwhelming criticism for any use of military force.

The night was coming to an end, but a new day was about to dawn. Franks stood once again to speak.

"It has been a long night. We have one last item to attend to. The question on the table now is simple. If you believe, no, if you are *certain* that the plan of our forefathers is complete, and if you are *certain* that the time is correct to fulfill the very purpose of The Cause, then I ask you to stand. I ask this question knowing that history shall be our judge and jury. Please stand for freedom, for The Cause, and for the birth of The Federated States of America!"

Each Director, in turn, solemnly stood one after another.

"God bless the Federated States of America!"

"God bless the FSA!"

FIFTY-NINE

24 Hours Later
Austin, Texas

Margie Franks stood proudly behind a podium placed on a raised platform under the three-story high arched entrance to the Texas state capitol building in Austin. On either side, the governors of Alabama, Mississippi, and Louisiana stood waving and smiling at the jubilant crowd celebrating Margie's announcement.

Earlier in the day, The Cause had spread rumors through social media that these four states would announce their secession from the United States and the formation of a new country that evening. Like wildfires flamed by a hot wind, the unbelievable news flashed across the country and the world. Over the next few hours, over fifty thousand people filled the park and streets around the huge building to see if the rumors would become reality.

And just moments earlier, they did.

Most people celebrated. Some wept with joy, while a few wept with shame. Others shot guns into the air or waved confederate flags. Skirmishes broke out between protestors and supporters. Yet, overall, the mood was nothing short of euphoric.

With her final words, Margie announced the name of the new country before stepping off the platform to face the hordes of press.

"God bless the Federated States of America!"

The scalding hot story stunned the country and the world. One concise report from the United Kingdom stated:

BBC Report, July 28, Austin, Texas

What began as rumor hours ago has been proved to be true. State legislatures in the southern part of the United States of America, including those of Alabama, Mississippi, Louisiana and Texas, passed resolutions revoking the petitions made in the nineteenth century requesting statehood. Simultaneously, the same state legislatures passed what have been entitled Ordinances of Secession from The United States of America.

These types of actions have been taken before. Since the American Civil War period, various state legislatures in this widely diverse country have passed laws touted to be articles of secession or requiring a certain state to leave the United States altogether. No such law or ordinance has ever been signed into law by the Governor of any state and these actions have been widely seen to be mere statements of political dissatisfaction with the U.S. federal government or its policies.

However, today, at six-thirty p.m. local time, the Governors of four states stood together on the steps of the state capitol building in Austin, Texas. And, to the approving roar of a gathered multitude, signed both the resolution rescinding their respective states' petitions to join the United States and the Ordinances of Secession. These documents purportedly remove their states from the jurisdiction, control, and protection of the United States of America. The Governors made no other formal statements before or after the short ceremony.

In very brief post-ceremony interviews, spokespersons for the Governors denied their actions were political theatre and expressed, in gravest terms, a warning that the federal government of the United States not interfere with their rights as sovereign entities. Further announcements and information are scheduled for tomorrow.

There has been no comment from President Kimberly Mallory to these unprecedented events.

For now, the world waits. But this writer must ask whether this is the beginning of the end of the United States of America as we in Great Britain and those all around the world have come to know it?

And more importantly, what will happen tomorrow?

SIXTY

The White House Situation Room
Washington, D.C.

The President of the United States sat at the end of the long maple table. On the wall across the room, huge maps glowed and changed while news reports ran on screens to one side. Four of the six members of the Joint Chiefs of Staff, the president's principal military advisers, sat along the right side of the table barking orders into telephones or having discussions with various staff members, who walked briskly in and out of the room or sat along the walls talking quietly into cell phones.

The Secretary of Defense sat at the other end of the table, looking back and forth at the maps, posing questions to the chiefs, and issuing orders to his staff, who periodically had to scoot past uniformed military trying to get in and out of the single door.

On the president's left, Secretary of State Bradly Wall spoke quietly into his telephone. While the rest of the room generated nervous and barely controlled tension, Wall sat slightly reclined with a smile on his face. If she hadn't known better, the president might have believed Wall was chatting about last night's baseball game to an old friend.

President Kimberly Mallory was dressed casually in a white blouse and dark blue skirt. She had pulled on her lightweight leather jacket emblazoned with the president's seal on the way down to the situation room. Despite the number of bodies in the relatively small space, the room could be cool. Just an hour earlier, she and her husband had been attending a quiet dinner with Her Majesty's Ambassador to the United States, Sir Nigel Smithson, when her chief of staff brought her one of the small folded notes she hated so much. The president immediately excused herself, leaving Sir Nigel with her husband. Her pleasant, casual evening, the kind presidents rarely get to enjoy, had morphed into a nightmarish crisis.

The small folded note revealed that four Southern governors had stood up and proclaimed their states were no longer part of the United States of America.

"Gentlemen," the president said, trying to get their attention. The noise in the room barely diminished. Despite the heavy male presence and accompanying testosterone-fueled need for action, this room belonged to her. Mallory calmly reached into her pocket and retrieved a wooden gavel – a useful souvenir from her term on the California Supreme Court before becoming the state's first woman governor.

Banging the gavel three times directly on the table had the intended effect. Every eye in the room now looked her way. Once she had their attention, she paused a beat, and then snapped, "Let's settle this room down! Now!"

Telephone calls ended and staff disappeared either out of the room or into chairs against the wall. Generals and cabinet members took their seats.

"Okay, people, let's do this right. First, I want a summary of the political actions taken to date and an analysis of the constitutional issues. Juan will handle the politics and Attorney General Adams has joined us by teleconference to address the constitutional issues. Then, I want to hear what overt action has been taken and what we can do about it. Let me be clear. I expect briefings. Discussion will wait until afterward. No exceptions. Let's define the problem before we try to work it. Okay, Juan, you're up."

Juan Driggs, the president's chief of staff, stood and quickly walked to the front of the room. Wielding one of the sharpest political minds in the country against Mallory's opponents had won him this job. As the second most powerful person in the White House, Driggs' public notoriety skyrocketed, which he fully planned to exploit in his own eventual presidential bid. But tonight's situation threatened to derail his long-term plans. If the union disintegrated, there would be no need for a President of the United States.

A map of Texas, Louisiana, Mississippi, Alabama, and the Florida panhandle appeared behind Driggs' head as he stepped behind the podium.

"Madam President, at seven-thirty p.m. Eastern Time, the governors of these four states appeared at the Texas State Capitol building and signed the purported documents of secession, as well as resolutions revoking each state's original application to join the United States. The near riotous approval of the gathered crowd has caught the attention of the nation and the world. Since that time, the Ordinances of Secession, as they have been titled, have been circulated widely and copies are in your briefing folders, along with the Application for Revocation resolutions."

"Juan, could this be just another publicity stunt? Haven't we seen this kind of thing before? State legislatures passing resolutions and laws to secede from the union to placate disgruntled voters?" the president asked.

"I'm afraid not, Madam President. These four governors took this action openly and publicly. Afterward, the governors made not-so-veiled warnings that we not interfere. Further, we have just received information about communication problems at scattered military bases," Driggs reported.

"Alright. Thanks, Juan. Let's hold that last part for a moment. I want to hear from the attorney general. Charles, what the hell are they trying here? Is this even legal?"

The Attorney General of the United States, Charles Adams, appeared on the big screen. He was seated at a small conference table in a private jet returning from a trip to his hometown in Alaska. Athletic in his youth, at sixty-six years old, he now carried twenty more pounds than he should. Nonetheless, his long history as a federal prosecutor and constitutional scholar had toughened his skin and sharpened his mind. He had been offered nominations to the federal bench on several occasions but had declined them all to remain in the courtroom. Mallory offered Adams his current job mostly due to the man's stubbornness and tenacity.

"Madam President, I wish I could report that the Constitution is unequivocal on whether a state can choose to leave the union. Unfortunately, that is not the case. While our founders realized that other states would be formed from the western frontier and provided the means, requirements, and procedures for applying for statehood, they simply did not address whether or how a state might leave the union. Speculation and scholarly research are abundant on why, but that isn't relevant tonight," Adams replied.

"Surely there has been law generated on this subject at some point," the president commented. "I would think this would have been a crucial question for the courts either before or after the Civil War."

Adams answered the question directly. "Before the Civil War, and especially after the election of Abraham Lincoln, tensions and tempers were already so inflamed that no legal process could have averted the conflict. After the South lost, the issue was moot, irrelevant for the most part. The rebellion was snuffed out of existence and the Confederacy became conquered territory. However, there is one case that addresses whether a state, once admitted, can ever leave the union. White vs. Texas."

"One case? That's it?" the president asked, shocked. "I would have thought a constitutional amendment would have been at least considered to deny states the right to leave the union."

"Perhaps, but without getting deep into the intricacies of federal law and states' rights, the horrors of the Civil War made contemplation of secession intolerable. Plus, nobody wanted to pass an amendment that kept states from leaving the union in fear of legitimizing the actions of the Southern states as having taken place *before* such an amendment," Adams replied.

"So, what about this White case, can we do something with that?" the president asked, frustration seeping into her voice.

"Probably not," Adams answered. "In short, that case was about some bonds issued by the State of Texas before the Civil War. The Supreme Court held that the bonds remained a valid debt on Texas after the war because Texas never, in fact, left the union. The attempt at secession was never legitimate. So, it's weak at best. And there's another problem."

"What's that?" the president asked.

"The Supreme Court of the United States could hand down an order that any attempt to leave the union is illegal and void tomorrow morning. But it appears these governors would ignore such an order, just as this government would ignore an order from the Supreme Court of Canada or Mexico. We don't recognize a foreign country's authority over us and they, by all appearances, no longer recognize our authority over them. It's now a question of sovereignty and not a question of law," Adams explained.

One of the joint chiefs had heard enough. "This is treason. Open, stinking, two-faced treason!"

The president knew tensions were high, so she acknowledged the general with a nod and held her hand out to indicate she would get to that.

"Charles, is this an act of treason?" the president asked.

The attorney general paused to consider the question. "Not yet. The Constitution defines treason as levying war against the United States, adhering to its enemies, or giving its enemies aid and comfort. I'm a prosecutor, so I need evidence that one of these actions has occurred. We just don't know enough yet," the attorney general answered.

The president knew right then that she was about to join an elite group of former presidents - Washington, Madison, Lincoln,

Roosevelt, and Kennedy. Fate handed each of these men the same deal - succeed or lose the country. They all succeeded.

Would she?

SIXTY-ONE

The White House Situation Room
Washington, D.C.
Ten hours, thirty minutes post secession

The Chairman of the Joint Chiefs of Staff quietly waved away his aide, who had been whispering into his ear.

"Madam President, I believe I have a definitive answer to the question of whether this is an act of treason."

The president looked up from the notes she was jotting down. Ever since college, the president had taken notes on everything. Her semi-eidetic memory, the ability to later "see" written material and remember its content, worked most efficiently with her own handwriting.

"What have you got, General?" the president asked, her eyes looking over the top of red plastic reading glasses.

"Madam President, the Pentagon has lost several avenues of communications with our largest bases in the, and I think I can fairly use the term now, rebellious states," the general reported, keeping as much emotion out of his voice as possible.

The room once again began to churn with overheated voices.

"Go on please, General," the president commanded loudly, her tone quieting the room.

"I have been getting sporadic reports over the last half-hour of communications outages with Fort Benning, Pensacola, Camp Shelby, Fort Hood, and several other installations. Initial information pointed to a satellite malfunction, but we have continued to lose backup communications systems. Now we know why. The only way to get into those systems is from within. Entry requires code-word clearance and above. There is no doubt whatsoever. Unknown members of the United States military have sabotaged our network."

"General, a direct assault on our command-and-control communication infrastructure could be seen as a prelude to an attack. Am I right?" The president asked.

"Yes, Madam President. Disruption of command and control is always a part of any military engagement," the general said, stoically.

Mallory considered the general's answer and asked: "Do we have any intelligence or evidence they have taken any aggressive action so far?"

"Not yet," the general responded. "But we can expect something shortly. For now, the communication problems are severe, but we are developing work-arounds."

"Keep on it, gentlemen. I can't issue orders if nobody can hear what I tell them to do. Now, how could this happen?" the president asked as she rose from her chair. "How and why?"

"While it seems impossible, we have to be looking at a high-level conspiracy," the attorney general said from his aircraft.

"Yes," Secretary of State Wall agreed. "Well planned, organized, far-reaching, and I might add, successful."

"This is unacceptable! We must respond with force and immediately!" an admiral snapped, banging his fist on the table. The faces of the other members of the joint chiefs all showed the same emotion - outright fury at the betrayal of trusted officers and men under their command.

The Situation Room immediately transformed into a battle-planning session. Several of the chiefs were already on their phones issuing orders. Mallory had to maintain control of the entire situation.

The president stood and repeatedly slammed her gavel on the table so hard that the wood handle cracked on the last blow.

"Everyone, sit down and shut up!" the president demanded.

When order was restored, the president sat back down and said, "Now, get this straight, we are not starting the Second Civil War tonight."

"We cannot just sit by and let these traitors cripple our national defense! We have to act! Now!" the general protested, rising from his seat.

"Sit down, General. You heard my orders," the president said firmly.

"But..."

"But nothing. If you can't follow the orders of your commander-in-chief, then resign and leave. That goes for anyone else who wants to interrupt me. Everyone understand?" she asked.

Nobody moved or spoke.

The president's chief of staff stood and leaned over the table. "Your president asked you a question. Answer it."

A quiet chorus of "Yes, Madam President" calmed the turbulence.

"Now, get me that bitch Margie Franks on the phone."

SIXTY-TWO

Governor Margie Franks' office in the Texas State Capitol held a new sense of power. Franks sat behind a magnificently carved oak desk used by all thirty-nine previous governors. But, this morning, Franks wasn't the chief executive of one state. She led the newest and yet one of the most powerful countries on earth – The Federated States of America.

Less than twelve hours old, the FSA claimed the territory once considered the states of Alabama, Mississippi, Louisiana, and Texas. The FSA had also just announced the annexation of the panhandle area of Florida. In just a few hours, Franks would be named, officially and publicly, as the Acting President of the FSA.

Alone in her office for the first time in several days, Franks took a moment to celebrate her accomplishments by pouring two fingers of fine scotch whiskey, throwing it back, and twirling around twice in her office chair. *Damnation! Raw power felt good!*

It had been a long night. She and the other Directors had closely monitored public and governmental responses to that evening's declaration of independence from the United States. But the linchpins of their success would be General Sean Brady's plan to disrupt and confuse the U.S. military and her strategic use of the fabulous Revolution I aircraft.

So far, news reports and snap polling indicated wide-spread and majority support among the citizens of the fledgling country. Yes, things were going very well. In fact, far better than expected. But Franks and the Directors knew that these were only the opening moves in a supremely complex game. The next move belonged to President Mallory. And that move would be forthcoming very quickly indeed.

A loud knock on her office door jolted Franks from her thoughts. An aide stepped in and announced, "Madam President, the President of the United States is on the telephone."

Goddamn! I love being called that!

"Alright, we knew that old hag would call and complain! Where's the Revolution I now?" Franks asked.

"Per your orders, it left our Mobile hangar where it has been undergoing armed shakedown testing. It is now loitering four point eight miles off the Virginia coast," the aide responded quickly.

"Stay by the door and be ready to relay my order to proceed with our plan when I give you the signal," Franks said, giving the somewhat nervous young man a confident smile.

The aide nodded and Franks picked up the telephone.

This was going to be fun!

SIXTY-THREE

"Governor, just what the hell are you doing down there?" the president demanded as soon as Franks picked up the handset.

"I suppose we'll just dispense with the small talk about our families, last rounds of golf, and other niceties, Madam President," Franks said, with as much pretend mirth as possible.

"Yes, let's. Now answer my question," the president demanded.

"Well, to begin, you can stop barking at me. Next, I would hope my announcement last night rather clearly conveyed what's going on down here," Franks said, without emotion.

No governor had ever been this disrespectful to the President of the United States. Franks thought she heard several gasps over the phone.

"Since you have people with you there in the Situation Room, it would be impolite of me not to greet them as well. So, greetings, ladies and gentlemen. I know that Juan Driggs and Brad Wall must be there. So, a pleasant good morning to you both!" Margie said, unwilling to show any deference to the president.

Brad Wall caught the president's eye and silently asked if he could respond. The president nodded.

"Margie, it's Brad. I think posturing is of no real use at the moment. Perhaps you might do us all the favor of an explanation," Wall said smoothly. "While I believe their language to be too strong, there are some here that believe you and whoever else is complicit in this act are traitors."

"Oh, Brad, always the diplomat," Margie responded. "'Traitor' is your word. Mine is 'patriot'. But there's no use in arguing over semantics right now."

"Governor," the president said, "you have to realize that the United States cannot just turn its back while a group of rogue governors declare independence and steal away a major part of American territory. Your actions are mad and cannot and will not be allowed to stand."

"The FSA exists. The territory we claim is no longer part of the United States. Plus, if you will look at the news reports, our people have already approved our actions by acclamation. Madam President, empty threats cannot change what is now a matter of history," Margie responded, knowing what the obvious response would be.

The president had had her fill of Franks' attitude and lashed out. "Whatever the reason for this insanity, you cannot be so deluded as to think this will actually succeed. So, don't even begin to be bellicose with me about history and the acclamation of the people. You did this without even consulting the very people you claim to represent. This is an illegal coup d'état and will be dealt with as such. Your petitions and resolutions and acclimations are all horseshit - something you should be well acquainted with. And I'm tired of your pugnacious attitude. I advise you and your compatriots to reverse course. Maybe you can still avoid a sharp needle in the arm while strapped to a metal table!"

SIXTY-FOUR

Margie Franks looked toward the heavy oak double doors where her aide stood ready for orders. Franks pointed directly at him. The meaning of the gesture was unmistakable. The aide nodded and disappeared.

"Governor? Do you have a response you would like to make? If you do, now is the time," Franks heard the President of the United States say over the phone.

In the cockpit of the Revolution I, pilot Daniel Zafran received the order to proceed with their mission via secure data link with the temporary FSA military command headquarters in the Texas capitol. The message simply read: "Proceed to target."

Zafran's co-pilot, Dave Knox, looked at Zafran and smiled. "Major, are you ready to make history?"

"Proceeding to target number one per orders," Zafran responded, without emotion.

If his mission today produced the expected results, Zafran felt sure his government would quickly recognize the new country, whether he liked it or not. The FSA had promised Israel one of the new gravity wave craft in exchange for diplomatic recognition. But the FSA also possessed documents that gave them undeniable leverage over Zafran's beloved country and Israel wanted those returned and destroyed.

Zafran pushed these thoughts from his mind and concentrated on the mission at hand. Utilizing the incredible speed of the gravity wave propulsion system, it took mere moments for the Revolution I to skim over the top of the United States capitol and come to a stop directly over the White House. Dave immediately sent confirmation that they were in position.

In the Situation Room, alarms sounded.

"Turn those damn alarms off! And find out what the hell is happening," the president ordered.

Secret Service flooded into the room and first advised, and then demanded, that the president move immediately to the secure bunker located several levels underneath the White House. When the president didn't move, an agent grabbed her by the elbow and started physically lifting her from the chair.

"Stop! Now!" the president ordered, pulling her arm away.

"Madam President, we may have only seconds before the White House sustains an attack. You have to go!" her personal-protection detail leader explained emphatically.

"If an attack is so goddamn imminent, then we won't make it to the elevator anyway. I'm not leaving and that's final. I'm the president – so back off!"

One of the joint chiefs barked an order to change the forward screen to the exterior video security feed. The screen flashed and the familiar south lawn of the White House appeared. The entire room gasped in astonishment.

Even the determined Secret Service agents froze momentarily. Three seconds passed before someone spoke.

"Oh my God!"

Margie Franks listened to the confusion with great amusement through the still-open telephone line.

Nobody moved. By the dim light of the grey early morning sky, they saw a black, triangular craft, hovering menacingly, directly over the White House. The spell finally broke when the general rose slowly from his seat. Still staring at the screen, he turned to the president and said, "They did it. They actually built it!"

"General, what is that?" the president asked in a hushed voice as if the thing on the screen might be able to hear her speak.

"That, Madam President, is the Revolution I."

At first, President Mallory didn't know who spoke, but then she looked down and noticed the speakerphone. Not taking her eyes off the screen, she said, "Governor Franks?"

"Yes, Madam President, you are looking at what your black research project dubbed the GW-1, or Gravity Wave-1. Please let me assure you that it is not present for attack purposes, so your Secret Service boys can calm down. You see, I knew you would get all riled up when the FSA announced its independence. So, we had to take some precautions. One of those precautions is on a screen in front of your nose. And a damn effective one, if I do say so myself," Franks said, not being able to keep from gloating.

"How did it get over the White House?" the president demanded, glaring at everyone in the room, especially the joint chiefs.

"Madam President, we just don't know. I'm sorry," the general said. "But we can sure as hell shoot it down!"

The general turned to his staff, "Get that...that thing out of our sky!"

Margie Franks heard the order. "I don't think you want to do that."

"Hold that order!" the president shouted. Then into the phone, she asked, "What are you talking about, Franks? Better speak up, we have a missile battery on the roof and an inbound squadron of F-22 Raptors that will be overhead in minutes. Your aircraft has violated secure airspace and I have every right to destroy it." The president looked to the Air Force general who nodded confirmation of the threat the president just made.

"Okay, then. Go ahead. Order one of your missiles to fire at it. I assure you there will be no aggressive response. No return fire," Franks said dismissively.

The president's blood boiled. This woman was actually taunting the President of the United States!

"General, you may fire on the craft," the president ordered, making sure Franks heard her. She was done bantering.

Everyone turned their attention to the screen. The video surveillance camera zoomed in on one of the Marines protecting the White House. Dressed in black combat gear, the soldier raised a long tube to his shoulder, flipped open the sight, armed the weapon, pointed at the bottom right side of the Revolution I and pulled the trigger.

A long tongue of flame shot from the back of the tube. A few milliseconds later, the Stinger missile jumped from its encasement.

The president followed the course of the evil little missile. Riding on a long slim triangle of flame, the missile flashed skyward, straight up toward the bottom of the intruding aircraft. The president braced for the devastating impact and fireball. She had seen the Stinger used on multiple occasions in reports from Afghanistan and other war zones and it always ended the same way. A jet fighter or helicopter hammered by an immense explosion followed by the target tumbling out of control into the ground.

The missile's flight took only two seconds. It couldn't miss.

Then, nothing.

The president leaned forward, trying to comprehend what she was seeing. "Zoom in!" she ordered.

The strange aircraft grew on the screen until only its underside was visible. There, directly under the aircraft, the Stinger missile hung motionless in mid-air still twelve inches from the body of the craft, its solid-propellant motor smoking and spitting small bits of flaming material as if frustrated and angry at its predicament.

"You'll want your men to be careful," Margie Franks warned over the phone.

"What? What are you talking about?" the president asked, completely distracted by the sight of the huge black craft and unexploded missile.

"I said, you'll want to be careful with that missile. It's still armed," Margie Franks advised. Franks had been watching the encounter from the Revolution I's onboard camera system.

As she finished speaking, the black aircraft gently descended, with the missile still "stuck" to its underside, directly toward the very Marine staff sergeant that had just launched it skyward. All at once, the Stinger fell the last few feet to the roof.

Less than a second later, the Revolution I disappeared from the screen. The Marines on the roof gave away its direction, staring straight up into the morning clouds.

The Revolution I's visit to the White House lasted less than three minutes. But many Washington residents had seen the huge aircraft appear, almost magically, over the president's home, and shaky cell phone pictures and videos began flooding social media. News outlets, still reporting on the shocking secession announcement the previous evening, now had a second major story to cover. White House correspondents, already clamoring for a statement from the president, now became rabid for an official government response.

President Mallory couldn't believe her eyes. As the still-smoldering missile rested harmlessly on a reinforced metal section of the roof, her thoughts raced. An aircraft capable of penetrating the most highly protected airspace on earth with such impunity could eviscerate American military superiority. Mallory had to buy time.

"Impressive show, Franks. Now you listen to me. You have twenty-four hours to recant your announcement and withdraw any claims of sovereignty. Otherwise, we'll take any action necessary to bring about your compliance!"

The president slammed her hand down on the speakerphone and turned to her advisors. "Franks knows empty bluster when she hears it. I need options, people, and damn quick. I'll be in the Oval Office."

As the president stood from her seat, Juan Driggs said, "Madam President, as your chief of staff, I must advise that we remain in the situation room. Another option would be to board Air Force One. The Oval isn't the safest location."

"Juan, I appreciate your concern. The people will expect to see me in the Oval and I won't run away." The president turned and left the room. *Not to mention that I would be forfeiting the next election - if there is a next election.*

SIXTY-FIVE

Margie Franks knew she had won the round the second the president hung up on her. President Mallory and her staff had been dumbfounded by the overpowering show of force. And, Mallory spitting out an ultimatum meant that their plan had worked to perfection. At least so far. Mallory had nonetheless been right, of course. The seceding states could never stand up to the might of the United States military, even with the Revolution I. But The Cause never planned to rely on a military confrontation for its success.

Franks left her office and met the other Directors in a sumptuous conference room just down the hall. She couldn't keep a grin off her face. Walking into the room, the other eleven Directors, all men, stood.

"Madam President, I trust your conversation with President Mallory bore fruit?" the Governor of Mississippi asked for the cautiously optimistic group of men around the table.

"Please be seated, gentlemen," Franks said. "As expected, President Mallory, uh, voiced her objections to our announcement from last night. In response, as I'm sure you've already seen on the news channels, our new aircraft blunted those objections considerably."

"Did you get a sense of whether or not Mallory intends to confront us militarily? Either now or in the future?" General Brady asked from his seat.

"Oh, Mallory was all spit and piss, to begin with," Franks answered. "But, after the appearance of our wonder weapon, she went silent for a long time, like a big cork got shoved into her mouth. The only thing left for her to do was to blurt out a threat and hang up!"

The fact that Mallory had no viable response meant two things. First, it would take considerable time for the U.S. government to form one, giving the Directors time to solidify their claim as a nation. Second, it meant the U.S. government had no idea, before today, the gravity wave technology had been made operational in a military aircraft.

SIXTY-SIX

At Deal's headquarters, the pressure to find Donnelly and the gravity wave technology increased five-fold after the Revolution I's appearance over the White House. The FBI's nationwide scramble to find any additional evidence had met with no success and the president demanded answers. Deal knew he would have to make a breakthrough quickly or face a stinging failure, and worse, its consequences.

As Deal poured through the latest NSA intercepts, which were now focused on the four rebellious state governments, Stella Sims turned her attention to Drew Campbell's wife, Lex. Other than Drew, only Lex could have known the FBI was responding to the kidnapping of Michael, Sarah, and Bubba. If anyone warned the skinhead kidnappers of the FBI raid, it had to have been Lex.

A quick background check revealed Lex Campbell, born Alexandria Monroe, came from an extremely wealthy family of real estate investors. Lex was the only child of Alexander Monroe, CEO of Monroe Enterprises. Lex had refused to go into the family business, choosing instead to attend law school - where she met and fell in love with her husband, Drew. Despite choosing a different life path than her father encouraged, Sims couldn't find any evidence of estrangement between Lex and her father. On the contrary, they talked on the phone regularly, met for holidays, and occasionally vacationed together.

Sims had found the theory that Lex somehow warned the kidnappers unlikely and almost dismissed it altogether. Then she uncovered the telephone call.

Cell tower records from that night showed Lex made one call eleven minutes after Zach's call to Drew. Following up on the tower information led to a suspicious dead end. The number Lex called was unassigned. Plus, the call came from the parking lot of a grocery store two miles from the Campbell home. Since Lex's call lasted less than fifteen seconds, Sims might have concluded Lex had simply called the number by mistake, but she didn't think so. Lex had driven away from the house, perhaps to conceal the call from Drew, and then dialed a non-existent telephone number. The circumstances were too suspicious to ignore.

Digging deeper into Lex's background, Sims found she had attended Southern University and had been president of the same sorority that drew Michael and his friends' interest.

A theory started to come together in the young FBI agent's mind. Could the fact that Donnelly, Knox, and Lex Campbell all joined a Greek organization at prestigious universities be some kind of connection?

Wait. No. It was more. They were all members of these organizations at universities in the South - and therefore members of The Tyros. And, they now faced a very real second Southern revolution. Whatever conspiracy led to the current attempted formation of a second confederacy, it had to be connected to The Tyros.

Sims knew her theory was so thin as to be almost invisible. But she knew she was right. She just needed something to back it up.

She didn't know it yet, but that corroboration had just walked into Agent Deal's conference room down the hall.

"Dammit, I told you to stay out of this!" Deal said, jabbing his finger at Michael and Zach.

"Well, you said for us to stay out of trouble. We didn't get into any trouble, really," Michael responded, a bit sheepishly in the face of Deal's boiling temper.

"No? Do I look like you aren't in any trouble?" Deal said, his face a mask of disapproval.

"Agent Deal?" Zach said, drawing Deal's ire in his direction. "Yes, we overstepped. But my friends got kidnapped and their lives were threatened. That, sir, was at least part Hunter Ewell's doing. We weren't going to let him get away with it. You really need to listen to this."

"God almighty! Fine. Play it. But it better be worth interfering in an FBI investigation," Deal threatened.

Zach found the audio recording he made the previous day and pressed play.

"Alright, I'm not a traitor to The Tyros. If you had given me two seconds yesterday, I would have told you it was me that made the call about what Michael and Bubba were doing."

"Bullshit. You're telling me you called the Directors?"

"Of course not. I called my father. He called the Directors. Like I told you before, my family has been loyal to the Tyros for decades."

After listening to the entire recording twice, Deal asked, "So you went back to Hunter and claimed to have made the call warning the skinheads about the FBI's pursuit?"

Michael nodded. "Hunter's ego gets him into trouble. All Zach had to do was suck up to him a little, make him feel like a big man, and he just blurted out all that stuff."

"Who are 'the Directors' Hunter talked about?" Deal asked.

"I don't know. He mentioned them first, so I just played along. But they sure are connected to The Tyros. Like their bosses, probably," Zach answered.

"I think I have an idea," Sims said, entering the room. She had been standing at the door unnoticed.

Sims explained her theory. Donnelly, Knox, and Lex Campbell were part of The Tyros when they were in college. Without question, The Tyros is part of a much larger organization - the very conspiracy that had just announced the creation of the FSA. Lex had reported the threat to someone who warned J.P. Hoffman and his crew. And, from Michael and Zach's recording, they knew she must have reported to people called The Directors.

"But we still don't know the identity of these 'Directors', Deal observed.

"No, but Lex Campbell does," Sims said. "Her father is ultra-wealthy and extremely well-connected. Maybe even one of these 'Directors.' And if we get our hands on one of the Directors - we can find Donnelly and the gravity wave plane."

Deal picked up his phone and called his Red Team leader.

"Pick up Alexandria Campbell. Bring her here."

"No warrant, boss?" Sims asked.

"No time," Deal responded.

SIXTY-SEVEN

"What's going on here?" Lex demanded, once seated in Deal's conference room.

Fifteen minutes earlier, two of Deal's Red Team, dressed in civilian attire, had entered Lex's law office and politely requested she accompany them to Deal's headquarters in the federal courthouse. It wasn't lost on her that she had just warned the Directors of an imminent FBI raid. She considered refusing based on the agents' admitted lack of an arrest warrant, but they had requested only voluntary cooperation. She had correctly concluded too much reluctance on her part would raise suspicion.

"We just have a few questions. We appreciate you coming all the way down here," Deal responded. He wouldn't start out strong-arming the accomplished lawyer. He'd only go heavy if necessary.

"Am I being interrogated, Agent? Your helpers didn't say what this was about. If so, I'll need a lawyer present," Lex replied smoothly.

Deal smiled. *This lady is good. Cool as a cucumber.*

"Well, I really only have a couple of questions. I need to know about the Directors and why you warned them about our operation to recover several students taken by their people."

Oh my God! Lex thought. *It's out! For over ninety years, the existence of the Directors and The Cause has been carefully concealed. Now, a Special Agent of the FBI is looking me in the eye. And he knows!*

Every lawyer knows that the first sign of deception is looking away from the person asking the question. The second indicator is hesitation - and Lex hesitated.

"The what?" Lex responded. "I don't know what you're talking about."

But it was too late. Deal had successfully thrown her off balance by his casual mention of the Directors.

Deal went in for the knockout punch. "You know, the leaders in charge of the secret organization behind this rebellion, secession, or whatever you want to call it. The organization responsible for the FSA? Come now, Ms. Campbell, the organization led by the Directors? Are you seriously trying to tell me that you don't know your own father is one of these 'Directors,' whatever that means?"

This moment was crucial. If his suspicions proved correct, Lex would have most of the information they needed to get to the bottom of this entire conspiracy – including the disappearance of Dr. Rick Donnelly and the gravity wave technology. Sims had suggested this long-shot bet - inferring that Lex's father was a Director. Deal knew it was a risky play, but he was out of time.

Locked in a battle of wills, neither said anything, while each gauged their opponent for any weakness. As a lawyer, Lex often judged the strength of her adversary solely on their demeanor. But now, Lex faced her greatest challenge. She didn't have any idea of the extent of Deal's knowledge and she certainly didn't know what information Deal had about her family's relationship to The Cause. But she wouldn't back down without a fight.

And neither would the FBI agent. Deal had confronted some of the most dedicated and motivated terrorists on earth while hunting biological and chemical weapons from the deserts of Iraq to the mountains of Afghanistan. He knew his evidence against Lex fell between slim and none. But his surprise question about her warning the Directors had worked and they both knew it.

But he could also see Lex still had plenty of steel in her spine. He'd have to turn up the temperature.

"Ms. Campbell, let me just cut the bullshit. We have you interfering with an FBI investigation, but that's nothing compared to actual treason against the United States of America. The Directors have made themselves enemies of the United States. You have aided and abetted the Directors, making you a traitor. You have a choice, right now, today. You can remain loyal to the Directors in which case I'll have no choice but to take you downstairs for enhanced interrogation and I'll learn everything I need to know anyway. I assure you, the psychological drug regimen will extract your knowledge, but will leave you, well, insane. Eventually, you will probably be executed. Or, you can help us. Clear your name and return to your husband and two daughters tonight. You have ten seconds to decide."

Lex didn't respond. She sat for a moment, her mind swirling around a dilemma she couldn't solve. The Cause she had been loyal to her entire life - or her family? How big of a sacrifice does political allegiance require? Was she willing to lay down her life for a dream she had been taught to believe in?

"Time's up," she heard Deal say.

Deal could see Lex breaking. He could see her eyes flashing about, searching for a way to remain loyal to the Directors and still save her family. And, it just wasn't there. A moment later, she gave up.

"What do you need from me?" Lex said, looking down at the wedding ring on her left hand.

"Everything," Deal said, motioning for a technician to enter the room and set up recording equipment.

When the room was prepared, Deal said, "Alright, go ahead. I'll only ask questions if I need to. If you lie, voice stress analysis will catch it and our agreement is void. Understand?"

Lex nodded, gathered herself, and began speaking.

"My name is Alexandra Monroe Campbell and I'm the only child of Alexander Monroe, one of the Directors, or leaders, of an organization known as The Cause. There are eleven other Directors. I don't know their identities.

"The Cause began back in the 1920s. A group of very wealthy southern men met in Atlanta, I think, to discuss the ongoing changes being, as they believed, forced on the South and its people. To be honest, I don't know much more about the early days of The Cause."

"What is their objective?" Deal asked.

"Basically, they achieved their original objective yesterday. Since I am part of it, I suppose it would be more accurate to say 'we'. In a nutshell, the Directors have worked for decades to remove the South from the United States and form a separate country. A new Confederacy, if you will. Although, in recent times, the Directors' motivations have changed. They still want a new country. But now, the Directors want the power and control that comes with basically owning an entire country."

Deal leaned back in his chair running a hand across his closely-cropped hair. Lex's revelation explained a lot. The pre-arranged 'government' of the FSA, the immediate popular support and appropriating the gravity wave technology must have been in the works for decades. The sheer audacity of such a conspiracy simply boggled the mind.

He now knew The Cause, whatever its scope, was behind the creation of the FSA. But Lex's revelation alone didn't help him. His assignment wasn't to stop the FSA's political agenda. His job was to find and stop the gravity wave aircraft. If the FSA could dominate the sky, it had a fighting chance to succeed. It didn't take a genius to see that carving up United States would profoundly weaken the most powerful country in the world – all but forfeiting that title to the Chinese or the Russians.

"Ms. Campbell, what else do you know?"

"Like I said, my own father is one of the Directors. But I never really believed that they would *actually* try to secede from the

Union. I honestly had no idea, none, that the Directors were about take this drastic step. And, the first I ever heard about the airplane or whatever was on the news this morning."

"And that's what I'm focused on right now. Where is that plane?" Deal asked.

"If I knew, I'd tell you," Lex responded. "Really."

Deal looked at his technician seated across the room. The tech gave him a nod indicating Lex had told the truth.

"Alright then. You'll have to go talk to your father. And you'll be wearing a wire," Deal said. "We don't have a choice and, I'm afraid, neither do you."

Lex hated the thought of lying to her father's face and betraying The Cause. But she knew Deal was right, she had no choice. After a moment, Lex nodded, agreeing to Deal's demand. "Getting to my father right now might be problematic. He's most likely in Austin with the other Directors; and, he might not even agree to see me."

Deal picked up his phone, pressed one button. "Get me a location on Alexander Monroe."

After a few seconds, Deal hung up. "He's at home. Arrived today at zero six thirty-two by helicopter. At the moment, he's entertaining a group of Chinese business representatives. They're discussing terms for open access to docks on the Gulf of Mexico."

"How the hell do you know that?" Lex asked, astonished.

"You really don't want me to tell you," Deal responded, while he fiddled with his cell phone.

An hour later, Lex drove her Cadillac SUV under the portico of Alexander Monroe's classic Southern mansion. She told Drew she wanted to run down to see her father for the afternoon and asked him to pick up the girls from school. She had taken a few hours out to visit like that before and Drew suspected nothing.

Lex sat in her parked car for a minute gathering her thoughts and trying to get her emotions under control. She needed to find a way to talk to her father without him becoming suspicious.

In the end, she focused on her family. Lex had no doubt Agent Deal would keep his word and she would never see them again if she didn't cooperate. She also remembered the fact that The Cause now not only wielded a weapon of enormous destructive potential but also seemed willing to use it. She had never been taught The Cause would turn to violence, and this gave her reason for doubt. She knew she needed to cling onto that doubt to get through what she had to do next.

Steeling her resolve, Lex got out of the car and made her way to the front door. Before she was halfway across the expansive front porch, the door opened, revealing her father, smiling like a church greeter on Sunday morning. She forced herself to smile back.

At seventy-five, Alexander Monroe exuded the looks and energy of a man thirty years younger. His tanned skin contrasted with wavy hair he had let turn grey. His conservative but tailored suit gave away the fact he was conducting business at his home that afternoon. Otherwise, he would be wearing a pair of Levi's and a casual shirt.

"Congratulations, Daddy!" Lex said throwing her arms around her father's neck and kissing him on the cheek. Her deception didn't come easily and she had to be careful. Her father knew her well and could easily tell if she was upset.

"Well, this is a pleasant surprise!" Alexander Monroe responded. "I wasn't expecting you tonight."

"I know. I'm sorry for not calling, but I wanted to see how you were doing after the big announcement," Lex said innocently. "But if this isn't a good time..."

"Don't be silly! Come in. I can bring you up to speed. It's about time you knew more anyway," Monroe responded without hesitation. "We need to have a drink to celebrate together – and I won't take no for an answer this time!"

Lex couldn't help but notice her father had already been celebrating – probably with his Chinese friends.

Monroe led Lex into his private office and poured them both a drink.

"To the Federated States of America!" Monroe said, lifting his glass.

"To The Cause," Lex responded, just before they both threw back the fiery liquor.

"So, Dad, is the plan working?" Lex asked, referring to the scheme devised by Edward Young Clarke decades earlier.

"Oh, yes! Yes, it is my dear! And I cannot wait to introduce you to the other Directors. You will be a Director one day, of that there is no doubt. Our own governor is one, as you might have guessed. A neurotic dolt to be sure, but he has been useful."

"I assumed he was," Lex said, trying to stay casual. "Probably the other governors as well. I can't see how it could be otherwise. But I'm just guessing."

"Yes, of course, you're right," her father replied.

"Dad, do you think President Mallory will retaliate? I'm worried about Drew and the girls," Lex asked, seeking reassurance.

"No, Alexandra. She won't. I promise. We have worked extremely hard to be sure she will not be able to use force against us. We have hobbled their military bases within FSA territory by disrupting their communications. Even if we hadn't, President Mallory would never use military force on people she considers citizens of the United States. Plus, we have another, uh, deterrent in our hands now. So, don't worry, it's a done deal."

"That strange aircraft I saw on the news over the White House?" Lex asked.

Monroe got up and poured himself another hefty shot. He held up the crystal decanter to Lex, who shook her head.

"It's amazing, Lex," Monroe said, sitting down close to his daughter. "It works by manipulating gravity. The technology is astounding! That thing flew from Mobile to Washington D.C. in a matter of minutes! We got the French down there helping us build several more right now. Very soon, The Cause and our creation, the FSA, will be secure and invulnerable. The Directors have also arranged to sell the technology to our, uh, friends, for enough money to buy a few good-sized *countries!* I put several of their representatives on my chopper and sent them down to Mobile to take a look at it for themselves.

"But all that's a secret," Monroe said, slurring his words just a bit and putting a finger to his lips.

"Our friends? Allies of the FSA?" Lex asked, hoping she hadn't pushed her father too far. But she didn't have to worry - the combination of power, riches, and liquor had made Monroe uncharacteristically effusive.

"Yes, but more importantly, friends of The Cause. We created the FSA for our own benefit. Like every other country and government in the world, the Federated States of America serves those with the drive, ambition, and ability to control an entire country. Leaving the country in the hands of the masses would lead only to anarchy. The fine people of the South need The Cause, and we have answered that call," Monroe said proudly, looking across the room at several oil portraits of his direct ancestors and raising his glass in their direction.

Lex stood and walked over to her father and turned her gaze to the portraits. "What about a government of the people, by the people, and for the people?"

"Well," Monroe said, smiling with self-satisfaction, "that's just some bullshit our forefathers invented to soothe the rabble of the day. But it sure sounds good, doesn't it?"

In a black SUV parked two miles from Alexander Monroe's property, two FBI agents looked at each other before keying their mics.

"White Actual, Red One. Did you get all that?"

"Red One, White Actual. We got it all. Follow Ms. Campbell back here at a very discreet distance," Deal responded.

SIXTY-EIGHT

"Do y'all have satellite coverage over Mobile, Frank?" Bubba asked over the helicopter's intercom system.

"Dammit Bubba, call me 'Agent Deal' or 'Agent'. This is serious."

"Okay, boss," Bubba replied. "You'll need a satellite with infrared, microwave, and radiation detection available if you want to find the gravity wave aircraft is all I'm saying. If you don't, is it alright if I look out the window? This being my first helicopter ride and all?"

Deal rolled his eyes and didn't respond. But Agent Stella Sims couldn't help but let out a chuckle.

"Sorry, sir," she said.

Deal looked at Bubba and shook his head. Bringing him along on their flight to Mobile violated numerous FBI policies. Recruiting civilians into active FBI operations could get him fired, if not thrown in jail. But this entire case wasn't normal in the least. Deal had been sorely tested in his search for Rick Donnelly and the gravity wave technology. While he had run extremely intelligent suspects to ground in the past, Donnelly and his cohort, Dave Knox, were geniuses of the first order. He needed his own genius, and he hoped the fat kid across from him filled the bill. He desperately needed someone who could understand the technology; and, he had no time to find someone else.

Sims broke into Deal's thoughts. "We have been assigned all the time we need with the Air Force's newest surveillance platform. But we won't get the feed. It's classified way above the FBI's pay grade. NSA will provide us a location and data when they find it."

Deal handed Bubba his laptop. "Bubba, we have about forty minutes before we set down in Mobile. This is classified, but I need you to take a look and see if you understand this stuff. I get the gist, but we may need to put our hands on the actual hardware."

Giving Bubba access to the top-secret technology briefing material from Area 51 couldn't have been more illegal, including gross violations of the National Security Act of 1949.

Bubba took the laptop without a word and began devouring the file. After sitting engrossed and utterly silent for fifteen minutes, he closed the top slowly.

"I presume you want to know how to defeat this technology?" Bubba asked seriously, his country persona gone.

"Yes. Can it be destroyed?" Deal replied. "Or at least temporarily disabled? We have next to no information about its defensive capability other than the fact that it caught the Stinger missile over the White House."

Sims added, "We do know that Governor Franks boasted to the president that it was invulnerable."

Bubba only nodded, absently stroking his chin.

Determining how the craft defended itself wasn't the challenge. Bubba had figured out that the gravity waves were simply manipulated to absorb or deflect incoming objects as soon as he saw the video of the missile shot from the White House. His mind now churned through possible ways to defeat the gravity waves that both powered the aircraft and defended it from kinetic threats.

Kinetic threats! That was the key! Kinetic energy is the energy an object possesses because of its movement. It is defined as the work needed to accelerate a given mass from rest to any certain speed. A bullet shot from a gun or a missile flying by rocket power hits its target with kinetic energy. Gravity works on objects with mass!

Only something with no mass, or very, very little, could penetrate the gravity wave shield. He had it!

Bubba's gaze turned back to the impatient FBI agents.

"We need a laser."

Bubba now believed that a laser with enough power could penetrate the gravity waves surrounding and protecting the incredible weapon. As the helicopter swept low over thick pine forests, Bubba ran complex calculations on Agent Sims' laptop. His conclusions surprised him.

The laser didn't have to be powerful at all to penetrate the gravity waves. While science had proved that gravity could bend light over a hundred years ago, the test that proved Einstein's general rule of relativity had measured gravity's influence on light over interstellar distances and as light passed through the gravity of the sun. Any deflection of light through the relatively weak gravity waves generated by the new aircraft would be insignificant. Even a small commercial, hand-held laser-pointer could place a red dot on the skin of the craft.

But, unless they could obtain a laser weapon powerful enough to punch holes in metal in the next hour or so, they couldn't possibly cause enough damage to the craft itself. Then it hit him. They didn't have to punch holes in the thing, they only needed to disable it! Bubba had an idea about how to do just that.

"Agent Sims? Do y'all have laser sights on your weapons?" Bubba asked.

Sims drew her weapon. Sure enough, a small, but powerful, aiming laser was pre-mounted along the side of her Beretta M9A3 9mm handgun. Sims removed the laser and handed it to Bubba.

Bubba studied its power rating, smiled, and handed it back to Sims.

"Well?" Deal asked.

"Well, boss, my daddy used to say that even a blind pig will find an acorn every now and again. But I don't believe a blind pilot can find anything but the ground," Bubba said.

"What the hell does that mean?" Deal demanded.

"Agent Sim's gun can't shoot through the gravity waves, but the laser can. We can use the laser to effectively blind the pilot," Bubba explained.

"Oh, that's great! Your big idea is to shoot the laser in the pilot's eyes? You don't think he might have the presence of mind to just turn the airplane away from it?" Deal responded sarcastically.

"No, that's not what I mean at all. The laser on Agent Sims' gun can do a whole lot more than that. We just have to get close enough to use it while the plane is in the air!"

Bubba went on to explain his theory and how it would work.

"*Will* it work?" Deal asked, astonished at the elegant simplicity of Bubba's theory.

"I guess y'all didn't hear. I'm the smartest country boy in the world. Sure, it'll work. You get me close enough, and the only place that big old plane is going is nowhere."

SIXTY-NINE

Deal's helicopter landed five miles from the colossal airplane assembly buildings located on the north end of the Brookley Airfield, near Mobile. The European consortium, Airbus, chose this location for its primary manufacturing facility, taking advantage of massive tax incentives and other government support mostly arranged over the past couple of years by the Directors.

Almost eighteen months ago, the French arm of the European consortium found itself the beneficiary of a lucrative contract from a shadowy "investment group" to build a new triangular aircraft. To date, the French completed one new aircraft and had two more airframes under construction.

Assembly of gravity wave craft took place in an enormous, gleaming white hangar, placed several hundred yards away from the two equally-sized buildings housing the assembly lines for commercial aircraft. Security at the gravity wave aircraft building was tight but not as tight as the protection surrounding a much smaller and dingier hanger perched at the opposite end of Brookley's long runway.

A cursory inspection of the old, rusty hanger would reveal very little. A bored-looking security guard sat outside in a chair, smoking a cigarette. The guard's fifteen-year-old white SUV was parked under a dim street lamp, its side emblazoned with the name of a non-existent private security company.

The innocuous appearance of the facility was a façade, meant to turn aside any interest. The ancient-looking hanger housed the original gravity wave aircraft – the Revolution I - for armed testing and while certain interested parties were in town. Safeguarding this critical asset required unprecedented security measures. This one aircraft was the key to the continued life of the FSA and its only deterrent to the federal government moving to squash the FSA into a footnote in American history.

Rings of sensors on the ground and mounted on surrounding buildings monitored any ground vibrations out to a range of two hundred yards. Radar concealed in the roof constantly searched the sky for fifty miles in all directions. Finally, several teams of ex-special forces operators patrolled the surrounding area by car and could be deployed in seconds to investigate possible threats.

As Deal and his team approached Mobile by helicopter at tree-top level, Sims pointed out the hangar identified by the NSA's satellite.

After landing at an abandoned car dealership three miles north of their target, Deal's team drove several rented cars, all different colors and makes, to within a mile of the airfield. Taking different routes through quiet residential and light commercial neighborhoods, the team finally reunited behind an abandoned building that once housed a dry cleaner.

Deal succinctly laid out the plan. "From here we go in on foot. Blue One, take your team and circle around a few blocks to the west and approach from behind. Keep your eyes open for patrols. Blue Two, you will provide security for Agent Sims, Mr. Adcock, and me. Sweep for security personnel, cameras, and motion detectors. But let's not start a firefight out here. Take out sentries only if absolutely necessary."

The teams moved into the early morning darkness, disappearing like ghosts into the deep shadows.

"So, how close do we have to be to the building, assuming it's in there now?" Deal asked Bubba.

"Fifty yards should be close enough. But the aircraft has to be outside and powered up. Once it is, Agent Sims should have no problem placing the laser at the precise point we need. Right, Agent?" Bubba asked.

"If it's a matter of aim, make it a hundred yards," Sims replied.

"I don't doubt your skill, Agent. It's atmospheric interference with the beam that dictates the distance. We can't afford to have the laser's intensity diluted by the morning mist, fog, or the like," Bubba explained.

"Fifty it is," Deal said, moving toward the target hanger following Blue Two's team.

After a few minutes, Bubba stopped and, in a loud whisper, said, "Hey, y'all slow down. This fat country boy ain't trained for all this runnin' around. And I haven't even had any breakfast neither!"

"Move your ass, country boy!" Deal hissed.

Bubba picked up his pace a little. "Well, okay, boss. But you're buyin' after I ground this bitch for you!"

Inside the secret facility, Rick Donnelly and Dave Knox fussed over their baby, the deadly Revolution I. So far, its only real action had been during the FSA's show of force over the White House. It carried no weapons on that mission, but it would not fly again without teeth.

Rick and Dave directed the arms-loading process, choosing ordnance that would be used only in the event President Mallory ordered military action. The FSA had no desire to start a civil war. But their secret weapon wouldn't be much of a threat without the ability to shoot back – if needed. At least that's what most of the people in the hangar that morning believed.

"Why are they loading an Exocet AM39?" Rick asked as the techs rolled the white, fourteen-foot missile under the Revolution I.

"Capability. That thing can sink an aircraft carrier or destroy a large building," Dave Knox responded. "She's a beauty. Our invention can carry one of those plus just about anything else. Right now, the plan is to mount a range of air-to-air missiles and a few Mavericks for ground attack."

"I know for a fact there are no carriers in the Gulf of Mexico and that it would take at least three days for them to deploy one within striking distance of FSA territory. So, if it's not that, you and the Directors have another target in mind."

"We do," Dave said, smiling. "But don't worry Buddy, it's only a threat. As much as she might like to, President Margie Franks isn't going to blow up the White House."

Rick's brow furrowed. "I'm *not* reassured. Margie Franks can be compulsive, even reckless. The very fact that she ordered us to deploy the Revolution without finishing its test protocols is but one example. Do *you* condone this?"

"This what? Loading the missile or blowing up the White House? Let me save you some time, 'yes' to the first, 'no' to the second and 'it doesn't matter' to both. We take orders from her. She wants the big missile; she gets the big missile."

"Wait! You're not telling me that's the *nuclear*-tipped Exocet are you?" Rick demanded, his eyes so wide, they might have fallen out of his skull.

"Calm down. Calm down. No. You know the nose on those nukes are yellow. I checked that both the nukes are still safely under lock and key in the armory," Dave responded.

But it wasn't true. Dave had secretly switched warheads, inserting the nuclear warhead into the white nose section of the Exocet being loaded in front of them. The conventional warhead now rested inside a yellow nose cone in the secured armory. The weapon being loaded at that moment indeed carried a thermonuclear warhead with enough punch to vaporize Washington D.C.

Completely unaware of Dave's actions, Rick relaxed slightly. Ever since the two nuclear warheads arrived, his anxiety level had spiked. While loyal to The Cause, Rick had doubts about some of the decisions being made by the Directors. He didn't understand why they had offered the gravity wave technology to Israel and showed it off to the Cubans - other than as an incentive to obtain those countries' formal recognition of the FSA.

Rick, above anyone else, possessed a full understanding of the Revolution I's capabilities and he strenuously objected to arming it with nuclear weapons. But, as usual, Dave effectively managed to quell his anxieties, arguing that the presence of the nuclear ordnance at their location was a necessary precaution. Not against any action by the United States, but as a deterrent against aggression by a third nation hoping to take advantage of the new country's vulnerability.

Despite Rick's impressive technical intelligence, he was quite susceptible to the influence of others – particularly his best friend, Dave Knox. Always seeking acceptance after a strained and lonely childhood, Rick believed Dave's explanations, even though they were mostly concocted by Dave to maintain Rick's allegiance.

Dr. Dave Knox complied with Franks' order because his ambitions went way beyond being Frank's favorite scientist. He desperately wanted to move to the top of the food chain. The unimaginable wealth available to the top ranks of The Cause attracted him like a fly to cow manure. He didn't expect that the Exocet would be used at all since their plans had worked to perfection so far. But Margie Franks believed they needed a "nuclear option," an irresistible force on her side that could change the game.

"Is there another mission planned?" Rick asked casually.

"Not until early tomorrow morning. Everything is quiet for now. If it stays that way, our baby will stay out on patrol, and probably make a few fly-bys of Washington. Margie wants to keep it front and center in the president's mind," Dave responded, folding his arms across his chest. "Once done with that, we'll get her back home to Texas."

Rick didn't notice Dave's defensive body language.

"Will you be co-piloting again?" Rick said.

"Yeah, you want to go along?" Dave responded, knowing what Rick's answer would be.

"No, thanks. I'll leave the driving to you," Rick replied.

"How close are we to having the second bird ready?" Dave asked – also knowing the answer to that question.

"All ready for advanced testing. Rev II took her first spin around the block late last night and performed beautifully," Rick replied. "You haven't seen the data yet?"

"No, I've been kinda busy. Margie's been on the phone every thirty minutes wanting me to hold her hand. Anyway, if *you* think the data's good, I'm satisfied." Dave put his hand on Rick's shoulder.

"I have to admit I've been anxious ever since we made the secession announcement," Rick said, confiding in Dave. "Do you think we'll be able to avoid, you know, real fighting over all this?"

"Yeah, nobody wants that. Nobody," Dave said trying to assure Rick.

He was wrong.

SEVENTY

Captain Paul Jennings emerged from the turret of his M1 Abrams tank into the fresh evening air. The temperature had dropped considerably since his battalion rolled north out of Fort Benning. But things were about to heat up considerably.

Jennings plugged his headset into the tank's secure communication equipment and contacted General Brady's office.

"Sir, phase one of Operation Longbow is complete. My platoon is in position approximately one klick south of the Georgia National Guard base. We are under cover at the moment at the crest of hill number 7-A. We can see two battalions of older Abrams on the firing range below supported by a platoon of Bradley Fighting Vehicles. Shall we commence phase two?"

"Captain, you may commence phase two. And good luck," Brady replied.

After acknowledging Brady's order, Jennings disappeared back into his own tank and closed the overhead access hatch. Once in his seat, Jennings got on the command network that allowed him to communicate with every tank at once.

"Commander to all tanks. Prepare to fire on your designated targets on my order with HE rounds only. I expect accuracy. If vehicles or personnel appear within your kill zone, hold your fire and report. We just want to make them mad gentlemen, not kill anyone."

A moment later, all tanks reported ready.

"Fire!"

Almost simultaneously, fire erupted from the 105mm barrels of five Abrams tanks, the four members of Jennings's first platoon and his own command vehicle.

Jennings watched as the rounds flashed across the open space in front of him and impacted open ground surrounding the National Guardsmen.

Chaos erupted as the surprised Guardsmen tried to determine what had just happened. Jennings could only imagine the scope of confusion he had just created.

While the Guardsmen tried to come to grips with the fact they had were under attack, Jennings ordered a second salvo. Geysers of dirt, thrown high into the air by the high explosive shells, fell back to earth spattering the 'enemy' tanks with red Georgia clay.

Finally, Jennings could see the Guard organizing themselves and forming into a ragged echelon formation. The Guard could only roughly determine the origin of the incoming rounds but were at least beginning to react. Jennings needed to draw their attention.

Jennings ordered two of his tanks into the open while the entire platoon sent a third group of rounds into the midst of the Guardsmen's tanks.

So far, the placement of the HE shells by his men had been perfect. While the shots impacted close to the other tanks and BFVs, none had caused any significant damage. The intent behind Operation Longbow included drawing the Guardsmen out of their base and pursuing Jennings's battalion back toward Fort Benning. Neither General Brady nor Captain Jennings wanted to engage in an actual battle between American servicemen. They just wanted it to look that way.

But they didn't anticipate the professionalism and ferocity of the Georgia National Guard's response.

After some initial confusion, Jennings could see that whoever was in command knew his business. Several tanks had moved toward a flanking position to Jennings's right, while the main group of almost fifteen tanks and four BFVs had tightened their formation and swung their turrets in his direction. Jennings began to fear General Brady had underestimated these weekend warriors.

"Alright, Platoon, we've shaken the hornets' nest. Retreat as planned. Repeat, retreat as planned," Jennings ordered.

As Jennings's five tanks backed away from their firing positions, the first rounds from the Guardsmen hit the ground they had just vacated.

Close. Way too close. Jennings thought.

"Jennings to all tanks. Retreat at flank speed. These boys mean business and there's a hell of a lot more of them. Move out!"

But in less than ten minutes, Jennings would face a threat more deadly than National Guard armor.

SEVENTY-ONE

Margie Franks slammed down her telephone nearly breaking the hard plastic handset.

"Where is General Brady?" she yelled through her open office door.

Almost immediately, one of her aides appeared and informed her Brady was in his office just down the corridor.

"Shall I ask the general to come see you?" the aide asked, with some trepidation.

"No. I'll find that sonofabitch myself," Franks replied, marching out of her office and turning down the hall.

Every head in Franks' outer office turned to watch her leave, thankful they were not her target.

Entering Brady's office, several staff members jumped to their feet. Franks didn't acknowledge their presence before crashing through the general's private office door.

"Madam President," Brady said, pulling himself out of his tufted-leather office chair. "How may I be of service?"

Franks was in no mood for Brady's insincere charm.

"What the hell have you done? Are you trying to start a war, you idiot?" Franks screamed as she leaned across Brady's desk.

"You are referring to the situation in Georgia, I believe. I was just on my way to brief you," Brady replied, smoothly.

"You're damn right that's what I'm here about. I just got off the telephone with Mallory. Apparently, some of your men have attacked the Georgia National Guard base south of Atlanta. Are you insane?"

Brady walked deliberately to a side wall and turned on a screen displaying a map of Georgia.

"I deployed several units from Fort Benning north to a point near LaGrange. Several units of mobile infantry had moved south toward our forces with the intention of securing Benning. I issued the orders to block the move on my own authority," Brady explained.

"You initiated *combat,* is what you did! Without my authority!" Franks blurted.

"They attacked us. I had no choice," Brady responded.

"Bullshit. Mallory has clear satellite imagery of your tanks leaving Benning. I've seen it. They set themselves up on a hill and shelled a National Guard base. You should know that their satellites can see the tits on a squirrel and there wasn't so much as a firecracker shot off by the Guard before your attack. Those are our own people dammit!"

Brady remained unphased. "Ridiculous. Why would I order such an attack?"

"You want my job. You think if you can make yourself out to be some kind of hero, you'll be elected when the FSA holds its first elections," Franks replied, standing up straight and staring the general in the eye.

Brady leaned over his desk and sneered in Margie's face. "Even if that were true, it doesn't matter. The facts on the ground are this: we have engaged forces of a hostile nation – the United States of America. They have launched an airstrike that will be over our forces in nine minutes."

Margie took a step backward.

"Yes, I know. The president informed me she had ordered an airstrike in response and told me in no uncertain terms what was about to happen to our men. And now you want the Revolution I to come and save the day, repel the airstrike. Am I right?" Franks said, feigning some resignation to Brady's plan.

"It's simple. You order the Revolution I to respond in defense of FSA forces or they die. A-10 Warthogs are deadly tank-killers. Yes, I'll be the hero for stopping an attack, but you'll certainly be railroaded from office if you let our boys be killed," Brady explained with a maniacal grin.

Franks gave Brady a broad smile and in one smooth motion, pulled her Smith & Wesson .38 caliber snub-nosed revolver from her waistband and shot General Sean Brady between the eyes.

Blood and gore exploded from the back of Brady's crew-cut, splattering framed pictures and military awards with his own treacherous blood.

Franks walked around the desk, calmly removed Brady's .45 caliber automatic from its holster and tossed it by his side.

A second later, stunned security guards burst into the room to find the President of the Federated States of America holding a pistol and standing over the body of the new country's top general.

"General Brady tried to kill me. Get his stinking carcass out of my capitol," Franks ordered, calmly walking out of the room.

As she entered her own office, Franks barked, "Get Knox on the phone. Now! I need the Revolution in the air immediately."

Having heard the gunshot and seen the revolver still in Franks' hand, her staff moved very quickly indeed.

SEVENTY-TWO

Agents Deal and Sims, with Bubba in tow, made their way toward the old hanger suspected of housing the gravity wave aircraft. Its extensive security measures had slowed their progress considerably. Using high-tech detection equipment, they managed to avoid being discovered. But, as they approached the target, the density of security measures increased.

Deal raised his hand to call yet another halt. "Infrared and two motion detectors ahead. Take a break while I move west and try to find a way through," he whispered.

"I'm fine with that," Bubba said quietly sitting down in the vacant lot's weeds. "I'm sweatin' like a stuck pig."

"We're close," Sims said, handing Bubba a bottle of water. "I can make out the building, but that's about it. Maybe we should have just set up surveillance and called in a chopper when it appeared."

"Good thought," Bubba said. "But by the time a chopper got into the area, it would be too late. From what I've seen, that thing can pop into the air like Fourth of July fireworks, and nobody even has to light a fuse."

"Yeah, I suppose you're right," Sims said, still standing and looking toward the building. "But I can't see how ... hold on! Bubba look! I think the doors must be opening! I see some faint light coming out!"

Bubba stood. "Yep, what do we do? I'd bet my daddy's truck they're going to roll it out."

Sims radioed Deal, "Sir, we think the craft is being deployed. If so, what are your orders?"

"Take your shot, agent. It's our only choice."

"Acknowledged. Out," Sims said. "Bubba, how far away are we?"

"Too far. Way too far," Bubba replied. "At least five hundred yards. Probably more."

Sims drew her weapon and made sure the laser sight was ready. "Agent Deal said to take the shot."

"Well alright, Annie Oakley," Bubba quipped. "Aim for the big holes in the wings. Otherwise, just go for center mass."

"Understood. On the ground or in the air?" Sims asked.

"As it lifts off. You'll see the result if you get a hit. If you do, keep the laser on that point. Yep, I see movement on the ground." Bubba exclaimed. "Here it comes!"

"I see it too. Barely."

"As soon as it moves upward, I'll put my laser on it." Sims replied, sighting her gun on the object and holding her breath to steady her aim. She didn't have to hold it very long.

Focused on her target, everything else disappeared. She had one shot. Like a kicker trying to win a big game in the last second with a fifty-yarder, she knew her chances were slim. But she had won every FBI commendation available for marksmanship, so she knew she had a chance.

When she saw the craft move slowly into the air, she fired.

A faint bubble of pink light briefly surrounded the craft just before the plane disappeared straight up and out of sight.

She missed.

"Sir, the aircraft is gone. Shot missed. Repeat, shot missed. Sorry, sir," Sims said into her mic.

"Acknowledged, Sims. Good try. All teams, all teams, we're going to plan B. Take the building. I want everyone in there alive. No shooting unless absolutely necessary. Assault in sixty seconds from...now! Sims, stay with the kid until we have secured the objective. Then bring him in," Deal ordered.

"You didn't miss, Agent Sims," Bubba said. "Like I was saying, atmospheric conditions blocked most of the beam. But did you see that little blink of light just after you shot?"

"Yeah, I thought I saw something, but I wasn't sure. What was that?" Sims said.

"That, Ms. FBI Agent, was proof positive you made the shot. If we could have gotten closer, the laser would have spread around the plane, completely blinding the pilot."

Sims felt better knowing she had done everything possible to ground the gravity wave craft. But her nerves frayed at the thought of where it was headed now.

SEVENTY-THREE

Just minutes later, the Revolution I flew in a slow circle around the periphery of the tank battle taking place below. High tech surveillance gear painted a picture of the battlespace, designating FSA and Guard forces with blue and red triangles. While the blue Guard units outnumbered the red FSA forces two to one, the FSA tanks were moving away quickly under covering fire.

"Margie? Where's General Brady? I need to know how to handle this," Dave asked over secure coms. "How did FSA forces end up in LaGrange, Georgia?"

"I've relieved Brady. Permanently. I'm in charge. Put the fear of God in the Guard so they don't try anything stupid. Then provide cover while we pull our men out. The A-10 counter-attack is two minutes away. We have to get out of this shit, and now! Once that's done, head toward Washington, D.C. in case Mallory gets any cute ideas."

"Roger that, out," Dave said looking over at Zafran in the pilot's seat. As usual, Zafran could have been on his daily commute to work with as much emotion as he showed on his face.

"You heard all that, Daniel. You're the pilot. How do we do this?" Dave asked.

Zafran answered immediately. "We have no choice but to neutralize the A-10 force approaching from the northeast. I have seen these aircraft in action. If they engage your tanks, you will lose them all. We will block their flightpath, but fire only if we have no alternative. Agreed?"

Zafran had been analyzing the situation from the beginning of the mission. His faith in the FSA's ability to actually succeed with forming a new country evaporated in the firefight raging below. The decision to reach into U.S. territory militarily didn't make sense. It revealed a profound lack of control by the FSA leadership. But his country's agreement with the FSA included Israel receiving one of these magnificent crafts, and the technology behind them. Israel critically needed a gravity-wave craft and a simple plan immediately came to mind. He controlled the aircraft; and, the intellect that best understood the technology sat in the seat next to him. He would do what was necessary.

But first, he would resolve the situation below. Escalation of this conflict would not be in Israel's best interest.

Zafran pulled the Revolution I into a steep climb and then plunged down and through the formation of deadly A-10s at supersonic speeds. The Marine pilots had no choice but to ride out the shock wave that threatened to smash them into each other. After barely recovering control, the Marines were confronted with a sight they would never forget.

The massive black aircraft seemed to materialized in front of their formation – flying backward! The lead A-10 pilot could see Zafran and Knox through the Revolution I's windscreen. Later, one of the pilots swore the black craft tilted its nose slightly skyward, revealing a massive load of air-to-air missiles. They had no choice but to turn away and await further orders.

As the A-10's disappeared, Zafran slowed and dropped the Revolution I to treetop level, giving Dave a chance to launch three Maverick missiles at the ground in front of the Guard units. The resulting wall of fire, combined with the black aircraft's terrifying presence were more than enough to dissuade any further pursuit of the FSA troops.

"Make your heading zero-seven-zero," Dave ordered. "We're going back to Washington."

SEVENTY-FOUR

Washington, D.C.

In the Situation Room, FBI Director Glover put down his telephone. The report from Deal wasn't good.

"Madam President," the director said, interrupting a discussion she was having with her chief of staff.

"Yes, Director Glover. Go ahead," the president responded.

The room quieted.

"My agents on site report that the Revolution aircraft was deployed from its base in Mobile, uh, three-and-a-half minutes ago, Ma'am," the director reported looking at his watch.

"Dammit! General, what's the latest from Georgia?" the president asked.

"It looks like the Georgia National Guard is in trouble. The FSA's surprise attack caught the lightly-defended base by complete surprise. Per your orders, we have Marine A-10s overhead, but they are sitting ducks to that damned gravity wave plane, Madam President," the general reported succinctly.

"Alright, gentlemen. Operation Witchcraft is authorized. You may launch, Admiral," the president said.

The evening before, the joint chiefs recommended Operation Witchcraft as a response to the FSA using the Revolution I for military purposes. The operation depended upon two key elements: the willingness to fire on Americans on American soil, and the immediate ability to communicate with available FSA leadership. The plan called for launching a non-nuclear air-to-surface missile at the capitol building in Austin. If Franks withdrew the Revolution I, the missile could be aborted long before impact. Mallory didn't relish playing such a deadly game of brinkmanship, but a real and imminent threat was the only counter-play she had given the Revolution I's astounding capabilities.

Twenty miles off the coast of Texas, flames erupted from under the wings of an X-47B stealth pilotless aircraft, armed to the teeth with one air-launched cruise missile or ALCM. Part of the Navy's Unmanned Carrier-Launched Airborne Surveillance and Strike (UCLASS) program, the X-47B gave the Navy deep surveillance and strike capability without risking the lives of on-board crew. The remote-controlled craft could easily enter enemy airspace and attack without warning.

As the strange robotic aircraft gathered power for launch, it squatted deeply into its landing gear, like a sprinter coiling his muscles in the starting blocks.

In a darkened space far below the decks of the cruiser Toledo, Lieutenant Calvin Baker pressed a button labeled "Launch." Instantaneously, the X-47B catapulted into the night sky, only its twin blue jet exhausts marking its position - until even those disappeared into the distance.

"Time to target, fourteen minutes," Lieutenant Baker reported. Baker had no idea how he found himself piloting a warplane against an American target. He figured it must have something to do with the crazy announcement that several states seceded or rebelled or whatever. But he had to set his personal thoughts aside. He was a naval aviator on a mission ordered by his Commander-In-Chief. It wasn't his job to ask questions.

If ordered to fire, he would – without question. *But damn!*

SEVENTY-FIVE

Mobile, Alabama

Agents Deal and Sims stood in the secret hangar, looking around in disbelief. Nobody would guess that the dingy, run-down old building at the end of a runway actually contained a sparklingly clean, even antiseptic interior, and ultra-modern equipment of every sort.

The FBI's assault on the building lasted only minutes. Deal's team found and disarmed FSA security forces both outside and inside the building. Scientists and technicians wearing white lab coats gave up without resistance and were herded into a corner.

Best of all, the long hunt for Rick Donnelly ended when he simply identified himself voluntarily, stepping gingerly out of the gathered techno-nerds with his hands comically high above his head.

A hurried search of the facility unearthed an incredibly large cache of missiles, bombs, and other weaponry. Most of the high-tech air-to-air and air-to-ground ordnance bore Chinese, Russian, and French markings. But the collection's crown jewels were three immense Exocet missiles. And it didn't take a rocket scientist to recognize the yellow and black nuclear warning labels on two of the three.

Deal wasted no time dragging Rick Donnelly into the armory.

Once inside, he dismissed everyone else from the room and ordered the door closed. Handcuffs restrained Rick's hands, which shook uncontrollably behind his back. Without introducing himself or producing his FBI identification, Deal shoved Rick down into a kneeling position and pressed the barrel of his pistol against the side of the scientist's head.

"I'm going to ask each question once," Deal said, menacingly. "I will execute you here and now as a traitor if you fail to answer any question immediately and honestly. Do we understand each other?"

Rick's entire body twitched and quivered. Sweat rolled off his nose, splashing on the polished concrete floor.

"Ya...ya...ya...yes," Rick replied.

"Good. Are these the only nuclear weapons at this facility?" Deal asked pressing his gun a bit deeper into his captive's scalp.

"Yes, yes, uh, yes, sir!" Donnelly stammered.

"Is the gravity-wave plane armed with an Exocet?"

"Yes...uh...yes, sir. One."

"Is there a nuclear warhead on board?"

"No. No, sir. Only two nukes. Those," Donnelly said, looking across the room. "Uh, the two with yellow noses."

"Where's the plane now?" Deal asked.

"Ordered, uh, President Franks...uh...to Georgia somewhere to stop, like, fighting between US and FSA...that's all I know about that! I swear!" Rick said, his body shaking so hard he had trouble staying upright on his knees.

"Where's Dr. David Knox?"

"On the Revolution I."

"What is the mission's target? Why would they load an Exocet to interdict a land battle?" Deal demanded, walking around to stand directly in front of Rick and pressing the gun to his forehead.

"I...I asked Dave, uh, Dr. Knox the same question. He...he said they might as well take it along. Weight doesn't matter," Donnelly tried to explain.

"Bullshit! Too bad, I thought you were going to survive this for a second there," Deal said, making a show of jacking a round into the chamber of his pistol.

"I swear! I swear! If I knew I'd tell. Please...please, sir! If I knew... God! Please!" Rick pleaded pitifully, his head slowly lowering toward the floor. Tears now mixing with the puddle of sweat.

"Is the Revolution I the only gravity wave aircraft you have now?" Deal asked, intentionally sounding less threatening.

"No. No, sir. We...we have three more. One of those is ready for flight tests. The other two are still being assembled," Rick replied, his head still resting on the floor.

"Get up!" Deal demanded, pulling Donnelly up to his feet.

"Manufacturing is done at the annex to the airliner manufacturing facility at the north end of the runway. Revolution II was going to be moved down here today," Rick offered without hesitation.

Deal made a show of taking his pistol away from Donnelly's head and replacing it in his holster.

"Keep cooperating and you might, *might,* live through this. Lie once and I'll splatter your skull against the nearest wall. I'd like that. You've been a pain in my ass far too long. Understood?" Deal said, staring Rick in the face.

"Yes, sir."

Deal meant every word.

SEVENTY-SIX

As soon as he got the chance, Bubba began exploring the hangar. This place was nothing less than heaven on earth to a genius aerospace engineering student.

While Deal interrogated Rick Donnelly, Sims took the opportunity to pick Bubba's brain.

"What do you think?" Sims asked.

"I think I'll just hang out here for the rest of my life! Ridiculous hardware loaded with the best engineering-design software money can buy! High speed, advanced milling. Metallurgical and chemical analysis stations – all top of the line! Aerospace and space-ready instrumentation – all new and still in their boxes. And, best of all, what appear to be prototype gravity wave generators!" Bubba exclaimed.

"It's actually better than that, Bubba," Deal said, walking up on the discussion.

"I sure don't think so, boss. Not unless I got my hands directly on the gravity wave plane itself. Yeah! I'd like that," Bubba answered wistfully.

"If everything goes to plan, I'll have the second plane here for you in about twenty minutes. No way to get anyone else here quick enough, so I'm going to have to rely on you to give us an initial rundown on its capabilities, how it works, and anything else you can think of," Deal said seriously.

Bubba's eyes opened wide. "Excuse me a moment," he said, before running out one of the side-entrance doors and closing it behind him.

A moment later Deal and Sims clearly heard "Wooooohooooooo!" from the other side of the door.

Bubba calmly walked back in and said, "Sorry, Boss. I'd be quite pleased to be of assistance."

"For now, go check out the armory. That should give you some idea about its capabilities," Deal said.

Bubba found the armory at the rear of the massive hangar. Once inside the enclosed space dedicated to storing weapons, the Exocet missiles drew Bubba's attention immediately. As a student of everything aeronautical, he recognized the extremely powerful weapons immediately. His interest sharpened when he noted the nuclear warnings and yellow nose cones on two of the three.

After a brief overview of the other ordnance in the room, none of which excited him too much, Bubba turned back to the Exocets. He knew the sleek, powerful weapon was generally intended to sink ships - and had been used to do so in the past. Originally designed decades ago, Bubba recognized these as the latest model, the AM-39.

Bubba's technical mind demanded more information about the nuclear aspects of the Exocet's construction, including the amount of shielding necessary to contain any radiation emanating from the core. Bubba looked around for a few moments, finally grabbing the Geiger Counter he knew would be nearby.

Running the instrument across the warheads one by one, Bubba noted the ionizing radiation coming from each warhead. His results didn't make sense, so he ran them again.

"Awe, hell!" Bubba exclaimed. "Agent Deal! Agent Sims! Y'all need to come on back in here!"

When the agents arrived, they found Bubba sitting atop one of the nuclear-armed Exocets like he was riding a horse, closely examining something on the nose cone.

"What the hell are you doing?" Deal demanded.

Bubba held up one finger while he quickly finished his inspection.

"Well, folks," Bubba said looking up and pointing to his right at the only white-nosed Exocet. "This one here is not nuclear. I confirmed it with this." Bubba held up the Geiger Counter.

"Yeah, so? We know that already," Deal countered.

Touching the yellow nose of the missile to his left, Bubba said, "This one here is nuclear."

"Bubba!"

"Now for my big announcement," Bubba said, patting the yellow nose of the weapon he was sitting on. "This one here is supposed to be nuclear, *but it's not*. Someone has opened it up and taken the warhead out."

"Where is it, then?" Sims asked, her stomach turning to ice.

"Where indeed?" Bubba said simply.

Deal's face turned red. Without a word, he turned and ran out of the room.

A moment later the FBI agent had Rick pinned against the wall of the small kitchen where he was being kept under guard.

"One nuke is missing. Where is it?" Deal demanded.

"What? No! There were only two! I checked before Dave took off. He had one of the conventional ones!" Rick answered, once again terrified.

"No. A warhead was taken from one of the yellow missiles! And it's not here!" Deal shouted, slamming Rick against the wall.

"Someone switched warheads! That's the only explanation," Rick pleaded.

"Who could do that? Who had both access to the weapon and the ability to do something like that?" Deal demanded.

"Only me and Dave. I didn't...I wouldn't! I hate those things. I made sure...but...but... I didn't look inside before it was loaded. Why would I do that?" Rick explained quickly.

"How can I know you're telling the truth, scumbag? Give me a reason not to break your neck right here and now!"

Deal's fist encircled Rick's neck.

Rick thought quickly. "Let me talk to him. Dave. You can listen."

"Do it," Deal said, throwing Rick toward the door.

Rubbing his bruised throat, Rick walked out to the communications console and sat down. Deal stood behind him.

"One wrong word and you're dead," Deal hissed into his ear.

Rick nodded and made contact.

"Hey, Ricky! Man, you should have seen our baby perform! Completely shut down a whole freaking battle in like two minutes flat! What's up?" Dave Knox said over the radio.

"Dave, we have a situation here. One of the nuclear warheads is missing. One of the techs ran a routine radiation check. Someone definitely removed the warhead from an AM-39," Rick croaked through his damaged throat.

"You okay? Sounds like you're choking. Well, listen. Sorry, Buddy. I thought it best you didn't know. Orders. Everything's cool," Dave said, in his usual lighthearted banter.

"Are you insane?" Rick blurted. "Please bring it back! You know as well as anyone what using it could lead to."

"No can do, Ricky! But don't worry. It's just a precaution Margie ordered. See you soon! Out."

Rick turned to Deal and shrugged. "I'm sorry. I had no idea."

Deal turned away, pulled out his phone, and reported to Washington that the Revolution I was confirmed to be deployed and armed with a nuclear warhead. And that he had no information concerning the plane's location or whether the Directors intended to use the nuke or not.

Not! Please, God! Not!

SEVENTY-SEVEN

Deal found Sims and Bubba still examining the various weapons in the armory.

"We have a problem that needs an immediate answer. Donnelly spoke with Dave Knox on the Revolution I. Knox didn't know we captured this facility. He confirmed that the Exocet is on board and packing the nuke. We don't know if there's a plan to use it or not," Deal explained solemnly.

"Uh, that's crazy, dude! What would they gain by popping a nuke? That's just stupid," Bubba declared.

"Motives aside, gentlemen, the question is what *can* anyone do about it? From what we have discovered, nothing can catch the Revolution I. Bubba's idea with the laser doesn't stand a chance unless we get close," Agent Sims observed.

"You are both correct and incorrect," Bubba responded. "Yes, we have to get close enough to the actual craft to have a chance at disabling it with the laser. I can't see that working while it's in active flight. But there is something that could catch the Revolution I. The other gravity wave aircraft," Bubba said.

Agent Deal uncharacteristically grinned and plucked a small radio from his belt. Not moving his gaze from Bubba and Sims, Deal pushed the "talk" button and said, "Bring her in."

The hangar doors opened slowly revealing the pointed nose of a second gravity wave aircraft. Bubba and Sims stared as the monstrous black plane came toward them, growing to fill the previously empty building.

"Well, I'll be damned! Good timing, boss!" Bubba said slapping Deal on the back.

"You can say that again," Sims added.

SEVENTY-EIGHT

Deal and Sims looked on as Bubba walked slowly around the entire craft, spending a few minutes examining the gravity wave reflectors in each wing. He ran his hand over the skin of the craft, opened avionics access hatches, and peered into the gravity wave generator's compartment. Finally, Bubba opened the crew access door and disappeared inside.

After several minutes, Bubba's upside-down grinning face appeared out of the same opening.

"I seen two-headed snakes, a fat woman ridin' a sway-backed pig, and my grandpa kick a bull in the nuts, but I ain't never seen nothin' this cool! Come on!" Bubba exclaimed just before his head disappeared once more.

Deal looked at Sims. "Go on. I'll update Washington."

"Yes, sir!" Sims said enthusiastically.

Sims walked quickly under the plane, climbed the crew-entry ladder, and found herself in a tight corridor behind the cockpit.

The no-nonsense interior reminded her of several other military and FBI airplanes she had flown in over the years. No comfort. All business.

Bubba sat in the pilot's seat, pouring over what looked to be a flight manual and checklist. He didn't notice Sims maneuver herself into the co-pilot's seat next to him.

Sims had no flight training but was surprised to find only a few instruments. A simple display showed an outline of the triangular craft both from the top and the side. Another showed their position on a map, much like the GPS in her car. A digital display marked "MACH" showed double zeros and she found a joystick where her right hand rested to the side.

"This is it?" Sims asked.

When Bubba didn't respond, she touched his shoulder. "Bubba?"

Bubba had to pull his eyes away from the flight manual. "Yeah? Oh, hey there, good-looking. I didn't see you come in. Cool, right?"

"God, Bubba. You understand this stuff? And you shouldn't refer to me as 'good looking'," Sims replied.

"Why not? Ain't a lie if it's true. And, yeah, this is as easy to fly as a video-game," Bubba said absently, his attention already back on the manual.

Sims blushed just a bit at Bubba's compliment, even if it seemed a little offhand.

"So, you're saying you can actually *fly* this thing?" Sims asked.

Without looking up from the manual, Bubba replied, "Oh, yeah. No problem at all. Pilots of conventional aircraft have to deal with a host of delicate interactions between the air, the ground, and their aircraft. With gravity waves, it's just a matter of telling it what to do. A ten-year-old could do it. I'm just reading up on the fuel. That's where the magic really comes from. And we're in luck. We have a full tank – so to speak."

At that moment, Deal pulled himself into the cabin. "Did I hear right? You can fly this? Now?"

"Yeah, boss. Open the doors, push me out, and it's up, up and away!" Bubba said swooshing his hand up like an airplane taking off.

"Can you catch the Revolution?"

"No problem there. But we have to know where to look," Bubba replied.

Deal frowned. He didn't like what he was about to do, but he didn't have a choice

"Get in the air. Head toward Washington, D.C. If they launch that nuke, Washington will be their target. I'll get you more information as it comes in," Deal ordered.

"Oh man! You got it, boss!" Bubba crowed.

"I need to stay here and coordinate," Deal said, turning to leave.

"What about me?" Sims asked.

"Looks like you're in the co-pilot's seat. So, you know, co-pilot," Deal replied without looking around.

"Alright, good-looking. Let's go hunting!" Bubba said, beaming a wide grin at his surprised co-pilot.

Sims looked back wide-eyed. "Oh, crap."

SEVENTY-NINE

Austin, Texas

"Madam President, we just intercepted a communication that the U.S. has launched a missile at us!" Governor G. Hunt Smith of Alabama blurted as he burst into Margie Frank's office.

"What? Calm down, Smith! What are you trying to say?" Franks replied, getting up from her desk.

"They've shot a damn missile. It's aimed at us! We have to get out of here!" Smith stammered.

Franks had been awake for over thirty hours, and her normally perfect haircut was a little disheveled. She had been managing all parts of the secession plan and now, due to General Brady's treachery, she also bore the burden of cleaning up the mess he created in Georgia. And now this?

"Goddamnit, Smith! If that's all you can tell me without crapping your diaper, get your ass outta my office!" Franks shouted, physically shoving Smith through the door. She didn't have time or patience to handhold a coward.

"Mr. Snow! Get in here and tell me what's going on," Franks ordered, as Smith disappeared.

Snow had been invaluable to Franks leading up to the secession and she knew he would have accurate information.

Appearing immediately, Snow reported. "We have one inbound cruise missile, fired from what must have been a stealth aircraft. Tracking began two minutes ago and shows an impact point on this building. I recommend immediate evacuation and response."

"How long do we have?" Franks asked.

"Approximately twelve minutes, Madam President. Your orders?" Snow responded.

"Evacuate the building and surrounding two blocks. Say it's a terrorist threat. Get my chopper on the roof ready to lift off. Then get back here," Franks barked. "And get me the Revolution I. I want to talk to Dr. Knox."

A moment later, Franks' private phone rang.

"Margie! Your wish is my command, my dear president!" Dave said.

"Shut up and listen, you jackass," Franks replied. "That goddamned bitch Mallory has launched a cruise missile at us! At me! Personally! I'm about to get on a chopper. She wants to bring down *my* house? I'll bring down her city!"

"Are you seriously giving me the launch command? Margie, don't be rash here. We blow Washington away, the country and maybe the whole world goes to shit. You *know* that!" Dave pleaded.

"They nuke us. We nuke them. That's how all this works. Yep, the *United States* will end up in ruins. But guess who is going to be around to pick up the pieces? Us. The Cause. And more important my brilliant friend – you and me! Do it. Do it now and we win. You win. We have a contingency plan for this scenario. Believe me, we'll come out on top," Margie said calmly.

Franks didn't reveal that the incoming missile wasn't nuclear at all.

"So, I'll be a Director?" Knox wanted assurance his near lifelong dream would come true. The Directors held all the power and Dave wanted in.

"Yes. You can have General Brady's chair," Franks said, glancing at the clock. She needed to convince Dave to act.

"It's empty?" Dave asked.

"Yes, his chair became vacant when I put a bullet in his head. If you want to sit down in it – *pull that damn trigger!*"

Inside the Revolution I, Dr. David Knox, hyper-intelligent aerospace engineer and theorist, child of two public school teachers from Georgia, son of the South, and supreme egotist, flipped up the cover protecting a small red button mounted on the joystick to his right.

And pushed it.

The pilot, Daniel Zafran, didn't have time to react before the Exocet fell from the Revolution I's fuselage and passed through the gravity wave field. Zafran watched in horror as the Exocet's rocket motor ignited, propelling the missile to its pre-programmed path. The shocked Israeli pilot never thought he would witness the beginning of a nuclear war.

"What have you done?" Zafran shouted. "Why did you release that weapon?"

"Just a small retaliation for a similar missile launched at our government by the U.S. My people will enter the self-destruct code if the U.S. President does the same. No worries my friend," Knox lied.

"Then, may we return to your home base in Mobile?" Zafran asked, placing his left hand on the grip of his 9mm pistol. He had no intention of returning the marvelous aircraft to the FSA even if Dave gave the order.

"No, Daniel. We shall fulfill my people's promise to yours right now. Let's take our craft to *your* home base in Israel. We'll call it an incentive for your country announcing its formal recognition of the FSA today!" Dave replied. "Does that meet with your approval?"

Zafran looked at Knox. The pilot's usual strict adherence to protocol making him question the motive for Dave's seemingly ad hoc decision. But Dave's pronouncement also just simplified his mission exponentially. Before that moment, Zafran fully intended to shoot Dave if necessary and return to Israel anyway.

Zafran shrugged. "Let us go then. With this magnificent aircraft in our hands, Israel shall never have to fear again."

As the Revolution I made a ninety-degree turn and flashed out over the Atlantic, Dave turned to take a last glance at the U.S. coastline.

Israel may be dangerous. But it will be far safer than the United States in just a few minutes.

EIGHTY

Washington, D.C.

"Alright, get Margie Franks on the phone," the President of the United States ordered from the Situation Room.

"Ringing, Ma'am," the Navy signals officer in charge of communications said a moment later.

Through the speakerphone resting near the center of the conference room table, the assembled crisis team listened as the other end of the line rang. After five rings the president looked up.

"Do we have the correct number, sailor?" the president asked with a grin. A few tense chuckles followed.

"Yes, Ma'am," the Navy ensign replied, looking at his screen just to be sure.

They waited.

Ten rings. Fifteen. Twenty.

"I'm sorry, Ma'am. No answer," the now concerned young ensign said, looking back at his screen.

The president looked around the room but found only blank faces looking back.

Suddenly, the lights in the room all turned red and a quiet, but urgent, alarm began to sound.

Before the president could even ask its meaning, she was bodily yanked from her chair and lifted clear of the floor by three extremely large Secret Service agents, who ran with her from the room.

Too startled at first to object, it took several seconds for her to react. "What the hell is going on?"

The lead agent of her personal protection team grabbed her feet. "We have an imminent nuclear attack inbound. Continuity of Government protocols."

"COG?" the president gasped. "Put me down!"

The only response was a curt, "No, Ma'am."

If anything, the three agents carrying her one hundred and thirty pounds ran even faster.

At that moment, The President of the United States had no control or power whatsoever. The one and only duty of the secret service was to get her, and her family if possible, out of Washington and onboard Air Force One.

Outside, the agents sprinted across the South Lawn, up the three steps into the waiting Marine Corps helicopter and dumped her unceremoniously into a seat. The three agents jumped out of the aircraft and slammed the door. The pilot yanked up on the collective and applied full power, sending the aircraft leaping into the sky.

A crewmember fastened the president into her seatbelt. "Three minutes to Andrews Ma'am."

"My husband?" the president asked getting her feet back under her literally for the first time in the past several minutes.

The young marine in dress blues spoke into his microphone then turned back to the president.

"One minute behind us."

"Dear God."

In Austin, Texas, nobody heard the ringing telephone on President Margie Franks' abandoned desk.

EIGHTY-ONE

It took several minutes for Sims to get over the profound disorientation of gravity-wave travel and several more to overcome her intense fear that Bubba wouldn't be able to fly the strange craft. But her confidence in Bubba's ability grew with each passing moment.

After being pushed out of the hangar, Bubba tentatively brought them up to one hundred feet and slowly maneuvered the craft in several directions to get a feel for the controls. Marveling at the ease of operation and the craft's incredible capabilities, he insisted on using the call-sign "Hot Dog."

"You okay over there, Bombshell?" Bubba asked.

Sims didn't react to the almost objectionable nickname. She was trying to get used to the view out the window and align it with her senses – which demanded that they weren't moving at all.

Bubba contacted Deal on the radio. "This is Hot Dog Adcock to the boss. I got this thing in hand and have set course for D.C. My co-pilot Bombshell Sims is a little green right now, but improving quickly. Anything new on our situation?"

"Dammit, Bubba...!" Deal began, but cut himself off. He had to get this kid moving. "Okay. Alright. Hot Dog. Yes, how long to Washington?"

"I've got us at Mach 4.3 and climbing. We're over Virginia now. Two minutes to Washington," Bubba replied.

"Okay, listen, son. This is critical. We have confirmation they launched the Exocet. Repeat, the Exocet has been launched and is headed toward Washington. We have no information on the location of the Revolution I. Bubba. Sims. You two have to stop it."

Bubba flipped on the tracking radar. The news wasn't good.

"Boss, I have it on radar. It's bad. The missile is thirty seconds from impact. I, I just don't know if we have time," Bubba responded, pushing aside the fire erupting in his guts.

"Bubba, we have to try," Sims said. "Go!"

Bubba's mind went into hyper-drive calculating the relative speed and closing rate of the two supersonic objects. He immediately recognized the best intercept point would be directly over the city. Bubba pushed the control stick forward and down accelerating the aircraft to unbelievable speed, leveling off at just two thousand feet above the ground.

Sims sat motionless and silent, allowing the genius in the pilot seat to work.

"Boss, it's Hot Dog, we'll have one chance and it's going to be tight."

Sweat dripped down the side of Bubba's face, while his hands deftly worked the control stick making continuous minute adjustments to speed and course.

Sims could see their track on the computer screen - two lines were coming together quickly. The Exocet approached from the southeast while they charged ahead from due west. The intercept point would be directly above the Smithsonian Air and Space Museum.

In the last few seconds, Sims wondered if she was actually about to die.

The Exocet screamed over the rooftops of the Virginia suburbs causing sonic booms that shattered windows and set off car alarms for miles around. The missile's computer brain worked to place its warhead two thousand feet over the Washington Mall. When the weapon arrived at the precise location, it would unleash a fireball hotter than the sun itself and a mile wide.

Washington D.C. would cease to exist. But the damage to the country and the effect on the rest of the world would be even worse.

It happened in an instant.

Sims caught a brief glimpse of the gleaming white monuments and buildings of Washington. Then, as if by magic, a large, white missile just appeared in front of her as if stuck in mid-air a few feet in front of the cockpit window!

The gravity waves that both propelled the craft and protected it from missiles, bullets or anything else, had reacted just as Bubba predicted. Like the much smaller missile fired by White House security earlier, the gravity waves ensnared the Exocet before it reached its preprogrammed detonation point. When the missile's brain detected it was off its intended course, it automatically disarmed the nuclear warhead.

"Yeah, Baby! Yeah!" Bubba hollered as he slowed the craft back to cruising speed. "Caught that son-of-a-bitch! Ha! Stuck like glue, baby!"

"You did it! You did it! Oh my God!" Sims said impulsively leaping from her seat and hugging Bubba around the neck.

"*We* did it, Bombshell!" Bubba said, pulling Sims into his lap and planting a kiss on her cheek.

"This is Hot Dog! We got it! We got it. No impact. Repeat, no impact! Returning to base, boss!" Bubba shouted into the microphone before kissing Sims again – this time right on the mouth.

Sims didn't resist but untangled herself afterward. "Hey Hot Dog, this ain't the end of a James Bond movie. Take me home."

Bubba just gave her a big toothy grin.

"Awe, now, what's the fun in that? Seems to me I'm the only one that can fly this beauty, so maybe we ought to take a ride over to Paris, France, buzz the Eiffel Tower, and pick up some snails for dinner!"

"I'm pretty sure that would be a bad idea. You might have noticed the nuclear warhead out there?" Sims said pointing out the cockpit window. "Home, Hot Dog."

"Yes, Ma'am."

At that moment, one thousand five hundred twenty-three miles to the southwest, the beautiful old capitol building of the State of Texas disintegrated. The missile entered a second-floor office window, just before terminating its long flight in a massive fireball. The overpressure of the explosion burst the magnificent stone structure like a balloon, sending glass, brick, stone, and metal hundreds of feet into the air. Any walls remaining upright after the initial assault quickly fell to the ground.

The entire building was utterly destroyed, from within, by a single deadly shot.

EIGHTY-TWO

Margie Franks watched the explosion from the safety of her personal helicopter. But, thanks to the quick work of the Texas Rangers and Austin police, the explosion caused minimal casualties.

Franks' horror quickly morphed into pure rage. Her revenge would be the sweet news reports that Washington D.C. had been obliterated in a nuclear holocaust. But her hunger for revenge would not be satisfied.

Snow sat to Franks' right, focused on a laptop computer.

"Well? Stop screwin' around with that thing, Snow. Tell me that every stinking, lowlife, talking head is stammering about Washington burning!"

Snow looked up at the woman he had served for many years. "No, Madam President," Snow said in a low voice.

"No, what? Speak up!" Franks demanded.

"There is no news of anything happening to Washington. Nothing. I'm sorry, Madam President," Snow reported, anticipating Franks' reaction.

"Nothing?" Franks checked the diamond-encrusted Rolex on her wrist. "The attack should have happened almost ten minutes ago! Goddammit, all! Get me over to the hotel and get me Knox!"

As the Revolution I sped over the Mediterranean Sea, Dave Knox answered the call from Franks.

"Margie! I'm so glad you called!"

"Shut your mouth. Why the hell didn't you nuke that bitch? Answer me!"

"Whoa there. We did! Washington should be gone! What are you trying to say?" Dave responded, taken aback by Franks' attack.

"I'm tryin' to say you didn't do your job. I'm sayin' you're dead!" Franks screamed.

"Margie, we fired the Exocet as you ordered. Calm down. Daniel?" Dave said, turning to Zafran, "tell her."

"The weapon was released as you directed," Zafran said into his mic.

"See? Maybe the warhead failed. I don't know. What I do know is that I'm tired of taking your shit, *Madam President*. I've been assured that the Israeli government will be quite happy to accept my services. Not to mention how generous they will be with their thanks. So, in a language I know you'll understand - *fuck off!*"

Dave ended the call and looked over at Zafran. "Now, how about we go home?"

"Mine or yours?" Zafran asked, smiling for the first time Dave could remember.

"Ours," Dave said, pointing at the approaching Israeli coastline.

EIGHTY-THREE

Banebridge, Alabama

Sarah, Michael, and Zach stood inside the small campus radio studio waiting for the morning host to arrive. It had been a long night and the few hours of sleep they managed didn't do much to relieve their exhaustion. But their plans for the morning and their excitement to carry them out energized their spirits.

"What do you think will happen to Hunter?" Sarah asked. "Once we release your recording where he admits attacking Mary O'Dell, somebody has to do something."

Zach answered Sarah. "Like all bullies, he's really a cowardly asshole. Willing to beat up little guys, but will run away when there's a chance he could get beaten up himself."

"And he sure did run!" Michael added.

"Really?" said Sarah.

"Oh, yeah. We saw his slimy, hung-over butt sneak out to his car and high-tail it away from campus," Michael chuckled. "I bet he's running back to his mamma as we speak."

"I called a friend from the university newspaper. She'll be here and she promised to run a story in the next issue, with a transcript of the good parts," Zach added.

"Awesome! Good job, buddy! Now, who's going to do the talking? We all three can't fit in there," Michael said pointing to the broadcast booth. "I think you two should do it. A lot of people know you, Zach, and it was Sarah's idea."

After Zach and Sarah reluctantly agreed to do the interview, the host showed up and agreed to the plan. As a journalism and broadcast major, he wasn't going to pass up the chance at a story this juicy.

For the next half hour, the host played the usual mix of popular music interspersed with teasers about Zach and Sarah's interview that would reveal the actual purpose of The Tyros and the real-world conspiracy supporting it.

Buzz around campus grew as more and more students tuned in to the morning broadcast.

Finally, Zach and Sarah sat down, put on headphones and were introduced.

"We have Zach Self and Sarah Marshall in the studio this morning to give us some insight on The Tyros as promised," the host began. "Zach you're an SGA senator and an Eta. Sarah, you're a member of Pi, correct?"

"That's right, Jack," Zach said to the host.

"Yes," Sarah added.

"And I understand you want to talk about The Tyros. That's always controversial, but you are both Greeks and I take it members of The Tyros?"

"Well, yes and no," said Sarah. "When you join a fraternity or sorority, it's not like you get a Tyros membership card or something. They tell you that it's really important for the Greeks to vote together to get 'our people' into office. You're expected to follow along; and, because you're in a group of people you identify with, you do."

"Sarah's right," Zach added. "I believed The Tyros was sort of like a political party, like being a Democrat or Republican or a support system to get like-minded people elected. But it's much more than that."

"What do you mean? What else does it do?" the host asked.

"A lot," Zach continued. "What nobody really knows is that The Tyros has a secret leadership committee that meets to make all the decisions, like, who will be picked to run and what The Tyros representatives and officers do once they're elected. This committee controls everything about The Tyros and a lot of what happens on campus."

"Really?" the host said, surprised. "Who picks the members of this committee?"

"Now you're getting to the real reason The Tyros exists," Zach said. "At least some of the members are hand-picked by the leaders of a group called the Directors. They are extremely powerful men and women who use The Tyros to find, recruit, and choose their next generation. It's really huge."

"This is starting to sound like one of the conspiracy theory shows you see on television. Come on, these Directors, or whatever, aren't real, are they?"

"Yes," Sarah broke in. "And we can prove it."

"You said you brought a recording you want us to hear?" the host asked.

Zach handed a thumb drive across the desk and the host brought up the sound file to play over the air.

"This is a recording made last night at the Eta house. It's me confronting Hunter Ewell, Eta's president, about his actions as a member of The Tyros leadership committee. Please play it for your listeners. It's important."

"Alright then ladies and gentlemen, I'm going to let this play through. It's several minutes long and then we'll discuss what it reveals, if anything," the host said, giving Zach and Sarah a look as if to say *this better be good!*

Zach and Sarah both nodded.

The host played the recording Zach made in Hunter's room.

"Wow! The independent candidate was Mary O'Dell. She left school entirely right before the election. She never said anything," the host observed.

"She was scared. I don't blame her at all," Sarah said.

"This is, well, incredible. How could this happen? Here!" the host said, expressing what almost everyone listening felt.

Sarah answered. "It's not how it happened that's important. We had the wool pulled over our eyes. But most of us in frats and sororities just didn't think it through. We all have to accept some responsibility. But the important thing now is to fix it, become aware, ask questions, and don't blindly follow along. Because this is what happens. This conclusively proves there is corruption and crime here on our campus and at our school. It should end here and now."

Zach added: "And I'm resigning as an SGA senator and I challenge all Tyros representatives and officers do the same. We can hold new elections. Fair elections. This is just college. If politics and elections are this corrupt here, how much bigger is the problem in the real world?"

EPILOGUE

Santiago, Chile

Eleven men and one woman sat around a large round table in a very private room in Santiago's Pacifico Resort.

The arrival of twelve guests surprised the manager of the Pacifico. Not by their number, but because the private space and suite of rooms on the top floor had been reserved and paid in full for the past twenty years, without anyone ever coming to the resort. The top floor and meeting area had long ago become the topic of speculation, rumor, and legend with the resort staff.

So, when the unidentified guests arrived and claimed the rooms, they were treated with extreme deference.

Margie Franks sat next to Alexander Monroe. The other Directors filled the remaining spots.

The atmosphere in the room should have been despondent and tense. It was anything but.

"What's next?" Franks asked the room as a whole.

"We move forward with the rest of our plan," Monroe answered. "As you know, since the time of our ancestors' first meeting back in 1928, our goals have expanded considerably. The United States is divided and destabilized. It must look inward now and it will take decades before it can hope to reassert any substantial influence around

the globe. The door is open for us to manipulate our new allies and profit beyond measure. With the United States pre-occupied, Russia and China will have to compete for the power vacuum. With any luck at all, they'll go to war."

"And we'll be ready to pick up the pieces," Ex-Governor Burns of Mississippi said, raising his glass.

"With the gravity wave technology. Right Doctor Knox?" Margie Franks said to the newest Director on the other side of the table.

"I've already set up a new manufacturing plant in Israel. They are appreciative beyond measure and will be fast friends. By the way, nice rant at me over the radio. Zafran bought the act," Dave Knox said.

"How do we know they won't just take the technology for themselves and kick your ass out?" Monroe asked.

"Because they can make the aircraft, but only I can make the fuel," Dave answered, not without hubris.

"What about Donnelly? He knows the formula too," Margie observed.

Dave grinned. "Yes, but our sources say he isn't talking. But just to make sure, we have more than a few loyal inmates who are willing to make sure he never speaks again."

"Then the future is indeed bright! To The Cause!" Monroe exclaimed raising his glass. The Directors raised their glasses as one.

"The Cause!"